LEGACY OF MERLIN

THE ABDUCTION CYCLES

JOHN ELIJAH CRESSMAN

MAVERICK-GAGE PUBLISHING

ISBN: 978-1-954524-17-0 (Paperback)
ISBN: 978-1-954524-18-7 (Hardcover)
ISBN: 978-1-954524-16-3 (Amazon Kindle)
ISBN: 978-1-954524-19-4 (Audiobook)
Any references to historical events, real people, or real places are used fictitiously. Names, characters, and places are products of the author's twisted imagination.

Front cover image by Christina Myrvold
Editing By Celestial Rince.

Printed by Maverick-Gage Publishing in conjunction with IngramSpark, in the United States of America.
First printing edition 2021.
Maverick-Gage Publishing
Allentown, PA

info@maverick-gage.com
www.maverick-gage.com
John Elijah Cressman
www.johnecressman.com

In memory of my friend and mentor, Sam Losagio, Jr., who helped me at time when I needed it most and opened a new pathway for me that gave me the confidence to try new things - like writing.

Samuel C. Losagio, Jr
1947 - 2021

PROLOGUE

Two full moons and a sliver of a third moon illuminated the night sky as Ethan and his group sat huddled around the crackling fire. The orc shamans and their escorts were camped a short distance away. The distance wasn't just physical. There was now a coldness from the orcs that hadn't previously been there, and he hoped it wouldn't escalate into trouble.

"You really believe my father is alive?" asked Guinevere. The blond warrior woman sat on a rock, across the fire from him. Her face was dirty from days of travel and her blond hair was limp, but neither could hide the fact that she was beautiful.

Guinevere had been the wife of King Arthur and former queen of Camelot, a thousand years ago. She was also the daughter of Merlin, the legendary wizard. Back in that time, she had drunk from the Fountain of Youth and no longer aged - her beauty and youth immortalized by magic.

The concept of magic and fountains of youth would have seemed pure fantasy a year ago to Ethan. Back before any of this happened, he'd been just an average computer technician in a dead-end support job. Then he'd been abducted by aliens and dropped onto an alien world.

Ethan looked up into the sky at the moons and the strange configuration of stars as if to remind himself this was all real. Yes. It was all real - as was magic. In fact, he was a wizard. He could manipulate magical forces that back on Earth would seem impossible. He didn't fully understand exactly how he did it, but he could bend elements and even space to his will. And that wasn't the only strange thing.

Thinking about it, he opened up his HUD - his heads-up display. Like something from a video game back on Earth, the HUD displayed images about his stats. The words and numbers appeared in what appeared to be English, seeming to float in his vision. Yet, it was invisible to everyone but him.

He assumed the aliens had done something to him - modified him in some way - so that he saw the HUD. It seemed a logical assumption considering he'd discovered that the natives of this world didn't have a HUD and the few other abductees he'd met did have one. But what that meant was anyone's guess.

As he thought of other abductees, he glanced at his wife, Nia, on his right-hand side. He'd originally met three other abductees who had been dropped into the world at the same time he had. There had been Nia, Ainslee and Yuliana. None of them were human.

Nia was a foxgirl. She looked like a human, but had

fox-like ears that poked through her rust-colored hair. She also had a large, bushy fox tail. In addition, she had fine hair across her entire body. The hairs were rust colored on her back and sides and white all along her front.

She had a keen sense of smell and hearing, though her hearing wasn't as sharp as the elves he'd met. Nia was an extremely skilled warrior who came from a more primitive planet that adhered to some sort of male-dominated pack system where tribes followed a powerful alpha.

When they'd first met, she'd been unable to kill enemies due to orders from her previous alpha. This had hamstrung her in combat until they'd made love and she'd informed him that he was her new alpha and that they were married.

Ethan didn't know the legalities of it, but he wasn't about to argue with the deadly foxgirl. Besides, he actually did care for her and was captivated by her exotic beauty and inner strength. She was certainly leagues above the women he'd dated back home.

The other two abductees, Ainslee and Yuliana, no longer traveled with him. Ainslee, who looked and acted like the quintessential dwarf from fantasy novels, had never wanted to be an adventurer or fight monsters. She just wanted to work a forge.

After they had found Camelot, the dwarf had called it quits and had gone back to Hawkshead. They'd found enough money to fund her forge and Ethan hoped she was happy back there crafting items for the villagers.

Then there was Yuliana. The strange elf had come from a world where she and the other elves tended groves that were maintained by huge tree creatures. They'd found some of the same creatures around Camelot and Yuliana had decided to stay and tend their grove here on this planet.

He missed the two women. They'd all faced death together many times and Ethan owed his life to them. They'd been good comrades through their many adventures since arriving on this planet.

When they'd first arrived, they'd been completely lost and had managed to make it to a village called Hawkshead. The traitorous ex-mayor had set the village on a collision course with destruction.

The mayor had equipped one of the local kobold tribes with weapons to scare away the trade caravans and isolate the village while he hired bandits to terrorize the villagers. It hadn't worked out the way he planned.

The kobolds used the weapons to destroy the other tribes in the area and, with their competition gone, had turned their sights on the village. It had taken all of them working together to defend the village and kill the kobold leader.

That's when he'd met Par'karr, the little kobold on his left. Small and scaled, looking like a three-foot-tall humanoid lizard or dinosaur, Par'karr had been one of the few survivors of the kobold purge by the dominant tribe.

He'd joined with Ethan and revealed that he was a summoner. Using a type of magic Ethan didn't fully understand, he was able to summon large rabbits with unicorn horns, large teeth and glowing red eyes.

For his part in the defense, Ethan had been made mayor. But even after the village had been saved, it was still in danger of dying out. The kobolds had stopped the trade caravans and the village was being starved of the goods it needed to survive.

As mayor, Ethan had been tasked by the villagers to go to a nearby city called Castlehaven to re-open trade. But that hadn't been the only reason the villagers wanted him to leave. He'd learned of a much darker reason.

Ethan was a wizard. He found out that something had been going around killing wizards and sucking out their brains. Not only that, but people around wizards tended to get hurt when the wizards were killed. The villagers hadn't wanted him in the village, in case the same fate had befallen him. He'd been fine with leaving, eager to learn more about the world and more about the magic he wielded.

In Castlehaven, Ethan had found an order of sages with an immense library. The problem was, it was for members only. To become a member, they'd given him a quest to retrieve some tomes. The only problem was, no one who went into the lost library ever returned.

He and his friends had journeyed to the destroyed city of Patheos and retrieved the tomes, meeting the elven wizard, Michalus, along the way. The wizard had since become a trusted friend.

Looking across the fire at Michalus, Ethan knew anyone looking at him would never guess he was over 800 years old. Unlike when they'd first met him, Michalus appeared to be in his mid-20's in human years. In fact, he looked like a human except for the sharper features and long tapered ears.

Elves lived for nearly 1,000 years and Michalus had been an old elf when they'd met him. Now, thanks to a drink from the fountain of youth, the elf had been restored to his prime and would never age again.

Despite his young appearance, the wizard held centuries of knowledge about magic. Though, if Ethan was honest, Michalus was much more of an academic than a field mage. Even after plenty of battles, Ethan's own battle magic was much more potent than the wizard's.

Ethan shook his head as he thought about Michalus and the fountain of youth. The wizard hadn't been the only one to drink from the fountain. A fountain they'd found in Arthur's tomb.

When Ethan and his friends had returned from the library of Daemonium, in Patheos, they'd learned that a terrible high-pitched sound was scaring off all of the game around Hawkshead. They'd tracked it down to the tomb that the former mayor had uncovered.

After exploring the tomb and fighting the spider-like denizens, they discovered that it was the final resting place of King Arthur. Resting on his tomb had been the legendary Holy Grail - a cup with amazing healing properties.

Also in the tomb was a pool of water they had learned was the fountain of youth. A single drink from it made the drinker immortal. Or rather, it made them ageless. They would never die of old age but they could die from other wounds. Nia, Ainslee, and Yuliana had all drunk from the fountain. So had he.

After realizing that King Arthur had been real and had lived on this world, Ethan had decided to read a book he'd found in the library of Daemonium - a journal from Merlin, the fabled wizard of Arthurian legend.

In the book, he'd discovered directions to Camelot and he and his friends had set off to find it. Little did he know that he'd been subtly manipulated through magic by Arthur and Guinevere's son, Mordred.

Mordred had transformed into a tentacled demon and waited for them in the ruins of Camelot. Luckily, Ethan and his friends had defeated the prince-turned-demon and released his mother, Guinevere, from his mental control. The former queen had told them of the fate of Excalibur and they'd set off to find the most famous sword in history.

But finding Excalibur had been more complicated than he thought. The orcs had seized the tomb of Lord Bryan, the man who carried Excalibur away from Camelot. They demanded that he find the dragon Firestorm and discover why the dragon had begun attacking the area around the orcs.

Ethan had done so and to his surprise, found out there were two dragons. Firestorm's mate had been injured by a Doemenagg. The Doemenagg were a race of sentient praying mantis creatures that were responsible for the deaths of the wizards - and their missing brains.

Using the Grail, he had healed the dragon's mate and in return, Firestorm had given Ethan a glowing sigil on his chest. He still was not sure exactly what the sigil did.

One side effect of having it - and being declared Dragonfriend by Firestorm - was that the orcs had taken him to Excalibur. They took him to Lord Bryan's tomb and - with magic - Ethan had pulled the sword from the stone.

Looking at Excalibur across his lap, he remembered how he'd teleported himself and the sword out of the stone. During his trip through the Bifrost, he'd been approached by a ghostly apparition. The misty form of Merlin's head had appeared and told Ethan to find him. He'd even gotten a quest to do that very thing.

"Do you?" Guinevere repeated and Ethan realized he'd zoned out after the warrior woman had asked about her father.

Ethan looked down at Excalibur. The first time he'd traveled through the Bifrost with the sword, her father had appeared to him and spoke. The old wizard was alive. He nodded. "I think he is. We just have to find him."

1

"You really intend to go after Merlin?" Michalus asked, one eyebrow raised.

Guinevere frowned at the elven wizard for even asking the question but Michalus didn't flinch away.

Ethan nodded. "Of course."

"Do you have any idea where to look for him?" the wizard inquired, giving both Ethan and Guinevere a serious look. "He's been missing for quite some time. Where could Merlin be that he can't free himself?"

Ethan considered the wizard's words. As he did, he saw Guinevere bite her lip and look down. While the rest of them could only speculate on the fabled wizard's powers, only Guinevere - his daughter - would have a good understanding of the man's magical ability.

He turned to the former queen and daughter of Merlin. "Any idea where we would start looking?"

Guinevere shook her head. "I don't know where he could be." She sighed. "I thought he died in the explosion.

I thought he sacrificed himself to save me - and prevent the warlocks from having their library."

"That is the last time you saw him, my dear?" Michalus asked.

"Yes," she replied in a quiet voice.

"And when was that?" the wizard inquired.

"I'm not certain." The warrior woman shrugged. "Things were... strange... when I was under Mordred's spell. I lost track of time. It could be a hundred or two hundred years."

Ethan brought up his HUD and looked at the quest he had received right after the vision.

```
You      have    received    a    new    quest
"Legacy of Merlin - Part I"
    The  legendary  wizard,  Merlin,  has
spoken  to  you  in  the  Bifrost  and
asked you to find him.
    Find Merlin (0/1).
    Reward: 5000 experience, Unknown.
    Accept quest (yes or no)?
```

The quest was vague and really offered little insight into where he might be. It didn't even give Ethan a place to start looking.

"You've traveled through the Bifrost many times," Michalus said. "Why do you think he chose that particular time to contact you?"

Having been wondering the same thing, Ethan pointed to the sword that lay across his legs. "It has to have something to do with Excalibur."

Guinevere peaked an eyebrow. "What makes you think that? Plenty of people have touched the sword before."

"Yes," Ethan replied with a grin. "But none of them ever pulled it out before."

"Only Ethan," Nia said with a proud smile and a slight wink at him. "He is the strongest alpha."

The warrior woman rolled her eyes. "I'll at least concede that you are the first person to pull the sword out since my father put it in the stone. But why would that make a difference? You could be anyone."

Ethan furrowed his brow. Then he thought back to how the Akugyo, the fishmen, had used the Trident of the Kings as the focal point for scrying. Perhaps Merlin had done something similar. He'd been waiting for someone to pull the sword from the stone so he could reach out to them.

"I think I know!" A grin spread across his face. "I think he was using it like a scrying point. He wasn't waiting for me. He was waiting for anyone who would remove the sword because I think teleporting it was the only way to remove it from the stone."

"Are you saying that you believe only a wizard could have pulled the sword from the stone?" Michalus asked, his eyes wide with curiosity.

"Not just a wizard," Ethan retorted. "But a wizard with strong aether magic."

Ethan held up the sword, pointing to the Chymera crystal in the crossguard. It was both larger and more well cut than the crystal that had been in the Trident of Kings he returned to the fish people. "This is a Chymera crystal. This sword has to be meant for a wizard."

"Arthur wizard?" Par'karr squeaked, staring intently at the glimmering crystal in the crossguard.

"Interesting." Michalus sat back and scratched his chin.

Guinevere shook her head. "No. Arthur was many things, but a wizard wasn't one of them."

"You're certain?" Ethan asked, his own eyebrow raised. "He never performed any magic?"

"I knew him since I was a maiden," the warrior woman retorted. "I never saw him... oh... gods of Asgard!"

"What?" Ethan asked, looking behind him to make sure she hadn't seen enemies approaching. There was no one and he turned around to see Guinevere right in front of him. Without asking permission, the woman yanked his shirt open - revealing his bare chest and the glowing sigil put there by the dragon.

Nia growled, and Ethan, unsure what the warrior woman was doing, began to summon *Air* to bind the woman.

After staring at his chest for a moment, the warrior woman backed away and slumped back down on the log she had been using as a seat.

"What was that about?!" Ethan demanded, pulling his shirt back on.

"Sorry," the woman muttered. She had a faraway look in her eyes and Ethan began to worry about the woman.

Everyone stared at Guinevere, waiting for an answer. After a long pause, she looked up. "I didn't remember it right away - not even when I saw your tattoo..."

"Sigil," Ethan corrected.

"...sigil," Guinevere continued as if he hadn't interrupted her. "I didn't remember until you mentioned the possibility of him being a wizard."

"Remember what?" Nia asked, her hands on her weapon hilts and her eyes narrowed at the blond woman.

"I think I told you that the orcs once wanted to kill my father after he visited the dragon," she started, looking at Ethan for confirmation.

He nodded. Ethan did remember the conversation. She had said something about the orcs being untrustworthy after they tried to kill Merlin after he visited the dragon. It was the main reason she'd thought they would try to kill Ethan and his friends.

She sighed. "What I didn't tell you was that Arthur had gone with him."

Ethan shook his head. "Wait. What? Merlin and Arthur went to see the dragon? Why?"

Guinevere let out an exasperated breath. "I don't know. Neither of them told me why. It happened just before we were to be married. They both went and when they returned, Arthur had a tat...uh... sigil... like yours."

He remembered his own interaction with the dragon, Firestorm. The dragon had told Ethan that the sigils imparted the knowledge - very possibly even magic ability. He glanced down at the glowing lines on his own chest and then back to Guinevere, understanding dawning in him. "The dragon gave Arthur magical ability. It made him a wizard."

Drorm, who had been silent, nodded at Ethan. He glanced over at the orc camp, where his mother was, and spoke quietly. "It is said the dragon can awaken magic in those who had not done it before."

Michalus's eyes went wide. "If that is true..."

"If that's true," Ethan said with a shake of his head. "No wonder they want to keep it a secret. The dragon can turn anyone into a wizard - or in the case of orcs, a shaman."

The elven wizard was shaking his head. "This defies all magical lore. The very thought is... mind boggling!"

Ethan wasn't sure what made some people a wizard while other people couldn't use magic at all. But if a dragon could awaken it in people, or grant the ability outright, the ramifications were staggering. Anyone could be a wizard!

He corrected himself. No, that wasn't exactly true. The person would only get the type of magic the dragon had granted them access to through the sigil. Ethan looked down at his own sigil and wondered what, if anything, it had done for him. Had the dragons thought they were giving him magical ability when he already had it?

"I do not understand," Nia said. "The dragon made Arthur a wizard. What does that mean and how does it help us find Merlin?"

"I'm not sure," Ethan admitted. "It may not be relevant at all. But it does make sense then why I could pull it out when others couldn't."

"And why I never could," Guinevere said bitterly.

"And probably why Mordred couldn't either," Ethan pointed out, seeing the former queen flinch at the mention of her dead son.

"Then we are no closer to knowing where to look." Nia sighed in frustration.

"Are you in some kind of hurry?" Guinevere asked,

glaring at the foxgirl. "If anyone should be in a hurry to find my father, it's me."

Ethan held up his hands. "We aren't really any closer to knowing where to look for him, but it might help me better understand how Merlin was able to contact me and why he chose that time."

"Because only a wizard could have pulled the sword from the stone," Michalus surmised. "And wherever Merlin is, he must need a wizard to find him."

"Exactly." Ethan nodded and looked around the fire. "Wherever Merlin is, he must have used the sword like a focal point to contact me as soon as I pulled it out - much like the Akugyo king used the trident as a focus to scry on me for so long."

They all remembered the many battles they'd had with the Akugyo. And the fishmen were able to track them by *Scrying* on the trident and getting a fix on their location. It appeared that Merlin might be doing the same.

"So, what do we do? How do we find my father?" Guinevere asked. Ethan thought he heard a slight tinge of desperation in her voice.

Scouring his brain, he went back to his books and TV shows. How did they solve a murder or abduction? He thought for a moment before he came up with what he thought a detective might do.

"We return to the scene of the crime." Ethan grinned at his friends. "We return to Patheos."

2

"We are leaving," Ethan told the shamans a short time later.

Unandum Thunderflame, Drorm's mother and also a shaman, and Senamm Stonelash, another orc shaman, stood in front of them. Both frowned as they considered his words. Ethan didn't miss that both of their eyes flicked towards Excalibur at his hip.

Ethan's hand was on the hilt, allowing him to channel his magic through the large Chymera crystal in the crossguard if necessary. It was a gesture not lost to the shamans.

Technically, according to orc law, Ethan was the high shaman. He had been the first to receive a sigil from the dragon since it had awakened. According to their own law, that made him the high shaman - even though he was not an orc.

It was a loophole in the law. He guessed they never counted on anyone other than an orc receiving the sigil -

let alone being declared Dragonfriend. He was sure they would fix the law some time very soon.

"Where?" Unandum demanded.

Despite his supposed position as high shaman, he didn't think the orcs thought of him as the real high shaman. Given that he'd drawn Excalibur, he still wasn't sure whether or not they would let him go or if they'd pull a Julius Caesar and try to kill him - and the others - and take the sword.

"We're going to find Guinevere's father," Ethan told them, seeing no particular reason to withhold the truth from them.

Senamm arched a thick eyebrow. "Merlin still lives?"

"Yes," Ethan answered.

"It has been a long time since anyone has seen or heard from the wizard." Unandum looked doubtful. "You are sure?"

Ethan hesitated as he wondered how much he wanted to divulge. Finally, unable to see the harm, he told them about his vision in the Bifrost.

"We have heard stories of the Bifrost," Senamm said, exchanging glances with Unandum. "We have never heard of someone communicating in the Bifrost."

"I'm not sure exactly how he did it either," Ethan retorted. "But he did. He's still alive and we're going to find him."

The two shamans exchanged looks again. Unandum gestured to his side. "You will take the sword with you?"

"Yes," he replied flatly.

"You cannot..." Senamm started but was interrupted by Drorm.

"He is high shaman!" Drorm growled. "Are you defying the high shaman?"

Senamm fumed at Drorm but shut his mouth.

"The high shaman is not a king," Unandum told Drorm coldly. Ethan felt the tension between the two and hated to be the person causing it. Yet, he knew the sword was the key to finding Merlin. He wasn't about to let it go. "His word is not law."

"The sword is coming with me," Ethan said, hand still on the hilt of Excalibur.

The two shamans exchanged looks and then the Chymera crystals in their staffs began to flare up with pale blue light. Ethan reacted instantly with reflexes honed from years of playing video games. He ripped the staffs out of the shamans' hands with a quick conjuring of *Air*.

He and the others had discussed it and Drorm pointed out that the shamans most likely wouldn't allow him to leave with the sword. Like before, he expected treachery. Ethan had been ready for the shamans to make a move. This time, he'd been ready.

Unandum opened her mouth to call out to the orc soldiers but Ethan shook his head. "I won't give up the sword unless I'm dead. You do remember what Bal'Furtun said would happen if I was harmed, right?"

Drorm's mother glared at Ethan but shut her mouth. Senamm did the same, though he fumed as well.

"Michalus, you and Guinevere have the horses?" he asked.

"Ready to go," the wizard replied.

"We're leaving," he told the shamans again. "Don't

follow us and don't send any one after us. If so, I will kill them and I'll make sure word gets back to both dragons."

Both shamans blanched. They knew full well what the dragon had said would happen if Ethan or his friends were harmed.

"Are you sure you want to come?" he asked Drorm.

Drorm looked at his mother and then back to Ethan. He nodded sadly. "I have no place here, not any longer."

"Drorm..." his mother started to say but the big orc cut her off with a raised hand.

"No, Mother," he growled. "My people have betrayed their own honor. Not once, but twice. And you, my own mother, were at the heart of it both times."

His mother went rigid, but a defiant look came across her face. "There are things you don't understand."

"You are right," Drorm agreed bitterly. "I don't understand."

Unandum scowled and crossed her arms over her chest. She didn't say another word.

After a moment, Drorm nodded. "So be it. Goodbye, Mother."

The big orc stepped back and gestured to Ethan, letting him know he was ready. Ethan channeled *Mana* into the Chymera crystal of the sword. He noted how easily the magic flowed through him and into the crystal. It almost made channeling through the trident seem difficult.

He was still amazed at the difference in the Chymera crystals and how much it affected what he could accomplish with the same amount of *Mana*. Almost effortlessly, he opened a portal to his right.

There was a commotion among the orc soldiers as the portal appeared and Ethan gave the two shamans a sharp look. He gritted his teeth and tightened his hand on Excalibur's hilt. "Call them off."

Still glowering, neither shaman moved. Senamm glared daggers at Ethan while Unandum did the same to her son.

"Between Michalus and I, and with this sword, we can kill them all," Ethan said through gritted teeth. He wasn't completely sure that was true. He was counting on the fact that they didn't know exactly what the sword did.

Skill increase: Bluff +1%.

He saw the skill increase flash across his HUD but kept his expression neutral, maintaining eye contact with the two shamans.

The soldiers now watching their exchange must have sensed the tension. Several of them began to come closer.

"Last chance before we kill them all," Ethan said. "Or one of them accidentally kills me and sets off two very pissed-off dragons."

"Everything is fine!" growled Drorm's mother, casting a glance over her shoulder at the approaching orcs. "We'll call you if we need you."

The soldiers stopped, looking over Ethan and his group. Slowly, as if they weren't sure they were doing the right thing, they turned around and walked back to the others.

"Good choice," Ethan told her.

"Michalus, Guinevere," he snapped. "Take the horses through the portal - now. The rest of you follow."

The pair, who had been holding the horses, walked them to the glowing portal and disappeared inside. Par'karr went next, along with his rabbits.

Drorm frowned at his mother. "I am sorry it has come to this, Mother. I hope you will find your honor again."

"I am not your mother," the female orc spat. "I have no son."

The big orc grunted as if hit by a blow. His scowl deepened. "Goodbye.... Shaman."

Spinning, Drorm stalked into the portal and disappeared while his mother stared straight ahead.

Ethan wanted to defend his friend but he guessed any arguments he made at this point would fall on deaf ears.

"Go," he told Nia but the foxgirl shook her head.

"I will go with you," she told him.

"Fine," he grumbled. "Let's go then."

He started to turn towards the portal but Unandum caught his eye. Her lip twisted in a scowl. "We will not forgive you for this."

"If that's the case," Ethan said coolly. "Then if I see any orc anywhere in the north, I'll just assume it's there to assassinate me and I'll send a mental message to my good friend, Firestorm."

"You are bluffing. You could not send a message that far." Unandum scoffed.

AM I?! Ethan thundered into heads, pushing a good portion of *Mana* into the communication.

Both shamans fell to their knees, clutching their

heads. As they looked up, Ethan saw blood dripping down their noses.

Ethan blinked. Had he done that? He hadn't intended to hurt them, just shout in their heads. He looked down at the crystal in the sword. Had the sword amplified his power somehow and not just channeled the magic?

Looking up, Ethan knew he'd have to explore that possibility later. The soldiers were reacting to the two shamans' pain. They grabbed their weapons and began rushing towards them and Ethan knew it was time to go.

"Don't come after me," Ethan warned them. With that, Ethan grabbed Nia's hand and jumped through the portal.

Instantly, Ethan was in the Bifrost with Nia. Like before, as long as they were touching when they entered the Bifrost, the two of them would be able to see each other.

Mist appeared again from the sides of the rainbow tunnel. This time, it didn't gather around the sword first but instead moved right in front of Ethan's face. Like before, it seemed to solidify into a human head made of mist.

The head turned and seemed to look at him. Then a ghostly wail issued from it. "Find me! Find me!"

"Where are you?" Ethan shouted but before he could get an answer, they were suddenly out of the Bifrost. They stumbled for a moment and then looked around.

"What's wrong?" Michalus asked.

"I saw Merlin again..." Ethan said began but his wife interrupted him.

"I saw the misty head too," Nia said, wide-eyed. "It was like a spirit."

Guinevere perked up immediately and thrust the horse reins at Par'karr. She moved next to the pair. "What did he say? Did he tell you anything new?"

"Same thing as before," Ethan replied. "He asked us to find him."

"Did he say where?" Guinevere demanded, almost frantic.

Ethan shook his head. "No. There wasn't enough time."

The warrior woman cursed. "Then what do we do?"

"We stick to the plan," Ethan told her. "We go back to Patheos."

The Queen clicked in frustration, lashing out at one of her nearby elite guards. The guard might have been able to dodge the blow but like the obedient slave it was, it just stood there as the Queen's scythe-like forearms slashed off its head. The triangular head rolled a dozen feet away and the body collapsed on the ground. She paid it no mind.

She had been getting closer to where she'd last felt the human wizard. He had used his Aether magic to create a small portal that was not a portal. Unlike other portals, which had an origin and exit point, this one just seemed to be a flare of Aether magic with an exit point. She didn't fully understand it, not yet. Once the Queen devoured the human wizard's brain, she'd know his secrets.

But now that would be longer. She had sensed the wizard creating a portal further north. Several days' north. The Queen knew the dragons were still killing the remainder of her brood, but how long before they finished and then came hunting for her.

The Queen needed to find the human wizard, eat his brain and absorb his knowledge of Aether. With that information, she could finally create a portal back to her homeworld. Then, she would find the new queen and kill her.

It would be simple now. She had magic. Magic that none of the other Doemenaggs possessed. With that magic, the other queen would be no match for her. She would destroy her and take her rightful place as Queen. All she needed, was the human wizard. And now, he was even further away.

Clicking in anger, she looked down at the decapitated corpse of her elite guard. There was no use in letting it go to waste. She sliced off a large portion of the body and picked it up. She sent a mental message to the others with her as she took a bite.

Eat.

3

The group had appeared at the outskirts of Highshire, where they'd met with the shamans. Ethan had left the runestick he'd made for Michalus at the spot, in case they needed a quick getaway. Now he was glad he did.

"Let's mount up and ride out," Ethan told them as he retrieved his horse from Guinevere.

"You think they will come after us?" Michalus asked, bending down to retrieve the runestick.

"I don't know. I hope they don't, but given what just happened..." He trailed off and looked to Drorm. "Do you think they will?"

"You embarrassed my mother. She does not forgive such insults." Drorm scowled.

"You didn't see what he did after you left," Nia chimed in. She was looking at Ethan with a strange look that almost bordered on admiration.

Everyone was mounted and Ethan motioned for

Drorm to take the lead. The big orc led them east towards the dragon's lair again.

"Do you think the orcs on the wall saw us?" Ethan asked quietly, changing the subject.

Drorm nodded. "They saw us."

"Good." Ethan grinned.

It was a ruse to throw the orcs off their trail. Ethan had suggested porting right to Hawkshead but Nia had suggested setting up a false trail for the orcs to follow. After hearing the foxgirl's idea, he agreed.

"What did you do?" the big orc asked, breaking Ethan from his thoughts.

"I might have used a bit too much mana when I sent them a telepathic message," he admitted, feeling some-what bad that he'd done it to Drorm's mother. "It was powerful enough to send them to their knees."

"And made them bleed out their noses," Nia added cheerfully.

Drorm frowned and didn't speak for nearly a minute. Finally he spoke without looking at Ethan. "You may have made an enemy out of her."

Ethan shrugged. "I don't know if they were ever friends. They've betrayed us at every turn. First wanting to kill us after we spoke to the dragon, then basically attacking us once I got the sword."

"She did not actually..." Drorm began but Ethan cut him off.

"They were channeling mana," he told the orc. "They were about to do something. And whatever they were planning, I'm sure it wouldn't have been pleasant for any of us."

Drorm lapsed into silence again. Ethan knew it couldn't be easy for the big orc. His own mother had disowned him for doing nothing more than upholding his honor.

Ethan shook his head as he thought about the shamans. To him, they seemed like the politicians back home. They professed one thing, and then did another, all while telling everyone it was in the best interest of everyone. They had given up their honor for power.

"They were wrong to attack you," Drorm said, breaking his silence. "They dishonor themselves by attacking the high shaman."

"But I wasn't really the high shaman," he pointed out. "And I certainly wasn't an orc."

"The law does not say the high shaman must be an orc," Drorm retorted. "It only says it is the first one to be chosen by the dragon and given his mark."

"Maybe," Ethan said, with no real strength in his words. He didn't really believe it. He'd seen corporate politics at play before. Just because something was in black and white, didn't mean the higher-ups interpreted it the way you thought it should be interpreted.

The group rode east along the river highway until they were out of sight of the city. Once they were certain no one was around, Ethan opened a portal to Hawkshead. The others went through, one by one. Once everyone was through, Ethan urged his mount into the portal.

Ethan was once again in the shimmering rainbow tunnel that was the Bifrost. Almost immediately, mist appeared from the sides of the tunnel.

It quickly formed in front of Ethan's face, merging into

the face of a bearded man. The face he now knew belonged to Merlin.

The head looked at him and the ghostly voice spoke. "You have the sword. Find me!"

Ethan wanted to ask where but once again, before he had a chance to ask anything, he and his horse were next to the others in Hawkshead, surrounded by a very surprised group of visitors.

From out of sight, Ethan heard a familiar voice. "Bout time you lot show back up, now that all the work is done!"

Glancing in the direction of the voice, he saw a familiar face pushing her way through the curious villagers.

"Wizard-boy!" thundered a loud dwarven voice. He knew the voice instantly. It was his companion turned blacksmith, Ainslee.

AFTER TYING up their horses and greeting some of the familiar villagers, Ethan and the others gathered in the inn.

"We're glad yer back!" Fearghas said, clapping him on the back as the dwarf passed out mugs of mead.

"It's good to be back," Ethan told him. And it was the truth. In this new world, Hawkshead had been the only home he'd known. Yet despite this, he felt like he'd actually spent very little time in the village.

"Yes," agreed Elspeth, Fearghas's wife. "We were starting to get worried something had happened to you."

"Bah!" Ainslee saw with a dismissive wave of her hand.

She paused to take a long draw from her mug, then wiped foam from her mouth. "I told them you could handle yourselves."

Fearghas and Elspeth exchanged looks and then chuckled. "Weren't you the one in here every night, drinking all our ale and telling us how you hoped they were alright?"

Ainslee sputtered and looked sheepish but then took another long draw from her mug, finishing up the contents. She slapped the mug on the table and wiped a hand across her mouth. "I may have been... a little... concerned. I mean, without me, who knows what sort of trouble they'd get into."

Fearghas rolled his eyes at Ethan's friend. He started to say something but Ainslee tapped her mug on the table.

"How about another?" she asked, giving Fearghas a pleading look.

"Fine. Fine," the innkeeper said and stood up from the table.

"So what trouble did you get into after I left?" Ainslee asked, leaning closer. "You went to find the sword, right? Is that it?"

The dwarf was looking at Excalibur, leaning against the wall of the tavern. Without a scabbard, it was just too dangerous to keep in the leather loop on his belt. He was afraid someone would trip over it and slice off their foot.

Ethan nodded. "That's the sword."

Ainslee nodded appreciatively. "Exceptional crafts-manship, but a bit plain for a magic sword. The gems are a nice touch though. A bit impractical though."

"They're Chymera crystals," he explained. "They hold

the enchantments on the sword and I can channel through the big one, like Michael's staff."

Ethan cast a glance at Michalus, who was looking a bit awkward. Since he'd drunk from the fountain of youth, he looked nothing like the Michalus the villagers remembered. He was young now.

Instead of risking knowledge of the fountain, they'd introduced him as Michael, Michalus's nephew. Ainslee knew the truth since she'd seen after he had gotten younger. The others seemed to accept the story. Some even said they saw a resemblance.

"I can make you a scabbard for it," Ainslee offered. "I am the town smith now."

"That would be great." Ethan grinned. "How's the smith going?"

"It's going great," Fearghas said, returning with a pitcher of mead. "It's been a blessing being able to get items crafted right here in the village. Since she re-opened the smith, I think she's gotten more orders than she can handle."

Ainslee grinned. "Much better than almost being eaten by monsters."

Ethan nodded. The dwarf had originally been their fighter, or tank, in video game terms. But she had never wanted to be an adventurer. All she really wanted to do was craft. Now she had that chance.

He understood that. Ethan wasn't certain he wanted to be an adventurer either but it seemed like things kept cropping up and he and his friends were the only ones who could do anything about it.

"She's the most popular person in town right now,"

Fearghas acknowledged. "Everyone needs or wants something from her."

Finishing up her mead, Ainslee let out a belch. "It's nice to have a hammer in my hand, again. And not just to bash some monster in the head with!"

"I'm glad it's working out for you," Ethan told the dwarf honestly.

"Enough to buy me some of Fearghas's spirits?" Ainslee asked. She looked at the innkeeper. "Now that I'm making some money from the forge, he makes me pay for my drinking now."

"Ha!" Fearghas chuckled. "Since you started drinking all of my stock, you mean!"

Ainslee shrugged and then she looked back at Ethan. "So, you gonna buy a round or not?"

Ethan checked his coin purse. He still had quite a bit of gold and at the moment, he had nothing to spend it on. Plus, he had an idea.

Nodding, Ethan pulled out some gold. "Sure, a round for the house."

4

First thing the next morning, Ethan and Nia found Odelina and her father at their house. Odelina, the village's butcher and tanner, had told him a story about her mother. Her mother had been a wizard and had been killed by what Ethan now knew was a Doemenagg. Her father had witnessed it.

Unfortunately, the Doemenagg had done something to her father, Ark, and he had been an invalid ever since. His condition was too similar to how Firestorm's mate had been affected to be a coincidence. Whatever the Doemenagg had done to the dragon, they'd also caused the same condition to Ark.

Ethan had used the Grail to cure Firestorm's mate and it appeared that she had made a complete recovery. Now, he hoped the magic of the cup would do the same for Odelina's father.

He and his companions had agreed to keep the Grail a secret, lest those seeking its powers destroy Hawkshead -

and possibly even start a war. Not only did the Grail rest in King Arthur's tomb, but so did the fountain of youth. A cup that healed nearly any wound and a fountain that gave youth would be something that kingdoms would go to war over.

Luckily, Ethan had come up with a cover story. It was a stretch of the truth that would hopefully alleviate any suspicion about how they cured Odelina's father. He hoped.

"Ethan! I'd heard you were back!" Odelina called out as they approached the barn where the woman slaughtered animals. She buried her large butcher's blade into the slab of meat she'd been cutting and wiped her bloody hands on her apron. "You need some meat?"

"No. No meat," he replied with a smile. "I'm actually here about your father."

"My father?" the woman replied, her brow furrowing in confusion. Her expression became wary and she put her hands on her hips. "My father ain't been causing no trouble. I don't know who complained but..."

"No one complained about your father." Ethan held his palms up in a placating gesture. "In fact, I'm here because we think we discovered something that may cure your father."

Odelina blinked, her face going pale. "Wha--- What?"

"We have a potion that should cure your father," Ethan repeated.

Odelina furrowed her brow again. "We saw the best healers. None of them even knew what had happened to him, let alone were able to help."

"We ran into a dragon..." Ethan started.

"A dragon?!" Odelina exclaimed, eyes going wide. "An actual dragon?!"

"Yes, and the dragon's mate had a similar affliction." Ethan said with a smile. He had a prepared lie, although he preferred to think of it as a bending of the truth - not an actual breaking of the truth. He just couldn't reveal the nature of the Grail's magic. "I worked with the dragon to create a potion that healed her. And thinking of your father, I brought some back."

"You what?" Odelina said, shaking her head. It was clear she was having a hard time processing what he was saying.

"I have some of the same potion that cured the dragon," Ethan said, keeping his voice even and friendly. "I think it will cure your father."

Odelina just stared at him open mouthed for a long time, jaw moving but no words coming out.

"I was there," Nia added. "I saw it work. The dragon was as your father is now. After drinking the... potion... she was fine."

The butcher looked from Nia to Ethan and then back. Finally, she shook her head and gave them a wary look. "Are you sure it will work on a human? It won't cause other problems, will it?"

Ethan shook his head. "It won't. It's completely safe for humans. I even tried a little sip myself, just to make sure."

"You did?" Odelina said, her voice cracking with emotion. Her eyes were watery and it looked like she might burst into tears at any moment. "And it's safe?"

"No bad effects at all," he told her.

"And you really..." Her voice broke up and she cleared her throat. "You really think it will fix my da?"

"I do," Ethan told her, trying to give her his most reassuring smile. "And it won't hurt him, so I think it's worth a try."

Odelina nodded her head and then wiped her hands on a nearby rag to get any remaining blood off. "Da's inside. I'll take you to him."

Ethan and Nia followed the butcher out of the barn and into the small house next door. Her house was simple. There was one main room that acted as the dining room, kitchen and living room, and then two doorways that led to what appeared to Ethan to be bedrooms.

In the living room, sitting in a rocking chair was Ark. He rocked back and forth, staring at nothing.

Odelina walked over to her father and squatted down next to him. "Da. Ethan is here to see you. Remember Ethan? He's the new mayor."

Ark continued to rock back and forth, staring into space. He showed no reaction to his daughter or her words.

Ethan reached into his portal pouch. The pouch had been enchanted with Aether magic, or portal magic, to link back to the spot in Arthur's tomb where the Grail lay. Through it, he would reach in and take the Grail or replace it, anytime he needed.

Pulling out the Grail, Ethan held it up. There was some golden liquid at the bottom already and he smiled. He'd taken some of the dwarven spirits from last night and a bit of honey and put it in the chalice ahead of time.

He figured if she expected a potion, he had to make it seem convincing.

"How did you..." Odelina started and then stopped. "It's one of those magic bags, like the backpack you gave us, right?"

He nodded. Ethan had created a magical backpack that linked to a chest here in the village. It allowed the villagers to go further and hunt more, without having to carry the meat all the way back to the village. Given that Odelina did much of the hunting, he shouldn't have been surprised she would know what it was.

"Nice cup," she commented, her eyes locking on the gold chalice with its many gems.

"Something the dragon gave me for helping with his mate," Ethan lied. He frowned inwardly. Another lie. He didn't like to lie, but secrecy of the Grail was too important. What was the old saying: loose lips sink ships, right?

Ethan handed the Grail to Odelina. "It only takes a single sip. Just put it to his lips and pour some in his mouth."

Odelina took the offered chalice. She sniffed it and frowned. "It smells like alcohol... and maybe... honey."

"That's what I said," Ethan agreed with a smile. "It tastes like Fearghas's spirits, but it works."

The butcher looked back down at the liquid in the cup and then shrugged. "I hope you're right."

Moving the cup to her father's mouth, she placed it on his lips. Gently pushing down on his lips, she opened his mouth slightly while tilting the cup so that some of the contents poured into his mouth.

Ark didn't move but merely coughed. Having felt the

burning alcohol on his own throat only the night before, Ethan didn't blame the man.

Odelina's father continued to cough, blinking his eyes. He brought his hand up to cover his mouth as he coughed a few more times. He moved his head to scan the room, his eyes appearing focused for the first time. "Wha... what was that stuff?"

"Da!" Odelina's eyes went wide. "Da! You can talk?"

"What? Of course I can..." Ark had turned to look at his daughter and had stopped talking. He cocked his head, looking the woman in front of him up and down. "Ody? Is that... is that you? What happened to you?"

The Grail fell from Odelina's hands as she threw her arms around her father, hugging him. With a thought, Ethan reached out with *Air*, grabbed the falling chalice and pulled it to his hand. He quickly replaced it through the portal pouch, back in its place atop Arthur's tomb.

To keep the Grail away from Mordred, Merlin had enchanted it to emit a hypersonic sound that humans couldn't hear but which drove animals - as well as elves and foxlings - nuts. The longer the Grail was away from the tomb, the louder the sound became. Because of that, Ethan had created the portal pouch to the tomb so they could use the magic of the Grail and then replace it without driving the local wildlife crazy.

"What happened to you? You're... old?" he heard Ark say.

Odelina nodded, tears streaming down her cheeks. "You've been sick for a long time, Da. A very long time."

"I have? Sick?" Ark said, obviously confused. "Where's Marium?"

Odelina backed up and wiped her eyes with her sleeve. "Da. Mum's dead. She died the night you got sick."

"What?" Ark muttered, his face in shock. "Your mum's dead? How?"

Ethan touched Nia on the shoulder and nodded his head towards the door. "I think they have a lot to talk about. We should go."

They quietly left the house but had barely made it a dozen paces before the door burst open and Odelina came running out. She practically tackled Ethan in a bear hug, planting a big wet kiss on his lips that was made even more wet by her tear-streaked face.

After a long moment, she released Ethan and hugged Nia just as hard. When she was done, she backed away and wiped the tears from her face again. "Thank you both! Thank you so much! I have a lot to tell him but he's back to his old self. Thank you! Thank you!"

"I'm glad it worked," Ethan told her and then made a shooing motion with his hand. "Go on back and spend time with him."

Nodding, Odelina spun and hurried back to the house. Ark was standing at the door and looked out in confusion. Ethan remembered Odelina telling him they had lived in the city when her mother was killed. Now they were in a tiny hamlet in the middle of nowhere.

He guessed Odelina was right. She and her father had a lot to talk about. Reaching down, Ethan took Nia's hand and they walked back to their house.

5

─────────

"**I** got a feelin' you ain't stayin'," Ainslee said, taking a bite of her roasted pheasant.

The group had gathered at the inn for lunch, along with Ainslee, Fearghas and his wife. Ethan looked around at the others and nodded. "You're right. We only stopped in to resupply and then we're heading back to Patheos."

"That ruined city where that crazy warlock ambushed us?" Ainslee said with wide eyes. "Why in Loki's balls are you going back to that gods forsaken place?"

Ethan bit his lip for a moment. He hadn't planned on giving everyone a rundown on their plans, but these were people he trusted. There didn't seem to be any harm in letting them know what they were up to.

"We're going to look for Guinevere's father," Ethan replied. He gave Ainslee a meaningful look, hoping she wouldn't reveal the truth of who Guinevere was. That might lead to questions about how she was still alive.

Ainslee cocked her head and took a long sip of her ale. Then she nodded as she glanced between Guinevere and Ethan. "Uh... I thought he was dead."

"We don't think so," Ethan replied. "Once I got Excalibur, I... ah... got a vision or something in the Bifrost. A message from him saying to find him."

The dwarven smith screwed up her face. "And he said to go back to that old city?"

"That was the last place anyone saw him alive," Ethan said. "He had... ah... gone to the library there."

"You mean the one that was trapped? The one you and foxgirlly almost didn't make it back from?" Ainslee retorted. "Maybe he was trapped on the other side and died there."

"I thought my father was dead too," Guinevere added. "But with this vision that Ethan has had, it's possible he survived somehow."

Ainslee took a long draw from her mug, let out a loud belch, and then wiped her hand across her mouth. "Not sure where he would be. That place was a wreck."

"It's the last place I know he was," Guinevere retorted. "I'm not sure where else to start."

Shrugging, the dwarf took another sip of her mead. "Good luck then... and glad I'm not going with you."

"You seem much happier as a smith," Ethan noted.

"I get to practice my craft." Ainslee nodded. "And I don't have to worry about trolls and demons and that stuff..."

"Don't forget the most important reason," Fearghas chuckled. "She gets to drink every day!"

Ainslee raised her mug. "I'll drink to that."

"I know I said it before," Fearghas said with a glance at his wife. "It's a blessing having her here. Just having a fresh supply of nails has been a godsend."

The blacksmith rolled her eyes. "Bah! That doesn't take any talent. Just pour some molten lead in a mold and let it cool."

"Maybe so," Elspeth said with a smile. "But until you got that forge going, there was no place to do even that. And those nails are needed everywhere."

Ethan raised an eyebrow. He'd never thought of nails being so important, but when he thought about it, it did make sense. And given the amount of rebuilding they'd needed to do after the kobold attack, no doubt nails were scarce.

"I'm glad things are going well for you, Ainslee," Ethan told his former companion.

"And I'm glad you're all still alive," Ainslee said, holding up her mug. "And glad I'm not going on any more of your crazy adventures."

"When are you leaving?" Elspeth asked, turning her attention on Ethan.

Ethan looked around at the others. He didn't think anyone was overly excited to get back on the road again. They could all use a little rest. Yet, seeing Guinevere's anxious expression, he knew they really didn't have that luxury.

"Within a day or so," he replied.

Elspeth, Fearghas and Ainslee exchanged looks. He wasn't sure what the looks meant, but he had a feeling they were about to give him bad news. "Is something wrong?"

"Tell him, dear," Elspeth prodded her husband with her elbow.

Fearghas rubbed his arm and sighed. He took a long draw of his own mead. "I take it you will be heading north - through Castlehaven."

Raising an eyebrow, Ethan nodded. "That was the plan. Is something wrong with that plan?"

"Just tell him," the innkeeper's wife prodded her husband.

Rolling his eyes, Fearghas took another draw of his mead. "There's dark rumors coming out of Castlehaven..."

"Really dark," Ainslee added.

"What rumors?" Nia asked, voicing the question before Ethan could ask.

Fearghas cleared his throat. "The last caravan, about a month and a half ago, mentioned that the city had really stepped up its slave trade. Even people who committed crimes were being made slaves..."

"They make slaves of their own people?" Drorm asked, not bothering to hide the disgust in his voice.

The innkeeper nodded. "The caravan master, a halfling named Athalia..."

"Athalia?" Ethan interrupted, the name ringing a bell. "Why does that name sound familiar?"

"It was that obnoxious halfling we talked to in Castlehaven to get the trade restarted," Ainslee answered. "I didn't recognize her either, but she remembered me. Said she had an eye for faces."

The memory came flooding back to him. They'd talked to a female halfling about restarting trade with

Hawkshead. She hadn't been particularly helpful, but she had put them on the right track.

"Anyhow." Fearghas cleared his throat. "She was worried. She said in addition to elves, foxlings and other races, any non-human citizen committing a crime was being sentenced to slavery and then sold off to the temple of Hel. To be sacrificed."

There was silence around the table as everyone absorbed what the innkeeper had just told them.

"And the prince is okay with that?" Guinevere asked, her lip curled in disgust.

"From what she said," Ainslee said in an uncharacteristic somber tone, "the new laws are coming from the prince. Apparently, he's a convert of the temple of Hel."

Ethan's eyes went wide. "Are you serious?"

Fearghas, Elspeth and Ainslee all nodded in unison. Fearghas looked down and fidgeted with his mug. He purposefully didn't look at Drorm. "She also said that Highshire had fallen to the orcs."

"Ha!" Drorm laughed. "They surrendered the city to us when the dragon began attacking. We did not wage war on them."

Fearghas held up his hands in a gesture of peace. "It's just what she said."

Ethan frowned, thinking about all of the people who must have been sacrificed. He wished there was something he could do, but his small group couldn't take on an entire city.

"The point we were making was," Fearghas continued, "that you should stay clear of the city."

"And bands of slavers," Ainslee asked, giving Fearghas a pointed look. "Remember?"

"Ah... right." The innkeeper nodded. "The slave trade is so lucrative, there are bands of mercenaries who are collecting people and turning them over to the city or to the temple directly. Villagers, travelers, merchants, whoever they can find. They've even sent the army north to Moonpoint."

"Moonpoint?" Michalus said with alarm.

His group had rescued some elves from a band of slavers and they'd gone north to Moonpoint. Later, they'd found a handful of elven children who had avoided capture. They'd met Michalus shortly after and he'd agreed to take them to Moonpoint to reunite them with their families. Now it seemed, they could all be in danger.

"That's what she said," Elspeth replied with a bob of her head.

"Trying to get more slaves," Ainslee spat. "They're despicable."

Ethan looked to Michalus. "Do you know a way to bypass Castlehaven? Another route that will avoid the city and the surrounding countryside?"

Michalus nodded. "We could take a more direct route. But, that's rough country."

Guinevere smirked. "Is there any other sort?"

"We can make it," Nia said confidently.

"I agree with Nia," Drorm added. "After trolls and giants..."

"And dragons," Par'karr squeaked.

"And dragons," the big orc added with a nod to the kobold, "I think we can manage it."

Ethan was nodding, but not at their conversation. An idea had popped into his head, one that would allow them to bypass the city and shave weeks off their journey. He smiled.

"There's another way too," Ethan told the group. "And it might save us a whole lot of time."

"Oh?" Michalus asked, his eyebrows raised in interest. "A different path?"

"Not exactly." Ethan grinned. "I was thinking more of portaling directly to your house."

"My house?" the wizard said with surprise. Then he cocked his head and scratched his chin. After a moment, he began to nod, then he smiled. "You know, that just might work."

6

The plan was simple. Michalus's portal pouch led to a chest back in his house. For that to work, there were three unique runes created by the wizard carved into the bottom of the chest. All Ethan had to do was memorize the runes, scry the area and then open a portal. Simple, right?

Not quite, it turned out. Memorizing the nonsensical runes that Michalus had created turned out harder than he thought. It took him nearly an hour of repeatedly shaping them with Earth magic before he finally had them memorized.

Then, there was the *Scrying*. He spent the rest of the day trying to *Scry* the runes but getting nothing. It wasn't until just before dinner he realized why. It was the same issue the fishman king had encountered when he'd placed the trident inside the boulder. You couldn't see anything because it was pitch black.

After talking over the situation with Michalus over

dinner, Ethan went back home and practiced *Scrying* the chest and then shifting focus. From what the wizard said, it was possible to change the focus on an object - like zooming in and out. The problem, as usual, was that Michalus only had a theoretical knowledge of how it was done.

But after two hours, Ethan was finally able to shift his focus out of the chest and into the wizard's house. Another hour later, he was able to stretch his focus just outside the wall of Michalus's home.

With an effort of will, Ethan opened a small portal to the location he was *Scrying*. Immediately he felt the strain on his mind as he kept the portal open and the scrying open. His head began to throb. Knowing he had little time before a full-fledged headache came on, he tested the portal by sticking his hand through it. Sure enough, he saw it in his *Scry* vision.

With a little cheer, Ethan let the magic go and slumped back in the chair. He was mentally exhausted but felt great about actually getting the *Scrying* and portaling work at the same time.

"You did it?" Nia asked, propping herself up on her hands. She had come in earlier from hunting and flopped on the bed.

Ethan hadn't been able to pay much attention to her while he had been concentrating but now he realized she was naked, except for a sheet. He grinned. "I did!"

"I knew you would," she said confidently. "You are a great wizard."

"I'm okay," he retorted, thinking about the power that Merlin must have, not to mention the dragons.

"I think you are a great wizard," she said, moving so that the sheet slid off half of her. "And you probably have lots of mana to be restored."

Ethan looked over the curves of his wife's body and his grin grew wider. He nodded. "Oh yes. Lots of mana."

Quickly stripping off his own clothes, he joined his wife in bed.

THE NEXT MORNING AT BREAKFAST, Ethan related his success to the group. He told them of being able to *Scry* Michalus's cabin and open a portal just outside it.

"That is quite remarkable," Michalus said when he'd stopped talking. "So much progress, in so little time. I guess at this point, I shouldn't be surprised."

"Hey," Ethan countered. "You gave me plenty of useful hints. I think I'd still be trying to work it out if it weren't for your suggestions."

"Always nice to know that the books you dedicated your life to studying are finally useful," the wizard said.

"Does this mean you're leavin', wizard-boy?" Ainslee asked. Once again, the dwarf had joined them for breakfast. At the moment, she was wolfing down a half dozen eggs and some fried potatoes with onions.

Ethan glanced around the table at his companions. "Do you want to leave today?"

Guinevere bit her lip and looked around the table before answering. "I'm ready today. But I understand if some of you need more time."

"I am ready, as well," Drorm said. He was working on the same breakfast as Ainslee.

"Par'karr ready," the little kobold squeaked. As Ethan watched, Par'karr broke open a raw egg and poured it into his mouth. Seeing the kobold do it, Ethan hoped his friend was immune to salmonella.

Michalus nodded. "It would be nice to be home, even if for a short time."

Nia gave Ethan a nod. "I am ready when you are."

"I guess it's settled. Let's get everything packed up..." Ethan started but Ainslee interrupted him.

"Whoa, wizard-boy!" she said. "Not so fast. You need to wait until this afternoon before you go jumping through your portal!"

Ethan furrowed his brow. "Why?"

"I told you I was going to make you a scabbard for that sword of yours," she retorted, glancing over at the sword against the wall. He'd placed it there again to prevent hurting anyone.

He started to object but Nia put a hand on his shoulder and looked at Ainslee. "We can wait a few hours. A scabbard for his sword would be most helpful."

Turning towards his wife, Ethan gave her a questioning look.

Nia grimaced. "You almost cut me four times yesterday and three times this morning."

Ethan made an apologetic expression. "I'm sorry, I didn't even..."

"We need to work on your swordsmanship... and your awareness of the blade," she told him. Her tone held the promise of many long hours of muscle aches. He grimaced but knew she was right. If he was going to carry the sword, he should know how to use it.

"I can help instruct him too," Guinevere offered. She gave Nia an evil wink. "I know some very grueling... I mean, helpful... drills."

Nia smiled at the warrior woman and Ethan groaned.

"You have women competing to see who can inflict the most pain on you!" Drorm laughed. "A lucky man indeed!"

"Oh yeah," Ethan muttered under his breath. "So lucky."

"Well then," Michalus said, giving Ethan a small sympathetic glance. "I guess we'll at least be here for lunch. I for one wouldn't mind another one of Mistress Elspeth's delicious meals."

The innkeeper's wife beamed. "I will make sure I make a fitting farewell meal, then."

"I guess I can break out another keg of mead," Fearghas said with a smile.

"Now we're talkin'!" Ainslee said, rubbing her hands together. Looking at her plate, Ethan saw that it was completely clean. He shook his head. Sometimes he'd swear the dwarf had a portal in her mouth, given how much she could eat.

Ethan reached into his pouch and pulled out some gold. Before he could hand them over to Fearghas, the dwarven innkeeper waved them away. "I ain't takin' your gold, mayor. After everything you've done for this town, it's the least we do. Besides, without the caravans coming through, we ain't got nothing to spend it on."

Remembering the previous conversations, Ethan nodded. There might not be caravans for a long time. And if things were as bad as they said, the next caravan that came to the town, might be a slave caravan. He turned to Ainslee.

"How much iron do you have?" he asked.

"A fair bit yet," she replied. "Why? You need something made?"

"Yes," he told her. He looked from Ainslee, to Fearghas and finally to Elspeth. "If you're right, it's possible the slavers might come south looking for more slaves."

Elspeth and Fearghas exchanged knowing looks and Ethan raised an eyebrow.

Fearghas sighed. "We thought the same thing. The halfling said there were already roaming mercenaries looking to make an easy buck by scouring the surrounding countryside."

"That's insanity," Guinevere growled. "If they take the farmers and other villagers who supply goods and trade with the city, how do they think they are going to get enough food for the citizens?"

Drorm scowled. "I doubt they are thinking that far ahead."

"That's the most basic rule of war," Guinevere said with a shake of her head. "Always keep your supply lines open. In this case, the surrounding farms and villages are their supply lines."

"From what Athalia said, the prince has lost his mind," Fearghas sighed. "I don't think he's considering the long-term impact."

Guinevere snorted. "It won't be that long. Without a regular supply of food, even the most noble city will end up turning on itself. People have to eat."

"Be that as it may," the innkeeper said. "We do worry that they'll make it here."

Ethan nodded. "That's why I want Nia to make spearheads. You can season some wood and make real spears, not the crude things we used against the kobolds."

Ainslee bit her lip. "That would take most of the iron we have. There won't be any left for things like nails, hammers, shovels and the like."

"Maybe so," Ethan replied. "But if the slavers make it this far, you'll be glad you had them."

The dwarf blacksmith sighed and nodded. "I guess you're right."

Remembering Ainslee came from a world that was slightly more advanced than this world, he hazarded a guess. "Do you know how to make crossbows?"

"For the most part," she said. "But I don't really do much with wood."

"Crossbows are fairly easy to use and will puncture most armor I've seen," Ethan said and then looked at Guinevere in her full plate. "Except hers. Having a few villagers with crossbows raining bolts down on attackers, might just make them pause."

Ethan remembered the cooper, Hamish. "Maybe draw up some plans and give them to Hamish to see what he can do. Even a half dozen might turn the tide."

"You really think we should be worried?" Fearghas asked. "I mean, that's a lot of work and resources you're talking about."

"Considering what this village has been through in the short time I've been here," Ethan replied. "I think there's a good enough chance that we should be prepared."

The innkeeper let out a heavy sigh, suddenly looking years older. "You may be right."

"And don't worry," Ethan told him. "If trouble comes, I'll give you a way to contact me. With portal magic, we can be here in no time."

Fearghas and Elspeth both brightened. The innkeeper's wife put a hand on her husband's shoulder. "I think everyone will be glad to know that our wizard-mayor will help us when we need it."

7

Ethan wanted to make some sort of message bag that they could use to exchange messages. He thought about using his chest, which was linked to a portal pouch he kept with him. Unfortunately the chest was frequently used for storing meat he managed to freeze with magic. He was afraid a message left there would be missed.

Going through the magical items he'd created, he remembered the noise-cancelling necklaces. He'd made them to protect Nia and Yuliana from the high-pitched sound the Grail emitted. But they really hadn't used them since they restored the Grail to its rightful place. There was also his first attempt at the noise-cancelling necklaces - the necklace of silence.

He looked down at the magical items. They had been some of the first items Ethan had crafted. It seemed almost wrong to destroy them. But, in the end, the needs of the village came before nostalgia. He needed the crystals in them.

Cannibalizing the Chymera stones from the necklaces, he had enough to create another portal pouch. He spent the rest of the day linking it to runes he inscribed on the inside of a small metal coffer. The tiny copper chest had most likely been used to store the previous mayor's money. Sadly, it had been empty when Ethan had taken over his former residence.

Once the new portal pouch was complete, Ethan gave the coffer to Fearghas. The innkeeper and his wife had both used the magical haversack and even Ethan's magical chest, so they were familiar with the concept.

"I'll try to check it during every meal," Ethan told the couple at dinner. "So if you drop a note in there, it should be at most 4 hours before I read it unless it's at night. I'll check it again before I go to sleep, so 8 hours or so at night."

"Hopefully, we won't ever need it," Fearghas said, taking the coffer.

"When are you leaving?" Elspeth asked.

"Tomorrow," Ethan answered, looking around at his companions for confirmation. Everyone gave him an affirmative answer or gesture. "First thing tomorrow morning."

"Not quite enough room in my cabin for all of us to spend the night," Michalus chuckled. Then he scratched his chin. "Unless some of us slept out on the porch."

"Tomorrow morning," Ethan said again.

"Fine, fine," the wizard said with a dismissive gesture. "I was just thinking of ideas. If you want a cozy bed, I completely sympathize."

"Actually," Ethan said with a grin. "It was more Elspeth's food I was thinking about. So, make that... tomorrow after breakfast."

"I'll eat to that!" Ainslee said, holding up a half-eaten leg of mutton and taking a large bite out of it. "It'll give me time to put the finishing touches on your scabbard!"

THE GROUP ATE a breakfast of eggs, fried tomatoes, sausage, and beans the next morning. Once done with the hearty meal, they said their farewells to Ainslee and the villagers. Ethan wished they could have stayed longer, but he knew Guinevere was anxious to find her father. He couldn't blame her. He was looking forward to meeting the legendary Merlin too.

Ainslee, who was also at breakfast, presented him with a brand-new scabbard. "Here ya go, wizard-boy!"

Taking the scabbard, Ethan held it up to admire it. He whistled. "You created this just in... what... the last day or so."

The dwarven blacksmith shrugged. "Not my best work, but it was rushed. Might have had it done sooner if Hamish would have gotten off his wrinkly old arse and carved it out sooner."

Ethan shook his head and examined the scabbard more closely. The scabbard was made of dark wood that appeared to have been stained or treated somehow. The corners of the scabbard were reinforced with gray metal bands. The top and bottom of the scabbard were also trimmed in gray metal but looked like it had been inlaid with gold.

The thing which really caught his attention was the golden "E" that was affixed to the scabbard, about six inches below the top of the scabbard. He looked at Ainslee with a smile. "E for Ethan?"

Ainslee rolled her eyes. "Well, it WAS E for Excalibur, but E for Ethan works too."

He nodded. "So it does. What's the gold metal?"

"Uh... it's gold, wizard-boy," she retorted with another roll of her eyes. "I know you've seen gold before."

"Wait... how... why..." Ethan stammered, trying to figure out where she had gotten gold ore from and why she would use it on the scabbard.

"I melted some of my gold coins," she replied with a smile. Ainslee looked thoughtful. "Come to think of it, technically, I guess it was your gold... so, I'm just returning it."

"Very impressive," Guinevere told the dwarf. "As good as any smith in Camelot."

Ainslee beamed. "I guess they didn't have any dwarven smiths in Camelot."

"It suits you," Nia said. "Put it on so you can safely carry your sword around."

Ethan looked at the scabbard and then at his sword. "I hope it fits."

"Of course it will fit!" Ainslee snapped. "What do you think I am? A novice?"

He furrowed his brow, trying to think back to whether the dwarf had made any measurements of his sword.

Ethan didn't recall her doing so. "When did you measure it up?"

Once again, Ainslee rolled her eyes at him. "I knew the exact size of the blade the first moment I laid eyes on it. I told you, I'm a very good smith."

Ethan whistled. "You are indeed."

"Now," Ainslee said. "Do what your wife said and put it on."

Nodding, Ethan took the offered scabbard, and strapped it to his belt with the leather straps Ainslee handed him. He adjusted it to a comfortable position and then, taking Excalibur, he slid his sword into it. It fit perfectly.

Ethan whistled again. "Wow! You weren't lying. It's a perfect fit!"

"Of course it is!" Ainslee grinned.

With his new sword strapped to his hip, Ethan and his friends quickly finished up their meal. He and his group assembled in front of his home. When everyone was ready, he *Scryed* Michalus's house again. It was much easier this time. Once he locked on the area outside the house, Ethan opened a portal large enough for their horses.

One by one, Ethan's friends went through the portal. He saw them through the portal as they arrived on the other side. Finally, it was only Guinevere and himself. Nia had taken his horse through already and someone must have taken hers too. It was just the two of them.

"Go ahead," he told her.

"I want to go with you," Guinevere replied, biting her

lip. "Nia told me she saw my father too when you went through together. I want to see him."

Ethan nodded and mentally kicked himself for not thinking of it earlier. He felt like an idiot. Of course she would want to see her father! He should have offered earlier. "Yes, of course. Grab my hand."

Guinevere grabbed his hand, her palms calloused from years of swordplay. Definitely not the soft hands of a queen.

"On three, you go first and pull me in," he said. "1...2...3!"

On the count of three, she did just that. With surprising strength, she stepped into the portal and yanked him along after her. He crashed into her and they tumbled through the rainbow tunnel of the Bifrost.

Ethan had fallen atop of Guinevere and was holding onto her so they didn't separate. In order for her to see Merlin, she had to be going through with Ethan while he was wearing Excalibur. At least, that was his prevailing theory at the moment.

Mist began to form in the Bifrost, just in front of Ethan's face. The same man's face appeared in a ghostly pale visage and looked at Ethan and then Guinevere.

"Free me..." the voice started, in the familiar ghostly tone but then it stopped as the face turned back to Guinevere. Despite the ghostly visage, Ethan saw shock... and maybe happiness on the visage's face. "Gwenny? Is that..."

The two of them emerged from the Bifrost. Ethan landed heavily on the armored form of Guinevere but she didn't react at all. Her face had a similar look of shock.

Ethan tried to get up, but the warrior woman was still holding him. He looked down at her. "Uh... Guinevere?"

For a moment, she looked at him without really seeing him. Then her face grew excited. "That was him! That was my father!"

Guinevere pulled his head down to her and planted a kiss on his lips before pushing him off her and standing up.

His other companions were looking down at the pair in confusion. No doubt their strange entrance had made quite a scene.

Ethan found Nia looking down at him as well. She shook her head and rolled her eyes at him. "You males are all the same."

8

Michalus spent a little time checking out his home and making sure everything was in order. It had been months since the wizard had been back to his home and things looked a bit overgrown. He made some feeble efforts to clean things up before finally giving up.

"It will just have to wait until we get back!" the wizard growled in an exasperated tone, as he tossed the fallen branch he'd been moving to the ground. "My garden is ruined and I'll have to replant it."

"Animals?" Ethan asked, glancing at the area where the wizard's garden had been. It was now overgrown with weeds and it appeared that most of the vegetable plants had been eaten.

"Rabbits," Par'karr replied before Michalus could reply. The kobold pointed to several rabbits that suddenly sprinted from underneath a plant Ethan didn't recognize.

Michalus sighed. "Yes, rabbits. They ate everything."

"Sorry about the garden," Ethan said.

"If I'm not here to tend it," the wizard lamented, "they'll eat the entire thing - which they did."

Ethan cocked his head, a smile coming to his lips as he thought about the Grail and its animal repellent sound. "You know, maybe you could rig up a device that emitted a sound like the Grail - only much less powerful. It would keep the rabbits away."

Michalus brightened and scratched his chin. "You know, that might just be my next project. I'd have to make one of those necklaces you made or else it would drive me nuts too!"

"True enough," Ethan agreed. He looked around at the scattered branches that had fallen during his absence. "We could help you..."

"No, no," the wizard retorted, waving him off. "The day is wasting and I know the lady wants to get to Patheos."

Guinevere, who had been staring off into the forest, turned her head. "Assuming there is even anything there for us to find."

"It seems like a long distance to travel without knowing if there is anything waiting for you," Drorm commented.

The big orc had been quiet since they portaled away from his people. Ethan had tried to ask Drorm if he was okay, but the stoic orc had waved off his concerns. He knew it couldn't be easy for Drorm to leave his friends and family behind. But unless the orc wanted to talk about it, there was nothing else Ethan could do.

Ethan shrugged. "I don't know where else to start. The last place you saw your father was Patheos. And I found his journal in Patheos. Everything seems to point there."

He'd made a few portal attempts to try and get more from Merlin, but the ghostly apparition seemed either unwilling or unable to answer his question about where he was. That left only one option, return to the last place Guinevere had seen him.

"Anyone else have any ideas?" Ethan asked, glancing at his companions. "I'm open to suggestions."

They all looked around at one another for a moment and finally Ethan sighed. "It is a long distance to travel, but we can portal back here afterwards. So at least we won't have to travel back."

Drorm grunted but said nothing.

"Daylight is wasting," Nia said, looking up at the twin suns. "If we are going, then we should go now."

No one else had any objections so the group retrieved their horses and gathered near the edge of Michalus's clearing.

"You know the way to the road, right?" Ethan asked, not really remembering the way himself. It had been months since they'd been here and he couldn't recall the way.

Michalus chuckled. "Of course, my boy. I've been roaming these forests for over two hundred years. Follow me."

THE GROUP FOLLOWED the wizard east through the forest for the rest of the day. Just before dark, they found a small clearing. It appeared to be a perfect spot for a campsite, so they stopped for the night.

The group quickly tied up the horses and unpacked their bedrolls. Once that was done, Drorm and Guinevere started towards the forest to collect some firewood. Nia grabbed her bow to go hunting.

Unfortunately, they hadn't been able to stock up on any travel supplies while they were in Hawkshead. Elspeth hadn't had time to make them any jerky and no one else in the village had any. That meant they'd need to hunt on the way to Patheos and freeze any extra meat for when they reached the desolated area that surrounded the ruined city.

Ethan saw his wife stop at the edge of the clearing and that was when he noticed the forest had gone eerily quiet. She sniffed the air and started to call out when huge shapes burst from the forest with a bellow!

Two enormous humanoids bounded into the clearing. Ethan recognized them instantly, having fought them twice before. They were ogres - very large ogres. Running in front of the ogres were two huge grizzly bears on thick ropes that the ogres held!

Like the ones they'd encountered before, the creatures were twice as tall as a man, at least twelve feet tall. They had long, thick arms that dragged on the ground and shorter, under-sized legs, like a gorilla or other primate.

One of the ogres had large, drooping breasts that identified it as female. Since she was alongside the male, Ethan could see that the female was slightly smaller than the male. Despite that, judging by their equally thick arms, they were just as lethal.

Both the male and female ogres had some sort of white paint-like substance on their chests. It was crude and reminded him of the paint the Aboriginal people in Australia used. Ethan couldn't be sure, but it looked like a hand. Or maybe it was a fist.

While neither of the ogres wore clothing on their chest, they did wear crude furs that covered up their groins. Even from where Ethan stood, he could tell that the hides were untreated and in the process of rotting. But that didn't matter at the moment, as the creatures bore down on his group.

Despite her surprise, Nia managed to shoot the lead grizzly bear with an arrow. The shaft thudded into the bear's chest, but it didn't even pause. It charged forward and snapped at her with its large mouth.

Easily dodging the huge bear, Nia deftly rolled out of the way. Dropping her bow, she drew her scimitars in a smooth, fluid motion. She managed to get them out in time to deflect the snap of the second bear.

Drorm and Guinevere both spun, drawing their weapons, and hurried into the melee. Ethan, Michalus and Par'karr were slower to react. Ethan grabbed Excalibur's hilt and pulled the sword free of its scabbard.

Seeing the two bears snapping at his wife and the two ogres almost on her, Ethan created a wall of *Fire* in front of the charging ogres. He pushed the same amount of *Mana* into the wall of fire as he thought he had when he'd used it on the fishmen.

The wall of fire exploded out of the ground. Unlike his previous wall, this one was nearly fifteen feet tall and three feet wide. It appeared directly in front of the charging ogres. Ethan was nearly twenty feet away and he felt the heat from where he was, flinching away from the sudden heat and light.

The wall was larger and more intense than Ethan had expected and he guessed the flawless Chymera stone in the sword was to thank. Whatever the reason, the hulking brutes could not stop in time and plunged into the fiery wall.

```
You critically burn Bloody Fist Ogre
for 49 fire damage.
    You  critically  burn  Bloody  Fist
Ogre for 47 fire damage.
```

The sudden appearance of a burning wall also caused the bears to yelp and stumble back from the raging inferno. The distraction was enough that Nia could tumble between them and retreat to where Drorm and Guinevere were standing.

The ogres emerged from the wall of fire bellowing in pain. The fire had set the loincloths on their groins on ablaze, as well as set alight their hair and fur. The creatures dropped to the ground and began rolling around, trying to extinguish the flames.

Ethan cocked his head. Apparently, stop, drop and roll was a thing on this world too. Maybe it was just common sense, or perhaps some sort of instinct.

"Quick!" Drorm yelled, charging. "While they are on the ground!"

Drorm, Guinevere and Nia charged forward but were intercepted by the grizzlies. The large bears lumbered in front of them, growling and swiping. Like dogs protecting their masters, Ethan thought.

Small shapes blurred past the group and Par'karr's rabbits launched themselves at the two bears. One embedded its unicorn horn in the bear's shoulder, causing the creature to bellow and chomp down on the rabbit. The rabbit immediately disappeared into dust.

Through sheer luck, or amazing skill, the other rabbit launched itself just right. Its horn penetrated the bear's eye and embedded itself deep in the grizzly's brain. The creature stiffened and then dropped to the ground, lifeless.

The ogres bellowed again as a fireball cast by Michalus exploded between the two of them, burning them even more. The creatures bellowed even louder, though in pain or rage, Ethan couldn't tell.

Ethan still had the wall of fire up and was about to dismiss it when he got an idea. Channeling a bit more *Mana*, he caused the wall to collapse onto the ground, atop the two writhing ogres. The effect was a two-foot-tall field of fire that completely encompassed the two ogres.

```
You burn Bloody Fist Ogre for 28
fire damage.
    You burn Bloody Fist Ogre for 31
fire damage.
```

The two ogres' bellows became primal screams as they tried desperately to get out of the field of fire. They didn't make it. One of them collapsed as it was standing up and the other managed two steps before falling over.

```
You  burn  Bloody  Fist  Ogre  for  28
fire damage.
   You  burn  Bloody  Fist  Ogre  for  31
fire damage.
   You  burn  Bloody  Fist  Ogre  for  28
fire damage.
   You  burn  Bloody  Fist  Ogre  for  31
fire damage.
   Bloody Fist Ogre dies.
   You     gain     150     experience.
Experience to next level 23,140.
   Bloody Fist Ogre dies.
   You     gain     150     experience.
Experience to next level 22,990.
```

The second bear went down under a flurry of blows to its neck, including a massive chop of Drorm's axe that covered the orc in a spray of blood and dropped the grizzly. Ethan guessed he must have hit the carotid artery.

Ethan wrinkled his nose as the stench of burning meat assaulted his nostrils and he dismissed the wall of fire to reveal two charred corpses.

The group looked around for any more enemies but there were none standing. The two bears and two extra crispy ogres were all still.

Nia looked down at the bear in front of her then looked over to Ethan. "I hope you like bear meat."

~

THE QUEEN LOOKED DOWN *and saw that, in a fit of anger, she'd impaled two of her soldiers. She clicked angrily, knowing she couldn't afford to keep killing them. In her hive, she could have easily grown more. Now, without her hive and the special food her workers created, growing more soldiers wasn't an option.*

The infuriating human wizard had created another portal. Now he was east and even further north. She rubbed her antennae together, getting a fix on the location of the wizard. Then, mentally, she ordered her remaining minions to follow her as she sprinted towards the portal - and the human wizard.

9

Nia hadn't been joking and began to skin the bears. The old Ethan would have been squeamish but considering some of the things he'd seen, the new Ethan was barely fazed. Instead, he turned his attention to the charred ogre bodies.

"They reek!" Guinevere said, scrunching up her nose.

Drorm snorted and rubbed his nose. "That they do!"

"Ogre smell bad." Par'karr bobbed his head up and down.

"Perhaps we should drag the bodies away from the clearing," Ethan suggested.

"Actually, I think we should move on," Michalus spoke slowly as he stared down at the bodies.

"It's almost dark," Ethan pointed out.

"Even so," the wizard started and then bit his lip and then looked from the ogre bodies to the forest. "I think we should move on."

"They don't smell that bad," Ethan joked. "Plus, we're going to drag them away."

Michalus shook his head. "No, that's not what I mean. Those were Bloody Hand ogres, or is it Bloody Fist? I can never remember. They're a tribe that roams the forest west of here - or rather, they used to roam the forest west of here. It appears they've come east."

"Tribe?" Par'karr asked. "More ogres?"

Everyone stopped what they were doing and turned to Michalus. Ethan furrowed his brow as he thought of the implications. "Are you saying there might be a whole tribe out here somewhere?"

"Loki's Pale Balls!" Guinevere swore, reminding Ethan of Ainslee. "That's all we need, a tribe of ogres!"

Drorm frowned and looked around the clearing, peering into trees. "How many ogres are in a tribe?"

"Many?" Par'karr asked, head whipped back and forth as the little kobold looked around the forest.

Everyone looked at Michalus but the wizard just shrugged. "I have no idea. I've only seen a few, here and there, in my travels. They stayed west, I stayed east. It was a good relationship."

Ethan remembered the three ogres they'd killed the last time they were in this area. "Were the ogres we killed last time part of the tribe?"

"No, no paint. Most likely outcasts that wandered west." Michalus shook his head.

"Why do you think these tribe members have come east?" Ethan asked.

"I have no idea, my boy," the wizard replied with an

exasperated sigh. "They never ventured this far east before."

"Probably food," Nia called from where she was cutting up the bear. "Or expanding their territory."

"Food," Par'karr said confidently. "Ogres big. Always hungry maybe."

"Maybe," Ethan conceded. He imagined with as large as the creatures were, they must have large appetites. He wondered how much game an entire tribe would eat.

"But why choose this particular time to expand?" Michalus wondered aloud.

"What's west?" Guinevere asked, beating Ethan to the question.

"Some villages, several days' walk - as you know, a town, and then Castlehaven," the wizard replied.

Drorm growled. "Didn't the villagers say something about Castlehaven sending out mercenaries to find sacrifices? Do you think they would try to capture ogres?"

Ethan whistled. "I think it would take quite a few mercenaries to capture one ogre, let alone several. And a tribe? They'd need an army."

"I agree," Guinevere nodded. "An army would be..."

The warrior woman trailed off and looked west. Ethan peaked an eyebrow. "You have an idea?"

"An army..." she continued. "I was saying, you'd need an army. Didn't they say Moonpoint and Castlehaven are at war and that they sent an army to attack them?"

"Yes, I'm pretty sure that's what they said," Ethan replied. He remembered the conversation and being concerned over the elven children Michalus had escorted to Moonpoint. "What are you getting at?"

"Maybe the army scared them east," the warrior woman suggested.

Michalus frowned. "How? The army would have gone north to Moonpoint, up the coastal highway."

Guinevere sighed. "Sure, if they were doing a frontal attack - which Moonpoint would expect. A more tactical idea would be to march a few days east, then cut north. They could go north past Moonpoint and circle around the city to attack their flank."

"Where they don't expect an attack to come from." Drorm nodded his approval. "A sound tactic."

"Then you really think the Castlehaven army went east and then north?" Ethan asked. Guinevere's idea seemed feasible. He knew that in certain MMORPGs with player versus player (PvP), he'd seen guilds use the same tactic. But would that really work in real life?

Ethan frowned. "What about scouts? Villages along the way? Travelers who see them?"

"Villages will be sacked and travelers will be killed," Drorm said matter of factly. "It is war."

Guinevere nodded. "Drorm's right. It's war. They'll do whatever they have to in order to win. Plus, from what they said of the prince, I doubt he has any qualms about some collateral damage."

"And if they did come east and then go north," Michalus ventured. "That might explain the ogres' migration east."

"If there are more ogres coming, then we shouldn't camp here. Another group could stumble into us," Ethan said. He looked up at the fading light. "And we should put some space between us before it gets completely dark."

"Ethan!" Nia called to him.

Turning, he saw that she had some large cuts of meat lying atop one of the carcasses. The foxgirl gestured to the pile of meat. "Use your magic to freeze this and put it into your magical pouch."

"I'll freeze the meat," he told the group. Ethan gestured to the horses. "The rest of you get the horses ready to move. Let's get as far as we can."

The others muttered agreements and they all set about their tasks. Ethan walked over to Nia and began to freeze the meat and slip it into his pouch. He wrinkled his nose at the meat but said nothing. He just hoped it tasted better than it smelled.

After only a few minutes, his companions were ready to leave. Ethan quickly finished up freezing the meat and then joined them. Everyone looked at him.

"Nia," he told his wife. "Take the lead and keep your nose peeled for any more ogres. Everyone else, keep an eye out."

There were affirmative mutters and grunts and then Nia started their procession north. They moved as quickly as they dared in the fading light to prevent the horses from having a mishap.

After only thirty minutes, Nia called them to a halt. Ethan was about to ask the foxgirl why she'd done it but then he heard something to the west. Grunting and growling. Looking, he saw the flicker of light through the trees.

"Is that what I think it is?" Guinevere asked, though Ethan guessed she already knew the answer.

"Ogres!" Par'karr squealed softly. His rabbits seemed to sense his fear and huddled against the kobold's legs.

"Ogres," Nia hissed. The foxgirl sniffed the air, her ears twitching and rotating as she looked around the forest. "There are some to the west but others following us."

"More?!" Par'karr whimpered.

Ethan cursed. "Are they tracking us? How did they catch up..."

He had started to ask how the ogres had caught up to them, but stopped. The answer seemed obvious. Given the creatures' large size, their gait must be twice as long as a human stride. Ethan and his companions were forced to lead the horses through the forest. That meant it had probably been easy to catch up with them.

"They are using light," Drorm pointed out. "That means they cannot see in the dark."

"Probably right," Guinevere agreed. She looked at their rag-tag group. "But then again, neither can we - except for Nia."

"I think maybe six to the west and four or five behind us," Nia told them. "I also smell more bears to the west."

"Loki's balls!" Guinevere swore. She looked around. "If we're going to fight them, we need to find a defensible spot. Someplace where we can create a bottleneck to negate their numbers."

The warrior woman looked at Ethan. "Unless you want to risk starting a forest fire with that wall of fire trick you did in the clearing."

Ethan looked around at all of the leaves and vegetation on the ground. He shook his head. "Probably not a good idea."

"Then let's get moving," Guinevere suggested.

"Michalus, do you know any defensible areas around here?" Ethan asked the wizard.

"I can't think of... wait..." The wizard looked around. "Actually, a mile from here, there's a ravine. Would that work?"

"Let's hope so," Ethan said, looking at the lights getting closer. "And let's hope we can make it there before they catch up to us."

"Which way?" Nia demanded and Michalus pointed north. Yanking on her horse's reins, the foxgirl waved them northeast. "Come!"

They all fell in line, moving faster than they had been. The risk to the horses was still there, but it was less than the risk of being caught by the ogres. Ethan glanced behind him and then to the west. It was now a race to see whether they would reach the ravine before ogres reached them.

10

As they began to move away from the clearing, Ethan heard howls from behind them. They were immediately answered by howls from the west. The horses jerked on their reins in fear, trying to run ahead of them.

"Hold on to the horses!" Drorm yelled.

"They've sighted us!" Nia hissed, glancing behind them. "Come!"

Par'karr squealed, barely able to control his horse. It dragged him several feet before Drorm reached out and grabbed the reins. He gave the kobold a stern look but then more howls pulled his attention away.

The howls began to get louder and Ethan saw the torches and shadowy shapes moving through trees. He cursed. She was right. Like any other predator, once they saw the prey, they moved in quickly.

"Go! Go!" Ethan urged and the group began to jog,

keeping pace with the terrified horses. The safety of the animals was no longer a major concern - staying alive was.

"We need light!" Drorm called out. "The trees block out the last remaining bits of light!"

Nodding, Ethan pulled out his magical lightstone. He'd made it back when they'd been exploring the tomb of Arthur. He'd actually created five of them, one for himself and each of his companions. Now, he was glad he'd held on to this one.

The small, magical stone shed a pale light in a 10-foot globe centered around him. He blinked at the sudden appearance of light. Nia pulled out her own stone. Her light, combined with his, was enough that they could at least see where they were going.

"That's good!" Drorm thanked him.

With their light, they moved quickly through the trees as the terrain became steeper. Despite their breakneck pace, the ogres were gaining. Looking back, Ethan could now see some of the ogres as they loped after them, torches held high in thick arms.

The two groups of ogres had obviously caught up to each other and there was now a line of ogres charging through the trees at them. Preceding them, on thick ropes, were several grizzly bears.

Ethan cursed. He wasn't quite sure how fast grizzlies could run but he did remember some of the local hunters back on Earth had told him you couldn't outrun a bear. And you couldn't out climb them.

Looking back at the approaching mob of ogres and grizzlies, Ethan wondered why the ogres didn't release the bears to run them down - like hunters with hunting dogs.

Were they too primitive to understand the concept? Or had they discovered what had happened to the other bears and were cautious. Whatever the reason was, he was glad they didn't.

"They are catching up with us!" Guinevere called. "I'm not sure if we'll make it!"

"We're.... almost... there!" Michalus gasped between breaths. "A little further!"

The ogres were close now, maybe a few hundred yards away. While he and the others were starting to get winded, the ogres did not seem to be affected by the run. For all he knew, this was a casual walking pace for them.

Ethan almost stumbled on an exposed root as he looked back and only the quick reflexes of the nearby Guinevere kept him from face planting. Her hand snaked out and caught his shoulder just in time.

"Eyes forward!" the warrior woman said, releasing her grip on his arm.

"Right!" Ethan puffed sheepishly and turned his eyes to the area in front of them.

As Ethan looked up the hill where they were headed, he frowned. He looked over to Michalus. "We're going INTO the ravine, right?"

The look of horror on the wizard's face told him all he needed to know. Michalus's eyes got wide and his mouth opened but no words came out. He shook his head. He grimaced. "We're heading to the top."

Ethan yelled a curse.

"What?!" Nia called from in front of him.

"We're heading to the top of the ravine!" Ethan

answered and was given a look of utter disbelief by the foxgirl.

"The top?!" his wife yelled. "We'll be cornered!"

"Exactly!" Ethan yelled back.

"I'm sorry!" the wizard cried out. "I wasn't thinking!"

"Do we stop and find a way down?" Nia asked, slowing her pace.

As he was about to answer, the group broke through the treeline. They erupted into the clearing just in time to see the last of the suns dip below the horizon. He cursed. Inside the light's pale radiance, his night vision was gone and it was difficult to see anything outside.

From what he could make out, they were in some sort of clearing. The clearing stretched for several hundred feet to either side of them and several hundred yards in front of them.

"The ground ends in one hundred yards!" Nia shouted.

Ethan cursed again. He knew that, like a cat, Nia's eyes were more sensitive than his own. She had almost perfect night vision. "You're kidding?!"

"I am not kidding!" the foxgirl shot back. "We will be trapped if we don't turn right or left!"

"Which way do we go?" Drorm demanded, slowing his pace too.

Ethan glanced left, then right. Unfortunately, the lack of detail in the fading light prevented him from making out any details. All he could really make out was the silhouette of the landscape. He swore again. "Nia, I can't see outside of the light! Is there any way down in either direction?!"

The foxgirl shook her head. "Not as far as I can see!"

His companions had slowed their pace to a walk as they waited for Ethan to tell them which way to go. They all looked at him to make a decision and unfortunately, there was no good choice.

At that moment, the ogres broke through the treeline, fifty yards behind them. They paused then, seeing their prey. It was possible that they even knew they had their quarry cornered.

More and more ogres emerged from the forest until Ethan counted over fifteen, along with six grizzlies. Ethan swore under his breath. He was fairly certain he and his companions couldn't take so many - even with both Michalus and him using their magic.

The ogres howled and pounded their chests or the ground as they stared out at Ethan and his friends. And yet, they made no other move towards them. They didn't even release their bears.

"What are they waiting for?" Nia asked. "They have the advantage in numbers and we are within easy striking range."

"Perhaps they are gathering their courage," Drorm suggested.

"They don't need courage," Guinevere spat. "They have numbers and brute strength. Not even your wall of fire trick is going to stop all of them."

Ethan nodded in agreement. He'd been thinking the same thing. The line of ogres was simply too long. If he tried creating a wall that long, he'd use up all of his *Mana* in one shot and it wouldn't kill them - probably just enrage them.

Just in case, he checked his *Mana*.

Mana: 112

He might be able to do it. He might even be able to get two walls before his *Mana* was gone. After that, he'd be useless.

"Flee?" Par'karr asked, his little voice breaking in fear. His rabbits twitched nervously at his feet, obviously sensing his distress.

"No place to..." Ethan started to say but then looked behind him towards the ravine.

"Michalus! How far is the ravine? I mean... how far to the other side?" he demanded.

The wizard scratched his chin for a moment, looking thoughtful. "I don't think I've ever really..."

"Just say you don't know," Guinevere snapped.

Michalus looked indignant for a second but then shrugged. "I don't know."

"I can portal across it!" Ethan told everyone.

"Of course!" Michalus said and then scratched his head. "Why didn't I think of that!"

Ethan admitted the thought had only just occurred to him too. Despite having portaled dozens of times, the concept of being able to just be somewhere else by stepping through a portal just wasn't natural for him.

"We need to get closer to the edge so I can see the other side," Ethan told them. "If it doesn't work, we'll portal back to Michalus's place."

"We'll lose a day of travel," Guinevere pointed out, her face revealing her urgency to find her father.

"Better than dying," Drorm said.

"Exactly," Ethan said. He looked at the ogres, who were

still posturing at the forest's edge. He furrowed his brow. "What ARE they waiting for?"

No sooner had the words left his mouth when the center of the ogres parted and a large ogre strode through to stop a dozen paces in front of the assembled creatures.

The newcomer was larger than the others but it was more than that. There was something... off, about it. It looked deformed somehow. Unfortunately, in the dim light, he couldn't quite mark out the changes.

"The big one!" hissed Nia. "It has wings!"

"Nonsense, my dear," Michalus chuckled. "Ogres don't have wi..."

The wizard trailed off as the creature unfurled large, leathery wings and a red glow formed in its hands.

Ethan barely had time to react as the red glow grew into a ball and launched itself at the group. Swearing, he barely had time to counter it with his own magic. He summoned *Water* magic to cool the ball as it raced towards them, sucking the heat out of it until it fizzled only a few feet from them.

"You felt it?" Michalus breathed.

He nodded. Ethan had felt the *Fire* magic as it was being conjured but there was something else there too. A corruption. He'd felt that sort of wrongness before - from the magic used by Mordred. This wasn't a wizard they were facing. It was an ogre who had given himself over to demons to get power.

"Channeler!" he hissed.

11

———

The ogres looked around at each other and then towards the channeler. It was obvious they had expected some sort of larger display of power. Even the ogre channeler himself looked surprised. Most likely, he'd never run into anything that could counter his magic.

He tried to bring up the ogre channeler's stats but the winged channeler was out of range. Ethan cursed. He would have preferred to at least know the thing's level and possibly confirm its class. Not that it mattered at the moment. Right now, he only had one course of action.

"Kill it!" Ethan shouted and launched his own fireball at the channeler. Only a moment later, Michalus launched one as well.

The two fireballs raced at the ogre. The creature obviously saw them coming but made no move to counter them or even avoid them. Instead he just stood there. He wasn't sure, but Ethan thought he saw the channeler's face break out in what could have been a grin.

Whoosh! Both fireballs exploded, temporarily obscuring the channeler. There were howls of pain and Ethan looked at his HUD.

```
You  burn  Bloody  Fist  Ogre  for  19
fire damage.
    You  burn  Bloody  Fist  Ogre  for  22
fire damage.
    You  burn  Bloody  Fist  Ogre  for  21
fire damage.
```

The fire and smoke dissipated quickly revealing a completely unharmed channeler. On either side of him were scorched ogres. Two ogres on the channeler's left and one on his right were beating at flames in their hair and loincloths. But the channeler himself hadn't been affected at all.

"Well that sucks," Ethan muttered, realizing that he'd been right. The ogre channeler had been grinning. Probably because he knew he was immune to fire. He cursed. Obviously, their *Fire* magic would be useless against him.

Luckily, both Michalus and he were wizards. They had access to multiple elemental magics, not just one. Looking around, he saw that the clearing they occupied was peppered with small stones. He smiled.

Ethan could shape some of the nearby rocks into spikes and then hurl them at the ogre channeler with *Air*. It would be difficult, if not impossible, for the creature to counter stones with *Fire*.

It was almost like the old paper, rock, scissors game. Some elements were better at countering other elements. And some elements did a very poor job at countering certain elements.

He could counter *Fire* with *Water*, as they were opposites. Ethan didn't think the channeler could counter stone with fire - unless he was able to get his fire hot enough to melt rock. He didn't remember exactly how hot it had to get to melt stone, but from some of the science shows about volcanoes, he knew it was pretty darn hot.

Before Ethan could enact his plan, the ogre channeler pointed at their group and bellowed something in ogre speak. The other ogres howled and charged towards his group. Par'karr screamed.

Cursing, Ethan lost sight of the channeler as the mass of ogres surged forward. There were too many to fight - especially with an ogre channeler in the mix. He glanced over his shoulder at the ravine's edge. He made a decision.

"Everyone to the ravine's edge!" he cried. Spinning, he ran towards the edge of the ravine. Everyone except Par'karr hesitated for a moment and then followed him. The kobold and his rabbits didn't have to be told twice, they spun and kept pace with Ethan.

"Ethan have plan?" the kobold squeaked as he ran alongside.

"We'll portal to the other side of the ravine!" Ethan told him.

Almost a moment too late, Ethan felt a surge of magic. He threw himself sideways at his friend and knocked him to the ground just as a wall of greenish flame erupted in front of them.

Bloody Fist Medicine Man burns you for 9 fire damage.

His quick reactions had saved Par'karr and himself from running through the wall of fire, but the heat from the wall still scorched them. Ethan grimaced at the blistering heat. Grabbing Par'karr, he scrambled back from the heat.

"Rabbits!" Par'karr cried, hand outstretched towards the flames.

Ethan looked back at the wall of fire as a chorus of howls went up from the approaching ogres. There was no sign of Par'karr's rabbits. He realized that they hadn't been able to stop in time and had gone right through it.

"I'm sorry..." Ethan started but stopped, mouth agape. Par'karr's rabbits poked their heads through the flaming wall and then hopped through it like it wasn't there.

He blinked. The rabbits were unharmed. There wasn't a mark on them. Apparently, their demonic nature must give them resistance to fire or heat. It was good to know.

Ethan smiled down at a relieved-looking Par'karr. "It looks like they're immune to fire too."

"Uh," Michalus said, looking at the ogres. "They're still coming!"

Ethan pushed himself up to his feet. One hand on Excalibur's hilt, he willed *Water* to cool down the flames but there was so much heat, he had to exert a lot of will and *Mana*. It was much more difficult than just countering the fireball.

Even as the wall faded, Ethan felt another surge of magic. "Back!"

Everyone jumped back just as another wall sprang into life where they had been.

Bloody Fist Medicine Man burns you for 11 fire damage.

"Okay," Ethan said through gritted teeth. "This guy is officially annoying."

Pushing himself to his feet once more, Ethan saw the ogres were only seconds from reaching them. He knew a wall of fire could hurt them but not stop them completely. Then again, he was a wizard. As he'd just reminded himself, he did have more than *Fire* at his command.

There wasn't enough water around to make an ice wall. An *Air* wall would require constant concentration. But, they were near a ravine. That meant, below the ground was rock. Stone. Earth. He grinned. Oh yes, wall of *Earth* it was!

With a surge of magic, he willed the stone below towards the surface. It was difficult to manipulate and he had to be careful not to destabilize the part of the rock they actually stood on and cause it to collapse into the ravine. But he managed it - barely.

A terrible roar filled the clearing as a fifteen-foot wall of stone sprang up in front of the charging ogres. Ethan wasn't sure just how thick it was, but he heard yelps and cries of pain as ogres slammed into it.

Waves of dizziness overcoming him, Ethan staggered but was caught by Nia. She looked at him with concern. "Are you well?"

Ethan looked at his HUD.

Mana: 4

He shook his head, clearing it slightly. He'd just used over a hundred *Mana* in one shot! Apparently, the strain of doing so had left him light-headed. He gave the foxgirl a half-hearted smile. "I'm fine."

Nia frowned. "You do not look fine."

Feeling steadier, Ethan stood up and only felt slightly dizzy. He took a step away from Nia and managed to keep his balance. He smiled again. "See, I'm fine."

"You're not going to be in a few minutes," Guinevere growled. "As impressive as that wall is, they'll either go around it or climb over it in a few minutes."

Ethan looked at the massive *Earth* wall. He was impressed too. He hadn't been sure he would be able to pull it off. But given the choice between trying and possibly burning some stat points and being pounded by ogres and grizzlies, he thought he'd made the right call.

"My boy," Michalus whistled. "I've never even heard of anything this large being created in one use of magic!"

Guinevere rolled her eyes and even Drorm grunted. The big orc looked down at the wizard and then to Ethan. "What is the new plan? We have minutes - if that."

Looking slightly chagrinned, Michalus shrugged and looked at Ethan. "You have a plan?"

Biting his lip, Ethan shook his head. He gave the group a grim look. "I just used up all of my mana. I have nothing left for a portal."

Everyone exchanged looks. Par'karr was the first to speak. "We is... trapped?!"

"You are a wizard too," Drorm said, looking at Michalus. "Can you make a portal for us?"

The elf shook his head. "I am not nearly as skilled at Aether magic as Ethan. I'm afraid my feeble attempt wouldn't be large enough for anyone but Par'karr to fit through."

Guinevere looked between Nia and Ethan. "You two can have sex and restore his mana, right? Not that any of us really want to see it, but can you do some sort of... you know... quickie... and give him his mana back?"

Nia looked at Ethan with a raised eyebrow and he felt blood rush to his face. He shook his head. "Not sure that would work with... all the distractions."

"Then we are trapped," Nia said with a nod. "We should begin creating a plan of defense."

Drorm and Guinevere nodded and began looking around at the wall and surrounding area.

While they did that, Ethan looked out over the ravine. He could barely make out the other side and even if he did have *Mana*, wasn't sure whether he could target the area for a portal. He cursed.

While Nia, Drorm and Guinevere talked over a plan, Ethan walked over to the edge of the ravine and looked down. He saw the shadowy bottom, two hundred feet below. If they could somehow get down, he guessed it would take the ogres an hour or more to find their way to the bottom.

Unfortunately, they only had a small amount of rope with them. It wouldn't be enough to reach the bottom. And even if they had rope, it would take too long to climb down. The ogres would be on them long before half of them made it down.

Ethan frowned. If he had all of his *Mana*, he could levitate them all down with *Air*. But given his current *Mana* state, that wasn't happening.

He cocked his head as he looked at the side of the ravine. Bending down, he looked down at the sheer face of it. He nodded. It was all rock. All stone. An idea began to form in Ethan's head and he smiled. He called Michalus over.

"Yes, my boy?" the wizard asked as he crouched down next to him.

"Remember what we did with the trolls near the waterfall?" he asked. On their way to find the dragon, they'd shaped large stepping stones out of a sheer rock wall so that they could retreat from a pack of trolls. It had allowed them to bottleneck the trolls and hold out against superior numbers.

Michalus looked over the edge and furrowed his brows. "That's a long way down. That would be a lot of stepping stones and I doubt the horses would make it down."

Ethan shook his head, still grinning. "We don't need a lot of stepping stones - just one big one."

"One big one?" the wizard repeated. "Why?"

"I think you should be able to manipulate the stone to move down the mountain - with us on it!" he told Michalus. He didn't know whether this world had any sort of lifts or elevators, so he wasn't sure how else to explain it.

Michalus looked down and then his eyes opened wide. "Are you suggesting what I think you're suggesting?!"

Ethan nodded, still grinning. "Create a stone platform attached to the side of the mountain. When we're all on it, you magically move the platform down the mountain."

"I...ah... um... " Michalus stammered and then shook his head. "I don't know if that will work."

"They're starting to climb over!" Guinevere yelled, pointing to a large hand over the top of the wall.

"We don't have a lot of time!" Ethan told the elf.

"I don't think that is sound magical theory," Michalus countered. "We have no idea if we can manipulate an existing platform - with people on it - down the mountain!"

"Try a small one with me on it! Quickly!" he told the wizard.

Michalus's mouth fell open and then he shook his head. "No! If it doesn't work..."

"I have enough mana to float myself back," Ethan told the wizard, hoping it was true. "But the fact is, if we don't do something - we're all dead anyway."

A howl erupted from the ogre who had been climbing over as an arrow thudded into its hand and the hand slipped off the wall. Ethan saw Nia with her bow and gave her a thumbs up.

"Come on!" Ethan pressed the wizard. "Just try it."

Taking a deep breath, Michalus stood up and nodded. "Okay. I'll try it."

The wizard held out his staff and the Chymera crystal flared blue as the stone near Ethan's feet rumbled and groaned. In a moment, a three-foot-by-three-foot platform of stone formed at the edge of the ravine.

Ethan didn't hesitate. He stepped onto the platform. He purposefully didn't look down. He held Excalibur's hilt in a tight grip. If need be, he was ready to channel *Air* under him if this didn't work. He took a deep breath and let it out. "Okay... move me down."

Nervously, the wizard nodded. His staff flared with light again and Ethan began to fall. No, not fall! He was moving downward atop the stone platform - just like an elevator! It was working! He went several feet down before signaling Michalus.

"It's working! Bring me back up!" he yelled and the wizard did so.

Once the platform was back up, he stepped off. "Good job! Now, you need to make it large enough to fit all of us."

Michalus grimaced. "My boy, I don't know that I have enough mana to get us down."

"We don't need to go all the way down." Ethan smiled. "We just need to get out of reach of the ogres."

Michalus looked from the wall to the platform and back. "Yes. Right. Let me get started!"

Smiling, Ethan backed away and let the wizard work while he called his friends over. It was time to sell his idea.

12

"Tell me again," Drorm growled skeptically. The orc cast a wary glance over the side of the ravine. "How is this supposed to work?"

The ogres had stopped trying to climb the wall and things were oddly quiet on the opposite side now. He could hear the howls and growls moving away to either side of the wall. Ethan turned to Nia. "What's going on over there? Are they doing what I think they're doing?"

The foxgirl cocked her head one way, then the other, her ears twitching. "They are running around the wall. Half one way, half the other way."

"Any idea which way the channeler went?" he asked. He knew it was a long shot, but sometimes Nia's abilities amazed him.

Nia shook her head. "I do not know the sound of its footsteps, so I cannot tell which one it is."

Ethan cursed and turned back to face Drorm. "Michalus is creating a platform from stone. Like the ones we created to walk on at the waterfall. We will all get on it and then Michalus will lower it down the side of the ravine."

Drorm looked at him warily. "But how will such a thing work? Will it not have to be detached from the side of the ravine to lower itself?"

Sighing, Ethan shook his head. "No... it... it's magic. He already tried it with me and it worked."

"With a smaller platform," Guinevere said.

"Yes," he replied, almost regretting that he'd told them they'd tried it with a smaller platform. "With a smaller platform. But the concept and principles are still the same."

The warrior woman raised an eyebrow. "You're sure about that?"

"As sure as I can be." Admittedly, he wasn't 100% sure about it. After all, he'd only been practicing magic for several months. But his gut said it would work. He thought about the alternative. "And much more sure than I am that we can take all of those ogres and a channeler."

That earned some mutterings from his friends. They looked at each other, as if hoping someone else would come up with a better idea. No one did.

"I go where you go," Nia said, giving the others a defiant look. "Ethan's magic has saved us many times. We should trust him."

Drorm looked thoughtful but Guinevere rolled her eyes. She shot Ethan a look whose meaning was clear. She thought Nia was just saying that because they were sleeping together.

Ethan was sure the sex had nothing to do with it. If

anything, since she had decided that he was her new alpha, she went along with whatever he did. She rarely even offered input. Although, she had been more than clear with her feelings on the dishonorable actions of the orcs.

She had spoken out about the orcs and his deal with them despite their treacherous intentions. But other than that, she always followed his lead. He almost wished she would give more input. She was a skilled warrior and the daughter of a chief. Her insight would be valuable.

He'd meant to talk to her about that very thing but there always seemed to be something happening, or something else for him to do or think about. He made a mental note to talk to her about it - knowing full well he'd probably forget again.

"Ethan?!" Nia snapped.

"What?!" he responded, snapped out of his thoughts.

Nia pointed towards the ravine's edge. "Michalus called you."

Feeling slightly embarrassed, Ethan spun towards the wizard. He was at the edge of the ravine, next to a large stone platform. Michalus had done it. He'd created a platform large enough for them to fit onto - with their horses.

"That looks good!" Ethan told the wizard.

Michalus frowned and looked unsure. He lowered his voice. "I have no idea if it will hold us all."

His other companions looked at Ethan sharply but he held out his hands placatingly. "Let's load the horses on it and we'll make sure it holds. If it doesn't work, better them than us."

Ethan knew it was cruel to use the horses as guinea

pigs but these were desperate times. Besides, the horses would die anyway once the ogres reached them. And a quick death by falling was probably preferable to being eaten by ogres.

"Hurry!" Nia shouted. "They are at the ends of the wall. They will come around any moment."

Grabbing all of the horses' reins from Par'karr, Ethan quickly led them onto the platform. He hesitated for only a moment before stepping onto the stone platform.

"Ethan!" Nia called as he walked onto the platform with the horses.

It was too late. Ethan was already on the platform and the horses followed obediently behind him. Right hand still on the hilt of Excalibur, he waited to see if the platform was going to crack or break off. Nothing happened.

The howls of the ogres grew suddenly louder as they rounded the sides of the wall on either side. As the ogres came running around the wall, they released their grizzlies. The huge bears, now free of their leashes, sprinted ahead of the ogres - directly at Ethan and his friends.

Ethan swore. "We're out of time! Get on! Now!"

His friends looked at the approaching ogres and bears and then hopped on. Ethan prayed it would hold. When the platform didn't break off, Ethan smiled. He spun towards Michalus. "Quick, Michalus! Down! Down!"

The approaching creatures were only a few dozen paces away when Ethan felt the platform lurch. It moved only a foot before coming to a halt.

"Michalus?!" Ethan shouted.

"Odin's Eyepatch!" Michalus grunted. "That is much

more difficult than moving you. It took a huge chunk of my mana!"

"What are you saying?" Guinevere said, grabbing the wizard by both arms. "What are you saying?!"

"I'm saying I don't think I can get us all the way down!"

The bears were right on top of them now. Another second or two and they'd be close enough to swipe at them or bite them.

"Go go, Michalus! Go down as far as you can!" Ethan yelled.

The wizard must have seen how close the grizzlies were because he paled. His staff flared blue and they began to quickly drop.

The grizzlies reached them but because of the height difference, the bears skidded to a halt. They growled and made other noises but didn't jump onto the platform. Instead, they looked down at Ethan's group in confusion. Clearly, they were intelligent enough to realize that stepping off a cliff was a bad thing and were hesitant to fling themselves after the group.

Ethan turned to look at his companions as the platform continued to descend. Guinevere, Nia, Drorm and even Par'karr, were all ashen. His friends looked down at the long fall and at the wall of the ravine with wide eyes.

No doubt, to them, the concept of an elevator-type platform was a completely new idea. Being on a platform that moved down a very steep cliff appeared to be terrifying to them. Unfortunately, Ethan didn't have time to think about their distress as the ogres reached the area where they had been.

Several ogres thrust their heads over the side of the

ravine to look down at his group. A few of them leaned down and tried to grab at them with their long, thick arms. Luckily, they were just out of reach of the ogres. Even as more of them tried, Michalus continued to move them lower.

About twenty-five or thirty feet down, the platform came to a halt. Alarmed, Ethan glanced at Michalus. He opened his mouth to ask the wizard why he stopped but then shut it. Michalus was breathing hard and sweat beaded his face. Looking at him, Ethan knew exactly what had happened. "You're out of mana."

Michalus nodded and leaned against one of the horses. "It's much... more difficult... than... I thought."

"Wait," Drorm said, eyes wide. "We are... stuck here?"

"Until Michalus or I get enough mana to..." Ethan responded but was cut short by a scream from Nia.

"Heads up! They are throwing rocks!" the foxgirl cried.

Ethan looked up just in time to see several large stones coming straight towards them. Luckily, he had enough *Mana* to deflect them with *Air*. Some of his *Mana* had regenerated but if the ogres kept raining stones down on them, eventually he'd run out.

"We're an easy target!" Guinevere pointed out.

"And there were many stones up there!" Drorm added.

"We be crushed by rocks?!" Par'karr squeaked.

Ethan swore. At this point, he was willing to have sex with Nia in front of everyone, just to restore his *Mana*. Unfortunately, even if he could overcome the embarrassment, that wasn't even an option now. And without *Mana*, they were going to get pelted by rocks.

Flinching as he brushed his burned arm against one

of the horses, he let out an involuntary cry. Nia looked at him with concern but he waved it away. "I rubbed the blistered part of my arm against one of the horses. I can use the Grail to heal it later..."

He stopped and blinked. Ethan played his last thought over in his head. The Grail! It healed, yes. But it also restored *Mana*! Without a moment's hesitation, Ethan reached into his portal pouch and pulled out the Grail.

The horses whinnied as he did, the high-pitch sound it emitted hurting their ears. Ignoring the horses, Ethan channeled water into the cup and took a sip. Instantly, he felt the burns disappear and felt a surge of energy. He checked his HUD.

Mana: 112

Ethan thrust the Grail at Michalus. "Drink! It restores mana too!"

The wizard took the golden chalice just as another group of rocks were hurled down on them. Now full of *Mana*, Ethan didn't just deflect them but sent them soaring back at the throwers!

Michalus drank from the Grail and then handed it back to Ethan. He slipped the Grail back into the portal pouch and then turned to the wizard. "Deflect the rocks. I'm going to see about getting us out of here."

"I don't think even you have enough Mana to get us all the way down," Michalus said.

Ethan smiled. "I have something else in mind."

Immediately, Ethan summoned his *Air Elemental* and sent it soaring to the far side of the ravine. He used *Clair-*

voyance to look through its eyes and then commanded it to circle the opposite side of the ravine.

With the elemental's sight, he was able to pick out a unique formation of rocks that he could latch onto. Committing the location to memory, he severed his connection to the elemental just in time to see a fireball soaring down at them.

It fizzled just before it hit them and Ethan knew Michalus must have countered it. Unfortunately, other ogres had taken the opportunity to throw more stones and the wizard couldn't deflect both at the same time.

Ethan was forced to use *Air* to barely deflect the large rocks just before they slammed into his friends. He swore at how close a call it had been.

"Get ready to get out of here!" he yelled and then opened a portal at the edge of the platform that led to the opposite side of the ravine.

"Go!" he yelled. "Everyone get through the portal."

His friends started to move but it was difficult to maneuver the horses and themselves in such tight confines. After what seemed like an eternity, but was probably only a few seconds, Guinevere led her horse through the portal.

Michalus countered another fireball and Ethan had to split his concentration between the portal and deflecting some more rocks. It was difficult and his head began to pound with the exertion.

Drorm went through, then Par'karr. Nia hesitated. Ethan shook his head. "Just go. I'll be right after you."

Nia looked defiant for a brief moment but then nodded and pulled their horses into the portal.

Michalus countered another fireball just as Ethan pushed away some more rocks. Ethan gritted his teeth as his headache grew. "Go!"

The wizard grabbed his horse and hurried through, leaving Ethan alone. Looking up, he saw the demonic-looking ogre channeler glaring down at him. The creature formed a large, green-tinted fireball in his hands, then threw it at him.

Ethan wasn't able to counter magic and maintain the portal at the same time. Luckily, he didn't have to. Hesitating long enough to flip off the ogre, he jumped into the portal just as the fireball hit.

~

THE QUEEN STOPPED her running and cocked her head. Her antennae rubbed together, trying to verify what she'd just felt. She'd detected Aether magic from the human wizard. She knew it was him. He was the only one she had detected who could use so much of the magic at once.

She tilted her head in the opposite direction. It felt like the wizard had created a portal, but it seemed to barely move. It was as if the wizard created a portal to the same place. That didn't make sense to the Queen.

With what the humans might call a shrug, the Queen continued running in the direction she had been. Her prey was still there and she was getting closer.

13

For a moment, Ethan was in the familiar rainbow tunnel that he had come to know as the Bifrost. As usual, the rainbow colors swirled around him with glimpses of stars, galaxies and nebulas just beyond the translucent swirl of color. Then everything went south.

Something hit him in the back, causing searing pain along his legs and lower back.

Bloody Fist Medicine Man burns you for 19 fire damage.

More than just burning him, something shoved him against the side of Bifrost and nearly through it. Suddenly, Ethan was tumbling along the surface of the Bifrost! As he made contact with the surface, multicolored sparks flew.

He tried to scream as he tumbled along the side of the Bifrost tunnel. Not only did Ethan tumble along it, he tumbled around it as well. It was suddenly as if he were in a giant clothes dryer and someone put him on tumble dry.

Ethan began to panic! It wasn't the somersaulting through a rainbow tunnel that he was afraid of. He began to wonder what would happen if he somehow "broke through" the Bifrost. What was on the other side? Space? Could he break through and end up in outer space, freezing solid in seconds? The thought was terrifying.

Then mist began to form around him. In moments, the spectral head of Merlin appeared. Once more the wailing voice in his mind said the same thing. "Find me!"

Ethan wanted to yell to the voice to help him but he suddenly found himself rolling across rocky ground. He tumbled for almost ten feet before coming to a halt, face up on the uneven terrain.

"Owww," he groaned as the world continued to spin.

"Ethan!" Nia yelled. "Are you well?"

"What the heck was that?!" Ethan said after things came into focus.

"What was what?" Michalus asked, coming to stand over Ethan. The wizard looked down at him. "Are you okay, my boy?"

"I'm not sure," Ethan said, pushing himself to his feet. He flinched as his singed flesh stretched and sent shooting lines of pain up and down his legs and lower back. "I caught part of a fireball... I think... maybe... the shockwave or something in the Bifrost..."

"You what?" Michalus said, eyes opening wide.

Nia noticed his scorched backside and made a face. "You are injured! You should heal yourself with the cup."

"I can't," Ethan replied. "I already used it. I have to wait 24 hours."

"My boy," Michalus interrupted, taking Ethan by the arm. "Go back to what you were just saying before. Tell me what happened to you in the Bifrost."

"Later," Guinevere said sharply. The warrior woman pointed to the opposite side of the ravine. "They know where we went and I think they mean to catch us."

Glancing across the ravine, Ethan saw the torches were starting to move to the left. He cursed and looked over to Michalus. "How long before they can get here?"

Michalus stuttered for a moment as he looked around. "I... ah... don't really know exactly. Maybe half an hour."

Ethan cursed again. "That's not much of a head start. Grab the horses, we need to get moving."

"It will be slow going," Nia said. "Even with your lights."

"Not to mention, the lights will give us away," Guinevere added.

Ethan cursed yet again. She was right. Only Nia could see well in the dark. The rest of them would have to use light but that light would act as a beacon for the ogres.

Looking back across the ravine, Ethan saw that the torches from the ogres were already disappearing into the woods on his left. Just like he could mark them by their lights, they would be able to do the same for him and his group. Or would they?

An idea formed and Ethan checked his stats.

Mana: 81

He'd already regenerated some and opening the portal hadn't taken as much as he thought. He glanced down at the Chymera crystal in the crossguard of Excalibur. He guessed it must be true that the better the crystal, the easier it is to channel magic through it.

Ethan glanced over to the opposite side of the ravine. He had a plan, he just wasn't sure if it was a good plan. He turned to the others.

"The ogres are coming for us," he told them and there were mutters of agreement from everyone. "I think that ogre channeler wants us in a bad way. I'm not sure why unless it's because we killed two of their number. Unless there's a channeler reason why they'd want us dead?"

He looked at Michalus but the wizard shrugged. "Not that I am aware of."

"You never know who the ogres were that we killed," Guinevere suggested. "They could have been someone important to the tribe... or to the channeler."

"They may be primitive," Drorm added, "but that doesn't mean they don't have a social structure."

Ethan cursed. He hadn't even thought of that. Had they inadvertently killed the channeler's wife or daughter? Maybe his sons? He growled. "Great. Just great."

"Monsters with family ties... who would have guessed," the warrior woman said.

"It could be a matter of honor," Nia offered. "We killed members of the tribe. If the channeler is the leader, he may be honor bound to avenge them. If not, his leadership might be seen as weak. He could be challenged."

Thinking of the warped ogre's physical changes and the magic power he wielded, Ethan didn't think any of the other ogres would be able to take him. Then again, the channeler had to sleep sometime. A knife across the throat would kill a channeler or normal ogre just as quick.

"Whatever the reason," Ethan continued. "It seems like they will be coming for us - probably tonight."

"All the more reason to get moving," Drorm pointed out.

"Hear me out," Ethan said, making a placating gesture. "What would happen if the ogres got here and we weren't here?"

"They would follow our scent and try to catch up with us," Nia replied. "It is what I would do."

"Exactly." Ethan nodded. "Now, what if you got here and there was no scent and no trail. What then?"

"I would think they used magic to go further away," the foxgirl retorted.

"Which way?" Ethan asked, a smile on his face.

"The way I knew you to be heading," she replied and pointed north.

"Exactly!" Ethan grinned. "Exactly! If they get here and we're not here and there is no trail, they'll assume we went north!"

His companions exchanged looks. Guinevere screwed up her face. "But we are heading north. We're going north to the road, then cutting east."

Ethan's smile broadened. "No we aren't."

"My boy," Michalus said, confusion written on his features. "Did you hit your head on something? You aren't making any sense."

"What if we don't go north and then east," he told them. "What if we go east and then north."

"They'd still follow our trail," Drorm pointed out the obvious.

"Unless there is none," Ethan told them. The group looked even more confused.

"Are you talking about portaling?" Guinevere asked. "I thought you didn't have a portal spot that direction."

"I don't," Ethan replied. "But I can make a portal to a place I can see."

Everyone continued to look at Ethan in confusion. He sighed and turned to the ravine. He pointed across the gap to the opposite side. "We can leave a lightstone here to keep them targeting this area. Then I portal us to the opposite side. We go east and keep going east until we run into the road we took to Patheos. Then we head north along the road."

The others looked at him, blinked and then looked at each other. They seemed to mull it over for several minutes before Michalus spoke up. "That might work."

"As long as we have no light sources, we should be fine," Ethan told them with a grin. "They're using torches which means they don't have night vision. They won't be able to see us."

"We won't be able to see either," Drorm reminded him. "How do we go east in the dark?"

Ethan smiled even larger. "We don't. We hang out over there until morning, then we go."

"What if they get here and then circle back around?" Guinevere asked.

"That's the beauty of it," Ethan explained. "I have mana now. I can carve out a hole inside the stone wall for us to wait until morning. Even if they come back, they won't see us."

"They could smell us," Nia said.

"Even if they do, that's a ton of stone," Ethan told her, gesturing to the stone wall in the distance. "With that much stone nearby, I think Michalus and I can take them. What do you think?"

Everyone exchanged glances, seemingly unable to come up with any objection. Finally, Michalus shrugged. "It sounds like a logical argument to me."

"I agree," Drorm said. "It is worth a try."

"I hope you're right, Ethan," Guinevere said.

"Me too," Ethan said under his breath. "Me too."

14

The group portaled to the opposite side after dropping a lightstone. Ethan and Michalus immediately hollowed out the wall and the group slipped inside. They created some air holes on the ceiling before sealing themselves in. Ethan also left a small hole open facing the opposite side of the ravine.

From the safety of his makeshift shelter, Ethan kept watch on the lightstone for a half hour before he saw the tell-tale sign of torches moving on their former position. It was too far for him to make out details.

"Nia," he whispered, unsure how good the ogres' hearing was. It was dark in their shelter, dark enough that he couldn't see anyone around him.

The foxgirl brushed against him, startling him momentarily. The wall was only a few feet thick, barely wide enough to fit the horses. This forced them to be uncomfortably close for the duration of their stay.

Combined with the darkness, it was an awkward situation.

"What do you need?" she asked.

"The ogres are across the ravine. You've got better eyes than me," he said. "Look through here and tell me what the ogres are doing."

Without a word, Nia squeezed in front of him and looked through the hole. Her position forced her bushy fox tail up and into his face. He sneezed softly as the soft fur tickled his nose, then gently pushed her tail to the side.

He also noticed that the rest of her body was pressed tightly against him and was starting to make his breeches feel a bit tight in the front. He tried to think of other things. Luckily, no one else could see.

Nia must have felt him against her and wiggled her hips against him. Ethan was about to squeeze out from behind her when she began to softly narrate what was going on across the way.

"They picked up the light stone," she told him. The others must have heard her speaking and perked up, judging by the rustling in the darkness. He guessed all of his companions were just as interested to know whether or not their ruse worked. "The channeler ogre is speaking now. I believe he is waving around."

"Waving at what?" Ethan asked.

"I believe he is having them search the area," she replied, eyes still glued to the scene across the way.

"Let's hope they don't decide to come back and search over here," Guinevere whispered from his right. He wished he had Nia's night vision. Being completely in the dark was disconcerting.

"No reason for them to," Ethan replied. "They just came from here and there's no logical reason for them to come back and search here."

"Who said they were logical," the warrior woman retorted.

Ethan had no reply to that. She was right. Ogres weren't human. And the ogre channeler wasn't even a full ogre any longer. A demon had twisted his body and probably his mind as well. He couldn't count on him acting like a normal ogre. He turned the direction of Guinevere's voice. "Good point."

"More talking," Nia said and everyone fell silent. "The channeler is angry. He is yelling."

He wished he or Nia could understand what the ogres were saying. He seemed to share a common language with the humans and demi-humans of this world. How that worked, he had no idea. He just knew that it did work.

The monsters were different. At least, what he considered monsters. He hadn't been able to understand anything but the most basic speech from the monsters. Trolls, ogres and even dragons seemed to have their own language that didn't translate into what he thought of as English.

"They are leaving," Nia whispered, breaking Ethan from his train of thought. He glanced past her and could just make out the lights of the torches fading from the top of the ravine.

"And now we pray that they do not come back and

search here," Drorm said. "I can barely move, let alone fight."

Ethan shook his head before realizing no one could see him. "I told you. We can easily turn this wall into a weapon, if it comes to that."

Drorm was silent for a long moment. "I just do not like being this... confined."

"You and me both," Guinevere agreed.

Nia squeezed by him, deliberately wiggling her hips against him until she was off to his left. He felt her sit down in the darkness and he did the same. It was going to be a long, uncomfortable night.

"Now we wait," Nia whispered.

Ethan sighed. "Now we wait."

THE NIGHT WAS as uncomfortable as he had expected. Like the rest of them, he had gotten very little sleep in the cramped quarters. By the time dawn's first light touched the air vents in the ceiling, Ethan was ready to leave.

After opening up holes on every side, they scanned the surrounding clearing. Ethan didn't know if ogres would lay an ambush for them, but he wasn't taking any chances.

"Anything?" he called out softly.

"Nothing on this side."

"Nothing here either."

"This direction is clear," Drorm reported.

Not trusting the ogre channeler, or rather the demon influencing him, Ethan opened a larger hole in the roof of the shelter and lifted Nia up onto it. The foxgirl easily grabbed the top of the structure and pulled herself up with the grace of a gymnast.

She disappeared out of sight for nearly a minute before poking her head over the edge of the hole. "There is no sign of them and their scent is old. They have not been back."

Sighing with relief, he heard the others make equally relieved noises. Everyone was tired and it showed.

Ethan channeled *Earth* and opened up the walls of the shelter, opening them up to the early morning air. And not a minute too soon. Since the horses had been in the shelter too, they'd stunk up the place with their droppings.

Groaning, everyone got to their feet and shuffled out onto the ground. Ethan stretched and rubbed his aching neck. He also flinched as his stretching pulled on the blistered skin of his back. Sadly, it was still hours before he'd get to use the Grail to heal the damage. He'd have to bear it until then.

The group gathered up the horses and allowed them to graze on the grass of the hill while they all walked around and stretched their legs.

"We don't have anything to eat do we?" Guinevere asked hopefully.

Ethan started to shake his head but then hesitated. "Actually, we do. We have some frozen bear meat."

Guinevere made a face but then shrugged. "At this point, I'm hungry enough to eat an ogre."

"Someone start a fire!" Drorm agreed. "Bear isn't that bad."

"Par'karr never eat bear," the kobold looked between his companions with a grin. Of all of them, he seemed less affected by the confined space. Given his diminutive size, it was no wonder.

The group quickly gathered firewood, started a fire and cooked the bear meat. While looking for wood, Drorm stumbled upon a wild raspberry bush and they supplemented their meat with some fruit.

All in all, the bear wasn't the worst thing Ethan had ever eaten. It was gamey and greasy, and it left a strange taste in his mouth. But after the long night and no dinner, he was willing to overlook its flaws and just be thankful that they had something to eat.

"See," Drorm said, halfway through his bear. "It's not bad."

"Par'karr like!" the kobold grinned.

Guinevere shrugged. "If you eat a bite of the bear meat with one or two of the berries, it cuts the flavor a bit."

Curious, Ethan tried the warrior woman's suggestion and found that a couple of berries did make the meat slightly more palatable. Slightly.

Once they were finished the group packed up and made ready to head north. Unfortunately, it would be a longer trek north to the road but it was better than fighting the ogre channeler and his tribe.

Ethan knew they still had several days to Patheos and he still had no idea what to expect there. And that was if he could expect anything at all. Ethan and his original group had already been to Patheos and there had been no sign of Merlin.

Then again, they also hadn't been looking for Merlin

either the first time. They'd been fixated on the library and retrieving the tomes. Plus, he'd been new to magic. Now that he was a bit more seasoned, maybe he would pick up on something. Maybe.

But there would be time to think more on that during the journey. Now, it was time to go. With a tug on the reins of the horse, Ethan started the procession on their journey.

THE QUEEN WAS CONFUSED. Once again, the wizard had used Aether magic. But once again, it seemed to go nowhere. Either that, or the destination was so close to the point of origin, that there should be no reason to create the portal.

Her mandibles clicked together. Did the wizard know she was coming for him? Was he trying to throw her off his trail? She clicked in amusement. It wouldn't work. She would still sense where the destination was.

Mentally signaling her remaining soldiers, she once again broke out in a sprint. It wouldn't be long before she ate his brain.

15

The journey north took two days before they finally reached the same road they'd traveled the last time they'd gone to Patheos. Like the area of road they'd previously traveled on, this section of road also ran parallel to a river.

Unlike the previous section of road, on the opposite side of the river, the area was lush and green. The previous area had been barren, just like the land around Patheos. The only thing that they'd seen live there was those Balweer creatures they'd encountered.

"Wow," Ethan exclaimed. "That's quite a difference."

"The plains?" Guinevere asked, following his eyes across the river. "The desolation doesn't start for another day to the north."

Ethan whistled. "And that desolation was caused by the explosion at Patheos?"

"It was all as you see here before that explosion." Guinevere nodded and gestured to the area in front of them. "I have no idea what my father did, but the area has never healed."

"It's breathtaking to know that magic caused this level of destruction," Michalus murmured.

"Yeah," Ethan agreed with a shake of his head. "I can't even fathom how he would have generated this much power."

The wizard just nodded and the conversation stalled. The group led the horses onto the road and Ethan looked up and down it.

"We built this highway," the former queen said as they came to a halt on the road. Her voice was sad and her eyes had a faraway look in them.

"Camelot, I mean," she clarified. "We built this highway to intersect with the northern kingdoms when they were our allies."

"I don't remember reading about that," Michalus interrupted.

"Probably because we stopped just as the war with the Doemenagg started," she replied bitterly. "Arthur had great plans..."

Guinevere faded off for a moment, her mind drifting back to another time. A moment later, she sighed and seemed to remember what she was talking about. "Anyway, the knights oversaw the building of the highway - that's why it was called the Knight's Road, or the Knight's Highway."

Ethan whistled. "So this goes all the way back to Camelot?"

The warrior woman shook her head. "Not any longer. It goes for a few dozen leagues before it disappears into the forest. The trees have long since broken it apart and it's just a scattering of stones now."

Nodding, Ethan remembered the partial road they'd followed through Sherwood. It had also been overgrown. He looked up and down the road. "At least part of it still remains."

Guinevere chuckled bitterly. "Oh yes. The road still exists. A road to nowhere."

"We know it goes past Patheos," Ethan said cheerfully, trying to raise the mood. "And that's where we're headed."

The warrior woman turned her head to face him, staring into his eyes. Her eyes were practically begging him. "Do you really think my father is alive?"

Ethan wrinkled his brow. "You saw his face in the Bifrost. He spoke to us. He has to be alive."

Guinevere bit her lip. "I've seen my father... make images of himself appear when you do things. When I was a child, whenever I would go near the pantry, he would appear and tell me not to eat too many sweets."

"Like a hologram?" Ethan asked, earning a look of puzzlement from the group.

"What is a... holly gram?" Drorm asked, cocking his head. "I have not heard this word before."

Frowning, Ethan tried to think how to explain it. Nearly everyone on Earth would instantly know what a hologram was. They'd been used in sci-fi movies long enough that they were part of pop culture. Not to mention, there were actually machines that could generate holograms now - they were just really expensive.

After a moment, he gave it his best attempt. "It's like an image of someone or something that is displayed in the air. It looks like the real thing, but sometimes it's just... ah... light."

"I thought you said magic didn't exist on your world," Michalus said with raised eyebrows.

Ethan shook his head. "It's not magic. It's technology. We have machines that create the holograms...er... the images."

The wizard made a face. "It certainly sounds like magic. Or, at the very least, enchanting!"

"It's not," Ethan retorted. "It's just... ah... technology. It's just that our technology has advanced so far, I'm sure someone who hasn't seen it before might think it was magic."

"What we saw may have been one of those... holly grams," Guinevere spoke up in annoyance. "It may not be coming from him."

"I'm not sure," Ethan said. "One time, I did ask his name and he seemed to understand me and respond."

Guinevere brightened. "Then maybe he is alive... but where?!"

Ethan shrugged. "I'm not sure. And since Patheos was the last place you saw him, it's as good a start as any. Maybe I'll find some clue to where he might have gone."

"Let's hope you are right," Guinevere replied and led her horse out onto the road. "Now that we have an actual road, we can ride for a change."

Nia nodded and looked up at the twin suns. "Yes, we still have many hours of daylight. We should use them to our advantage."

With that, everyone mounted their horses. On Ethan's signal, the group headed north on the Knight's Highway.

THE NEXT DAY was thankfully uneventful. While the area had remained lush, Ethan had asked Nia to do some extra hunting. He remembered how the food had been scarce once they hit the desolate area and he wanted to freeze as much meat as possible.

When they finally did reach the barren wasteland he remembered, they had more than enough food to last them for the remaining trip.

They stopped at the unnatural divide between the green and lush plains and the gray, barren wasteland.

"The way it just ends like that is really very interesting," Michalus murmured. "I can't imagine how that was accomplished."

Ethan didn't know and wasn't sure he did want to know. Now that he was seeing the wasteland again, he just wanted to get to Patheos, find Merlin and get back to this lush green area.

The group pushed on until dark and then camped on the forest's edge. He suggested double watches due to the proximity of the Balweers. Guinevere shook her head.

"No need," she told him. "They don't cross the river."

Ethan exchanged a glance with Nia. They both remembered a near fatal encounter with the Balweer, which had actually swum the river and attacked them on this side.

He turned and gave Guinevere a wary look. "That hasn't been our experience. One crossed the river and tried to eat us."

"Really?! There must be even less game for them to

hunt now." the warrior woman exclaimed. She looked across the river to the desolate wasteland and shook her head. Her countenance fell as her eyes got a faraway look again. "The last time I was here was on my way to Camelot after my father... you know... did what he did. They never crossed the river back then."

Ethan looked to Nia for confirmation. "When we were on the other side, we saw nothing other than the Balweers."

"And crows," Par'karr supplied helpfully. "Par'karr see crows last time."

"And birds," Ethan said with a nod.

"This much destruction is unfathomable," Drorm said with a shake of his head. "If you had not told me about your father doing this, I would only believe dragons capable of this magnitude."

Ethan smirked. "Merlin was apparently not someone who's bad side you wanted to be on."

"So true." Guinevere cracked a smile.

Looking around, Ethan pointed to a flat spot near the treeline. "Let's set up camp there and do the double watches. Those Balweers are vicious. If one sneaks into the camp, it could kill a couple of us before we even raise the alarm.

"Nia." He turned to his wife and pointed back towards the lush area. "Can you go into the forest back there and see if there is any game. I think we have enough food, but I think I'd prefer to eat fresh tonight."

The foxgirl nodded and slid off her horse. She pulled the bow and quiver from her horse. She looked at Ethan with a smile. "You should come too. I may need help drag-ging the corpse back."

Ethan grinned. He knew exactly what his wife was hinting at - a little alone time in the forest. Despite that, he guessed she hadn't been lying about the other part. She would let him drag the corpse home. He shrugged. It would be worth it.

He slid off his own horse. "I'm going hunting with Nia. The rest of you, set up camp and gather some wood for a fire. We'll be back soon."

With that, Ethan and Nia walked into the forest and out of view of the rest of their group. He was grinning the entire time.

16

No Balweers attacked them that evening and no ogres either. Ethan hadn't really expected the ogres to be able to track them. Yet, he hadn't still discounted that they might double back to the wall and catch their trail. If so, they might show up at a very inopportune time.

Ethan glanced out across the barren lands on the other side of the river. Another two days and they'd have to go back into those lands - with the Balweer. He still remembered how fearsome the creatures had been. Despite leveling up, he wondered if his group could take one - let alone two - of the Balweers.

He turned his attention to his friends. It was a different group this time. Last time, it had been Ainslee, Yuliana, Nia, Par'karr and himself. Now, Guinevere and Drorm had taken the place of Yuliana and Ainslee. Both were experienced warriors. Would that allow them to overcome one? What about two? Three?

If the ogres did catch up with them, would they dare the deadlands? Could the ogres handle Balweers?

Thinking about it, Ethan nodded to himself. Yes, with the ogres' larger size and the sheer number of them, he guessed they could take out a few Balweers. Maybe not without casualties or injuries, but they would definitely come out victorious.

"What are you thinking so hard about?" Nia asked, coming to sit next to him. She handed him a steaming leg of the lizard turkeys they'd killed last night.

He smiled and accepted the hot meat. It smelled delicious and his stomach grumbled. Ethan took a bite, flinching as the scalding juices burned his tongue. He was so hungry, he didn't care and chewed anyway.

When he finished chewing, Ethan glanced back to the south, the way they had come. "I'm wondering if the ogres might have doubled back, caught our scent and still following us."

Nia finished chewing a bite of what looked like a chicken breast, the foxgirl followed his gaze. "It is possible."

Ethan nodded. "I'm worried they'll hit us when we aren't expecting it."

"I am always expecting an attack," Nia assured him.

"Me too," Drorm said, obviously eavesdropping on their conversation.

"At least out here, in the open, we will see them coming for several miles," Guinevere added.

"Only during the day," he reminded the group. "The only one who would be able to see them that far at night is Nia."

"Mmm...hmmm." Nia nodded, chewing a mouthful of her turkey lizard.

"Worrying about it, won't change it," Guinevere told him with a shrug. "If they attack, we'll deal with it then. We're on the road. It's not like we can build fortifications or choose the high ground. We have no idea where we'll be when and if they attack."

"She speaks the truth," Drorm said. "There is not much we can do, other than be vigilant."

Ethan looked to Michalus and Par'karr, who were busy eating their meal. Neither seemed very interested in the conversation. "What about you two? Any ideas?"

Par'karr looked up and shrugged, then went back to alternating between taking a bite of his turkey lizard and feeding pieces to his rabbits.

"If you're asking if I have some magical way of warning us," Michalus replied as he finished up a bite. "I think you already know the answer. I don't."

He nodded at the wizard's words. He had asked the wizard about some sort of alarm spell or early warning spell but Michalus wasn't aware of any.

Ethan thought back to the lights in the library of Patheos. They had been motion activated. When someone was near, they had created light. Maybe a spell couldn't alert them, but perhaps an enchanted item could.

Cursing, Ethan remembered they had no Chymera stones left. Then he remembered that Michalus had some back at his place. He looked at the wizard hopefully. "I don't suppose you grabbed your bag of Chymera stones?!"

Michalus snapped his fingers and flashed Ethan a disappointed look. "No, my boy. I completely forgot."

"Why don't you portal back there?" Guinevere asked. "Before we get started."

Ethan had been thinking the same thing. Now that he knew the area, he was confident he could. He gave the wizard a questioning look. "You up for a quick trip?"

Mouth full, Michalus nodded. He finished chewing and held up the rest of his breakfast. "As soon as I'm done."

"Good point," Ethan agreed, looking down at his own turkey lizard leg. "Let's finish eating and then go."

"I will go with you," Nia said, her voice leaving no room for argument.

"Of course." He grinned. He never minded having the foxgirl with him.

The three of them finished eating and then gathered a short distance from the fire. Ethan took Michalus's rune stick and laid it down on the ground.

The wizard had carried it with them since Ethan had created it on the dragon's mountain. Originally, it was to allow him to find Michalus and the group after speaking with Firestorm. But since then, Ethan had used it as a marker to return to when they needed to portal somewhere and then come back to where they were.

"Okay," Ethan said. "If you're both ready, I'll open up a smaller portal, just large enough for us. Give me a second to scry the runes on the chest first, then I'll focus on the same spot we portaled to before - or I can focus on the inside of the house since we don't have horses."

"You might as well take us right inside the house," Michalus said with a shrug.

"Okay." Ethan grinned. "In the house it will be. You ready?"

Nia and Michalus both nodded, letting him know they were ready. Ethan then focused his magic on the runes of the wizard's portal chest. Then he *Scryed* the area.

Or rather, he tried to *Scry* the area. Nothing happened. Ethan frowned.

"Something wrong?" Michalus asked with a raised eyebrow.

Ethan furrowed his brow. "It didn't work this time. Let me try again."

Once more, Ethan focused on the three runes that Michalus had previously shown him. He focused on them in his mind until they were crystal clear. Then, he channeled *Mana* and tried to *Scry*.

Nothing.

He frowned again. "It's not working. Maybe I'm remembering the runes wrong. Can you draw them again for me?"

Not for the first time, Ethan wished he could make a list of the runes in a book and then just refer back to the book whenever he needed to look them up. Unfortunately, that wasn't how the magic worked.

In order to portal or *Scry* a specific place, the wizard had to know exactly where it was. The easiest way to do that was to create a unique set of runes that existed nowhere else. That way, when you envisioned the runes, there was only one place you could go.

Having the same runes in multiple places defeated the entire concept. Half the time, you'd portal or scry to the actual location. The other half, you'd end up at the place where you'd written them down.

"You okay over there?" Drorm called out and Ethan saw Par'karr and Guinevere look over at them.

"I forgot the runes to Michalus's chest," Ethan replied sheepishly.

"Here's the first one," the wizard said, leaning back so Ethan could see the rune he'd drawn in the dirt.

Looking at it, Ethan nodded to Michalus. "Yep. That's the first one I have memorized."

The wizard wiped away the first rune in the dirt and then drew the second one. It was the same as Ethan remembered too. Finally, Michalus drew the third and final rune. It too was the same as what he'd remembered.

"That's so weird," Ethan told them. "Those are the three runes I'm focusing on."

"Try again," the wizard told him. "After all, you're still new at scrying."

Ethan sighed. "True enough. Let me try again."

He did so and once again was unable to establish a connection with the place. Ethan cursed as he grew more and more frustrated. "Why isn't this working?"

"Have you been practicing it at all?" Michalus asked, his tone and expression showing he already knew the answer.

"No," Ethan said, letting out an exasperated breath. There hadn't really been time to *Scry* since he couldn't do it while walking his horse and they'd only recently reached the road where he could ride.

"I would suggest..." Michalus started but was interrupted by Guinevere.

"Try scrying something else," Guinevere told him. "Now."

"Why? What..." Ethan started to reply but the warrior woman shook her head.

"Just do it," she told him, her expression grim.

Seeing the woman's expression, Ethan nodded. He focused on the runes on his own portal chest and channeled magic. Instantly, his vision shifted and he was seeing the inside of his house back in Hawkshead. He moved his focus to look around the room and then severed the connection.

"It worked," he reported. "I was able to scry my place back in Hawkshead."

Guinevere's face fell and she bit her lip. She turned a pained expression on Michalus. "When was the last time you used your portal pouch?"

"The last time?" Michalus asked, forehead wrinkled in confusion. "Why would..."

"The last time," the warrior woman said more gently. "When was it?"

"Yesterday evening when I put some of the frozen meat away," the wizard said, his face and tone now alarmed.

"Try it now," Guinevere said with an almost apologetic expression.

Ethan wasn't sure what was going on but he started to get a bad feeling.

Michalus stuck his hand into his portal pouch and Ethan saw the pouch bulge and saw his hand hit the bottom of the pouch. The wizard went ashen.

"What is happening?" Nia asked, looking between Guinevere, Michalus and Ethan.

"My portal pouch isn't working..." Michalus said in a daze, his face still pale. "There's only one reason why it wouldn't be working..."

Ethan went pale too as he finally understood Guinevere's line of reasoning. His head twisted towards the wizard. "Michalus..."

"What?" Drorm and Nia asked at the same time.

"The only reason it wouldn't work," Michalus answered with a resigned sadness, "is if the runes had been destroyed."

"The ogres!" Ethan cursed.

"The ogres must have followed our trail back to his place," Guinevere said, coming over and putting a hand on the wizard's shoulder. "Given the channeler liked fire so much, he probably burned the place to the ground. That's why there are no runes to scry or portal to."

Michalus, face still pale, glanced down at what had once been his portal pouch and nodded numbly.

17

———————

They continued north all day. Despite attempts to strike up a conversation with him, Michalus remained silent the entire time. Not that Ethan blamed the wizard. When they finally stopped for the evening, the wizard sat alone. He barely touched his food.

It was sometimes difficult to remember that Michalus was nearly a thousand years old. Elves normally had much longer lifespans than humans and aged at a much slower rate. When they'd met him, he'd been a wrinkled old elf. Since he'd drunk from the Fountain of Youth, he now appeared no older than Ethan and would never age again.

Ethan had no idea how long the elf had lived in his house, but it was probably far longer than most humans lived. Losing the house must be traumatic. Who knew how many memories he had associated with that house.

Knowing the wizard, there were probably all sorts of books and other magical-related items that he had lost as well. The loss of that knowledge was probably weighing heavily on the wizard. But there were other matters that drew Ethan's attention.

With half of their food stores gone, Nia had tried hunting in the forest. Like before, there was a lack of any sort of game this close to the desolation. She returned after dark, with only a half dozen squirrels. Each one was enough to feed a single person for one meal. But that was still one meal they wouldn't have to worry about.

They went to bed full, but Ethan worried whether they would have enough food for the trip into Patheos, plus however long they decided to stay. As it was, they couldn't afford to stay more than a day before they would run out of food.

With those thoughts fresh in his mind, Ethan finished up his watch shift and then fell into a restless sleep.

THE NEXT MORNING, Michalus wasn't quite as lethargic. He made brief replies when anyone asked him things but otherwise stayed quiet again. They rode the horses as hard as they dared and reached the road to Patheos just as the suns were beginning to set.

"Let's camp for the night and tomorrow morning we can make a run for it," Ethan suggested, glancing out across the barren wasteland.

"You do not wish to use the night tactic we used before to reach the city?" Nia asked.

Ethan shook his head. The last time, Ethan and his companions had traveled by night to avoid the notice of the Balweers. They discovered the creature's sight was based on movement. With a little testing, they'd found the creatures' eyesight was very limited in the dark.

With that in mind, the group had traveled all night. When morning came, Ethan had used magic to dig a large hole and they'd stayed there until evening. That time, they hadn't brought horses. In fact, they'd gotten the horses from the warlock and the followers of Hel.

"Last time, we didn't have horses," he reminded his wife. "It would take too long to dig a hole large enough for all of us and the horses. Plus, there's no guarantee they won't try to climb out or be so noisy they attract a Balweer."

Nia frowned and nodded. "You wish to do the fast run we did on the way back last time."

Ethan smiled. They'd claimed horses from the warlock and her party who had tried to enslave them during their last visit. They'd ridden the horses hard and Ethan had used magic to cast a light spell directly into the eyes of any Balweer that attempted to intercept them. The strategy had worked and his group had made it back to safety in record time.

"Yes," Ethan confirmed. "We ride fast and I blind any Balweer that comes near us with a light spell in its eyes."

"Light spell in the eyes?" Guinevere questioned. "You sure that will work?"

Drorm looked dubious too. He glanced between Guinevere and Ethan, waiting for an answer.

Par'karr managed to get his words out before Ethan could retort. "It work! It work before! Ride horses fast! Ethan cast magic! Boom! Balweer not see!"

Ethan flashed the kobold a smile and then looked at the others. "It'll work. I mean, it worked last time."

"Are you fast enough to tackle several at one time?" Drorm asked.

"They seem to stay spaced out," Ethan replied, remembering their run. "Probably a territorial thing. But I should be able to keep up with them."

"I will help too," Michalus said quietly.

Everyone's attention immediately turned to the wizard. Ethan smiled at the wizard. "Are you sure?"

The wizard took a deep breath and then waved his concern away. "I might be over 900, but I'm not an invalid."

Ethan opened his mouth to apologize but the wizard just smiled. "I'm fine, my boy. Finding out my home was destroyed was tough. But I'm okay now - well, better at least."

"We are glad to hear you are okay," Nia told Michalus.

"There were a lot of memories there," the wizard said. "But also everything I owned, other than what I have with me." He paused and took a deep breath. "Including all of my research."

Ethan grimaced as he remembered the portal detector device the wizard had created. Michalus had created it with the help of Merlin, not even knowing at the time that it had probably been THE Merlin.

"I'm sorry," he told Michalus. "Maybe I can help you rebuild some of it. Heck, between the two of us, we can probably make you a house out of stone."

The wizard brightened at that idea but then shook his head. "No, I think I might settle somewhere else."

Remembering that Michalus and Yuliana seemed to

have gotten pretty close, Ethan gave the wizard a wink. "Maybe some place near Camelot?"

Michalus blushed slightly and nodded. "I was thinking maybe something in that neighborhood."

"Well, the offer is open," Ethan told the elf. "If you want me to help you build a house in Camelot, just let me know."

"Plenty of stone there," Guinevere agreed. She looked thoughtful. "Some buildings might just need a little repair to be livable."

"Thank you," Michalus said. "Both of you. But let's get through this adventure first and see if we can find your father, Guinevere. Then we'll worry about an old man like me."

"You're not as old as you used to be," Ethan said with a grin.

"Maybe not in the body, my boy," the elf said. He tapped the side of his head. "But up here, I'm still old."

A moment of sadness passed over Guinevere's face and she nodded. "I know what you mean."

The elf looked at her, cocked his head and then nodded. "I guess you do at that, my dear."

"Okay then," Ethan said. "Let's get to work. We'll stick to the plan. Camp here for the night and then make the run tomorrow morning. I'm going to make some containers for extra water and fill them down at the river."

"What about the Balweers?" Drorm asked, brow furrowed.

"I'm going to use a little invisibility," Ethan said with a smile. "We did it before."

"Then I will go with you," Nia said. "Just like last time."

Knowing he couldn't talk his wife out of it and confident he could cloak them both in invisibility, he nodded. "Alright. Let's get to it."

No one disagreed and they all went about their tasks for the night.

THE NEXT MORNING, they ate quickly and then rode the horses down to the road. Ethan looked out onto the barren earth in front of them and took a deep breath. Like last time, it would be a long ride and he'd need to be on his toes the entire time.

This time, they would ride two by two. Ethan would be in the front left while Michalus would be in the rear right. Between the two of them, they should be able to blind any Balweer that came near them - no matter which side they came from.

"Michalus, you ready?" Ethan called to the wizard.

"As I'll ever be," the elf responded. He'd been slightly more talkative since their conversation yesterday evening but still more reserved than usual. It would probably just take time for him to come to grips with the loss.

"Everyone else ready?" he asked.

There was a chorus of affirmative answers and Ethan nodded. Taking another deep breath and letting it out, he prepared to spur his horse forward. "Let's ride!"

With that, the group took off on their horses, doing the best to stay in a tight formation. The group thundered down the road and across the small bridge that stretched over the river.

No sooner had they cleared the bridge when Ethan saw a Balweer pop up from its burrow, a hundred yards on their right. It raced towards them on its many legs. He'd forgotten how quickly the creatures moved. "On your right!"

"I see it!" Michalus cried.

The creature got within a hundred feet and then suddenly skidded to a halt and began writhing around. Ethan had felt the wizard's spell just before the creature was struck and let go of his own ready spell.

No sooner had he done so when another shape appeared over a hill on their left, racing towards them. Another Balweer.

Ethan waited until it got within range and then triggered his own spell, blinding it. This Balweer had the same reaction and began writhing around.

So far, so good. Now, they just had to keep it up until they reached Patheos. Turning his attention back to their left, Ethan focused on keeping him and his friends safe.

18

They arrived in Patheos just as the twin suns peaked in the sky. Several hours of hard riding, followed by intermittent times of rest had gotten them to the city in record time. Now, as they looked down onto the ruined city from the hillside, Ethan wasn't so sure he wanted to go back in.

Once again, he was reminded of some of the pictures of war-torn areas back on Earth where the town or village had been bombed. He shook his head.

"What did this?" muttered Drorm, eyes wide as he surveyed the remains of the city.

"My father," Guinevere stated.

"Your father decimated this entire city?! Why?!" Drorm asked in disbelief.

"Warlocks and channelers were holding me hostage and forcing him to work on the library over there," she replied, pointing at the lone building standing in the center of the city. "When he had the opportunity, he portaled me away and did this."

"I'm not even sure the dragon could do this," the big orc breathed. He kept shaking his head, perhaps thinking the motion would clear his eyes and he'd see that he wasn't really looking at a completely decimated city.

"I had forgotten how bad it was," Michalus murmured.

"You've been here before?" Ethan asked.

"Shortly after it happened," he replied with a nod. "An explosion of that magnitude doesn't go unnoticed. And I wasn't the only one. Wizards from all over showed up, trying to figure out what had happened."

"Huh," Ethan muttered. "I didn't know that. But it does make sense."

"The cloud that it created could be seen for hundreds of miles," the wizard said. "It looked like..."

"A mushroom," Ethan finished, remembering Guinevere's account of being sent away.

"Yes." Michalus bobbed his head. "Like a mushroom. Strangest thing I ever saw."

Ethan looked down at the broken city and sighed. His chances of finding anything that would help him would be slim - probably even worse than slim. And yet, he had to try. "Well, let's go down there and start looking around."

"This rubble has probably been sifted through dozens, perhaps even hundreds of times since it happened," Drorm said. The orc gestured out to the city. "Do you really think we will find something?"

Ethan bit his lip but then remembered Excalibur hanging from his hip. He smiled. "Ah, but they didn't have Excalibur."

"You think the sword will lead you to my father?" Guinevere asked curiously.

"I'm not sure," Ethan admitted. "I portaled many times before seeing your father. It wasn't until I had Excalibur with me that I saw him in the Bifrost."

"You think he's linked with the sword?"

Ethan hesitated, unsure how to explain it. Then an idea came to him. "I think wherever he is, he's able to get a fix on the sword, like I use runes to get a fix on a place to portal to. Basically, the sword is like a rune."

"Or a familiar object used for scrying," Michalus added.

"True," Ethan agreed. The wizard had told him that when wizards were more abundant, they'd been used as spymasters. They would become intimately familiar with a small object that they would somehow place on a person. Once the object was with them, the wizard could use their familiarity with it to scry on the person at will.

It did sound a lot like what Merlin was doing. The main difference was, Merlin could somehow interact with them in the Bifrost. How exactly the legendary wizard was doing that, Ethan hadn't a clue.

"Daylight is wasting," Nia announced. "If we wish to search, we should do so now, while the suns are out."

"Good point," Ethan agreed. He looked over his companions. "Let's split into three groups of two, so we can cover more. Nia, you come with me. Drorm and Par'karr, you search together and Guinevere and Michalus, you will be the last group. Let's spread ourselves out on this side of the city and then work our way to the far end."

Muttering agreements, the group walked down into the city. They tied up the horses and then split into their groups before spreading out and beginning their search. Looking out on the town, Ethan knew it was going to be a long day.

AFTER HOURS of searching and making it to the library, the group called it quits for the night. They built a fire with some wood they'd brought and cooked the frozen squirrels Nia had caught.

There wasn't much meat on the little creatures, and the meat that was there tasted gamey. But it was enough to push away his hunger and get him through the night.

"Mmm," the kobold groaned as he ate his meat. "Par'karr like squirrel. Remind Par'karr of times in village."

"You ate squirrels in your village?" Ethan asked.

"Par'karr not warrior," the kobold replied. "Par'karr eat whatever he can find!"

Ethan nodded. Squirrel wouldn't be his first choice, but it was better than starving.

After dinner the group sat around the fire, relating their stories of picking through the rubble. None of them had found anything but Par'karr had nearly slipped into a basement when the rubble shifted unexpectedly. Only the kobold's quick reflexes had saved him.

Other than that, no one had anything to report. There had been no sign of anything related to Merlin or anything that might give them any other clues as to where he was.

Ethan sat there turning over Excalibur in his hands, looking for anything that might give him a clue as to where to look. Unfortunately, there was nothing. The blade was fairly plain, as was the hilt and crossguard. In fact, other than the Chymera crystal in the crossguard, it was completely unremarkable.

"We should practice with the sword," Nia said. "Since we finally have time."

Unable to think of any legitimate reason not to train, Ethan suppressed a groan and stood up. Then he paused and looked down at the sword in his hand. With his free hand, he smacked his forehead.

"What?" Nia asked, her expression confused.

"Now that we're here," Ethan replied with a grin, "I should portal with the sword and see if he says anything else or seems stronger.

"You think that will work, my boy?" Michalus asked from the opposite side of the fire.

"No idea," Ethan replied, starting to grow a bit excited. "I should definitely try."

"You could practice tonight and try tomorrow," Nia said, crossing her arms over her chest.

"It will just take a moment," Ethan assured the foxgirl. "And then we can practice."

"Fine."

"I'm coming with you," Guinevere told him, standing up from the fire and coming towards him. "If you do see him, I want to try and talk to him again too."

"Sure," Ethan agreed.

"Where will you portal to?" Michalus asked.

"Just over there," Ethan said, gesturing to a clear area a

hundred feet away. "I can do line of sight pretty easily and if he is going to do any extra talking, here is where it would be."

Ethan held out his free hand and Guinevere took it. With a force of will, Ethan channeled Aether magic and opened up a portal as large as they were. He could see through it and since the end point faced them, he could actually see himself.

He paused. Was that really him? He looked so different from the guy who had originally shown up in this world. He stood taller, was thinner and actually looked somewhat muscular. He smiled. All that walking and fighting was actually paying off.

"Are you waiting for something?" Guinevere asked beside him. She winked at him. "Or do you just enjoy holding my hand."

Pretending he hadn't heard her, Ethan pulled her through the portal and into the Bifrost.

Immediately they entered the rainbow tunnel that he was familiar with. He looked over and saw Guinevere with him, still holding onto his hand.

Ethan took a moment to look around the Bifrost, seeing the solar systems and galaxies as they raced by. Then, the mist began to form again and a few seconds later, he was staring at Merlin's face.

"Find me," the disembodied head said. "Find me!"

"We're in Patheos!" Ethan yelled. "Where are you?"

The head blinked and seemed to look around. Then, the head stared back at him. "Here. I am here."

And then Ethan and Guinevere were suddenly outside

again, a hundred feet from their group. He blinked and looked around.

"Did you learn anything?" Michalus called out.

"He spoke again!" Ethan yelled back. "He said.... He's here!"

THE QUEEN SKIDDED TO A HALT. The wizard had created another portal, but once again, it had to be so close that it made no sense to the Queen why he would have created it. He was further north and east now.

She knew exactly where it was. She had been there. Patheos the humans had called it, at least, the ones whose brains she had eaten. It had been a long time since she had been there. She'd gone to investigate magic so powerful, she was barely capable of fathoming what had caused it.

Aether magic had been used as well. Aether magic that had left a strong residue - one she'd been able to sense, even weeks after the event had occurred. The Queen had spent several weeks in the city.

At first, she'd been curious about what had caused it. She'd stayed in Patheos for a week, trying to discover what had happened and how - with no success. Then the first wizard had appeared.

The Queen hadn't hesitated. She'd killed him and eaten his brain, absorbing much of his memory. It had been delicious. Then more wizards had appeared. The Queen had killed them as well, sucking their skulls dry and absorbing all sorts of magical knowledge.

The wizards continued to show up, as well as large groups

of men. She knew she dared not risk exposure. Dared not risk drawing the attention of the Merlin. She'd fled back to her hive and continued to have her collectors bring her brains.

But now the prey was in Patheos. Why? Clicking her mandibles in frustration, she knew the only way she would find out was to eat his brain.

Without another thought, the Queen took off towards Patheos. And the wizard.

19

"What does that mean?" Drorm asked, glancing around the ruins. "If he is here, why does he not reveal himself?"

"Maybe him trapped," Par'karr suggested. The kobold pointed to the ruined buildings around them. "Maybe him under rocks."

Guinevere shook her head. "No. He would be able to portal out or even blast his way out."

The kobold hung his head. "Par'karr not know then."

Ethan reached over and patted his friend on the shoulder. "None of us know."

"How can he be here and not be here?" Drorm asked, his tone frustrated. "It makes no sense."

"Perhaps he is trapped in some sort of magical prison," Michalus suggested. "I remember reading..."

An idea hit Ethan like a slap to the face. He shot up, looking around. "Or... what if he's trapped right here... in the Bifrost."

It had hit him when Michalus mentioned prison. He remembered the fireball explosion that had almost thrown Ethan out of the rainbow tunnel he had come to know as the Bifrost... into the void outside. What if that happened to Merlin?!

"Eh... what's that? Trapped in the Bifrost?" Michalus said, losing his previous train of thought. He shook his head. "I've never read..."

Ethan nodded. "I know. You've never read about it. But trust me. I think it could happen."

Everyone was staring at him, obviously waiting for him to elaborate. "When that channeler hit me with an explosion just as I entered the Bifrost, it threw me for a loop inside the tunnel. I was tumbling through it and at one point, I hit the side of the rainbow wall and felt it give."

"But it didn't," Michalus pointed out.

"Right," Ethan agreed. "But that was a... relatively... small explosion. Imagine that Merlin opened a gate and stepped through just as this explosion went off."

He gestured around at the utter destruction around them. "The shockwave of an explosion like this might have been enough to throw him completely through the Bifrost wall and into... well... I'm not really sure what's outside that wall."

Ethan looked at Michalus with a raised eyebrow. "Do you?"

Michalus shook his head. "I've never read any definitive works about it. But I did read some speculations about what is just outside the Bifrost."

"Oh?"

"There are many theories. The prevailing one is that it is a space between dimensions, where time and the laws of our universe don't apply."

"So," Ethan guessed. "Some sort of void."

Michalus considered. "You might think of it like that."

Ethan shot a quick glance at Guinevere before turning his gaze to the wizard. "Can someone survive in the void?"

Shifting his own eyes to Guinevere and then back to Ethan, Michalus shrugged. "I don't know, my boy. I just... don't know."

"They can survive!" Guinevere said, putting her hands on her hips. "My father is obviously alive and if that's what happened to him, then yes... you can stay alive there."

Michalus rubbed his chin. "It might be a place outside of time. The perception of time could be completely different there."

"Like the Bifrost itself," Ethan said excitedly.

The wizard raised an eyebrow. "The Bifrost?"

Ethan nodded. "Yes. Going from point to point through a portal looks instantaneous for anyone watching from outside the portal. But once you enter the Bifrost, it's like time slows down. You travel the rainbow tunnel for much longer than it appears you should."

"True, my boy," the wizard conceded. "But that's inside the Bifrost, or perhaps I should say, the Bifrost tunnel. We have no idea what the effect would be outside the Bifrost tunnels."

"Maybe," Ethan admitted. He looked at Guinevere. "But she's right. He's communicating with us. That means he's been alive all this time."

"If he is inside your portals," Nia asked. "Can you not open one and bring him out?"

Ethan turned to Michalus. "Can we do that? Can we open a portal and somehow fetch him or allow him to come through the portal?"

"I... don't think so. At least, not easily." Michalus rubbed his chin again, his expression faraway. "I think... if you created a portal between two points and the line between them crossed the place where he was trapped - assuming he's there at all - you might be able to see him or even grab him as you went through... theoretically, of course."

"How do we do that?" Ethan asked, his excitement growing. Michalus's theory seemed plausible. It made sense that if you opened a portal between two points and that line formed by those points intersected something, you should be able to latch onto that something and carry it with you.

"First, and most importantly, you would need to know precisely where he was," the wizard said pointedly.

"How can we tell where he is if we cannot see him?" Nia asked.

"Ah," retorted the wizard, raising a finger. "Therein lies the problem. There's no known way to see what's in the Bifrost."

Everyone went quiet. Ethan's hopes began dissolving away. He barely could make the Bifrost tunnels, but he really had no concept of how they worked.

Guinevere looked pleadingly between Michalus and Ethan. "Is there nothing we can do?"

Michalus gave her a sympathetic look but shook his

head. "I've never read anything about seeing into the Bifrost, my dear. Nothing."

Ethan scratched his own chin. He chuckled. He was starting to pick up Michalus's habit. "Okay, maybe we don't see into it. But would there be some way to detect an object, or person, in the Bifrost? Some spell?"

The wizard shook his head sadly. "There's really no spells to detect anything about the Bifrost. That's one of the reasons I had to build my..." Michalus faded off as his eyes opened wide.

"What, Michalus?" Ethan asked. He thought he already knew the answer but he wanted to hear the wizard confirm it.

"That's why I had to build my portal detector," he replied. "To detect portal activity."

Ethan felt his excitement returning. "Do you think we can use your equipment to find Merlin?"

Michalus's face suddenly fell. His voice lost all of its energy. "Not anymore."

"The Thor's cursed ogres!" Guinevere spat and the wizard nodded solemnly.

Cursing, Ethan remembered that the ogres had destroyed the man's home - and most likely all of his equipment too.

"But if you still had it," Ethan asked, still hopeful. "Do you think it could help us find him?"

The wizard took a deep breath and scratched his chin. "It might. We might be able to pick up residual portal traces and triangulate his location within the Bifrost."

"Can you build another one of your machines?" Nia asked. "We can help."

Michalus shook his head. "No, my dear. I'm afraid that's impossible. It was quite delicate. It took me years to build."

Ethan cursed but then brightened. He grabbed Michalus by the shoulder. "It was all metal and crystal right?"

The wizard nodded.

"It might have survived a fire," he suggested.

Michalus gave him a doubtful look. "I can't imagine that it..."

"But there's a chance," Ethan pressed.

"A small chance..." Michalus admitted.

Ethan grinned. "That's better than no chance. It's at least worth a few days' ride back." He looked around. "I can create some runes here so we can portal back here if we find it."

"What about the ogres?" Nia asked. "They may still be there."

"They have most likely moved on," Drorm said. "There would be no reason to wait around."

The foxgirl shook her head. "They may be laying an ambush for us."

"They have no idea when we'd be coming back," Guinevere said. "I agree with Drorm. Ogres aren't known for their patience. By the time we get there, they will be long gone."

"Then it is decided," Guinevere said. "We will go and see if Michalus's detector is there and still working. If it is, we portal back here and find my father!"

Ethan shared a glance with Michalus. They both knew Guinevere was oversimplifying the situation. Neither of them knew whether or not the detector would even work the way they wanted it to. Nor did they know whether their theory of making a portal between two points would work to allow access to someone trapped in the Bifrost.

There were a lot of unknowns. He looked at Guinevere and held his tongue. There was no reason to burst her bubble at the moment. For the time being, he'd let her enjoy her hope. If it didn't work, she'd have to come to grips with it at that time.

"Alright," Ethan said loudly, getting everyone's attention. "Tomorrow, I'll create some runes to teleport back here and we'll head back to the road and then on to Michalus's home."

Everyone nodded or muttered their agreement and started making their bedrolls ready. All except for Nia. She looked at him and smiled. "That is for tomorrow. Tonight, you still have sword practice."

Realizing he wouldn't win this argument with the foxgirl, Ethan groaned and followed his wife to a clear area where they could spar. He sighed. It was going to be a very painful lesson.

20

They spent the next three days on their way back to Michalus's home. Their time was uneventful. No monsters bothered them and they passed no one on the road. That meant that each night Ethan received two sword lessons.

After the first night of Nia teaching him how to handle the bigger sword, Guinevere had pointed out some different techniques that she had learned over the years. After a brief discussion with Nia, the warrior woman had offered to train him as well. And the way both Guinevere and Nia looked at him, it was an offer he couldn't refuse.

Now, a few hours from Michalus's home, Ethan was sorely regretting agreeing to the lessons. Sore being the operative word. His legs hurt from the footwork and drills. His arms hurt from the swings and thrusting. And his wrists hurt especially. Who knew wrists played such a big part in swordplay.

On the plus side, when he'd woken up that morning and looked at his stats, he had an increase in *Strength* and *Agility*.

```
Strength: 13
  Agility: 18
  Hardiness: 16
  Intellect: 44
  Intuition: 15
  Charisma: 12
```

He still had a long way to go, but it felt good to actually get an increase in his physical statistics. Had Ethan known sword training would have benefited him so much, he would have started it a long time ago. Then again, perhaps his gains were over time and he just happened to hit whatever magic threshold gained him a point while he was training with the sword.

The group had just entered a clearing near the wizard's house when Nia called out behind him. "Ogres!"

Ethan barely had time to register her words when there was a deep bellow from the other side of the clearing. Immediately, a half dozen grizzly bears charged out of the treeline opposite them. They were followed by more bellows as a line of ogres lumbered out right behind them.

Yelling a curse, Ethan reacted by starting to bring up a wall of fire. He had just reached for his sword hilt when he felt tainted fire being channeled. Behind his group, a wall of fire erupted, sealing off their escape.

Cursing again and trying to keep his horse under

control, Ethan scanned the opposite woods for the channeler. All the while using *Earth* to sense whether there
was rock under the soil. There wasn't. At least, not close
enough to help him form a wall.

The bears were almost on them when Ethan created
his own wall of fire in front of their group, effectively
walling them into a very narrow corridor of free space.
Space which began to get very hot, very quickly.

"We can't stay here!" Guinevere yelled, struggling to
keep her panicked horse under control.

"This way!" Michalus said and rode to their right.
"Quickly!"

Trusting his friend, Ethan rode after the wizard,
followed by the others. The horses, having scented the
grizzlies and ogres, needed no encouragement. They
thundered through the forest, as Michalus led them away
from the ogres.

Ethan glanced back, seeing the bears and ogres scrambling to follow them through the dense trees. It slowed
them down, but he wasn't sure if it would be enough to
outrun them.

To their right, a fireball exploded, setting the nearby
foliage on fire. He guessed it had been aimed at them but
must have impacted a tree. Lucky for them - unlucky for
the forest.

Michalus led them through several turns until they
finally came to a creek with a small waterfall. The wizard
slowed and gestured for them to follow him. "Quickly! Get
across!"

The creek was no more than ten feet across and barely

three feet deep, but Ethan knew immediately why Michalus had led them here. The entire area was rock.

Once everyone was across, Ethan slid off his horse and handed the reins to Par'karr. "Get them back a ways and tie them to the trees so they don't run off."

Nodding, the kobold gathered up everyone's reins and led the horses a dozen paces away. Ethan looked to Michalus, who had come to stand next to him. "What's the plan?"

"Plan?" the wizard chuckled, a bit out of breath. "I leave the plan up to you. I just brought us here because I know how much you like your earth magic."

Ethan smiled. "Hey, it works good... uh... well."

"I don't think a wall will work this time," Guinevere said from behind him.

Grinning, Ethan nodded. "I wasn't planning on making a wall." He looked at Michalus. "Keep an eye open for the channeler and see if you can keep him countered."

"You think you can handle the ogres on your own?" Drorm asked, brow furrowed. "There are over a dozen."

Ethan withdrew Excalibur. His sore muscles ached at the motion but for the first time, he actually felt comfortable holding the sword. He shrugged. "I'm going to try."

The bears and ogres were only a couple of dozen yards away now. They would be here in seconds. But that was okay. Ethan had a plan.

Gesturing with his hand, though he knew he didn't need to, Ethan channeled *Earth* and *Air* and carved off several very slender rods of stone, forming them into razor-sharp arrows of rock. There were four of them in total and maintaining them in the air was taxing his concentration. But he still had enough focus left to do what he needed to.

"Some of them are going to get by or be wounded," he told his friends. "Try to keep them off me as long as possible."

Nia, Guinevere and Drorm nodded. His wife growled. "None of them will reach you."

The bears were almost to the creek now, leading the charge. The ogres were right behind them. The forest had spread them out a bit, with some lagging behind. That might work for or against them - he wasn't sure yet.

The bears hit the creek's edge and barreled into the water. There were only five of them and Ethan thought he remembered there being six. Unfortunately, he didn't have time to wait for the last one.

With an effort of will, Ethan brought the stone arrows soaring through the air, slamming into the bears' eye sockets, embedding themselves deep into their brains.

```
You  critically  pierce  Grizzly  Bear
for 193 damage.
   Grizzly Bear dies.
   You     gain     110     experience.
Experience to next level 22,880.
   You critically pierce Grizzly Bear
for 186 damage.
   Grizzly Bear dies.
   You     gain     110     experience.
Experience to next level 22,770.
   You critically pierce Grizzly Bear
for 192 damage.
```

```
Grizzly Bear dies.
You      gain      110      experience.
Experience to next level 22,660.
    You critically pierce Grizzly Bear
for 189 damage.
    Grizzly Bear dies.
    You      gain      110      experience.
Experience to next level 22,550.
```

The bears who were struck yelped briefly, spasmed and then collapsed into the water. Ethan quickly pulled the arrows out and all four hit the final bear, causing it to twitch for a moment before it collapsed too.

```
You  critically  pierce  Grizzly  Bear
for 189 damage.
    Grizzly Bear dies.
    You      gain      110      experience.
Experience to next level 22,440.
```

Ogres reached the creek then, slowing as they saw the red-stained water and the unmoving bear corpses. Ethan didn't hesitate. He sent the stone arrows at them.

He aimed for eyes, and got some, but after a few of them went down, the rest snarled. Covering their heads with their thick arms, they attempted to wade across the creek. Big mistake. Very big mistake.

Once again channeling *Earth*, Ethan had six-inch-thick, sharpened pillars of stone shoot up from the ground, impaling most of the ogres as they tried to cross. More system messages flooded into his HUD, but Ethan had to concentrate on the pillars and the stone arrows at the same time and it was taxing him to his limit.

The second wave of ogres skidded to a halt, seeing what had befallen their tribe mates. Not waiting for them to decide what to do, Ethan sent the stone arrows into their midst. He managed to kill some of them and the others howled and growled in pain and frustration.

Two of the original ogres made it to the opposite side of the creek, but Drorm, Guinevere and Nia took them down while they were still in the water.

Taking a brief moment to look at his HUD, he saw that his *Mana* was below half.

Mana: 57

Ethan had used a lot of *Mana* so far and continued to burn through it manipulating the stone arrows. He needed to slow down or he'd be completely out of *Mana* and be forced to use the Grail to restore it. That would work once, but then he'd be without the Grail's powers for a day.

Suddenly, at the same time, the remaining ogres turned and, with bellows of rage, fled back into the forest.

Furrowing his brow in confusion, Ethan turned first to Michalus and then to the others. "Why are they fleeing?"

"We did kill half their number," Drorm pointed out.

"You mostly," Guinevere chuckled mirthlessly.

"Did anyone see the channeler?" Ethan asked, glancing around his friends.

Everyone shook their heads. Michalus shrugged. "I didn't see or sense his foul magic at all."

"I saw the fireball go off earlier," Ethan commented. "The channeler has to be around here somewhere."

As if on cue, Ethan felt the channeling of dark magic and realized their mistake. He cursed. They'd forgotten to look up.

21

Ethan was blasted backwards by a fireball that threw him into the creek. He landed hard on one of the bear corpses and nearly lost his grip on Excalibur.

Bloody Fist Medicine Man burns you for 19 fire damage.

Cursing, he stood up in the water just in time to have the channeler come slamming down atop him, driving him backwards.

Bloody Fist Medicine Man crushes you for 10 damage.

Staggering from the blow, Ethan barely managed to get Excalibur up to deflect a blow from the ogre channeler's staff. The ogre's wooden weapon hit Excalibur and the blade severed the staff in half. This threw the channeler off balance and Ethan managed to regain his footing and put some distance between them.

The channeler unfurled his wings and began to beat them. He started to lift off the ground until Drorm leaped on the ogre's back and wrapped his hands around the creature's throat. The orc looked a bit singed but otherwise okay.

Falling back into the water, the ogre didn't even try to dislodge the orc. Instead, his eyes glowed and then greenish flame erupted all over the creature's body. Drorm yelped in pain and pushed himself away from the ogre.

Ethan snickered. He knew this trick - elemental armor. He hadn't used it in a long time, but the ogre was putting it to good use. The flames were hot enough to keep them away and once again he began to flap his wings.

"Two can play at that game," Ethan snarled and activated his own elemental armor, choosing water to counter the ogre's fire. He shivered as a barrier of ice formed around his body. It was cool - literally and figuratively - appearing like his skin had become a layer of sparkling diamonds.

Wasting no time, Ethan sprang forward and lunged at the ogre. He felt no heat as he got closer. As he had hoped, his ice armor negated the channeler's fire armor. His momentum carried him into the ogre's space.

He caught sight of the ogre's wide eyes as he realized the fire would not deter Ethan and then Excalibur plunged into the creature's thick leg. The blade slid into the ogre's leg all the way up to the hilt. The channeler bellowed in pain and rage.

**You pierce Blood Fist Medicine Man
for 21 damage.**

Ethan got a grim satisfaction from the ogre's pain.
Given the damage the ogre had done to him, he was eager
for payback. But something happened that surprised him.

The flames surrounding the ogre channeler died out,
leaving him unprotected. At the same time, Ethan felt a
surge of energy coming up the sword and into his body.

You gain 5 points of Mana.

He blinked. He wasn't sure where the energy had
come from but he wasn't complaining. Then he saw the
ogre looking down at his leg in horror. The thing howled
and then tried to jerk away from the blade.

You gain 5 points of Mana.

Panicking, the ogre started to slap at Ethan and he was
forced to retreat. He was perilously low on *Health* and a
good blow might just kill him.

As he did, he slid Excalibur out of the creature's legs
with no effort at all. It was like a hot knife through butter.
Even as he did, so Nia sliced both of her scimitars across
the ogre's other leg, hamstringing him and causing him to
go to his knees.

Drorm then buried his axe into the channeler's shoulder, eliciting another howl of pain from the ogre. He
pulled the axe free and prepared for another strike.

While Nia and Drorm were making their attacks,

Guinevere slipped in and chopped her sword down on the medicine man's wing. There was a crunch and the wing sagged downward, unusable. The ogre bellowed again in pain, unable to determine which way he should turn.

That's when a stream of water erupted from the creek, freezing in midair and burying itself into the ogre's stomach. Throwing his head back, the channeler let out a howl of agony. This gave Ethan the opportunity to rush forward and slam Excalibur into his chest.

```
You   critically   pierce   Blood   Fist
Medicine Man for 43 damage.
   You gain 5 points of Mana.
   Blood Fist Medicine Man dies.
   You      gain      160      experience.
Experience to next level 21,530.
```

The ogre channeler went limp, his eyes rolling back into his skull. Ethan just had enough time to dance away as the creature collapsed face first into the water.

Ethan looked around. All of his companions were singed and breathing hard. He noticed his skin was still encased in ice and dismissed it.

"That hurt," he said, looking at the red blistered skin on his exposed body.

Guinevere, whose armor repelled magic, hadn't come away completely unscathed either. The woman's face was blistered and some of her hair was burned away. Nia's fur too had been scorched by the channeler's fireball.

"If you don't mind, my boy," groaned Michalus, limping into view. The wizard's hands and face had been blistered, and part of his left sleeve was completely burned away. "If you would be so kind as to retrieve the Grail, I think we would all appreciate it."

Nodding, Ethan reached down to his belt to retrieve the Grail, only to find that the pouch had mostly been burned away. All three of his portal pouches were ruined - the Grail pouch, the pouch that led to his chest and the new pouch he'd planned to use for messages to Hawkshead. All gone! He cursed loudly and kicked the channeler's corpse.

"What is wrong?" Nia asked as she dropped into a fighting crouch.

"It burned away my portal pouch!" he growled. He kicked the ogre again.

Drorm, who was burned over most of his body from the elemental armor, sat down heavily in the water. "Then there will be no healing."

Ethan forced a chuckle. "It's still just a portal away. Give me a second."

Ignoring the pain of his own burns, Ethan conjured a portal to Arthur's tomb and, reaching through, retrieved the Grail. Bending down with a groan, he filled it with water and handed it to the orc.

For a second he thought Drorm might not take it, or insist that someone else use it first. But after a moment, the orc took it and sipped some of the water. As usual, the results were almost instantaneous. The burned skin on his arms, chest and face seem to dissolve away. Healthy skin replaced it, leaving him looking just the way he had before - except for a large patch of missing hair on the left side of his head.

Sighing in relief, the orc pushed the cup back at Ethan. He took the goblet and started to hand it to Nia but the foxgirl nodded to Guinevere. "Her first."

Guinevere gave the foxgirl a grateful smile that turned into a grimace as it pulled on the blistered skin of her face. The warrior woman quickly took a sip and then passed it back to Nia and then onto Michalus. Finally, it was Ethan's turn and he drank the cool water down.

Instantly, the burns, riding fatigue and even muscle soreness from the sword training all dissolved away as he was completely healed. With all the pain suddenly gone, he nearly laughed in relief.

"Everyone back to 100%?" he asked, looking around at his companions.

It had been the first time they'd all taken a blast from a fireball like that and they looked worse for wear. With missing eyebrows, missing or melted hair and burned clothes, they looked like quite the ragged bunch.

Guinevere looked up from checking out her reflection in the creek and shook her head. Much of the hair on her right side had been burned away and although the Grail had healed the skin, it hadn't restored the hair. Putting down her sword and shield, she pulled out her dagger. "Time to go short again."

Nia padded over to her and held out her hand. "I will do it for you."

Smiling gratefully, the warrior woman handed over the knife. "Thanks. I never get it quite right."

"Ethan," his wife said, ears flat against her head. She had a pained look in her eyes. "Can you..."

"Put the Grail back... sure," he replied, recognizing the

ultrasonic sound the cup emitted was starting to bother her. He opened up a small portal to the tomb and placed the golden cup back in its resting place. Taking a last look at it, he allowed the portal to close and turned to his friends.

"You two okay?" he asked, looking from Drorm to Michalus. He shot a grin at the wizard and nodded his head at the steaming spear of ice still stuck in the ogre's stomach. "Nice ice spear back there."

Michalus smiled, but it didn't reach his eyes. He looked at the ogre and shrugged. "A little bit of revenge, I guess. Unfortunately, it will not restore my house." He held up his sleeve. "Nor mend my sleeve."

"Revenge is always a bitter potion to swallow," Drorm said with a nod. "Even if sometimes the first sip is sweet."

A noise in the forest caused them all to look up but it was only Par'karr, returning with the horses. He grinned at them. Then, as he got closer, his grin slipped and he scrambled to them. Stopping a few yards away, the kobold took in the sight of his friends. "Ogre burn you?!"

Ethan nodded and pointed to the ogre's corpse. "But we got him in the end."

"That good," the kobold said. "Ogre bad."

Ethan nodded, looking down at the burned remnants of his portal pouches. "Very bad."

22

———

Ethan took the time to use *Air* to remove the bodies from the creek. He wasn't an expert, but he guessed dead ogre and grizzly corpses rotting in the creek wouldn't make for good water downstream.

Afterwards, they cautiously made their way to the wizard's home. They kept alert for any ogre attacks but there were none. It appeared their losses and the death of the ogre channeler had caused the others to beat a hasty retreat.

It took them fifteen minutes to reach the clearing where Michalus lived. Ethan had been holding out hope that maybe the ogres really hadn't destroyed the wizard's house. Those hopes were dashed when they looked into the clearing that used to be the elf's home.

The entire clearing was scorched and nothing remained in it but large piles of ash where his house and workshop used to be. Ethan cursed the ogres. Michalus's entire life had been in those two buildings. He cleared his throat. "I'm sorry, Michalus."

He continued to stare out at the charred clearing that had been his home and nodded. "It's not as if I didn't expect this. But seeing it... seeing it makes it real." Michalus shook his head. "All my books and experiments...."

The wizard looked at the still-smoking remains of his workshop and his scowl deepened. "I'm afraid my workshop is gone and the portal detector was destroyed."

Ethan cursed the ogres again. "Do you think there's anything you can salvage?"

The wizard chuckled mirthlessly. "I can't see how, but you're right. I should go and look."

"Tie horses here," Par'karr said. "Horses not like ash."

Nodding, Ethan and the others tied up their horses just on the outskirts of the burned area. They walked through the ash-strewn clearing, allowing Michalus to lead the way. Michalus went first to his home, looking around the smoking rubble.

Ethan could see there was nothing left. If he had to guess, the ogre channeler had fireballed it multiple times. Added to the fact that the wood used in the house was old and probably dry, it had burned very hot.

"I'm sorry," Ethan said again.

Michalus didn't say a word but gave a small nod of his head in acknowledgement.

Next, he went to where his invisible workshop had been. It was burned to the ground as well, but it appeared that a fireball had exploded inside the building. Not being as well built as the house, the concussion had blown the roof off and the walls apart.

Michalus shook his head as he looked down on the ashes that had once been his life's work. He said nothing, just continued to shake his head. Then he stopped.

Moving forward, he bent down and brushed some ashes away from something poking out. He wiped more away and then began furiously brushing at it, uncovering something. At first, Ethan wasn't sure what it was. But as Michalus uncovered more and more of it, he recognized the gyroscope-like device. It was the portal detector.

Rushing over, Ethan began helping Michalus uncover it. "Is this what I think it is?"

"Yes," the wizard said, voice hard. "But... no, let's wait until we retrieve it."

Ethan nodded and continued to help him uncover the device. He wasn't sure what the wizard's tone meant, but to his eyes, the device seemed mostly intact. It was made of copper and hadn't melted - which he thought was a good thing.

The two of them worked quickly, managing to excavate the portal detector from the ashes after only ten minutes. Lying there, it was bigger than Ethan remembered - probably three feet wide and four feet tall.

It still appeared to him to be a copper gyroscope with six different concentric circles. As he'd noticed before, embedded in each copper circle was a small blue Chymera crystal. To his untrained eye, it looked intact.

Michalus stood the thing up and then carefully moved each of the six circles. He moved them first one way, then the other. There was a slight creaking sound as several of them moved, but Ethan wondered if that was just ash caught in the mechanism.

Finally, the wizard stepped back and nodded. "We were... lucky, with the detector at least."

"It works?" Ethan asked hopefully.

"I believe it will," the wizard replied, turning his head to look at Ethan. "Only one way to be certain."

Ethan understood his meaning. "Gotcha."

He began walking to the edge of the clearing, but Michalus called out to him. "It's already pointing that way," The wizard pointed to the opposite side. "Maybe over there."

Stopping in his tracks, Ethan cocked his head as a thought occurred to him. "Wait. Which side of the portal does it detect?"

Michalus blinked. He opened his mouth and then closed it several times, looking almost comical. Finally he shook his head. "You know, I have no idea."

"Let's test it," Ethan suggested. He pointed to the opposite side of the clearing. "I'll portal from here to there. You watch what it does."

"Seems logical," Michalus said, his voice and demeanor resuming that of the magical scientist Ethan thought of him as.

Gripping Excalibur and channeling his *Mana*, Ethan opened a portal to the opposite side of the clearing. Without hesitation, he stepped through.

Once more, Ethan was traveling through the Bifrost. Even as he did, Merlin's face appeared, but not quite as solid as previous times. It looked him in the eye. "Find me. Hurry."

A heartbeat later, Ethan was out of the Bifrost, at the other end of the clearing. Turning around, Ethan started back to the wizard. "Did it work?"

"It did," Michalus responded. "And it actually tracked your point of origin and then turned to your point of re-entrance."

Ethan nodded. "So, unless you were watching it at the exact time the portal opened - like you were just doing - you would only have the point of exit. The destination location."

Michalus scratched his chin. "I believe your observation is correct. So all of my data..." The wizard paused and looked at the ruins of his workshop. He sighed. "My data would have been the exit points for the portals I had detected."

Giving the wizard a minute to absorb the information, Ethan asked the other question that had been on his mind. "How does this help us find Merlin? If it only detects actual portal activity, I don't see how it would help us?"

"It doesn't really detect portals," the wizard replied. "It actually detects portal energy."

Ethan frowned. "All portal energy?"

The wizard held his finger up. "Yes... and no."

"Yes and no?" Ethan repeated, brow furrowed. "You lost me."

"It does detect all portal activity," the wizard said. "But it is calibrated currently to detect portal energy of a certain magnitude. Otherwise, it would have kept going off whenever I used my portal pouch."

"Gotcha." Ethan nodded. "So it's set...ah... at a low

sensitivity, so it only gets powerful portal usage and we just need to set it to high sensitivity, then it detects any portal usage."

"Not just portal usage," Michalus said enthusiastically. "I believe it will even detect aether anomalies..."

"Like someone trapped in the Bifrost!" Ethan finished. "That sounds perfect! How do we set it to high sensitivity?"

Michalus's face fell. "I will have to enchant new crystals and replace these crystals."

Ethan made a face. "Can you do that without destroying it?"

"Oh yes." The wizard bobbed his head. "I designed it so the crystals can be removed and replaced. No... that's not the problem."

He almost hated to ask, but Ethan had to. "What's the problem?"

"The problem is the formulas I used to set the, what did you call it, oh yes, sensitivity," Michalus replied. "They were much too complex to remember and even the smallest mistake will cause issues. Merlin himself helped me with those formulas."

Getting a bad feeling in his stomach, Ethan sighed. "And where are the formulas."

"They were in a book in my workshop," the wizard said sadly, looking down at the ashes.

Ethan cursed. "So we're screwed."

Michalus held up a finger. "Not necessarily."

"You remember them?" Ethan asked, hopefully.

"No, no." The wizard waved away the idea with a hand. "Like I said. They were too complicated and I couldn't risk recalling them incorrectly. But, because they were so important, I did create a second copy of them."

Excited, Ethan grinned. "You've got a backup copy?!"

"A... backup... copy?" The wizard cocked his head.

"A second copy," Ethan clarified.

"Oh yes," Michalus confirmed. "I did make a second copy."

"Awesome!" Ethan exclaimed, then his countenance fell as he looked from the workshop to the house. "Oh geez. Please tell me it wasn't in the house."

"Oh no," Michalus replied, standing up. He bit his lip for a moment and then answered. "It's in the Order of the Scroll, in Castlehaven."

Ethan frowned, remembering Fearghas's warning of the events going on in the city. The slavery. The sacrifices. Fanatics trying to summon a dark goddess. He shook his head. "So we have to go to Castlehaven?"

"Indeed, my boy," the wizard said with a solemn nod. "Indeed."

23

———

"**I** don't like it," Drorm said as Ethan laid out his plan.

Ethan shrugged. "I'm not sure how else we would make it work."

"I don't like it either," Nia added her opinion. "I should be with you."

"The fewer people," Ethan countered, "the less attention we'll attract."

"What if you get in trouble?" Nia asked. "Who will have your back?"

He let out a frustrated breath. "Michalus will be there with me."

"As a slave," the wizard said distastefully. "Not exactly the way I had been expecting to return to Castlehaven."

Ethan sighed. "You're not really a slave. It's just a bit of acting. You know, make believe. They have theater on this world, right?"

"I've never thought of myself as a thespian," Michalus

retorted. "Besides, I know people at the Order. It will be humiliating."

"I don't like the idea of hiding out in the countryside, waiting for you to return," Drorm agreed.

"Neither do I," Nia added.

"Par'karr not mind staying in countryside," his kobold friend added with a toothy grin. "Par'karr not like human city and they not like Par'karr."

Pandemonium broke out as Drorm, Nia and Michalus all began talking at the same time and Ethan struggled to understand what they were saying.

"Enough!" Guinevere snapped in the authoritative voice that had once belonged to the queen of Camelot. Everyone quieted down and looked at the warrior woman.

She frowned at everyone for a moment before beginning. "Everyone wants to go. I understand that. I don't like the idea of waiting around either. But the fact is, we have to assume that Castlehaven is hostile territory. You don't just walk into hostile territory on a whim. You do reconnaissance, form a strategy and then execute the strategy."

Nia and Drorm nodded slightly, both of them experienced in war and conflict. Guinevere continued. "From what the dwarf said, the city has gone to hell. We have no idea what conditions are like. What type of forces we'll run into. We really know nothing at all."

"What do you suggest?" Michalus asked.

Guinevere smiled at the group, making eye contact with everyone. "I suggest that Ethan and I go in first, do some scouting and then report back to the group." She held up her hand to forestall any arguments. "He is a wizard and I am a warrior. And, more importantly, we are both human. Of all of us here, we have the least chance of attracting undue attention or being enslaved."

Nia opened her mouth but the warrior woman shook her head. "I know you want to be with him and protect him. I give you my word as a Knight of Camelot, that I will do my best to protect him in your absence."

The foxgirl bit her lip for a moment, eyes flicking between Guinevere and Ethan, before she finally nodded.

"Good." Guinevere turned to Drorm. "I know it is not in your nature to be sidelined but think of it like a military command. We are the scouts and you will be waiting with the others for our report. Once we return, we will make a plan that involves as many of us as is safe."

"That is reasonable," Drorm agreed.

"Michalus," she said, turning to the wizard. "Believe me when I tell you, I would feel the same way in your shoes. I have been a free woman from the moment of my birth and I have never been a servant to anyone. Even at the round table, I was equal to any man. I bent the knee to Arthur when he became king, but I did that by choice, because he was the best of us. Even in a deception, I would be loath to present myself as a slave."

The wizard nodded at her words, apparently sharing her sentiment.

Ethan didn't really understand the elf's reluctance. To him, it was just playacting. A role. It didn't mean anything. Pretending to be a slave no more made him a slave than pretending to be a kobold made him a kobold.

But Ethan came from a different culture, a different planet. Heck, perhaps even a different universe. He was used to TV and movies, where people pretended to be something they weren't all the time. Even the role-playing games he played involved acting and playing a role.

For him it was no big deal. But to Michalus - and Guinevere too, obviously - it was a big deal. It was something he didn't understand but something he had to accept and honor.

"I have an idea that may not require you to pass yourself off as a slave," Guinevere said and Michalus and Ethan both perked up.

"Oh?" Ethan asked.

Guinevere smiled. "Well, you ARE a wizard. You're also the best wizard I've ever met with portals after my father."

Ethan smacked his palm against his forehead. "You and I could get into the library and then I could portal Michalus directly to us."

"Exactly," the warrior woman replied. "Although, once we do get there, we may have a fight on our hands."

"You think the Order members would attempt to enslave me or turn me over?" Michalus said incredulously. "I've been a member for ...ah... four hundred and fifty years!"

"When was the last time you were in there?" Guinevere asked, giving him a knowing look.

"Well, I... uh..." Michalus replied, scratching his chin. "It might have been a hundred years or so."

Ethan nodded, realizing Guinevere's point. "There won't be any elves there and they're the only ones who will remember you."

Michalus frowned. "You have a point."

"Plus," Ethan added. "The last time I was there, the only people I saw were warlocks and channelers."

"Oh dear," Michalus replied. "I had almost forgotten the current state of wizards. You're right. For all we know, you and I might be the last two wizards alive. At least, in this part of the world."

"And my father," Guinevere said. "He's still alive."

"And your father," Michalus said with a nod of acknowledgement.

"So then, the plan would be," Ethan reiterated. "You and I go into the city while the others wait at a designated spot. We assess the situation. If it's safe, we come back and get the others. If not, we get into the Order and then I portal back to the others and then bring Michalus into the library to find the book he needs."

"Basically," Guinevere said. "Given the state of affairs as we know it, it is the plan with the best chance of success and the least risk to everyone."

"I still wish I was going with you," Nia said.

"I know," Ethan replied with a smile. "I wish you were coming along."

Nia nodded.

"I do not like that we have to go to Castlehaven," Guinevere continued, looking between Drorm, Nia, Michalus and Par'karr. "I do not know whether or not the priests of Hel can really summon her to this world, but I do know that demon lords have been summoned here before. And they are incredibly powerful."

"Ah yes." Michalus nodded. "I remember."

"There's a reason why warlocks and channelers were

banned for so long," Guinevere said. "It's folly to allow them to grow in power again."

"Has anyone ever summoned a god before?" Ethan asked, looking between Michalus and Guinevere.

"Not during my lifetime," Guinevere replied. "And not that I have ever heard of."

Michalus nodded. "I've never read about anyone doing it before and I would think that would be something that would have been recorded."

"Well, let's hope it's not possible," Ethan told everyone. "But even if it's not, that won't stop the fanatics from sacrificing people."

Guinevere nodded. "I suggest we don't spend any more time than we need to in the city. Get in, assess the situation, then you portal the others to us, we get the book and then you portal us out."

"That sounds like a plan to me." Ethan nodded. He looked around at his companions. "Is everyone okay with that plan?"

There was a murmur of consents and Ethan smiled. He looked around the area that used to be the wizard's home. "Okay, then. We will need to set up camp and then Nia, you and Drorm go hunting. We don't have portal pouches any longer so our food is gone and we'll only be able to take what we can carry."

Nia and Drorm nodded. Nia caught Ethan's eye and gave him a smile. "Perhaps you should come hunting with me."

Drorm rolled his eyes and stepped away from the foxgirl. He walked over to his horse and began unpacking his bed roll.

"Uh hmmm," Ethan cleared his throat. "You're right. There might be ogres out there and my magic could come in useful."

Guinevere chuckled. "Just go already. We'll set up camp. But do try to do some ACTUAL hunting too, I'm starving."

Slightly embarrassed, Ethan hurried over to Nia and the two of them headed into the woods.

24

They set off for Castlehaven early the next morning under dark, threatening clouds. Luckily, they were normal storm clouds and not a mana storm. The group managed to make it until just before lunch before the skies opened up and rain began to hammer down on them.

The trees of the forest offered some protection for them, but within only a few minutes, they were all drenched. Once again, Ethan tried to think of some way to use his magic to keep the rain off of them. Sadly, nothing sustainable came to mind. They were forced to ride through the downpour.

The group found a copse of fir trees near lunchtime, that shielded them from most of the rain and gave them a short respite. They built a fire and dethawed some frozen venison from Nia's kill the previous day. Ethan and Michalus also took that opportunity to refreeze the remaining meat.

After their short escape from the rain, they continued their ride until late afternoon when they came to the road west. The road that led to Castlehaven. Rather than start down the muddy road that late, Ethan and his group found some trees that offered shelter and quickly built a fire. Everyone was soaked and miserable and after a warm dinner, they set watch and turned in, hoping tomorrow would be a better day. It wasn't.

The rain continued the next day as they trudged westward along the muddy road. They reached the burned remnants of Silvershade before lunch and continued on. Ethan remembered the elven children they had found there and who Michalus had escorted to Moonpoint.

He frowned as he thought about Moonpoint and the fact that it might now be under attack from Castlehaven. For what? More slaves? He felt himself growing angry.

"Can the prince be supplanted?" Ethan asked aloud, raising his voice to be heard over the rain.

"Eh? What's that?" Michalus asked, riding up next to him. "Prince?"

"Can the Prince of Castlehaven be supplanted or overthrown? I assume it's not an elected office," he replied.

"I can't right say that I ever investigated human politics enough to know the answer to that," the wizard replied after a moment. "I'm not sure exactly what their government is based on."

"It's been a while," Guinevere said, riding up on Ethan's other side. "But it's been similar for hundreds of years. It's a hereditary office. I'm sure the current prince is the son, grandson, cousin or some relation of the current prince. Thus, if they were supplanted, it would need to be a relative."

"So someone couldn't just... ah... you know... kill the prince and assume his role?" Ethan asked.

"You mean, assassinate him?" Guinevere chuckled with a raised eyebrow. "Why, Ethan, I didn't know you had it in you."

"No." He shook his head. "I don't mean me. Given what's going on there, I'm surprised someone else hasn't."

Guinevere nodded grimly. "You'd be surprised at how much stock the common people put in divine right."

Ethan snickered.

"Not a believer in divine right?" she chuckled. Shrugging she got a faraway look in her eyes. "I might have believed once. But Arthur was the best of us... I mean, the very best... and... well... look at Mordred... look what he..."

The warrior woman lapsed into silence, staring off into the distance. Ethan let the conversation die, preferring not to break Guinevere's train of thought.

Instead, his thoughts turned to what he knew lay ahead, a place called Timberwell.

Timberwell was a logging town they'd visited before. In fact, it was where Ethan had first discovered Aether magic after unwittingly teleporting himself.

According to his memory, given their pace, they should reach it by sundown. Ethan was certainly looking forward to a nice warm - and dry - bed and a good, home-cooked meal. Yes, the meal would be nice. But the dry bed was what he really looked forward to. And a nice hot bath!

He blushed slightly at the memory of the last time

they'd been in Timberwell. He'd been taking a bath when a drunk Ainslee had passed out at the door. Ethan had gotten out of the tub to help drag her into the room when his towel slipped off. Somehow, he'd teleported himself back into the tub.

Ethan shook his head. It was an embarrassing memory but it had been how he'd learned Aether magic. In a way, it might have been one of the best things that could have happened to him. Portal magic was incredibly useful and versatile and had saved their butts more times than he could count.

Just then, the rain intensified, going from a steady downpour to a torrential deluge. He growled quietly. Just a few more hours. And then, dry bed and hot bath.

As HE EXPECTED, they reached Timberwell just before dark. With the dark clouds obscuring the twin suns, it was already dark. That was why they didn't see the wagons across the road until they were right on top of them.

Across the road, from the treeline of one side to the treeline of the other side was a barricade of wagons turned onto their sides. Confused, Ethan called his group to a halt. He squinted at the wagons.

Looking closer, he could see that some of them seemed to be nailed together with logs and boards. Only the center seemed capable of being moved and it was tied together at the top and the bottom.

"Slavers not welcome!" came a male's voice from the

other side of the wagons. "Turn around and go back to Castlehaven."

Ethan frowned, brow furrowed. "I have an elf, an orc, a foxling and a kobold as part of my group. Does that seem like slavers to you? Plus, I'm coming from the wrong direction to be from Castlehaven."

There was murmuring from behind the wagons and then Ethan saw movement near one of the space between the middle wagons. Someone was looking at them. It was hard for him to see in the dark but there was definitely someone watching them.

"Don't matter," another voice said, this one a bit deeper than the other. "No one allowed in Timberwell. We're a free city."

"Listen," Ethan tried. "We just want food and lodging for the night."

"Ain't got either," retorted the voice. "Inn's full with refugees and there's barely enough food for who's already here."

"We have money," Ethan explained. "We can pay..."

"What part of... no one gets in... did you not get?" the second voice called out.

Starting to grow angry and frustrated, Ethan considered ripping the wagons apart with *Air*. But he didn't. It appeared these people were taking a stand against the slavery and against Castlehaven. If nothing else, he respected that.

Not to mention, if they did break through the barricade, they could have a fight on their hands with the entire town. Even if they didn't, he doubted they could sleep soundly in a place where they had essentially forced their way into.

He cursed and looked at his companions. He could see their disappointment too. Apparently, he hadn't been the only one who had been looking forward to a dry bed. "What do we do?"

"It's too dark to circle around," Guinevere said, "especially in this rain."

Drorm looked around and then shrugged. "No good places to camp here."

"We can backtrack and find a spot," Nia suggested.

"You really ain't slavers?" the first voice asked.

"We're not slavers," Ethan replied, hoping that perhaps they would change their mind.

"Back down the road, about a mile," the voice said. "There's a path to the left that leads to a small farm. Sam and Cindy's farm. They got snatched up by the slavers a month ago. Place is abandoned but it's got a roof. Better than sleeping in this."

Ethan smiled. It was something. At least they might be dry tonight. "Thanks!"

"Yeah," the voice called out. "Just don't come back, you hear? Move on along to wherever you were headed."

"We will," Ethan answered and turned his horse around. "Come on, let's go find this farm."

Leaving the barricade behind, they rode back up the road until they found the path the men had told him about. Turning onto the road, they soon found the farm.

The place was small - only a single large room - but it also had a barn for the horses. They quickly checked to make sure no one was occupying it before they unpacked their gear and settled their horses.

Ethan and Michalus used *Fire* magic to dry everyone's clothes and bedrolls and then they cooked the frozen venison steaks in the fireplace. Warm food and a dry place to lay their heads changed the mood of the party and they actually stayed up a bit later chatting about all sorts of topics before finally turning in for the night.

25

It took them two more days and three fights with slavers to reach the outskirts of Castlehaven. He barely considered their scraps with the slavers to be fights at all. They had been little more than bands of thugs looking for a cheap buck by enslaving anyone they came across.

They'd only killed a few from each group before the rest fled. Ethan would have thought that a woman in plate mail and an orc would dissuade people from attacking them. Apparently not.

Most of the farms they'd run across had been abandoned. Either the families had been enslaved or they'd fled. Ethan hoped for their sake, it was the latter. He knew what fate awaited anyone who was enslaved. Human sacrifice.

The closer they'd gotten to the city, the more Ethan and Michalus had gotten a familiar feeling. It was the feeling of corrupted magic. Warlock or channeler magic.

And it was powerful.

As the feeling got stronger and stronger, Ethan finally asked Michalus. "Any idea what that is?"

The wizard shivered. "I have no idea, my boy. But it's powerful."

"Yeah," Ethan agreed. "Do you think it could be the summoning ritual?"

"Odin's Blind Eye!" Michalus exclaimed. "Let's hope not. To be honest, I didn't put much stock in the stories. No one's ever summoned a god here before. But feeling this... I'm beginning to wonder."

Ethan furrowed his brow. "You think they might actually be able to summon a god?"

The others, who had apparently been listening in on their conversation, turned to Michalus. The wizard looked off into the distance for a long time before answering. "The thing about gods is, they're gods. They can pretty much do as they please. Come and go as they please. Do they really need to be summoned?"

Nodding, Ethan considered his answer. "Maybe the ritual draws their attention to this place. If they are gods, then perhaps they don't focus on an area unless mortals do something noteworthy."

"Like lots of sacrifices," Nia added.

"Right," he agreed.

Michalus shrugged. "Oftentimes, I find the simplest solution is usually the right one."

"Occam's razor," Ethan said without thinking.

"Who's razor?" Drorm asked, confused.

"Occam's razor," Ethan repeated. "It's a saying or scientific principle or something. It basically says: All things being equal, the simplest answer is usually the correct one."

"Isn't that what I just said?" Michalus said with a smile.

"It is," Ethan agreed. "I just thought it was interesting that we had a similar saying on my world."

"Some principles transcend worlds," the wizard said.

"There," Nia said, pointing to an area of woods to the right. "We can wait for you in there."

Ethan moved them off the road, into the trees where there would be no clear line of sight to them. As his friends looked around the dense copse of trees, he cleared his throat. "Good call, Nia. This should help you avoid any more slavers."

"They will not be a problem," Nia declared. "They are cowards."

"Maybe," he agreed. "But there could be larger or better-armed groups. Best not to draw any attention to yourselves before I come for you."

"And keep the horses tied," Guinevere said. "I'm not sure how long it will take to get to the library. Be ready to come at a moment's notice."

Ethan shivered as a wave of energy washed over him, the same corrupted energy they'd been feeling. He shot a glance at Michalus. "Did you just feel that? Like a wave of energy passing through you?"

The wizard nodded, staring off into the city. "Whatever they are doing, I fear it is nearly complete."

"All the more reason for us to get to the library, get that book and get out of here," Guinevere said. "Come on!"

With a glance at Nia, Ethan turned and followed Guinevere out of the trees and back to the road. By time he had walked the hundred or so yards to the road, another wave of energy passed over him. He cursed.

"What?" Guinevere demanded.

"Another wave of energy," he said. "Whatever they're doing, I'm thinking it's building to a crescendo."

"Fools." The warrior woman's expression darkened. "Come, let's move faster."

It was another two hundred yards to the city gate and in that time, another wave hit Ethan. Each wave of energy seemed slightly more intense than the previous one. Whatever was going to happen, was going to happen soon.

"I don't think we have much more time!" Ethan said, breaking into a jog. "We need to get there now."

Nodding, the warrior woman broke into a jog and settled into a pace next to him. They ran the last dozen yards to the gate, only to find it open and unguarded.

"That's... not... normal," Ethan puffed as he jogged along. "There were guards there last time."

"No time to figure it out now," Guinevere shot back. "Keep running."

Ethan did, for several minutes, before another wave hit him. This one, he felt - physically - and nearly stumbled.

"Thor's hammer!" Guinevere cursed. "Was that... the wave of energy you were talking about?"

He looked at her in surprise. "You felt it too?"

"Oh yes," she replied. "I think my armor blocked my body from feeling it, but I felt it in my head."

"I don't think that's a good thing," Ethan told her. "Come on!"

The two of them ran past buildings and homes, not seeing a single soul outside. Ethan thought he glimpsed a few people looking out of cracked doors or shuttered windows, but no one roamed the streets.

"Where is everyone?" Guinevere put words to his unspoken question.

Another wave hit before Ethan could answer. This one was stronger than the last one and actually nudged him to his right. Then he noticed it seemed to be getting darker. He looked up.

The sky was starting to fill with dark clouds, seemingly centered on Castlehaven. Ethan cursed. "This sucks! This really sucks!"

Looking up, Guinevere just nodded. "Those fools will bring destruction down on us all!"

"Just keep going!" he yelled and broke into another run.

They turned a corner and nearly ran into a half dozen dirty-looking men in mismatched armor. Overcoming their shock, the men grinned. "More sacrifices."

Ethan barely stopped. They didn't have time to fight these men. Not with that energy building up. Gripping Excalibur, he channeled *Air* and slammed all six of them into the walls on either side of them.

The men hit with bone-rattling force, fell and didn't get up. They were either unconscious or dead, and honestly, Ethan didn't care which. They were slavers. They deserved what they got and probably much more. Though, judging by the lack of experience in his HUD, he guessed they were just unconscious. Too bad.

"That was impressive," Guinevere commented.

"I just did what I had to," Ethan told her. "I feel like we are running out of time."

As if in response to his comment, another wave of energy hit them. Then a huge crack sounded as lightning struck somewhere in the city ahead of them, the flash from it making him blink. "Great! Just great! As if we didn't have enough going on!"

"Go! Go!" Guinevere yelled. "Keep going!"

They continued to run as more lightning began to smash into the city. And this wasn't normal lightning. It was huge bolts, as thick as a man. He saw several buildings explode after being hit, throwing stone and wood in all directions.

Still, he and Guinevere kept going. They ran through the deserted city with reckless abandon. Waves continued to hit them, becoming more and more frequent. The lightning became more frequent too.

The two of them finally reached the street that the Order was located on and they both broke into a sprint. Finally getting to the large, ironbound door of the building, Ethan saw that it was discolored by black soot. Had someone tried to burn it down?

Looking around, he saw the side of the stone building was marred as well. It really did look as though someone had tried to burn the building down. But why?

Guinevere pulled on the door but it didn't budge. She let out a frustrated growl just as another lightning strike hit, followed by a wave of energy. "It's barred from the other side!"

"Get back!" Ethan said and was about to blast the door open when another idea struck him.

Instead, he summoned his water elemental. As soon as it appeared, he pointed at the door. "Get inside and lift the bar on the door."

Soundlessly, the dolphin-shaped elemental collapsed into a puddle of water. As he watched, the water flowed under the door until it was completely gone. A moment later, he heard a clatter from inside the building.

Guinevere pulled on the door and this time it opened. "Quick! Inside!"

Ethan hustled inside, followed by Guinevere. They shut the large door behind them and put the bar back in place.

"You are trespassing!" a voice said from behind them. "And you will pay the price!"

THE QUEEN WAS TORN. She knew the direction that the wizard been. He had been in Patheos. She hadn't detected a large spike of Aether magic since she had sensed him in the broken human city.

She had detected smaller uses of Aether, but those were unlike the human wizard. Another wizard perhaps? If she had any collectors left, she would have sent them to investigate. Having none, she had continued towards Patheos.

Then strange emanations of Aether magic had begun coming from the west. From the human city she knew from stolen memories to be Castlehaven. They started weak, but over the past few days had quickly gained in strength. Now, they were even stronger than the human wizard.

The Queen knew she needed to investigate. This much

Aether magic could be the key to her getting home. Yes. She had to find out more.

With a mental command, she and her remaining soldiers turned and headed west. Towards Castlehaven.

26

Ethan spun, ready to unleash his magic when he recognized the haggard and ragged form of Mertin Graystaff. Fire surrounded his hands and it looked as if he was about to blast them.

They'd met Mertin earlier, when Ethan had wanted to join the Order of the Scroll. He was a channeler who had been friendly, despite his somewhat demonic appearance. Now, the man looked like he'd been in a warzone. Given the current state of the city, perhaps that wasn't far from the truth.

"Mertin!" Ethan called out. "It's me! Ethan! Remember?"

Mertin blinked. He leaned his head forward, eyes squinting. "From Hawkshead?"

"Yes," Ethan replied, smiling. "Remember, I went to the library in Patheos."

The channeler let the fire on his hands die away. At the same time, the man sagged, putting a hand against the wall to support himself. "I'm afraid you picked a bad time to return."

"What happened?" Ethan asked, seeing that the inside of the building was in disarray too.

"Slavers. Looters. Desperate people," the man replied sourly. "You name it."

"And you and the others are defending the library?" Ethan asked.

"Others?" Mertin chuckled bitterly. "The others are gone. Captured, fled or dead. It's just me now."

"Why don't you leave?" Guinevere asked.

The channeler looked aghast. "And leave the library to the barbarian hordes?! Are you mad?"

"Something is happening out there," Ethan told the man, unsure whether he could feel the surges of power. "I'm not sure if they'll summon anything, but with that much power... who knows what might happen."

"I know." The channeler shuddered. "And I think they will summon something."

Guinevere looked alarmed. "The goddess?"

Mertin shook his head numbly. "I'm... well... you know what I am. I'm a channeler and we get our power from otherworldly entities..."

"Demons," Guinevere said flatly.

The channeler looked annoyed but then sighed. "Yes, creatures you know as demons. That notwithstanding, I am, shall we say, more in tune with the energies from the other dimension. That's why I don't believe it is a goddess they are summoning."

"Oh? What are they summoning?" Ethan raised an eyebrow. He had a bad feeling but hoped he was wrong.

"A demon lord," Mertin replied with a shudder.

"Gods of Asgard!" Guinevere hissed. "Those morons."

"Exactly," the channeler said. "They're deceived fools, duped by the demon lord into believing they are summoning their goddess."

Another wave of energy washed over them and they all shuddered.

Ethan cursed loudly. "We need to get a book and get out of here. You should come too, Mertin."

"We'll never make it through the city," the man replied.

"It's deserted now," Ethan said. He bit his lip. "Plus, I'm not going to be walking through the city again."

Mertin's brow furrowed in confusion. "You're staying?"

Giving Mertin a sheepish grin, Ethan explained. "I might not have been completely honest with you last time."

The channeler tilted his head. "Oh?"

"I'm a wizard," Ethan said and conjured several balls of light around the room.

Mertin's eyes opened wide. "Are you really? There are actually wizards left?! Wait... of course you are. I felt that magic. It didn't have the same feel as warlock magic! You are a wizard!"

"I am." Ethan nodded. "And I have another wizard with me just outside the city. He needs a book from the library to help us calibrate a portal detector that he created."

Mertin furrowed his brow. "A... portal detector?"

"I don't really have time to explain," Ethan told the man. "I need to go get him and bring him here."

The channeler's face grew even more confused. "Bring who? How?"

Another wave of energy hit them, even stronger than the last one. Ethan cursed. They were running out of time. "I need to go get him now! I'm going to portal away for a second and then I'm going to portal back."

Pulling the new rune stick off his belt, he dropped it on the floor. He'd made it before they'd come into town, knowing he'd need a marker to get him back inside the library.

A blast of energy hit him. This one was strong enough to unbalance him and force him to grab the wall to stop from falling over. Guinevere stumbled into him, grabbing his arm for support. Mertin windmilled for a second before falling to the ground.

"That was a big one!" Guinevere hissed.

"We're out of time!" Ethan told Mertin, reaching down to help the man up.

Nodding slowly, Mertin took the offered hand and scrambled to his feet. "Are you really going to open a portal? Big enough for us to go through?"

"I am," he told the channeler.

The channeler looked around the room and back through the hallway into the main library. He let out a breath. "Can I come with you? I don't think there is much more I can do..."

Before he could finish, an intensive wave crashed into them. So massive was the wave, it shook the ground itself and the walls of the building. It tossed them around and knocked him to the ground. Guinevere, who had still been holding his arm, crashed heavily on top of him, driving the air from his lungs.

Ethan groaned. He blinked his eyes as he struggled to

take a breath. Guinevere looked down on him and gave him a half-hearted smile. "Sorry about that. But thanks for breaking my fall."

"No... problem," he gasped.

Guinevere slowly pushed herself off of him, into a sitting position. Then, reaching out, she grabbed his arm and yanked him upright with surprising strength.

"Thanks," he breathed, sucking in a lungful of air. He was sore from the fall and from the warrior woman landing on him in full plate mail armor. Filling his lungs again, Ethan looked around for Mertin.

He saw the channeler, lying crumpled in a heap on the floor, next to the wall. A bloody smear ran down the wall.

"Mertin!" Ethan croaked, but the man didn't stir.

Scrambling over to him, Ethan flipped the channeler over. Mertin had a large, bloody lump on his forehead, just between his horns. He shook the man gently. "Mertin! Mertin!"

The channeler still didn't stir and Ethan cursed. "He's out cold!"

"The Grail?" Guinevere asked.

Reflexively, Ethan reached for his portal pouch. He cursed again, remembering the ogre's fireball had ruined it. "I have to create a portal to it."

Ethan focused his magic, centering it on the runes he knew were on Arthur's tomb, where the Grail lay. Focusing his will, he opened a portal to the tomb. Or rather, that's what he tried to do.

He blinked. Ethan had felt the portal trying to form, but there was some sort of interference. Something was preventing him from opening portals. He tried again with the same results. He cursed and tried opening a portal to his friends in the forest. Nothing. He cursed again.

"What?" Guinevere asked.

"I can't open a portal!" he growled in frustration. "Something's wrong!"

Guinevere opened her mouth to say something but another wave of energy slammed into the building at the same time the earth trembled again. Ethan had never been in an earthquake, but he guessed this was what it felt like. Luckily, he was still on the floor and not standing, so there was no risk of falling this time.

The tremor caused dust and pieces of the roof to fall down. Ethan stretched himself over the unconscious Mertin to protect him and then felt Guinevere cover his own body with her armored one. She smirked down at him. "If you're going to cover someone, you need tougher skin."

"Good point," Ethan thought and with a thought, he summoned his *Elemental Armor*, choosing Earth. In a second, his skin was covered in a hard, rock-like second skin. He felt a rush of relief that not all magic seemed to be affected, just the portals. "Like this?"

Guinevere rolled her eyes and then closed them as pieces of the roof fell onto her, banging off her armor. She grunted as something heavy hit her.

"Good thing you have magical armor," Ethan told her.

"Still hurts," she grumbled.

The shaking stopped and a moment later, there was a loud roar that they could hear clearly, even through the walls of the building. Whatever made that sound had to be large. Very large. Ethan swallowed unconsciously.

Their faces inches apart, Ethan and Guinevere exchanged glances. The warrior woman frowned. "Do I want to know what that was?"

Ethan swallowed and tried to hide his worry. "I think whatever they were trying to summon... they just succeeded."

27

F*lee, mortals! Flee before your new god!* The voice came unbidden into Ethan's head. He flinched and saw Guinevere flinch as well.

"You heard that too?" Ethan asked.

"Yes," she said, her face pained. "Reminded me a bit too much of... Mordred."

Ethan nodded. Her son, Mordred, had been a channeler and had given himself over completely to the demon giving him his power. He'd transformed into a Chthulu-type demon with incredible mental powers.

Mordred had been on the verge of taking over Ethan's mind when he had tricked the channeler. He had given Mordred exactly what he had wanted - the Holy Grail. Unfortunately for him, Merlin had enchanted the cup to admit a high-pitched sound that Mordred's demon ears couldn't stand. Once the Grail was within earshot, it disabled the demon and allowed Ethan to kill it.

He hoped it wasn't the same sort of demon. The one

that had possessed Mordred had been bad enough. A more powerful version might be able to knock down Ethan's mental defenses easily.

"Look after Mertin," Ethan told Guinevere. "I need to see what's going on out there."

Ethan started to rise but the warrior woman caught his arm. "I'm coming with you. You might be a wizard, but I'm a knight. I don't stay behind where it's safe."

"What about..." he started to say, looking down at Mertin.

"Mertin will either be fine, or he won't," Guinevere said. "I'm not a healer. There's nothing I can do to help him."

He nodded. She was right. And if truth be told, he would feel better with the warrior woman at his side. "Alright, leave him here and let's go see what's going on out there."

The two of them stood and, with one last look at Mertin, walked over to the door. The tremors had caused part of the archway to collapse and rubble now blocked the door from opening. After trying to shove the door open, Ethan used *Earth* magic to move the fallen stones.

Pushing the door open, the two of them were immediately assaulted by the sounds of screams and the smell of smoke and brimstone. Ethan looked towards the temple area to see flames everywhere. The city was on fire.

"Gods!" Guinevere spat. "Mertin was right. Those fools summoned a demon."

"And a powerful one at that," Ethan agreed. "Look at all that fire."

"This city is going to burn," Guinevere commented impassively. "Can you get us out of here?"

Ethan looked at her. "There are still a lot of people here."

"They'll get out once the fire gets closer," she said with a shrug.

"I thought you were a knight," Ethan growled. "Don't you want to help these people?"

"I AM a knight," she retorted angrily. "And these people summoned a demon and..."

I feel your fear, mortals! I will drink every delicious drop! came the demon's voice in their heads again.

"You want to leave them to that?" he demanded.

Guinevere glared at Ethan and then glanced at the burning section of the city. She set her jaw. "You're going to go try and help, aren't you?"

Whether the act of having to make the choice or some other cosmic or alien intelligence sensed he was going to make the choice, a prompt appeared in his HUD.

```
You     have    received    a    new    quest
"Defend  Castlehaven  from  the  Demon
Attack - Part I"
    You  have  been  given  a  choice  to
help  the  people  of  Castlehaven  and
fight  whatever  demon  that  has  been
summoned,  or  flee  the  city  with  the
others.
    Fight the Demon (0/1).
    Reward: 10000 experience, Unknown.
    Flee the City (0/1)
```

`Reward: Unknown.`
`Accept quest (yes or no)?`

Ethan shook his head at the quest prompt.

He forced a smile. Truth be told, he really didn't want to face another demon. He'd only killed the last demon he'd faced through sheer trickery. He had no tricks up his sleeve this time. And yet, could he really just stand by and let these people die if he could help? "I have to try."

Taking a deep breath, Ethan accepted the quest.

The warrior woman stared at him for a long moment. Her face softened into a slight smile and she shook her head. "You would have made a decent knight - well, if you could actually fight."

"Gee, thanks." He smirked. "I DO have magic, you know."

Her face grew serious again. "So will it. A lot of magic."

"You're probably right." He sighed. Magic had been his trump card in most altercations and he'd barely held his own against the casters he'd run into. How would he fare against a demon, who probably used magic as naturally as he breathed air.

"If it's a powerful demon," she said, "we're probably going to die."

Ethan nodded grimly. He knew that was a possibility. He didn't really want to die, but he wasn't sure he could just run away without trying.

He tried to create a portal but once again it failed. There would be no creating portals for a last-minute escape. Whatever magic had summoned the demon was interfering with the portal magic. Or perhaps it was the demon itself.

Cursing, Ethan forced himself to take a step towards the temple area. Then another. He licked his dry lips as Guinevere fell into step alongside him.

"You've got the heart of a knight," she told him with a smirk. "Even if you have the brains of a piece of ore."

"Gee," he said, rolling his eyes. "Thanks. You really do know how to compliment a guy."

"If we do die," she said softly. "At least I'll be with Arthur again."

Not knowing how to respond to that, Ethan kept walking. His heart pounded in his chest. Despite the fear, he forced himself to keep walking.

As they moved towards the temple area of the city, more and more people ran past them. The people were from all walks of life. Some looked like shop owners while others appeared to be average citizens. Some dragged or carried children with them.

Eventually, a group of men and women hurried past, pulling a wagon meant for a horse. The wagon was loaded with children and a few elderly. Behind the wagon, several more men and women pushed.

"Hel's priests summoned a demon!" one of the men yelled as they hurried past. "Get out of the city!"

More and more people rushed by them but Ethan and Guinevere kept walking until they reached the section of the city that was on fire. They stopped just outside the area.

"Are you sure you want to do this?" Guinevere asked.

Ethan took a deep breath, then nearly coughed as the

smoke-tainted air hit his lungs. He nodded. "If not us, then who?"

Guinevere looked down at the sword in his hand. "Remember, that's Excalibur. It will cut through nearly anything. Just get in close and try to take out a leg - or whatever this thing has that serves as legs. If we can cripple it, we might have a chance."

Looking down at the sword, he held it out to the warrior woman. "Maybe you should take it."

She shook her head. "You pulled the sword from the stone. Not me. Not anyone else in over 1,000 years. I think... I think you're meant to have it."

Ethan withdrew the sword and nodded. He didn't really agree but now wasn't the time to argue. If he spent any more time waiting, he was afraid he'd turn back around and run. He took a deep breath and let it out.

"Okay," he told Guinevere. "Let's go kill a demon."

They started into the burning city but didn't get far before Ethan was forced to tear pieces from his cloak and wrap them around his mouth. The smoke was getting thicker and breathing was becoming more difficult. There was also a stench in the air that he couldn't place. Whatever it was, it was foul.

Come, mortal plaything, come and meet your end. The voice sounded in his head. He didn't think the voice was talking specifically to him, but he shuddered nonetheless.

A crash sounded, followed by the sound of falling rubble. Guinevere pointed to their left. "It came from that direction."

Ethan swallowed and then nodded. "Let's go."

The two of them wound their way through the rubble

and blocked streets. Some streets were completely impassable. To Ethan, it looked like a crane with a wrecking ball had come through the street, leaving rubble strewn everywhere.

Stopping as he caught sight of fiery wings about twelve feet off the ground, Ethan froze. His heart seemed to be slamming against his ribcage as he caught glimpse. The demon had to be as tall as an ogre - maybe even a giant. How could they even hope to fight such a thing?

He only got a quick look at the fiery wings before they disappeared.

"Come on," Guinevere said, grabbing his wrist. "It's getting away."

Ethan rolled his eyes. Now she was suddenly gung ho. Great!

The two of them hurried to the corner of the street where the demon had disappeared. The buildings on both sides were on fire but the street itself was surprisingly clear. They moved out into the middle of the street and found what they had been looking for. About fifty feet down the street was the demon. And it was a big demon.

The creature was bigger than an ogre, perhaps 16 or 18 feet tall. The demon's body had dark-red skin and was thickly muscled - almost comically so. Its head was vaguely humanoid, but with a bestial look that was topped off by the large black horns that emerged from the sides of its head. Hooved feet and fiery wings topped off the demonic look, making it look like something from a nightmare.

It was just close enough for Ethan to scan.

Shadd'Rarr'Nor
    Demon Lord
    Level: 35

Ethan gawked at the information in his HUD. A demon lord? Level 35?! He cursed.

Just then, the demon lord looked their way. A wicked grin spread across its demonic face. *Ah, more playthings.*

28

The demon lord stalked forward on its large, hooved feet. As it turned, Ethan saw that in its right hand, the creature carried an enormous, jagged scimitar.

Guinevere shot Ethan a quick glance and then looked back at its legs. "Remember what I told you.

"Come on!" she yelled and charged the demon lord.

She only got a dozen feet before a wall of fire sprang up in front of her. Ethan thought the warrior woman might run through it, but she threw herself to the side just in time. She bounced off one of the buildings just in front of the flames. The demon was already bringing its sword down on the spot where she was and she rolled to the side as it slammed into the ground.

```
Quest Complete.
    Defend Castlehaven from the Demon
Attack - Part I
```

```
You have chosen to fight the demon
lord.
Fight the Demon (1/1).
Reward: 10000 experience, Unknown.
You gain 10000 experience.
You gain +10 Fame.
You have received a new quest
"Defend Castlehaven from the Demon
Attack - Part II"
Having decided to fight the demon
lord, you must now find a way to
defeat the vastly stronger foe.
Defeat the Demon (0/1).
Reward: 10000 experience, Unknown.
Accept quest (yes or no)?
```

Accepting and dismissing the prompt, Ethan pointed Excalibur at the wall of flame. Channeling *Water* through it, he doused the wall, causing the flames to die out. The demon immediately snapped its head towards him, focusing red, burning eyes on him. *You command magic. Interesting. You will make a fine meal.*

Ethan sensed *Fire* magic just in time to fling himself to the side, narrowly missing being consumed by a pillar of fire that slammed down on the spot where he had just been. Cursing, he scrambled to his feet just in time to see the demon bellow in pain.

Guinevere had used its distraction to rush forward and slice her sword across the demon lord's wrist. The thing reared back and bellowed, snatching its arm back.

Scrambling to his feet, Ethan ran forward. He channeled *Water* magic and created six-foot-long icicles that fell onto the demon's head.

Bothersome gnat. It growled in annoyance more than pain and summoned a blob of what appeared to be lava into its left hand. With a deft toss, it sent it hurtling at Ethan.

He sensed the molten rock and, with a quick use of *Earth* magic, he split the molten rock so that it flew to either side of him. The sheet of lava missed him by inches and he felt the hairs on his arm burn away from the intense heat.

Then he was through the lava and racing towards the demon's leg. He intended to chop the leg with all his might and hope that he cut deep enough to hobble the creature.

From the corner of his eye he saw the demon kick out with its other leg, its hoof slamming into Guinevere. The warrior woman managed to get her shield up in time to catch the blow, but the impact sent her flying backwards towards the wall of one of the buildings.

With a thought, he slowed the warrior with *Air* but the act cost him his opportunity. He barely managed to see the demon's fiery sword coming down at him in time. At the last moment, he managed to fling himself just out of the blade's path. The move saved him from being skewered but lost him his attack on the creature's leg.

Quick little ants. The demon chuckled. *I will enjoy drinking your souls and feasting on your corpses.*

Guinevere was back on her feet and running at the demon's leg. She managed to dodge its fist, which shattered the stone road, only to have another wall of fire appear in front of her, causing her to veer off her target.

Ethan had scrambled to his feet and raced back at the demon from the opposite side. He nearly got to the thing's leg when it suddenly jerked out at him. He twisted but not fast enough to avoid the hoof as it slammed into his side.

Shadd'Rarr'Nor slams you for 15 damage.

The blow staggered him and spun him around. Struggling to breath, he nearly dropped Excalibur. Then he almost missed another sword strike, but rolled behind the demon to avoid it. The move sent spasms of pain through the right side of his chest and he guessed he had at least one broken rib.

Guinevere managed to use the demon's distraction to get in close enough to the creature's other leg and slice her sword across the ankle, just above the hoof.

Roaring in pain and anger, the demon unleashed a wave of fire from itself that spread outward in a wave.

Ethan saw Guinevere raise her shield to cover her face before she disappeared into the flames. Not knowing what else to do, he activated his *Elemental Armor*, choosing water. The icy armor covered him a moment before the wall of flame hit him.

Shadd'Rarr'Nor burns you for 9 fire damage.
 Elemental Armor (Water) absorbs 23 fire damage.

He cursed as the flames scalded him. Seeing the message in his HUD, he was suddenly glad he didn't take the full brunt of the fire. Had he, it would have killed him.

Seizing the moment, Ethan darted towards the demon's leg. Whether the demon's spell required concentration or the demon just expected them both to be fried, it didn't react quickly enough to counter and Ethan sliced Excalibur into its ankle.

```
You critically slash Shadd'Rarr'Nor
for 37 damage.
     You gain 5 points of Mana.
```

The creature roared loudly and collapsed down onto its knee. Like with the ogre channeler, he felt a surge of energy flowing into him from the sword. Somehow, the sword was pulling *Mana* from the demon and giving it to him.

Distracted by the loss of his portal pouches, Ethan had completely forgotten about it until just now. He wasn't sure how such a small amount of *Mana* could help him. Then again, every little bit helped.

Ethan, still moving, barely made it to the other leg to prevent being squashed by the demon lord's leg as its injured ankle could no longer support its weight.

You will pay for that, worm! the voice thundered at Ethan and this time, he felt the pain in the demon's words.

Columns of flame began raining down on Ethan as he attempted to dodge them. He rolled one way, then dodged another and managed to extinguish another.

"Watch out!" he heard Guinevere yell.

Ethan turned to see the flaming sword coming right towards him. Not having time or room to dodge out of the way, he barely managed to get Excalibur up in time. He reinforced his arms and body with *Air*, hoping he could stop the blade from splitting him in two.

```
Shadd'Rarr'Nor  injures  you  for  2
fire damage.
   Shadd'Rarr'Nor  injures  you  for  1
fire damage.
   Shadd'Rarr'Nor  injures  you  for  2
fire damage.
   Shadd'Rarr'Nor  injures  you  for  1
fire damage.
```

He felt a jarring pain as pieces of molten metal pierced the skin of his arms and chest, going through his *Elemental Armor*. He cursed, both from the pain, as well as knowing he only had a few remaining points of *Health*.

Then he saw that the creature's flaming sword had been broken in two. The demon raised the broken weapon up to eye level and shook its massive head. *This is not possible!*

Guinevere used the opportunity to charge forward and bury her sword into the demon's good ankle. The demon swiped its left arm down, hitting the woman and sending her tumbling away. At the same time, it threw its head back and roared as it wobbled on its injured leg.

Seeing the demon lord distracted, Ethan grabbed Excalibur's hilt in a grip of *Air* and sent it racing at the demon's head. Somehow, the creature saw it. Dropping its broken blade, it moved its hand to cover its face.

It was a good strategy and it might have worked with any other sword on the planet. But this was Excalibur. A magical sword enchanted by Merlin himself and made virtually indestructible and sharper than any razor.

Excalibur shot through the demon lord's palm and emerged out the other side with none of its momentum slowed.

```
You gain 5 points of Mana.
   You gain 5 points of Mana.
```

Ethan felt energy rushing into him from the sword. He had no idea why, since he wasn't holding the sword any longer, but he wasn't complaining.

The now-bloody sword continued its path up and into the soft flesh of the demon's chin. Excalibur easily penetrated the demon's chin, traveling up into the mouth of the creature and then further up into its brain. A moment later, it shot out the top of the demon's head.

```
You critically slash Shadd'Rarr'Nor
for 867 damage.
   You gain 5 points of Mana.
   You gain 5 points of Mana.
   You gain 5 points of Mana.
   Shadd'Rarr'Nor dies.
   You    gain    3500    experience.
Experience to next level 8,030.
   Quest Complete.
```

```
Defend Castlehaven from the Demon
Attack - Part II
Fight the Demon (1/1).
Reward: 10000 experience, Unknown.
You gain 10000 experience.
You gain +50 Fame.
Congratulations!
You have reached level 9.
+1 Attribute Point.
New      ability:     Greater   Mana
Affinity.
```

The flames on the creature's wings and the burning in its eyes faded and the gigantic body fell forward. Ethan barely managed to roll out of the way before the massive creature slammed into the paved road beside him.

He still had Excalibur in a grip of *Air* and he brought it back to his hand as he scrambled to his feet.

Guinevere came limping over to him. The woman's face was bruised and burned but she was smiling. "You did it. You actually did it."

A cheer erupted from people who had somehow gathered at the cross street behind them. Mostly likely, they had been fleeing and stopped to watch the spectacle of a man and woman battling a sixteen-foot demon.

The people continued cheering until Guinevere stepped away from him and motioned for them to quiet. The people's cheering and hoots died down quickly, eager to hear what their new hero had to say.

"I am Guinevere," she yelled to them in a commanding voice - the voice of a queen. She motioned to Ethan. "And this is Ethan, the slayer of the demon! He holds the sword Excalibur, the sword of Arthur Pendragon, King of Camelot. He drew it from the stone where it has sat for over 1,000 years - waiting for the one true king to claim it."

The woman paused looking from the people to Ethan. "Behold, King Ethan, rightful ruler of Castlehaven!"

The people stared at Ethan and then erupted into cheers. Guinevere looked at him and winked. She hobbled back to him and whispered, "I just gave you the city."

Looking at all the people staring back at him and cheering, Ethan felt like he was going to vomit.

29

———

The people who had gathered began asking all sorts of questions and Ethan, who was sore and hurting, wasn't sure how to answer. Guinevere, who looked just as ragged as he was, took charge and began answering their questions and talking up Ethan and his accomplishments.

She turned back towards him and he could see the pain in her eyes. She must be hurt more than he realized. "Mind getting the Grail while I keep them busy. Then go get our friends and bring them here."

Nodding and trying not to wheeze, Ethan once again tried to summon a portal. Once again, the portal magic didn't work. He tried a second time with the same results. He frowned.

Ethan had thought the demon lord was somehow preventing portals from forming but the demon lord was dead. It couldn't be interfering with portal magic even after it had died, could it?

He remembered the energy surges that had taken place before the actual summoning. Had those been some sort of massive portal energy? Could they have somehow disrupted his access to the Bifrost?

"Portal magic still isn't working," he wheezed to Guinevere and heard the woman groan. He knew the feeling. At this point, he was quite certain he had at least three broken ribs. Every breath was painful. Unfortunately, without the Grail, he had no choice but to grin and bear it.

"That figures," she replied with a heavy sigh. "You need to talk to these people."

"But I don't want to be king," he hissed. He really didn't. Ethan knew nothing about ruling people. He couldn't really even manage Hawkshead. He was never there.

"Somebody needs to," Guinevere said. "Because I just found out that the prince was at the temple when the demon appeared."

"Dead?" Ethan asked.

Guinevere winced as she lifted her arm and pointed at a ruined area of the city that was little more than a smoking crater. "They're saying that it used to be the temple district, that's where Hel's temple was."

"And the prince is gone too, I take it?" he asked.

"That's what they're saying." The warrior woman nodded. "What remained of his family was there too, or already sacrificed."

"He sacrificed his family?!" Ethan gasped, pain shooting up his injured ribs.

"That's what someone said," Guinevere replied. "I don't know if it's true."

"What's the king going to do?" one of the people nearby yelled out. "Is he going to fix our homes?"

"What about food?" another one cried out.

"Is he a wizard?"

"How did he kill the demon?"

"Was the prince the demon?

"Is that really a magic sword?"

"What will he do now?"

More and more people began shouting questions until it was impossible to distinguish the answers. Finally, Guinevere appeared to have enough.

"Silence!" she ordered, her voice commanding.

"King Ethan will be directing repairs as soon as possible," she said. "Right now, it is important for all of us to search the rubble and find any survivors. The King is a wizard and can help extricate anyone who might be trapped."

The people looked around at each other, unsure what to do. They looked back at Ethan and Guinevere with blank expressions.

"Now go!" Guinevere ordered in a loud voice. "Check the area and the city for survivors! Spread the word! Tell everyone about King Ethan, Demon Slayer."

The people began to disperse, going in different directions, looking at the rubble and occasionally calling out.

Ethan shook his head. He flinched as he realized he'd somehow pulled a muscle in his neck and pain shot up his neck and into his head. He cursed quietly, aware that some of the people were still within earshot.

"I feel like..." he began.

Guinevere turned slowly, fatigue and pain showing on

her face. "Like you survived a fight with an eighteen-foot demon?"

Ethan chuckled, immediately regretting it as dagger-like pain shot out from his ribs. "Pretty much."

"Why isn't your portal magic working?" she asked.

"I'm not 100% sure," he told her. "I thought it was the demon lord at first."

Guinevere cocked an eyebrow. "Demon lord?"

"That's what its description said, Demon Lord," Ethan replied.

The warrior woman shook her head. "We're very fortunate then."

Ethan shrugged, another motion that he discovered caused shooting pain. He cursed again. "More lucky. Without Excalibur, I don't think we would have won."

Guinevere nodded grimly. "Honestly, I'm surprised we won at all. That was quick thinking, sending the sword up into his head."

"Honestly," he told the woman, "it was the only thing I could think of at the time."

"It worked." She smiled tiredly. "That's all that matters."

Nodding, Ethan made sure no one else was nearby. "Why did you tell them I was the new king?"

The warrior woman looked around at the people, who were moving off down the streets, looking for survivors. "Most of these people are good people. They've just been under the thumb of a madman."

"In a city where slavery was legal," Ethan pointed out.

Guinevere gestured around. "Do you think most of these people had slaves? Or even believed in it? No. These are good, hard-working people and they deserve a proper leader."

"You lead them," Ethan told her. "You were an actual queen."

She bit her lip, brow wrinkling, then shook her head. "I never wanted to be a queen. I wanted to be a knight. I believed in Arthur and I supported him. I played my part as queen, but I never wanted it."

"Exactly," Ethan shot back. "I don't want to be king."

The woman smiled at him. "Maybe not, but I think you would make a good one. Maybe not great, like Arthur, but a good one."

"Gee," he said with a roll of his eyes. "Thanks. Again with the heaping praise."

"Arthur was one of a kind," she said, her eyes getting a faraway look. "He was something special. A born leader."

Ethan shrugged. He had to admit, he was far from a born leader. If anything, deep down inside, he was just a nerd with magic.

"Besides," Guinevere said with a genuine smile. "I'm not going to throw you to the wolves. You can appoint me as your steward and I will help you out... for a while."

"Just a while?" he asked.

"Other than Camelot," she said, voice going bitter, "under the control of... Mordred, I haven't stayed in any one place too long. It's hard to form attachments when you know that..."

"They'll die and you won't?" he asked.

Guinevere nodded sadly.

"Just remember." He grinned. "Michalus, Nia and I

have drunk from the fountain of youth too. So you'd have some friends who won't age."

She nodded. "We'll see."

"What do we do now? How do we take control?" he asked.

"Mostly," she said. "We just act like we're in control. When anyone who believes they're in control comes to us, we show them the error of their ways."

"Oh?" he asked, raising an eyebrow. "And how do we do that?"

"The best way would be a demonstration of your power," she said.

He frowned. "What do you want me to do? Kill them?"

"If you have to," she said with a shrug. Her face grew serious. "This city was doing and did some of the worst things I've seen in my long years - at least, on this side of the continent. No one who was part of the old regime can be allowed to take control. That means, we are effectively leading a rebellion, or a coup or whatever you want to call it."

Ethan sighed and nodded. He knew she was right. He just didn't like it. He'd never really thought of himself as a real revolutionary. But at the same time, he couldn't just let the city sink back into slavery or possibly even summoning more demons.

"I'll do what I need to do," he said, trying to sound more confident than he felt.

"I hope so," she said. "Because no revolution is without a bit of bloodshed."

Flinching, Guinevere rotated her left arm. She looked

at Ethan, trying to hide the pain in her features. "I don't suppose you can try the portal again."

Ethan nodded and tried again. Still there was nothing. He cursed. "Sorry, it's not working. It might be some sort of portal magic residual from summoning the demon lord."

Guinevere cursed. "How long before it dissipates?"

"I don't even know if it will dissipate," he told her.

The warrior woman turned and pointed to the opposite side of the city. "The palace is on the opposite side. Let's start making our way there and hopefully you can open a portal there."

Nodding, the two of them started off for Castlehaven's royal palace, and possibly Ethan's new home.

30

___

As they walked, Guinevere yelled out to passersby that Ethan had defeated the demon lord, the prince was dead, and Ethan was the new king. Some just looked on in curiosity, others in confusion and a tiny minority in outright hostility.

A crowd formed behind them, following them to the palace. The closer they got to it, the more people joined in. He guessed they were more curious than anything else, but Ethan was getting more and more nervous.

He didn't really want to be king. It just wasn't something he really had any interest in. Being a king was about politics. And Ethan had zero interest in politics back on Earth, and no interest in politics on this world.

At the same time, he wasn't keen on the idea of someone taking charge of Castlehaven and leading it on the same path it had been on before. He had been involved in the decisions the prince had made before. He had no say or influence over what led to the city having slaves. If becoming king meant he was able to prevent it from enacting slavery and supporting human sacrifice again, he'd do it.

Every few blocks, Ethan tried his portal magic. Walking was causing him excruciating pain in the side with the injured ribs. He really wanted the Grail. Unfortunately, each time, it failed.

Then they came within eyeshot of the inner keep. He, Guinevere, and the mob behind them turned onto the street. Ethan stopped and tried his portal magic again. This time, when he attempted to open the portal, there was some resistance but, pushing harder, the portal formed.

Excitedly reaching through, Ethan took the Grail from Arthur's tomb and channeled water into the cup. He took a sip and then passed it to Guinevere. The warrior woman accepted it gratefully and took a large drink.

Instantly, Ethan felt better. There was a sharp pain in his ribs as they knitted back together and then he was feeling in perfect health. He accepted the Grail back from Guinevere and slipped it back on its resting place.

"That's better," Guinevere said, rotating her arms. "So much better."

"Definitely," Ethan agreed, excited to be able to take a deep breath without stabbing pain from his ribs. He looked back at the mob behind him and motioned them forward. "To the castle!"

The group reached the gates to the inner keep just as a group of guards attempted to shut them. No doubt, they'd seen the large mob of people approaching and wanted no part of it.

There were fewer guards than Ethan had expected. He guessed some of the guards must have gone with the army to Moonpoint. The prince must have taken some to the temple with him. How many did that leave?

The gate was almost closed and Ethan guessed that once it was closed, it would literally take an army to get through it. He had to stop it now. Still carrying Excalibur, Ethan simply channelled some *Earth* magic through it and warped the cobblestones in front of the doors. He fused and merged them together, effectively forming a doorstop for the two enormous doors.

Slamming into the makeshift doorstop, the twin doors rebounded, knocking over several of the guards.

"I'm sorry, I can't let you do that," Ethan told the men. Taking a deep breath, he realized he had to take on the role, even if he didn't want to. He poked out his chest and tried to look heroic. "I can't let you close the doors. That's my house now."

The guards looked at him like he was crazy and then managed to wiggle around the doors and see what had stopped them. The guards that did take a peek looked up at Ethan with a mixture of anger and fear.

"It's a channeler or warlock!" one of them spat.

"Neither," Ethan told them. "I am a wizard. And I am now king of Castlehaven."

Behind him, a few people cheered. Sadly, it wasn't nearly as many as he had hoped. Maybe the mob was just here to watch a crazy guy get killed by the guards. Hopefully, he would disappoint them.

Several of the guards scoffed. One of the older guards

looked him up and down. "What makes you think you're king?"

"One." Ethan held up a finger and began counting the reasons. "The prince is dead. He was killed by the very demon lord he summoned."

There were some exchanged looks and murmurs among the guards, but Ethan continued. "Two, Guinevere and I killed the demon lord that was summoned and pretty much saved the entire city from being destroyed."

More murmuring, but this time their expression was more skeptical, bordering on complete disbelief. Ethan sighed and continued and held up the sword. "I drew Excalibur from the stone and by divine right, I am now king."

The guards craned their heads to look at the sword he held. Some of them began shaking their heads, obviously not believing it was Excalibur. Ethan couldn't really blame them on that one. The sword did look a bit under-whelming.

Ethan half expected someone to yell out that taking swords from stones was no basis for a system of government. No one did. Instead, the guards just looked extremely skeptical.

"Ey," a voice called out from the parapets. "Ain't you that mayor of Hawk-something. Hawk-son? Hawk-eye? Hawk-town?"

Ethan squinted up at the man who had spoken and a flash of recognition hit him. It was Corporal Rollie, one of the guards he'd met when he'd come to Castlehaven. The man had been a bit of an arse, but he'd given him true directions at least.

"It's Hawkshead," he called back. "It was Corporal Rollie, right?"

"Sergeant Rollie now, thank you kindly," the man replied, pointing to some patch on his tunic. "And I command the guards at the moment. That is you, right? Ebert? Edmund? Ettin?"

"Ethan. And yes, I am the same person you talked to the first time I came to Castlehaven," Ethan replied. "But I might not have been 100% honest with you the last time we met."

"Yeah," the man agreed. "I got that impression. Is that really Excalibur?"

"It is," Ethan told the Sergeant.

"Don't look like much," he retorted. "Prove it. Prove that's Excalibur."

"I'm not sure how I can do that," he replied honestly. "But this is definitely Excalibur."

"Doesn't really matter if it is," the man said. "If the prince is dead, the throne goes to his next of kin, or their next of kin. Nothing about it going to someone with Excalibur. And since I'm his second nephew, on his mom's side... that might just be me."

Getting frustrated, Ethan reached out with *Air* and grabbed the man, hoisting him over the twenty-five foot wall he'd been standing on. He left him suspended in the air while he spoke. "Considering what the prince did to this city and many of its citizens by enacting slavery and summoning a demon lord, I'm not letting anyone related to him rule."

The man windmilled in the air, suspended there in midair. He screamed for help and for someone to get him down. Most of the guards just stared up at him but several men on the parapets brought crossbows up and prepared to fire.

"Kill him! Kill him!" Rollie screamed.

Ethan didn't wait for the men to fire their weapons. With a thought, he used *Fire* to burn the strings in their crossbows, snapping them. The three crossbow men uttered curses as the broken string snapped across their arms or face.

"Oh... and remember, Rollie," Ethan called up to him. "If anything happens to me, you fall."

"Fine! Fine!" the man yelled. "Let me down and no one will attack you."

Ethan looked at his *Mana* level.

Mana: 111

Since he'd so recently taken a drink from the Grail, he had been at his maximum *Mana*. The few things he'd done hadn't taken much. He could still do a lot more damage. Ethan just hoped he didn't have to.

"While I have you," Ethan said nonchalantly. "Who else is there in the castle that might have a claim on the throne?"

"Why should I..." Rollie started but then screamed as Ethan let go of him for a second before catching him in *Air* and hauling him back where he was. "Okay... okay... it's just me! Everyone else either fled the city or was with him at the temple."

Ethan raised an eyebrow. "You're the only one in the city that's part of his line?"

"Yeah..." Rollie answered but then stopped as his eyes went wide. "No! No! You don't have to kill me! I... uh... never wanted to be prince anyway."

"So then, you, as the last remaining heir in the city, acknowledge me as king?" Ethan said pleasantly, dropping him a few inches and hauling him back up.

"Yes! Yes!" Rollie screamed. "You're the king!"

Ethan nodded and smiled innocently at the man. "That's all you had to say."

Slowly, he lowered the man to the ground. He looked at the other guards. "Is there anyone else who does not wish to acknowledge me as king?"

This time, the guards didn't say anything.

"Good," Ethan said, gesturing at the gates and using *Air* to push them open. "Then it's time for me to see my new palace."

This time there were more cheers from the mob behind him and they began marching into the courtyard.

31

Ethan and Guinevere entered the inner keep, revealing a large castle courtyard. Inside the outer wall of the keep was an inner wall, the centerpiece of which was a large stone building. The inner courtyard itself seemed deserted.

"Where is everyone?" Ethan asked Rollie, who he had insisted come along with them.

"It's mostly just us," the Sergeant said with a shrug. "A lot of the guards went with the army. Others just deserted. Some were... ah..."

"Sacrificed," Guinevere finished with a scowl.

Rollie shrugged. "My uncle kind of went a little crazy there at the end. A lot of people went to the temple."

"That's over now," Ethan said sharply. "And it won't happen again."

"That's fine by me," Rollie said and the man actually sounded sincere.

The courtyard was empty, even though Ethan spotted

a number of buildings along the walls, including what appeared to be a smithy, barracks and stables. The one thing he didn't see were people.

"What about the people who worked in those buildings?" he asked.

The Sergeant shrugged. "I think the main smith went with the army - you know, to take care of shoeing and stuff. His two helpers... my uncle sent them to the temple last week."

Ethan shook his head, unable to believe the insanity of sending people to their deaths - and all to summon the demon lord. What idiots.

Noticing that there were no guards at the entrance to the main building, he pointed it out. "Where are the guards?"

"It's just us," Rollie repeated. "A couple of us normally stood watch inside and a couple others outside. But no reason to guard the main hall when the prince ain't in it."

Guinevere looked at Ethan and shook her head. "This is madness."

"It's been pretty crazy around here." Rollie shrugged. "To be honest, I wouldn't have wanted to be the next prince. Just seems like a lot of work to fix all this stuff. The balls and stuff, that would have been fun. But there ain't no more balls."

"And I don't think there are going to be any balls anytime in the near future," Guinevere growled.

Rollie made a face and nodded. "I reckon you're right. Ain't nobody left to come to no balls."

They reached the building Rollie had referred to as the main hall and pushed open the doors. It was like entering a different world. The inside of the great hall was well maintained and artistically decorated with paintings and tapestries.

It was hard not to be impressed. The main hall was something right out of a fairy tale castle. The large, main room was at least a hundred feet long and ended in a dais upon which sat a single throne. The polished marble floor looked clean enough to eat off of and was decorated with strategically placed silk rugs.

He shook his head and sighed. It was very ostentatious but he supposed that's how royalty lived and probably had to represent themselves to impress other royalty. Ethan had no desire to impress anyone.

Ethan felt himself agreeing with Rollie. He actually had no desire to be the king and have to oversee the rebuilding of the city. The Sergeant was right. It wouldn't be fun. It would be a ton of work.

A well-dressed man in his late fifties or early sixties appeared from one of the many doors along the walls. The man had a pale complexion and gray hair which was pulled back and fashioned into a bun. He was dressed in expensive-looking clothing that had obviously been tailored to fit him.

The newcomer stopped just outside the door and looked Ethan and Guinevere up and down. The man's face revealed only the slightest disdain before covering it up with a sickly sweet smile. It was the kind you saw on a used car salesman or on a predator, right before they ate you.

"Sergeant Rolland," the man said but Rollie cut him off.

"I told you, Rollie," the Sergeant growled. "Only my mom calls me Rolland."

"As you say, Sergeant Rolland," the man replied with a slight inclination of his head. His tone betrayed that he had no intention of calling the man Rollie. "And who are our... guests?"

Ethan scanned the man in his HUD.

Lucius Umbonius
> **Human**
> **Level 6**

"Lucius," Ethan replied. "There's been a change in management. The prince is dead and I am now the king." He gave the man a hard look. "Is that going to be a problem?"

Lucius gave Rollie a questioning look and the man nodded. "Uncle Marcus is dead. Big explosion in the temple district. He's the king now... oh... and he's a wizard, so watch it!"

Shifting his eyes from Rollie to Ethan, the man gave him a harder look and then did the same with Guinevere. He sighed. "Very well, your highness. My name is Lucius Umbonius, castellan of the late prince, and your humble servant."

"You handled that news rather well," Rollie smirked.

"Young master Rolland," Lucius replied. "I've served three generations of Lackners. People change, politics change, but the job does not change. I will continue to serve... the king.... King... uh..."

The castellan looked at Ethan expectantly. Ethan shrugged. "Ethan. Ethan Grower."

"King Ethan," Lucius said with a nod. "I will be happy to continue serving in my duties as castellan under your rule."

Ethan wasn't sure how loyal either Lucius or Rollie were but at the moment he needed them. He couldn't be watching them all of the time, but maybe he could do the next best thing.

"I hope you will both serve under me and help me rebuild this city," he told them. "But, I will warn you. I am a wizard...."

"The most powerful wizard since Merlin," Guinevere added.

Ethan shrugged and continued. "I won't force either of you to stay, but if you do stay, I will expect loyalty."

Using a bit of *Mana* and his *Mind* magic, Ethan opened a link to each of their minds. *And I WILL know if you are plotting anything.*

Both men started as Ethan's words echoed in the mind.

"Ey!" Rollie said. "No getting in my mind... uh... er... your highness. Uh... please."

Lucius handled it better. His eyes had gone wide when Ethan initially spoke to him telepathically but his features quickly arranged themselves. "I can assure you, there will be no plotting, your majesty."

"I appreciate that," Ethan said with a smile and gave Rollie a hard look.

The Sergeant swallowed. "What? I wasn't going to do nothing. I swear."

"Make sure the others know it too," he said. "If any of them want to quit rather than serve me, that's fine. They can go. If they stay, I expect loyalty."

"I guess that's fair," Rollie replied. He shrugged again. "I'll stay. Ain't got nowhere else to go now."

"Go make the same offer to the other guards," Guinevere said. "Tell them we want an answer in 15 minutes."

Rollie turned to leave, stopped and turned back around. "What about the crowd outside the gates?"

Ethan bit his lip and looked to Guinevere.

"They're going to want to hear something. They're common people. They want to know that there will be someone here, in charge, who is going to look after them and look after the city," she told him. "You're going to have to address them."

He groaned but nodded. He hated public speaking. "Tell the people I'll be out in 15 minutes to address them."

"Yes, sir," Rollie said and then looked embarrassed. "I meant, uh... yes, sire."

"Thank you, Rollie," he replied and gestured for the man to leave.

"Lucius," Ethan said, turning to the castellan. "If you can explain the current situation to Guinevere, I need to take a quick trip."

"A trip, your majesty?" The man blinked.

"Don't worry, I won't be gone long," he told the man, pulling out his rune stick and placing it on the floor. "But I will be returning with guests."

"Guests, your majesty?" Lucius stuttered.

Ethan grinned. "Including your new queen."

"The queen, your majesty?" the castellan repeated.

The man's mouth opened and closed several times before he mastered himself and smoothed his features. "As you say, your majesty. How long will you be traveling for?"

"About five minutes, maybe less," Ethan said and channeling his magic, opened up a portal to the rune stick he'd left with the others. He winked at the castellan. "I'm traveling by portal."

The gateway opened in front of Ethan and the castellan jumped back a step, eyes wide. Ethan nodded to Guinevere and then stepped through the portal.

Once more he entered the Bifrost and as had become the norm, Merlin's misty face appeared in front of him. "Find me."

"We're coming for you, Merlin," he said into the Bifrost. "Hang in there."

Then Ethan was outside the city in the woods with his friends rushing over to him.

THE QUEEN BLINKED HER BULBOUS, multi-faceted eyes and tried to pick herself off of the ground. It didn't work. Her head was pounding with a sensation that humans might have called a migraine.

One moment, she'd been rushing towards Castlehaven, following unbelievably strong emanations of Aether magic. The next moment, a wave of magic energy had slammed into her through her antennae and she had blacked out.

She had spent over a hundred years genetically modifying herself to better sense magic and she had just discovered a weakness. The Queen may have made herself too sensitive to magic. And she had paid the price.

Struggling, she managed to get to her feet. She wasn't sure exactly how long she had lost consciousness. Her antennae twitched painfully. The massive emanation of Aether magic was gone now.

But, she sensed a familiar use of Aether magic. A portal. Another close-range portal large enough that it had to be the human wizard.

The Queen clicked her mandibles in uncertainty. If the wizard was in Castlehaven, did that mean he'd created the powerful emanations?

If he had, he was even more powerful than she had hoped. And more dangerous. She would need to be wary.

She turned her head, ready to command her soldiers but as her eyes rotated around, she saw that they were lying dead next to her. The wave of energy must have killed them, or she had killed them when the wave hit her. Either way, the result was the same. She was alone.

The Queen would need to be extra careful but she would have the human wizard's brain. But first, she needed to recover. This was not a foe she could go after until she was at her peak.

32

"Ethan!" Nia cried, running over to him and flinging her arms around him. The foxgirl squeezed him in a tight embrace and then kissed him all over his face. Finally, she backed away, face angry. "What happened?! We were worried!"

"Indeed, my boy," Michalus agreed. "We all felt... well... I'm not even sure what we felt. I think it was some sort of magical energy coming from the city."

Ethan smiled down at his wife and then disengaged himself, but keeping her hand in his. "The priests succeeded in their summoning..."

"Priests summon god?!" Par'karr asked, wide-eyed. It wasn't just him. Everyone looked at him wide-eyed.

"Uh, no," Ethan explained. "I'm not sure if they were deceived or if they just told that to everyone else. They didn't summon a god. They summoned a demon lord."

"A demon lord?" Michalus gasped. "Thor's hammer! You're lucky to escape the city!"

Michalus blinked and looked around. Drorm did the same, his brow furrowed.

"Where is Guinevere?" the orc asked, his tone suggesting he was thinking the worst.

"She's fine," Ethan told them all. "She's back at the palace."

Nia looked up at him, confusion written all over her face. "The palace?"

"Ok. Hold on." Ethan held up his hands. "We killed the demon lord. I am now the king of Castlehaven and Guinevere is back in the palace, holding down the fort until I bring you all back with me... which I should do sooner rather than later, because I'm not sure who all in the guard might want to fight back."

Everyone looked at Ethan like he had gone mad. Par'karr stared up and then grinned. "Ethan is king?"

"For now, at least," he answered. "The prince and most of his heirs were at the temple when the summoning was completed. There was some sort of explosion and then the demon lord himself. They didn't make it. Instead of letting it fall into chaos or let it go back to slavery, Guinevere convinced me to... uh... take over."

"Good!" Drorm grinned. "You are now king and high shaman!"

Ethan blinked, unconsciously looking down at his chest, where the dragon mark was. Technically, he was the high shaman of the orcs - though he wasn't sure exactly what that really meant anymore, considering the other shamans had basically attacked and tried to take Excalibur.

"Let's discuss this back in the city," Ethan told them. "I

want to get back in case the guards decide to mount some sort of coup." He chuckled to himself. "Although, technically, I guess that's what I'm doing. Anyway... I'll open a portal. Michalus, take the runestick with you and as soon as you get there, take it outside. I'll portal the horses outside, instead of into the palace."

"Probably a wise idea," the wizard agreed. He reached down and took the runestick.

"Nia," he said, looking down at the foxgirl. "Can you stay and help me with the horses?"

"Of course." She smiled up at him, giving his hand a squeeze.

With that decided, Ethan opened a portal back to the throne room and sent the others ahead. Once they had gone through, he let the portal fade away.

"I was very worried for you!" Nia growled at him, once the portal had completely disappeared. She punched him hard in the arm to make her point.

"Ow!" he cried, rubbing his arm. She had hard, pointed, little knuckles. "Sorry, there wasn't much I could do."

"Next time, you take me with you!" she shot back. "I cannot protect you if I am not with you."

Ethan was about to point out that she couldn't have protected him even if she had been with him, but he thought better of it and simply nodded. "Well, we're abolishing slavery, so there shouldn't be any reason you can't come with me in the future."

Nia narrowed her eyes but she nodded. "Good. No leaving me behind anymore!"

"Okay," he said with a smile. "Let's go check out your new home, so people can meet their queen."

"Queen?" Nia gasped, eyes wide.

Walking over to the horses, Ethan untied them from the tree branch and handed half the reins to his wife. "That's right. If I'm king, you're the queen."

Speechless, Nia took the offered reins and walked through the portal as if in a daze, leading the horses through.

Chuckling, Ethan followed her through the portal and into the Bifrost.

Merlin's face appeared again and he asked to be found but once again, he didn't respond to anything else Ethan said. He wasn't sure what that meant - if it meant anything at all. But he did feel a renewed sense of urgency. They needed to find him and they needed to do it soon.

They appeared in the courtyard where they startled two guards who were approaching. Ethan recognized one as Rollie and scanned the other one.

```
Corporal Barnabas
    Human
    Fighter
    Level 3
```

Even though he knew him, Ethan scanned Rollie too.

```
Sergeant Rollie
    Human
    Fighter
    Level 5
```

Ethan thought he remembered Rollie being 3rd level when they'd originally met. That meant the man had gained two levels somehow since they'd last met. Idly, he wondered how he had done that. Through training, maybe? Had he seen combat?

"Your majesty," Rollie called out a bit frantically. "The people out there are starting to get... uh... upset."

Guinevere came out of the main hall at that minute and walked over to him, along with Lucius and the rest of the party. "You ready for your speech?"

Ethan, who had faced down a demon lord and a giant, and who had talked face to face with a dragon, suddenly felt his stomach lurch. He swore under his breath. He really, really didn't want to make a speech.

"You'd better say something," Rollie told him, glancing back at the gates. "Cuz me and my boys ain't going to be able to stop them if they decide to storm in here."

"I... ah..." Ethan started but Guinevere marched over to him and pointed to the gate.

"Go address your people," she said, then belatedly added, "Your majesty."

He glared at the woman. It had been her idea and now he was having to actually do kingly stuff. Ethan wanted to scream. This was exactly what he hadn't wanted!

And yet, he wanted to keep the city together and prevent someone else from trying to fill the power gap. The only way that was going to happen was if someone, meaning him, filled the gap first.

"Fine," he growled and spun towards the gate. "Let's go do this."

"Sire, perhaps a change of clothes before you address the people," Lucius suggested.

Ethan shook his head. "No, I'm going to talk to them and then I'm going to go into the city and see what we can do to help people. Michalus, I think two wizards helping would be better than one."

"Of course, my boy," the wizard said with a smile. "Whatever I can do to help."

"Come on," he said. "Let's go."

The group made their way across the courtyard to the gate. The handful of guards that were left were there, holding back the crowd. Ethan stopped a few yards away and motioned to the others to stay back while he proceeded forward.

Taking a few steps, Ethan realized he would need to get people's attention before he could talk with them. Looking around, he smiled as an idea formed in his head. He channeled *Air* and slowly began to lift himself off the ground.

He moved himself up slowly until people in the crowd saw him rising in the air. There was a collective gasp as he rose higher and higher until he set himself down atop the parapet, overlooking the mob of people who had formed.

"People of Castlehaven," he yelled out, trying to make his voice sound as kingly as possible. "The prince is dead. As are his relatives."

The crowd murmured at the mention of the prince but Ethan held up his hands for silence. "They summoned a demon into the city, one that caused unparalleled damage."

More murmuring from the crowds but these were

murmurs of both anger and agreement. Ethan continued. "They paid the price for their foolishness, killed by the very demon they summoned!"

There were scattered cheers from the crowd but most just waited in silence for him to continue. "I drew the legendary sword, Excalibur, from the stone where it was placed by the greatest wizard of all time, Merlin." Ethan held up the sword, watching as everyone stared up at it. "With the sword, I slew the demon that would have destroyed the city."

He stopped and waited for a reaction. Sadly, there was no cheering. More like stunned silence. Ethan suppressed a sigh and continued. "The city has seen much suffering lately. A prince is not enough to lead this city back to the time of prosperity. For this, you must have a king."

Ethan paused. "As the slayer of the demon and a wizard of no small power, I am willing to take this responsibility to help you and help this city rebuild and prosper. With your help and support, we can rebuild Castlehaven and make it the thriving city it once was.

"But," he continued. "A king cannot rule without the support of the people, for a king is a servant of the people. I pledge that if you support me, I will support you. I will help you rebuild. I will bring trade back to Castlehaven. I will bring prosperity back to our city."

There were some cheers this time. Not as many as he would have wished, but perhaps such things only happened in fantasy books and movies.

Guinevere stepped out in front of the people, her voice clear and commanding. "All hail, King Ethan!"

She repeated it several times until there was a giant chorus of people chanting it along with the former queen.

Ethan smiled nervously and then held his hands up for silence. "First, please, go now and check on your family, your friends and your neighbors. See if they need help - especially those around the temple area.

"I can move large objects and bend stone to my will," he told the crowd. Ethan reached down, picked up Michalus and levitated him up to the parapet with him, setting him on his left side.

"You might have warned me before you lifted me up," the wizard hissed to him through smiling teeth.

"This is Michalus," Ethan told the crowd. "My arcane advisor. He too is a wizard of great power. Either of us will be happy to help where we can. We will be going through the city as well. If you need us, find us and we will help.

"Second," Ethan said after a pause. "From this moment forward, there will be no more slavery. In this city, we are all equal. No more slavery will be tolerated."

He heard more murmurs from the crowd but from what he could see, most people were nodding their heads. They were probably sick of slavery as well, seeing where it led.

"And last, but certainly not least," Ethan said and gently lifted Nia up to the parapet and set her on his right side. "This is my wife, Nia, your queen."

"Queen Nia!" shouted Guinevere, and began repeating it until people joined in.

Nia looked down with wide eyes at the crowd chanting her name. He smiled at her and gave her a nudge. "Wave to the nice people."

They both waved for a few minutes, then Ethan called for silence. "Go back home now, help where you can, look in on your family, friends and neighbors. If people are trapped or need my help, find me or Michalus."

When the crowd didn't move, Ethan made a shooing gesture. "Go now. People may be hurt or trapped. Bring any injured people to us so that we can treat them."

The crowd began to disperse, turning around and heading back into the city. Ethan finally breathed a sigh of relief and looked down at Guinevere. The former queen returned his look and gave him a nod of approval.

33

———

The first thing Ethan did after the crowd dispersed was to go with Michalus to the Order of the Scroll. There, he found an awake Mertin, nursing a nasty lump on his head. After a sip from the Grail, the channeler was good as new.

Ethan left Michalus and Mertin to sort out the details about them borrowing the book while he went and tried to help anyone in need. After all, these were his people now. He had to at least do what he could. He was surprised to learn that he was extraordinarily suited for helping in a crisis.

With his mental magic, he was able to find people who were still alive but buried under rubble. He could use *Earth* magic to strengthen or repair stone walls. Ethan could use *Water* magic to quench fires and use *Air* to move things around - even heavy pieces of rubble.

In one case, he'd actually managed to use his *Aether*

magic to teleport a man who had been trapped under some debris. The rubble had been unstable and moving it risked bringing the collapsed building down atop the man.

Ethan had no choice but to attempt a risky teleport. Risky because he'd never attempted to teleport anything from a distance. Yet, despite his misgivings, it had worked. He'd instantly teleported the man from the middle of debris to his family on the road. After a sip from the Grail, the man had said he'd never felt better.

Michalus had joined him shortly after their visit to the Order. With their magic and the healing power of the Grail, Ethan and Michalus were quickly gaining popularity amongst the people they helped. But being popular proved to be a blessing and a curse to both of them.

All of the people they helped were very grateful and many of them said it was refreshing for a king to get his hands dirty. But they were only two wizards. They could only be at one place at a time. In addition, they had to take breaks to let their *Mana* recharge - although Nia had offered several times to help Ethan speed that process up.

Taking turns, the two wizards worked late into the night, finding and rescuing survivors of the demon lord's rampage. Finally, Guinevere found them and insisted that they come back to the keep.

After a side conversation with Nia, Ethan found himself escorted back to the keep between the two women. He had given a half hearted resistance but the truth was, he was exhausted. He'd used more magic today than he ever used in a single day. He was both physically and mentally exhausted.

When they reached the main hall, Lucius was up and escorted him to the master bedroom. Like the rest of the building, it was lavishly decorated, with a large king-sized bed. He chuckled. It was a king-sized bed and he was a king.

Sadly, he was so exhausted that he fell asleep as soon as he hit the bed, despite his wife's attempts to be playful. Of course, that didn't stop her the next morning.

AFTER A LITTLE FUN in bed the next morning, Ethan got dressed and he and Nia went downstairs. He was greeted by Lucius, who took him to the dining room for breakfast. He found the rest of his party there waiting for him. They were already enjoying breakfast.

"They said you would not mind if they started without you," Lucius said, showing Ethan to the head of the table. The chair to his right was empty and the castellan sat Nia there.

He quickly filled his plate with a pastry, something that he thought was French toast and some eggs. He was about to take a bite when he suddenly felt guilty. Here he was eating a large breakfast when some of his people didn't even have homes. How were they faring when it came to food?

"Anyone know what the status of food is in the city? Do people have food to eat?" he asked, looking around the table.

Guinevere leveled a grim look on him. "It is as we feared. From what I could gather, many of the local farmers and their families had been snatched up and sold to slavery - probably sacrificed."

Ethan remembered his conversation with Fearghas and the others about the rampant slavery and how it was out of control. Even back then he didn't see how the people would survive if they began taking the farmers as slaves. Unfortunately, their fears had been prophetic.

"Are there still farms nearby?" Ethan asked.

"There are," Guinevere replied. "But there's no one who can work them. Some even have fields ready to harvest."

"We need farmers and we need them fast," Ethan said. He snapped his fingers. "Guinevere, Drorm, I need you to find out what farms are empty. See if you can find out if there are any surviving heirs. I'll port back to Hawkshead and see if some of those villagers who lost their farms are interested in a move."

Drorm grunted affirmatively, shoving a forkful of French toast into his mouth.

Guinevere shrugged. "Even if we brought the entire village of Hawkshead here, we wouldn't have enough hands. We'll need more."

"Maybe we can check the nearby villages," he told them. "Find out if there is anyone able to take over one of the farms."

"After we check on the status of the farms, we can ride out to the nearest villages and ask around," Guinevere told him.

"Michalus," Ethan said, turning to the wizard. "Did you get the book you need?"

Nodding as he ate some of the eggs, he waited until he was done chewing before answering. "I have the book and it will allow us to make the adjustments to the portal detector. But... I'm not sure if it will be sensitive enough after all this time."

"Let's hope it works. Right now, it's the only shot we've got," Ethan reminded him. "How much time do you need to recalibrate it?"

"I believe I should be able to do it in a week," he said with a glance at Guinevere.

The woman gave him a small smile. "Let's just hope it works."

"So we have a week," Ethan told the group. "Let's do what we can to help out around here."

"Par'karr can help," the kobold offered with a grin.

Ethan wasn't sure how people would react to the kobold in the city and he didn't want to cause trouble at the moment. The people had been through quite an ordeal lately. Thinking quickly, he flashed the kobold a smile.

"Par'karr," he said. "I need you to do an important job for me."

The kobold bobbed his head up and down. "Par'karr do important job!"

"I need you to act as the communications officer," he told Par'karr.

The kobold scrunched up his scaly brow. "Communication officer?"

Ethan nodded. "I need you to stay here at our base. When anyone comes back with news, they'll tell it to you.

Your job will be to remember it and tell it to me when you see me."

Par'karr grinned and nodded vigorously. "Par'karr make good communication officer."

"I thought you would make a good one," he told the kobold. "It's an important job. I'm king now and news is important."

"I'm glad you feel that way, your highness," Rollie's voice said from the doorway. "Because I've got some news for you. Just heard it from a merchant coming from the north. He said there's an army coming towards Castlehaven south along the coastal highway."

"An army?" Ethan asked. He only knew one city north of them. That was Moonpoint. "Is the merchant sure it wasn't our army returning?"

"Oh yeah," Rollie said. Worry lines made the young man look older beyond his years. "I asked him about that. He said, it's an army of beast men, elves and others. It's probably..."

"From Moonpoint," Guinevere finished. She glared at the Sergeant. "They're probably retaliating for the army Castlehaven sent."

"An army which they must have defeated," Nia added.

Rollie held his palms up. "It wasn't me that sent the army. That was Uncle Marcus. I think we all know he was a few pints short of a keg."

"And without an army of our own," Drorm growled. "We are easy prey."

Ethan nodded. The city was in no shape to push back an attack by Moonpoint, let alone withstand a siege. They had no army and as far as he knew, the only troops he had were Rollie and the half dozen men in the keep.

He groaned as he realized his reign as king may come to a very abrupt end, very soon.

34

———

After speaking with the merchant personally, Ethan determined that the army was moving slowly and were about two days behind the merchant. That didn't give them much time. Not that a few more days would matter.

"A thousand?" Ethan repeated. The number didn't seem so impressive compared to the epic battles he watched in the movies and TV. In fact, a thousand people marching for a cause back on Earth, would probably not even make the news.

And yet, this wasn't Earth. Neither was it one of the epic novels where tens of thousands of dwarves, elves, men, and goblins fought in epic, cinematic battles. He paused and looked at Rollie. "How many people are there... or should I say... were there in the city before your uncle went crazy?"

Rollie scratched his head for a moment. "Maybe four or five thousand."

Guinevere shook her head. "We're lucky if there's half of that left. Maybe even a quarter."

"That much is true." The sergeant nodded. "The streets are deserted."

Ethan couldn't help but agree with them. Given the number of people he'd encountered the day before, the entire city had felt empty. Much emptier than the first time he was here.

"The first time I was here," Ethan mumbled aloud, a memory just on the edge of his awareness.

"First time?" Nia asked.

His mind seized a hold of the memory and he snapped his fingers. He spun towards Rollie. "Isn't there a mercenary guild in the city? Perhaps we can hire..."

Ethan's voice faded as both Rollie and Lucius shook their heads. The sergeant went first. "No more mercenaries. They up and left about a month ago. Left without a trace. We woke up one morning and they were gone."

"Ahem," Lucius cleared his throat and gave Ethan a serious look. "Even if there were mercenaries, your majesty, we couldn't afford to hire them."

"Oh? They're that expensive?" Michalus asked, turning around to look at the castellan.

"To put it bluntly, sire: The kingdom is out of money," Lucius told him, face impassive.

Ethan groaned. "You're kidding me!"

Lucius shook his head. "I am not jesting, your majesty."

"Dare I ask what we spent the money on?" Ethan grumbled.

"I am sad to say," Lucius answered. "Mostly on slaves and slave bounties."

"So the city is broke AND it's about to be invaded!" Ethan cursed and shook his head. He spun on Rollie, causing the sergeant to start and go wide eyed. "How many soldiers and/or guards do we have in total."

"Uh... how many?" Rollie stuttered.

"How many?" Ethan repeated, narrowing his eyes dangerously.

The sergeant cleared his throat. "Uh... eight... including me."

"EIGHT?! Including you?!" Ethan snapped back. He was trying to keep the frustration out of his voice, but he knew it wasn't working. "We have eight men?"

Rollie shrugged. "Like I said, everyone else went off with the army or they ran off. For all I know, they might have joined the army coming down here."

Ethan rubbed his temples as he shook his head back and forth. "Eight men."

"It is not good," Nia agreed. "If the deserters have joined the enemy army, they will have revealed any weaknesses in the city's defenses."

Ethan chuckled mirthlessly. "Defenses? We have no defenses. The most we can do is shut the outer gates. We have no army to man the battlements and I doubt very much we have the food for any sort of prolonged siege."

The sergeant bobbed his head. "That's true."

Turning to Drorm, Ethan bit his lip for a moment before speaking. "Do you think the orcs would help us, given that I am high shaman?"

Drorm stared off into the distance for a few moments

before shaking his head slowly. "I do not think so. The council has too much sway and the only ones who really know you are the high shaman is the council, a few guards and me. Besides, they would never get here in time."

"I was thinking I could portal them here," Ethan replied glumly. "But if they won't help, there's no reason to bother."

"Even if they accepted you as high shaman, I do not believe they would come to defend a city that was not theirs," Drorm explained.

Ethan was quickly running out of ideas himself. He looked around at his friends. "I'm open to ideas."

The group looked around at each other, obviously as bereft of ideas as he was. Ethan sighed. He turned to Rollie. "Take all but two men. Go into the city and see if there are any men willing to fight for the city...."

Pausing, he narrowed his eyes at the sergeant. "We still have an armory, right? I mean, if we find people, we have weapons and armor?"

Rollie nodded. "Some. Unfortunately, not the best stuff. That went..."

"With the army," Ethan finished with a nod. "Yeah, I figured. How many men can we equip?"

The sergeant squinted and moved his lips silently, finally he blinked and looked back at Ethan. "Maybe sixty with weapons and chain mail and another twenty or thirty with weapons."

"Bows?" Ethan asked. He knew the high walls would give them a huge advantage with bows.

"Oh yeah," the sergeant replied, licking his lips. "We got lots of bows."

Ethan heard a "but" in the sergeant's tone. He growled. "But..."

"But the arrows..."

"Went with the army," Ethan finished sourly.

Rollie shrugged apologetically. "Except for a few quivers."

Turning to Guinevere, Ethan smiled. "Guinevere, Drorm, do you think you can comb the city and see if you can find any fletchers? If you do, see if we can get them making arrows. Tell them I'll reimburse them somehow, but perhaps mention that there's an army coming here and for all we know, they might want revenge by killing every living soul."

"You really think so?" Michalus asked, shocked.

"No," Ethan admitted. "I mean, I hope not. But it might motivate the fletchers."

Guinevere nodded. "A man on a wall with a bow is worth ten at the bottom of the wall."

"Let's hope so," Ethan said grimly.

"Is there something I can help with?" Michalus asked.

"Yes," Ethan said. "Go back to the Order. Ask Mertin if he will fight with us. Also find out if there are any other channelers who stayed who would be willing to help."

"Channelers? Are you sure?" Michalus asked.

"I don't see that we have much choice," Ethan replied.

"True, my boy, true," the wizard agreed.

"Once you talk with him, see if he can point you to any books with spells for battles," Ethan said. "Something that might help us even the odds."

He stood up and started towards the door. "I will go there now."

Guinevere and Drorm stood up too. "We will go too."

"Uh, me too, your majesty," Rollie said, clearly anxious to get away from Ethan.

"Go," Ethan told him. "Get your men and see if we can recruit. Tell them their lives may depend on it... the lives of their families."

Rollie nodded and left behind Drorm. At the same time, Par'karr leaned forward and grinned. "Par'karr help!"

Having anticipated the kobold's request, Ethan had already thought of a job for him. "I have an important job for you."

Par'karr's eyes lit up and he nodded.

"You heard us talk about food and maybe a shortage of food if we get sieged?" Ethan asked.

The kobold bobbed his head.

"I need you to go out and count how many chickens, goats, cows, and sheep - and any other animals that might be usable for food," he told his friend. "So I know how much food we have, if it comes to that."

"Par'karr good counter!" the kobold replied and hopped down off his chair. "Par'karr count all animals!"

The little kobold scampered out of the room, followed by his two demon rabbits. Ethan watched them go and then looked around the room. Only Lucius and Nia were left.

"Lucius," he told the castellan. "Can you look around any vaults or other places where money and valuables might have been hidden and see if we have anything left?"

"As you wish, your majesty," the man replied with a small bow and then left the room.

That left him alone with Nia. He shook his head. "I don't see how we're going to win a fight against so many."

"You will think of something," Nia replied with a confident smile. "You are a mighty Alpha!"

Ethan shook his head. "Not so sure that makes a difference..."

"You slew the demon, did you not?" Nia asked.

"Well, yeah but..." he replied.

"You killed the Cthulhu and saved me from the creature's control as well, correct?"

"Yes, but..."

"You have ridden on dragons! There is nothing..."

"Wait," Ethan said, interrupting his wife. "What did you just say?"

Nia blinked. "What? That you have ridden on dragons?"

A smile crept across his face and he grabbed the foxgirl and gave her a big kiss. "You're a genius!"

Getting up, he started back towards their room where he would be undisturbed.

"Where are you going?" she asked, still confused.

"To make a long-distance phone call," he replied with a grin.

35

Ethan had contacted Firestorm and asked the dragon if he would repay the favor by coming north. Firestorm had told him that he and his mate were hunting down the last remnants of the Doemenagg. But, the dragon had a strong sense of honor and agreed to come north, while his mate continued to hunt down the vermin who had injured her.

While he was ecstatic that the dragon would be coming, the problem was timing. It was months of overland travel to get from Castlehaven to the nearest orc city. Could the dragon fly fast enough to get here in time?

He'd briefly considered trying to portal to the dragon and then open a portal back for him, but the dragon was enormous. Ethan couldn't be sure he could open a portal large enough to fit the dragon.

Ethan remembered Firestorm telling him that dragons didn't enchant objects and had to get Merlin to enchant their mountain against portal magic. Since the dragon hadn't mentioned portaling to him and had their mountain warded against portaling, maybe they couldn't use portal magic either.

Would the dragon get to them in time? That was the question. Unfortunately, Ethan had to work under the assumption that the dragon wouldn't get there in time. That meant he needed to check on the status of the tasks.

Hurrying out of his bedroom, Ethan nearly ran into Lucius. Luckily, combat and his recent training with the sword, allowed him to swerve out of the way just in time to avoid a collision. "Woah! Where's the fire?!"

"Fire, your majesty?" Lucius asked, looking around in both alarm and confusion. "Is there a fire in the residence?"

"Sorry," Ethan apologized with a sheepish grin. "It's a figure of speech. I meant, what's the hurry?"

"Sorry, your majesty," apologized the castellan with a bow. "I was merely coming to inform you that my earlier assessment was correct." The man held out a small leather bag. "This is all the coin that remained in the treasury."

Ethan frowned as he accepted the pouch. "That's it?"

"I'm afraid so," Lucius told him. "As I said, the former prince opened up the coffers in his final days, buying dozens - perhaps hundreds - of slaves to turn over to the temple."

Feeling himself getting angry all over again at the prince, he forced his feelings down. He would be upset later. At the moment, there was work to be done.

Lucius cleared his throat. "That is all of the coin. However, there are a few other things in the treasury."

He looked at the man hopefully. "Oh?"

Lucius shook his head. "Nothing of much value, I'm afraid." The man produced a folded piece of parchment and carefully smoothed it out. Ethan saw the man's eyes dart over the parchment before speaking again.

"There is a painting of Rolland III, the prince's father, and Rollie's namesake," Lucius began but Ethan chuckled and stopped him.

"You called him Rollie!" Ethan said with a grin.

A slight smile appeared on the man's face before he smoothed his features. "The man was an insufferable child, and sometimes we take pleasure in the small things. I will never call him Rollie to his face."

Chuckling again, Ethan nodded. "Your secret is safe with me. Anything else in the treasury?"

Lucius cleared his throat and continued. "There are also several marble busts of former princes, a few various knick knacks that were gifts from other cities. There are no jewels to speak of, but there is a small container of crystals. I'm honestly not sure where they..."

"Crystals?" Ethan perked up. "What kind of crystals? Do they look anything like this by chance?" He removed Excalibur and pointed to the light-blue crystal embedded in the sword.

"Smaller, not quite as fine perhaps, but they could be the same thing," Lucius replied. "Are they valuable?"

"Only to a wizard!" Ethan retorted, gesturing back the way Lucius had come. "Take me to the vault and show me the crystals."

The castellan bowed, turned and led him down the stairs. Then the man took him down several hallways, to a stone spiral staircase that led down. The castellan reached for a lamp on the wall but Ethan shook his head. "No need."

With barely a thought, Ethan conjured a ball of light between them. The light startled Lucius briefly but the man quickly recovered. He smoothed his clothes. "Ah, yes. Very good, your majesty. This way."

Following the castellan down the spiral steps for what seemed to be twenty or thirty feet, the stairs suddenly ended in a very sturdy-looking iron door. Lucius reached under his shirt and withdrew a large iron key on a leather cord.

Removing the key from around his neck, the man slipped it into the keyhole of the door, twisted it until the lock clicked, then withdrew the key and hung it back around his neck. He reached out and pushed the door open, allowing Ethan to step inside.

Ethan did. He stepped past Lucius into a long, stone hallway. He guessed the hallway was the entire length of the main hall. Glancing to either side, he saw that there were iron doors every fifteen feet on either side of the hallway. There was a pungent odor that reminded him of human sweat - and other human smells.

Somehow, he didn't think these were all vaults. He had a suspicion as to what the doors led to and turned to the castellan. "These aren't all vaults, are they?"

"No, your majesty," Lucius replied with a pained look. "They are cells."

"Cells," Ethan repeated, realizing his guess had been correct. That begged his next questions. "So this is a dungeon? Are there prisoners?"

The castellan shook his head. "No, your majesty. They were all... removed."

"Sent to the temple," Ethan guessed.

"Yes, your majesty." The man inclined his head and then moved smoothly around him. "The vault is at the end of the hall. This way."

Ethan followed Lucius past the cells. He counted ten cells on each side, for a total of twenty. It didn't seem like many for a city this large. He frowned. "So you could only hold twenty criminals at a time? Or did they share cells?"

The castellan stopped, causing Ethan to nearly run into the man. Lucius turned around and shook his head. This expression was grim. "I'm afraid these weren't for common criminals. These cells were for political prisoners."

"Political prisoners?" Ethan asked, his brow furrowing. "What kind of political prisoners?"

"The kind who have committed no crimes," Lucius said flatly, his expression blank. Ethan got the impression that man disapproved of the practice.

"You don't agree with that?" Ethan asked, testing the man.

Lucius bit his lip briefly but then smoothed his features. "It is not my place..."

"Speak freely," he told the castellan. "I'm not the prince. I take it you didn't approve?"

The man stared hard at Ethan, the castellan's eyes flicking around his face, probably judging whether Ethan was being sincere. Finally, the man sighed. "I do not agree with imprisoning people who have committed no crime, other than their wife or mother refusing the advances of the prince."

Ethan felt his face grow hot. "He imprisoned the families of women he wanted to sleep with?!"

The castellan nodded.

Fighting to control his temper, Ethan cursed. "If he wasn't already dead, I'd kill him myself."

Lucius bit his lip again. "I trust your majesty will not be continuing that practice?"

Ethan chuckled, some of his anger draining away. "No. I'm happy with just my wife. Although... I keep getting the feeling that she wants me to have more wives."

"Really?" Lucius blurted out without decorum. He cleared his throat. "Your majesty."

He chuckled. "It's normal in her culture apparently. Not for me though. I can barely handle one wife."

Lucius inclined his head. "As you say, your majesty. Shall we continue?"

"Of course," Ethan said and let the castellan pass him to unlock the iron door at the end of the hall.

The man used the same key and unlocked the door. Swinging the door open, he gestured for Ethan to enter.

The vault was a plain, unadorned room about fifty feet wide by twenty feet long. There were ten wooden tables scattered around the room. On the floor were several marble busts of noble looking men. Ethan immediately saw a resemblance to Rollie. They had the same eyes and jawline.

There were bundles of cloth on one of the tables and Ethan raised a questioning eyebrow.

"Tapestries," Lucius informed him; the man walked

over to a table to the right and picked up a small wooden coffer and offered it to Ethan.

Walking over to the castellan, Ethan took the coffer and opened it. He felt a broad grin forming on his face. They were exactly what he had hoped for - Chymera crystals!

"Are they valuable, your majesty?" Lucius asked, head cocked to the side.

Ethan grinned even bigger. "They are if you're a wizard who knows how to enchant things!"

36

With Nia's "help," Ethan spent the rest of the morning pouring *Mana* into crystals. He then used ten of them to create a portal pouch back to the Grail. For him, that was the most critical. The portal pouch wasn't just a convenience. Instead of everyone being dependent on him to get the Grail, he could just give the pouch to someone and they could retrieve it.

Counting the remaining crystals, Ethan found there were 43 remaining. The question was: how to best use them?

He and Nia went back downstairs, where they met Guinevere, Drorm and Par'karr sitting around the large dinner table. There were plates of vegetables, meats and bread in the middle of the table. Ethan greeted them and showed him the new portal pouch.

"That's good," Guinevere said. "It frees you from having to conjure a portal each time."

"And probably saves the ears of any livestock around," Drorm agreed with a nod.

"Speaking of livestock," Ethan said, turning to Par'karr. "How did the count go? Are you done already?"

Par'karr lowered his eyes and shook his head. "Uh... Par'karr not count many."

"Oh?" Ethan asked, feeling his forehead wrinkle.

"Yeah," interrupted Rollie as he entered the room. "I was just coming to tell you. Seems we had a number of complaints about a kobold trying to steal livestock."

"And you went to arrest him?" Ethan asked with a frown.

Par'karr gave Ethan a sheepish look and lowered his eyes again.

Rollie chuckled. "No, we went to save him from a small mob that was chasing him."

Ethan rubbed his temples. He groaned. "The people thought you were trying to steal their animals."

"Par'karr try to explain," the kobold said with a shrug, his expression apologetic. "But people not listen to Par'karr."

"Can't say I really blame them," Rollie commented. "You know, given what all has happened and the scarcity of food."

Looking down at his little friend, Ethan flashed the kobold a smile. "Sorry, Par'karr. I should have thought about that. Sorry you got chased."

Par'karr gave Ethan a toothy grin. "Par'karr fast runner. They not catch!"

Ethan turned to Rollie. "Can you assign one of your men to walk about with him and count the livestock."

Rollie frowned. "Only got two left and they're guarding the gate."

"The amount of prey in the city will not matter," Nia said. "Not if we face a long siege. It may mean an extra day or two, but no more."

Ethan thought of the dragon on his way. How long would it take Firestorm to get here? That extra day or two might make a difference.

Since he wasn't sure whether Firestorm would arrive in time, he hadn't mentioned it to anyone other than Nia. He didn't want to get their hopes up, in case the dragon didn't make it before the walls were breached. For now, they needed to work under the assumption that Firestorm wouldn't make it.

He turned his gaze to Guinevere and Drorm. "Any luck with fletchers?"

The two of them exchanged looks. Neither of them looked happy. The warrior woman gave him a sober look. "We asked around and found there were five civilian fletchers in the city."

"Civilian?" Ethan interrupted.

"There were some fletchers that..." Rollie answered but Ethan finished his sentence.

"...went with the army," Ethan sighed.

"Yep," Rollie said with a nod of his head.

"What about the five civilian fletchers?" Ethan asked.

Guinevere. "Only one is in the city and her workshop was destroyed by the demon's fire. She was actually one of the people you saved."

"You're kidding me!" Ethan growled.

"We are not joking," Drorm replied seriously. "She is

willing to make arrows if we can muster the supplies and tools."

"What about the other four?" Ethan asked.

"One is missing," Guinevere said, counting on her fingers. "His workshop was also near the temples and is now nothing but ash. One was an elf and he fled the city after the slavery laws changed. The other two disappeared within the last few weeks, their families believed they were snatched up as slaves."

Ethan cursed the former prince. He looked back at Guinevere and Drorm. "Check the workshops of the other three, see if any of them had supplies or tools we can use. If they do, confiscate them in the name of the city. Tell anyone with a claim on them that they'll be reimbursed... uh... eventually."

The two nodded and Ethan looked around the table. "No Michalus?"

Guinevere snickered. "You sent him to a place with books. Do you really expect to see him anytime soon?"

Rolling his eyes, Ethan chuckled. "Good point. Par'karr, check in on him and ask him to meet us back here at dinner time. Tell him I have Chymera crystals and need some ideas on how to best use them."

"Par'karr go get Michalus," the kobold agreed.

Ethan turned to Rollie. "Any luck with recruitment?"

The sergeant made a face. "The boys tell me we got a dozen recruits so far but that's it."

A dozen? That was nothing. That would put their numbers a little over twenty. Twenty versus a thousand. He was beginning to feel like Leonidas against the Persian army. He frowned, thinking about the story of the 300 Spartans. They all died.

"In my land," Nia said, interrupting Ethan's dark thoughts. "Each tribe makes their own arrows."

Ethan looked at his wife and raised an eyebrow, unclear what she was getting at.

Nia continued. "We passed several small villages to the south and to the east. Like in Hawkshead, they hunt. Will they not have arrows?"

Ethan grinned. "Good idea!"

"Also," Nia said with a small smile. "I know how to make arrows as well."

Looking at his wife, he shook her head. "Is there anything about weapons you do not know?"

Nia shrugged. "I cannot forge metal weapons."

Chuckling to himself and shaking his head, he looked around for someone to assign the job of going to the villages. Unfortunately, everyone already had a job.

"I will go," Nia told him. "I only need a fast horse."

He gave wife a kiss on the top of her head. "Thanks. But take Guinevere with you. Drorm, you'll have to check out the fletchers on your own."

Drorm grunted.

"You two ride south as fast as you can," he told them. He fished out the bag of coins Lucius had given him and handed it to Nia. "I don't know how much is in here but make the best deal you can. Just get any arrows they will part with."

"I have some coins too," Guinevere said, patting her own portal pouch.

Ethan gave the woman an impressed and somewhat curious expression. "Your pouch survived?"

She smiled and gave him a knowing look. "Daughter of Merlin, remember? He enchanted my armor to be invulnerable. You don't think he'd give me a pouch that could be destroyed by fire, do you?"

He nodded, wondering why he hadn't thought of that. Ethan sighed. He really did need some time to study up on things and figure out some of the stuff Merlin had done.

Thinking of Merlin, he looked at Guinevere and shot her an apologetic look. "I'm sorry about your father. I promise we'll get to him as soon as we deal with this army."

The warrior woman nodded. "I understand. I did sort of get you into this position and now you have to see it through. I've waited this long, a few more days won't matter."

Flashing her a smile, he nodded gratefully for her understanding. He really did want to help her father but he just couldn't leave these people to a war that their prince started. Not if he could help it.

"Grab horses and run by the Order," he said and looked at the sergeant. "Rollie can tell you where it is. Get his runestick and take it with you. I'll portal to you at dusk and bring you back."

"We will do that. We will leave now," Nia said. Going up on her tiptoes, his wife kissed him on the cheek and then, throwing a glance at Guinevere, headed for the door.

Ethan reached out and caught her wrist. He gestured at the table. "Eat something first."

Nia looked like she would protest but her stomach growled and she looked embarrassed. "I will eat quickly and then we will go."

"Fair enough," he told his wife with a smile.

Nia sat down and grabbed some of the meat from a plate on the table. She stopped and gave Ethan a dirty look. She patted the chair beside her. "You must eat too!"

Ethan was about to object but then his own stomach betrayed him with a loud grumble and he chuckled to himself. It appeared he needed to take his own advice. He walked over, sat down and filled a small plate with food.

37

After Guinevere and Nia had left to search the villages, Ethan wanted to go to the Order of the Scroll. He needed to find out what Michalus and Mertin had discovered. He also wanted to ask if the older mage had any ideas on how to best use the Chymera crystals.

As he was heading down the hallway out of the main hall, Lucius appeared from one of the many doors. Ethan chuckled. He realized he still didn't know where all them led. There just hadn't been time to explore the entire hall, let alone the keep.

"Ah, your majesty," the castellan said. "I've been looking for you."

Stopping, he turned to the man. "What do you need?"

"Actually, your majesty," the man said with an embarrassed expression. "It is rather what you need."

Ethan cocked his head. "What do I need?"

"Well, begging your pardon, your majesty," the

castellan replied. "But you need a bath, and a change of clothes."

Looking down at himself, he realized he did look a bit ragged. Between the battles, the blood and the fact that the Grail healed him but not his clothes, he guessed Lucius was right. Unfortunately, he had no other clothes. "You might be right about the bath but these are the only clothes I have..."

"Pardon me, your majesty," Lucius said with a slight inclination of his head. "But I had your valet, Charles, lay out a selection of clothing from the late Prince Ghregg, Prince Marcus's father, in your room."

"I have a valet?" Ethan asked, his brow furrowing. So far, Lucius had actually been the only one he'd seen in the hall.

"Indeed, your majesty," the castellan replied. "In fact, you have a valet, a cook, a maid, and a groom. There were more servants but they - how shall we say this, displeased the former prince in his final days. Given the grave circumstances we face, I felt it prudent to introduce you to the remaining servants after the current crisis is over."

Ethan frowned. "Makes sense. Why haven't I seen them around?"

Lucius cleared his throat. "The previous prince preferred to not see servants. After a few beatings, they quickly learned to stay out of sight."

"Please let them know that I don't mind if they are seen," Ethan told the man. "I assume they live somewhere in the hall, so this is their home too."

The castellan stared at Ethan for a long moment before nodding slowly. "I will tell them your wish, your majesty." Lucius looked him up and down. "As I was saying about the bath, your majesty."

"I really don't have time to..." Ethan started to reply.

"Begging your pardon again, your majesty," The castellan interrupted him. Apparently, Lucius had no qualms about being seen by or even interrupting him.

"Yes?" Ethan asked, raising an eyebrow.

"If you are going out," the man continued. "People will see you. If you wish to be treated like the king, then you should look like the king. These are common people. They will react to what they see. If you look like a - excuse my bluntness - vagabond, then they will think of you as such and treat you as such."

Ethan frowned. He didn't really have time to waste taking baths and picking out clothing. On the other hand, he did know from his previous job in computer support, he did know that people did judge you on the way you appeared. If he wanted to make this whole "king thing" work, he'd need to look and act the part.

He sighed. "Very well. But we'll need to make it quick. It won't matter how I'm dressed if the army shows up on our doorstep and we're not prepared."

"As you say, your majesty," Lucius replied, inclining his head. "I've already told Charles to expect you. He will also give you a shave and trim your hair."

Ethan started to object but changed his mind. In for a penny, in for a pound. "Fine. Where?"

"In your quarters, your majesty," Lucius replied.

Nodding, Ethan spun on his heels and quickly returned to his room. There he found a gentleman dressed in a crisp, dark outfit. The man, most likely

Charles, bowed as Ethan walked in and motioned to a polished brass tub next to him.

Charles was probably in his late 40's or early 50's, with salt and pepper hair and a well-groomed mustache and goatee. He wore a crisp black velvet tunic with gold trim and matching black breeches tucked into high, black boots. The boots were polished so well, Ethan could see the reflection of the room in them.

"Charles, I presume," Ethan said with a smile.

"Your majesty." The man bowed. "Lucius said you would require a bath, as well as a shave and haircut."

Ethan sighed again. "Apparently."

"I will help you undress," the valet said and took a step towards him.

"Charles," Ethan said, screwing up his face. He never called anyone Charles. "Can I call you Charlie?"

"Excuse me, your majesty?" the man replied, his expression telling Ethan that Charlie was apparently not a nickname the man preferred.

"Right," Ethan said with a smile. "Charles it is. Anyway, Charles, I can undress myself. The only person who helps me undress is the queen."

Ethan waited for a chuckle but the man's deadpan face showed no hint that he'd understood his attempt at a joke.

"As your majesty says," Charles replied.

Clearing his throat, Ethan began to strip off his clothes. "Alrighty then."

≈

AN HOUR LATER, Ethan was washed, shaved and sported a new haircut. He was also dressed in a very nice and surprisingly comfortable set of expensive clothes. The ensemble consisted of a lacy, silk shirt that was much more lacy than anything he had ever worn. When he put it on, he felt like some eccentric 80's rockstar.

Over the silk shirt he wore a navy and gold leather jerkin with chain mail reinforcement on the inside. While it looked a bit foppish, it was made in a way that it was more protective than his own leather armor.

To complete the outfit were a pair of navy leather breeches tucked into gold leather. Like the jerkin, the breeches looked like they had more form than function. But like the jerkin, they had inner padding and added leather protection on the thighs. The same with the boots.

After thanking Charlie, Ethan opened the door to his bedroom to go, only to find Lucius standing there.

"Geez!" Ethan exclaimed. "You startled me."

"My apologies, your majesty," the man replied in a tone that Ethan thought sounded like he wasn't really sorry at all. "When I was sorting through the clothes, I did come across this."

Lucius opened a wooden coffer he was holding to reveal a golden crown on a lining of velvet. The castellan offered it to Ethan. "While the current crown was lost with the prince, this crown was used up until about thirty years ago when Prince Adam II, commissioned a new, larger crown after seeing the prince of Knightmoor's crown."

"Knightmoor?" Ethan asked.

"The city north of Moonpoint," Lucius replied, still holding out the crown.

Ethan reached down and gingerly took the crown. It was smaller than he had imagined a crown. It was basically a circle of two-inch gold with some blue gems, probably sapphires embedded in them. Not exactly the crown of England. Not even close. It looked more like a golden headband.

Placing the crown on his head, he found that the inside of the crown was padded and fit snugly on his head. He moved his head back and forth a few times and the crown stayed on.

"Very regal, your majesty," Lucius said with the hint of a smile. "I believe you are ready to go out amongst the people."

Ethan looked down at himself. With Excalibur strapped to his waist, he did look like some renaissance noble. Perhaps a duelist of some sort. He smiled. "If nothing else, at least I smell better."

"As you say, your majesty," Lucius agreed. "Rollie is waiting for you downstairs."

"Rollie?" Ethan asked, his eyebrows raised.

"You are the king, your majesty," the castellan said. "You must have an escort."

"But I can..." Ethan started but once again Lucius interrupted him.

"Your majesty," he said, his face showing only a hint of frustration. "You are the king. The king simply does not walk around unescorted. Ideally, you would have a large retinue. Under the current circumstances, you should at least have the Sergeant with you."

"Fine," Ethan said and started to move past Lucius. He paused, looking at the castellan to see if there was anything else. When he said nothing, Ethan continued past him and down the stairs to where Rollie waited.

He smiled as he walked along. It really did feel good being in nice clothes. For a moment, he could almost forget that there would be an army on their front door tomorrow. Almost.

38

A half hour later, Ethan walked into the Order of the Scroll. Rollie, having escorted him here, waited outside.

"You clean up well," the sergeant had said when he first saw Ethan. He had hastily added, "Your majesty. You look like a proper king now."

After that, the two had spent the walk to the Order talking about the city. If Ethan was to be king, he needed to know everything he could.

Rollie seemed closer to the people than Lucius, actually interacting with them on a daily basis. Ethan had gotten the man to tell him everything he thought a king should know. And once Rollie started talking, he realized it was hard to get the man to shut up.

Ethan smiled as he walked through the hall of the Order. For the moment, at least, there was silence. But it was short lived.

Going into the main library area, Ethan found

Michalus and Mertin at a table with a stack of books. The two were arguing over something.

"Is there a problem?" Ethan asked as he got nearer.

Both men jumped at the sound of his voice, apparently oblivious to his approach.

"Ethan!" Michalus said and then cleared his throat. "Sorry, I guess it's, your majesty now."

Ethan rolled his eyes. "Just keep calling me Ethan. Come this time tomorrow, there might not be a city to be king of." He paused. "Unless you two found something that can help us."

The two men exchanged looks and then both men looked crestfallen. Mertin spoke up. "I'm sorry, your majesty. The books talk a great deal about some rather impressive-sounding war spells...."

"But..." Ethan said, sensing a "but" was coming.

Michalus nodded. "But, much like my exploration of scrying magic, you find many generalities but very few specifics."

Ethan rubbed his temples, feeling the start of a headache forming. He'd really been hoping the two of them would have found something. "So there's nothing?"

Both men shrugged. "We're still looking."

Shutting his eyes, Ethan massaged his temples harder as the headache began to fully form. "Okay. So no massive war spells. Can either of you two think of some sort of weapon we could make with some Chymera crystals?"

He opened his eyes and looked between the two magic users. "I can think of a few, but I'm looking for other ideas."

"How many?" Michalus asked.

"I had 40, but I used 10 to make a new portal bag..." Ethan started and stopped shy of saying Grail in front of Mertin. Instead he gave Michalus a meaningful look.

The wizard seemed to understand and nodded. "Good idea."

"So I have 30 left," Ethan said. "I was thinking of some sort of air-propelled rock launcher, similar to, but larger than, the boomstick I made for Par'karr."

"Launching rocks might be somewhat effective," Mertin said. "But as I learned when I first got these powers, something that's innately magical causes normal people to hesitate."

Ethan cocked an eyebrow. "What do you mean?"

"Well," the channeler explained. "If I was facing two men with swords and I pulled out a sword, they looked at me and figure they had the strength in numbers because basically we were on even ground - sword vs sword."

Mertin paused and looked at him. Ethan nodded and motioned him to go on. "Makes sense."

"Right. But, if I make a flaming sword appear out of my hand," the man said with a grin. "Now, the thugs aren't really sure. They know what a steel sword is, what it can do. It's familiar. But a flaming sword. That's new. They don't know how it works - and that scares them."

"That actually makes a lot of sense." Ethan nodded. "Rocks flying over the wall at them is something they might be used to in a siege. Even if it wasn't, a rock is a rock. They know what it is and what it does."

He felt his headache receding slightly as an idea began to form. "But if we create something they won't expect and aren't prepared for - that might make them think twice. So... shock and awe, huh?"

"Shock and awe?" Mertin repeated and then cocked his head. "Yes, I suppose that's one way to put it."

Belatedly, Mertin looked embarrassed. "Ahem... your majesty. Sorry, I have to get used to that."

Ethan rolled his eyes. "Let's get through the enemy army at our gates tomorrow and then you can worry about whether or not to call me your majesty."

"Oh!" Mertin's eye brightened. "And thank you for that healing draft. I have to admit, after that, I felt so much better. Even the knee I broke when I was a kid doesn't bother me."

After he'd left the castle yesterday, he'd made a point to stop by the order and use the Grail to heal Mertin. He hadn't had time to stick around but now it seemed he owed the man an explanation.

"Ahem." Michalus cleared his throat and gave Ethan a small nod. "I took the liberty of explaining that the drink you gave him yesterday was a special enchanted elixir you created. A secret wizard recipe that was passed down to you."

Mertin nodded enthusiastically and chuckled. "It certainly works! I can attest to that. You could actually become quite wealthy just by bottling that and selling it."

Thinking quickly, Ethan shook his head. "Sadly, I've never been able to make it last longer than 24 hours. It just so happened I made some right before coming to the city."

A little of the enthusiasm drained out of the channeler. "Too bad. It really is quite potent."

"Okay," Ethan told the two men. "Keep looking. Tell me if you find any sort of spell that you think we can use."

"We will," Michalus said.

"And Michalus, I will need you back at the keep around dinner time," he told the wizard. "Nia and Guinevere rode to the nearby villages to see if we can get any arrows. I'll need your help charging the crystals."

The wizard raised an eyebrow and suddenly Ethan felt his face warming. Obviously, Michalus knew how Nia "helped" him by recharging his *Mana* with sex. He cleared his throat and quickly clarified. "Uh, I will give you half to charge and I will charge the other half."

Michalus chuckled at Ethan's embarrassment and nodded. "I will be happy to help charge some of the crystals."

Still feeling embarrassed and wanting to leave as quickly as possible, Ethan spun on his heel and walked back to the door. He reached out to open the door when it suddenly burst open.

Standing in the doorway was Rollie and a sweaty, out of breath soldier.

"Your majesty, I sent Dave out this morning to do some scouting," Rollie explained. "He just got back. You should hear what he said."

The man Rollie introduced, Dave, was a medium-height man with a shaved head and a thick, blond goatee. His face and head were tanned from hours in the sun and he looked to be in his late thirties. He bobbed his head at Ethan as he caught his breath. "Your majesty."

"Report," Ethan told the man, giving him a nod of acknowledgement.

"I took one of the horses and rode north to the pass," he said, stopping to catch his breath. "From there, I could see the vanguard of the army."

"How many?"

Dave shrugged. "I could only see the forefront but it stretched as far as I could see."

Ethan sighed. So the reports of the army's size weren't exaggerated. He nodded to Dave. "Thanks..."

Rollie shook his head. "That ain't the part you got to hear."

Feeling his stomach do a little flip-flop, Ethan let out a breath. "What's the other part?"

Rollie nudged Dave with his shoulder. "Tell him."

Eyes darting around like a trapped animal, Dave finally looked down. "They'll be here sometime tonight."

"TONIGHT?!" Ethan exclaimed, eyes going wide. "Tonight?!"

Dave flinched as if he expected Ethan to strike him or, probably knowing he was a wizard, maybe burn him to a crisp.

Ethan cursed loudly. Tonight was too soon. He wouldn't even have time to build any enchanted items.

"Is something wrong?" Michalus said from behind him.

Turning, Ethan saw Michalus and Mertin hurrying down the hall. Ethan growled. "The Moonpoint army will be here tonight."

"Tonight?!" Michalus and Mertin said in chorus, both men suddenly looking as worried as Ethan felt.

Michalus opened his mouth and then closed it. He blinked. "I thought they said..."

"Tomorrow?!" Ethan spat. "Apparently not."

Mind racing, he quickly began to change his plans. He pointed to the library. "Mertin, keep looking for anything that will help us."

He pointed to Dave. "Dave, good job. Go get some food and some rest if you can, then report to the wall.

"Make sure every city gate is sealed," Ethan said, turning to Rollie. "Then, go get every able-bodied man you can. Dress them in armor and get them on the wall. Have them nap in shifts until the army arrives. We need them rested in case they try to siege tonight."

Finally, he gestured to Michalus. "You come with me. We'll need to work on the crystals now and see what we can come up with before tonight."

Seeing that no one had moved, Ethan clapped his hands together. "Come on, people, move!"

With that, everyone sprang into action. Gesturing for Michalus to follow him, Ethan hurried out the door and back towards the keep. He had a lot to do, and not much time.

39

Ethan and Michalus worked on charging crystals until it was time for him to portal to Guinevere and Nia. Unfortunately, being inside, he didn't realize it was already dark until it was too late. Cursing himself for being too focused, he got the wizard's attention.

"I have to go get Guinevere and Nia," he told the elf. "I'll be back."

Michalus looked up and nodded tiredly. "I'll be here."

Running up to his room, Ethan grabbed his own runestick and hurried down the stairs and out into the courtyard. Dropping it on the ground so he had a return point, he focused on the runestick that Nia carried. With his hand on Excalibur, he focused his *Mana* through the crystal in the sword, opened the portal and stepped through.

Appearing along the coastal highway, Ethan immediately looked around. He spun around and spotted the women sitting on a fallen log.

"I thought you said sunset," Guinevere growled, pushing herself to her feet. She looked him over and whistled. "You cleaned up well. I approve."

"You look very attractive... for a human," Nia said with a nod of approval.

Ethan looked down at himself, remembering he was now wearing the clothes of royalty. With everything that had happened, he had forgotten. "Uh... thanks... and sorry I'm late... things have... changed."

Both women perked up, obviously sensing his foreboding tone.

"What has changed?" Nia demanded.

"The Moonpoint army will be here tonight," he replied.

"Tonight?!" Guinevere shot back. "I thought that merchant said tomorrow!"

Ethan shrugged. "Either he was a bad judge of timing, or the army moved faster than he anticipated. But one of Rollie's scouts spotted them. He said they'd be here tonight."

"Perhaps it is their advanced scouts that he spotted," Nia suggested.

"It doesn't matter at this point," Ethan responded. "Even their advanced scouts outnumber us. I've already sealed the city."

"That was a good move," Guinevere said with a nod. "Enemies will sometimes try to slip in as villagers or merchants before a siege, then cause problems from within."

"How did you two do?" he asked, not wanting to think of the possibility of already having spies within the city.

Nia grinned. "We did well."

The women parted, revealing the two horses. Both had several large bundles of arrows strapped to their back.

"Nice!" Ethan shared her grin. "How many?"

"Six dozen from the three villages we managed to get through," Guinevere replied, she patted her purse. "But it cost us."

"I'll reimburse you," Ethan promised but the warrior woman waved him away.

"I did kind of get you into this," she admitted. "It's the least I could do."

Ethan smiled. "It's very much appreciated." He turned around and grabbed Nia's runestick. "Let's get back."

"One moment," Guinevere said from behind him and he turned around.

"We were talking while we waited for you," Nia said, sharing a glance with Guinevere.

Ethan narrowed his eyes. "And?"

"I know you are preparing to defend the city," Guinevere said, "but perhaps you should surrender the city to them."

"I do not agree," Nia said, placing her hands on her hips. She let out a breath. "But sometimes when the opposing clan is much stronger, and there is no chance of victory, it is acceptable."

"Surrender?" Ethan repeated. "Are you serious?"

"Or at least find out what their terms would be," Guinevere explained. "They are coming to defend themselves against the incursions of the former prince. Once they find out he is dead, they may not want to continue the war."

Ethan raised an eyebrow. "You really think so?"

Guinevere bit her lip and shrugged. "I know nothing about Moonpoint. They may not want a war any more than we do at this point."

"You do not have to talk to them if you don't want to," Nia assured him. "You are the Alpha!"

"You don't have to," Guinevere agreed with a sideways glance at Nia. "But you do have a bit of leverage."

"Oh?" Ethan asked, cocking an eyebrow. He hadn't told anyone that he'd asked the dragon to come. Had they figured it out?

"You're a wizard," Guinevere stated.

Ethan furrowed his brow, not sure how that made a difference.

"They're rare at the moment," the warrior woman explained. "And your portal abilities are far beyond the average wizard."

"And you think me being a wizard will persuade them to not attack?" Ethan asked, trying not to sound as uncertain as he felt. It seemed a stretch to him. But then again, what did he know. He hadn't even been on this world a year.

"I'm not saying that," Guinevere retorted. "I'm just saying, it's something that might work in your favor."

Ethan nodded, still not sure if it would do any good to talk with them or not. But he supposed it wouldn't hurt. If anything, it might buy them a little time. And the more time he could get, the better. That was more time he could give Firestorm to show up.

He briefly toyed with the idea of telling the two women but then dismissed it. At the moment, he had no idea when or if the dragon would get here. Even the dragon hadn't known. He simply never bothered to learn the names of human cities. To the dragon, who had lived tens of thousands of years, human civilizations came and went. He had slept through the rise and fall of certain cultures.

Having drank from the Fountain of Youth, Ethan wondered if he would ever feel that way. He was immortal now and would never age. Even just talking about a thousand years was like watching history from the dark ages to modern times. He couldn't even imagine 10,000 years, let alone tens of thousands of years. That would be like watching man from caveman days to the modern day.

Of course, all of that was assuming he actually lived that long. He might be immortal, but he wasn't invulnerable. He could still die through wounds - he just wouldn't age.

"Ethan?" Nia asked, causing him to snap his attention back to the two of them.

"I'm sorry," he said sheepishly. "I zoned out for a second."

"I asked what you were going to do?" Guinevere repeated.

Ethan shrugged. "I don't see how it will hurt to talk with them. If we can resolve it peacefully, then no more lives need to be lost."

"And what if they call for your removal as king?" Nia demanded, crossing her arms over her chest.

"That will depend on what will happen to the people

of Castlehaven," he replied. "I met quite a few of them when we were helping and looking for survivors. They seem like decent people. I wouldn't want anything to happen to them."

"Moonpoint might want them punished," Guinevere told him.

"For what?" Ethan growled. "They didn't do anything!"

"You don't know that," the warrior woman reminded him. "For all you know, some of the people you met turned people in as slaves."

"I... uh..." Ethan started to reply but snapped his mouth shut. Guinevere was right. The people he'd met seemed nice, but he knew nothing about them. For all he knew, one of the people he saved from the rubble could have been a slaver.

Guinevere nodded. "It's heavy, isn't it?"

"What's heavy?" he asked, his forehead wrinkling in confusion.

"The crown," Guinevere said, nodding her head at his crown. "That's one of the reasons I let Arthur do most of the ruling. It's not like the battlefield, where you know who your enemy is. In politics, it's never clear. Arthur had patience for things like that. I never did."

Ethan removed the crown from his head and stared down at it in his hands. He knew she wasn't talking about the physical weight of the crown. It weighed next to nothing, despite being made of gold.

No, it was the responsibility he assumed by wearing the crown. The responsibility for the people of the city, as well as a responsibility to seek justice.

Maybe he wasn't really cut out to be a king. After all, what had he really done as mayor of Hawkshead? Nothing. He'd helped save the town against a kobold invasion and then stopped the noise driving away all of the game. But what had he done to actually help build up the town? Nothing. He hadn't even been there for weeks at a time.

Maybe it would be better to just turn the city over to Moonpoint. He could let them sort out justice and just go find Merlin and then chill out back in Hawkshead. Was he really cut out to be a king - even if it was just of a single city?

Letting out a long breath, he slowly put the crown back on his head. He turned around. "Let's get back. The archers will need these arrows."

Not waiting for a reply, Ethan fixed the other runestick in his mind and, with the force of his will, opened up a portal back into the courtyard of the keep.

THE QUEEN CLICKED ANGRILY, *unable to hide her frustration. She had no more soldiers to take out her anger on, so instead, she sliced through several nearby trees.*

She was finally recovered and ready to go into the city to get her prize, but then a portal had formed nearby. She skirted the city to investigate but had seen no sign of the human wizard.

Then, she had circled the city, to find the best entry point, only to find a great number of the bipedal creatures coming towards the city. Too many.

The Queen knew the humans uttered curses when things didn't go their way, but she had no curse that could adequately convey her displeasure. Instead, she sliced through nearby trees, the action not really making her feel better.

For now, she would need to bide her time and wait for the opportune moment.

40

The moment they returned, Ethan asked Guinevere to go help Rollie organize the recruits and gather all the bows and arrows together on the north parapets. There was really no time to spare.

Lucius met him outside, carrying the two items he'd asked the man to procure. The castellan held them up and gave Ethan a questioning look. "Are these what you were looking for?"

Ethan grinned and nodded. "Those are perfect. Follow me."

He quickly led Lucius and Nia to the large room that he and Michalus had confiscated for their workroom. The place might have been a small ballroom at one time, but now had parchment lying all over the floor.

On his hands and knees, scribbling some notes on a piece of parchment, was Michalus. The wizard looked up at the group as they entered the room. His eyes roamed over the group and then settled on the two items that Lucius carried.

"You're sure those will work?" the wizard asked.

"I hope so!" Ethan replied. He motioned to a clear spot on the floor. "Set them there."

"How are we doing with crystals?" Ethan asked.

"The same as when you left," the wizard admitted. "My mana still isn't back to full strength to charge up another one."

Ethan grinned. He reached down and took a handful of the remaining crystals.

"I have these covered!" he said, scooping his wife in his arms. She cried out in surprise and then giggled as he spun her around towards the door. Then he carried her up to the bedroom and spent the next hour charging up crystals with her help. And as always, she was an enthusiastic helper.

He wished he could have enjoyed it more, but he had too many things on his mind. His attention was split between the coming army, the lack of soldiers and resources and the uncertainty of whether or not the dragon would show up in time, and a million other tiny details.

Guinevere was right. The crown was heavy. Knowing the people in the city depended on him to defend them was heavy weight. There was so much riding on his decisions.

Ethan had flashbacks to the time he'd defended Hawkshead against a tribe of marauding kobolds, shortly after first arriving here. The odds had been overwhelming then too but they'd still managed to defend the village and repel the horde. He and his friends had managed it then. Could they do it again?

THEY FINISHED CHARGING the remaining Chymera crystals and then the two of them got quickly dressed again. Ethan sent Nia to help Guinevere, then he rejoined Michalus in their makeshift workroom.

The wizard looked up in surprise. "That was quick."

"That's what she said," Ethan retorted without thinking and sighed as the wizard just furrowed his brow. "Nevermind. Here are the other crystals."

Nodding, Michalus pointed to the two items on the floor. "I don't think the wood will stand up to what you have in mind. I think they'll go up in smoke after a few shots. Not to mention, I'm not sure exactly how we will affix the crystals."

Ethan had already thought of that and had come up with an answer in between his and Nia's lovemaking sessions. He held up a finger. "One moment."

Leaving the room, Ethan walked down the hallway and out into the courtyard. He looked around and found several small, loose stones. Grabbing them, he spun and hastily made his way back to Michalus. Arriving, he held out his hand.

"Stones?" the wizard muttered, confusion etched all over his face. Then he brightened. "Yes! Stones! I think that will work!"

"It had better," Ethan said, handing two of the stones to Michalus. "Otherwise, there goes our secret weapon."

THE MOONPOINT ARMY began gathering a mile north of the city two hours after dark. It was easy to see because of the number of fires, probably torches, in the distance. And there were a lot of them. From this distance, they looked like a field of fireflies.

Ethan and his friends stood on the parapet. Lining the parapets with them were the guard and the about forty volunteers. Given the hundreds of people who were left in the city, he was disappointed that they had so few.

Not that it really mattered. Even with another 100 people, they would still be vastly outnumbered. If it came to a fight, Ethan was counting on Michalus's and his magic to even the odds. Even then, he wasn't sure whether they could repel the army of fireflies which continued to swell.

Looking down the line, Ethan could see bundles of arrows scattered every ten feet. Each bundle had ten or eleven arrows, but he knew there were only ten bundles. He shook his head. A little over a hundred arrows versus an army of a thousand. Even if every arrow miraculously killed two people, they'd barely make a dent in the army.

"Many torches," Par'karr muttered, eyes glued to the torches in the distance.

"It's been a while since I saw an army gathering," Guinevere said from his left. "And compared to some of Camelot's skirmishes, it's a relatively small army."

Drorm, next to Guinevere, grunted. "If we gathered our full army, we would have five times that number. All warriors."

Ethan breathed out a long breath. By modern, Earth standards, a thousand-man army was relatively small. But given how many "soldiers" he had, a thousand-man army seemed overwhelming. Glancing to his right, just beyond Nia were two items sitting on a canvas tarp. His secret weapons.

They'd come up with the name, Fire Bows, or Fireball Crossbows. They were old crossbows that Lucius had managed to either find or procure. Ethan and Michalus had used *Earth* magic to cover the wooden parts in a very thin layer of stone using the rocks Ethan had collected.

The layer of stone did two things. First, it prevented the wood of the weapon from catching fire when the fireball launched. Second, it also allowed them to embed the crystals into the weapon without special tools. And the end result was impressive in function, if not so much in form.

He and Michalus had only tested them a few times, but the tests exceeded their expectations. When he'd demonstrated the Fireball Crossbows to Drorm and Guinevere, both had been shocked by the results - and even more shocked when he'd told them they could use the weapons too - not just wizards.

But there was a catch. He'd first considered creating them similar to the boomstick he'd created for Par'karr. The problem with the magical shotgun was, it took the crystals almost a full minute to recharge. One charge every minute wasn't going to help them much. That meant he needed a different way.

Like the necklaces he'd created to protect the wearer from mental attacks, Ethan had geared the weapons to draw from the user's *Mana*. In this way, the Fireball Crossbows could be fired several times by a person in rapid succession.

The catch was, with the exception of himself, Michalus and Par'karr, no one else had a *Mana* pool worth mentioning. At most, they'd each get a couple of shots off before running low on Mana. And without a HUD, they could inadvertently use up all their Mana and fall unconscious. To mitigate the issue, they'd come up with a plan.

The crossbows would be fired once per person and then handed to the person next to them. That person would then fire and hand it to the person next to them. And it would continue all the way down the line. The last person on the line would run it back to the first person, who would start the cycle all over again.

At least, that was the plan. If they did that until the first person passed out, he hoped they'd be able to get at least 100 fireballs off per side - maybe more. If that didn't shock and awe the Moonpoint army, he wasn't sure what else would.

Well... except for a huge dragon. But Firestorm wasn't here. And the army was.

"They are moving!" Nia hissed, pointing out to the gigantic number of torches in the dark. "They are coming this way."

Ethan cursed and looked out at the massive army. Nia was right. The torches were no longer gathering. Instead, they were shifting. They were starting to come towards the city. Given their pace, they'd be here in twenty or thirty minutes.

"So." He let out a breath. "It begins."

41

Ethan didn't have a stopwatch but he thought he had guessed correctly. Somewhere around twenty minutes later, the army marched within eyeshot of the city, stopping just outside of bow range.

Unwilling to enter within the range of his archers, the mass of people then began spreading out to either side. For some reason, now that they were closer, they didn't look like quite as many as he had thought. Ethan wasn't sure if that was a good thing or a bad thing.

The army spread out about a hundred yards to either side of the main gate. He cocked his head. The line of soldiers was about the length of a football field, though not nearly as deep. But it seemed nearly every man, or perhaps every other man, carried a torch.

There were so many torches that the light was actually bright enough to make out details about the army. The first thing he noticed was the fact that they were garbed in a mishmash of armor and the weapons they carried were equally as varied.

It looked less like an army and more like a collection of farmers intent on storming a castle. He frowned. Was this even an army?

"They don't look like an army. They look like peasants, farmers, even craftsmen," he commented, adding the last one as he noticed a big man to the left. The man not only wielded a hammer, but appeared to still have a thick leather blacksmith's apron on.

"What do you think an army is?" Guinevere asked without looking at him. "Those men either volunteered or were conscripted. And yes, many of them are farmers or craftsmen."

Ethan scowled. "So if we fight them, we're fighting normal people off the street?"

Guinevere kept her eyes sweeping over the battlefield, not bothering to look his way. "That's war." She frowned and gestured at several places. "They cut down trees. They'll either try to ram the door or use them to scale the walls. Probably both. That's what I'd do. Split our forces and attention."

He looked where the warrior woman had indicated and was able to make out groups of men carrying large tree trunks. Ethan's scowl deepened.

"We should be able to hold them off with the Fireball Crossbows," he said aloud.

"There are other foxlings," Nia said softly.

Trying to see where his wife was staring, Ethan followed her gaze until he saw what she was looking at. In the front lines was a group of three foxlings. They looked remarkably like Nia, but they were obviously males.

As he squinted up and down the line, he picked out a variety of races. There were foxlings, cat-people, halflings, dwarves, elves and humans. Ethan shook his head. He really didn't want to fight these people - especially not if they weren't even soldiers.

He cursed but quickly lowered his voice when he saw the soldiers closest to him look his way. Ethan remembered he was king now. He had to act composed and confident. That's what a leader did, especially in the face of adversity.

Ethan put a smile on his face, the cockiest smile he could muster. He tried to relax his posture and then turned to the soldiers who were still looking at him. He sighed. "Darn. That's going to be a whole lot of bodies for us to bury."

The guards chuckled and then relayed the message down the ranks. He heard some other chuckles further away but went back to focusing on the battle lines. As he did, he saw a man start forward with a pole flying a white cloth.

Turning to Guinevere, he raised an eyebrow. He kept his voice low. "I assume that's a symbol for parlay and that they're not surrendering to us."

Guinevere chuckled and shook her head. "You are correct. They are not surrendering. They will send a rider to find out the rules of parlay. Once you vouchsafe the meeting, the leader or his or her immediate subordinate will come to offer us terms."

He looked into the warrior woman's eyes and she

stared back at him. She didn't say anything, but the message was clear. It was the same thing she had said back on the road. Find out what their terms are. If they're reasonable, he should agree. He gave the woman a small nod of his head, indicating he understood.

Looking back at the approaching man, Ethan saw that the man coming forward was dressed in chainmail, with a dark-blue tabard decorated with a large white circle - presumably a moon. He had an actual sword belted around his waist. Ethan guessed that meant he was most likely either a Moonpoint guard or an actual soldier.

He waited patiently for the man to get within shouting distance, at which point he stopped and looked up. The soldier's eye scanned the parapets until he stopped on Ethan. His face remained impassive, but Ethan thought he saw his eyes narrow.

"Prince Marcus!" the man began but Ethan held up a hand.

"It's Ethan, King Ethan!" Ethan yelled back. "Prince Marcus was a victim of his own foolishness! He is dead!"

Confusion washed across the soldier's features for a moment, but then his expression turned grim again. "No man has claimed the title of king since..."

"Since Arthur and Camelot and the sword Excalibur!" Guinevere called down. "King Ethan has drawn Excalibur. He is rightfully king!"

Ethan drew Excalibur and held it aloft. He channeled just enough *Mana* to make the gem glow, shedding a pale blue light along the blade.

The soldier stared up at the sword, his face unreadable. Then his face resumed its former countenance. "Nevertheless! The Princess wishes to discuss terms. Will you vouchsafe the parlay?"

"Princess?" Ethan said softly. "Moonpoint has a princess?"

Rollie, standing nearby, leaned closer. "Yah, Princess Melody, and quite the looker I hear. Uncle Marcus was trying to marry her for years." He shrugged. "Kept turning him down though."

"I will vouchsafe the parlay!" Ethan called back to the soldier.

"You must say 'On my honor'," Guinevere said quietly under her breath.

"On my honor!" Ethan yelled.

The soldier narrowed his eyes. "We will see how much honor you have."

"He insults you," Nia growled, hands going to her weapons.

"He doesn't know me," Ethan pointed out. "All he really knows is the former prince, who didn't have much honor."

"You can say that again," Rollie said in a hushed tone.

The soldier stayed where he was but waved the white flag first one way, then another and finally up and down. When he was done, three people from the enemy line began walking forward.

The one in the middle immediately caught his eye. She was a beautiful, dark-haired woman dressed in well-crafted chain mail that seemed to cling to all of the woman's generous curves. She was short, but walked with a grace that Ethan thought reserved for models on a catwalk. Ethan knew this had to be the princess. He also knew, by her long tapered ears, she was an elf.

To her right was a large catling, or maybe Ethan should say, a lion-ling. He was at least six feet tall and muscled, wearing chainmail and a tabard similar to the first man. Strapped on his back was a huge two-handed sword. Probably also a soldier - maybe a bodyguard or general or other high-ranking military man.

On the princess's left was a tall, willowy man in robes. He appeared to be a human but looked old. He sported a large, gray beard and long gray hair peeked out of a cone-shaped hat. In his hand was a staff with a blue crystal in it. His entire outfit and demeanor shouted "wizard" and he looked like he should be asking a halfling if he wanted to go on an adventure.

Michalus pressed in close. "I know him! That's Tibold! Tibold Keldord!"

"A wizard, I assume," Ethan said wryly.

"Oh yes." Michalus nodded. "Quite good. It's wonderful to see him still alive!"

Ethan turned and looked at his friend. "You do know he's on the other side, right?"

The wizard looked at him sheepishly. "Well, there is that."

Looking back down, he saw the three people stop next to the first soldier. There was a quick discussion between the original soldier and the newcomers. During the talk, more than one of them glanced up at Ethan, who smiled down at them.

Finally, their conversation ended and the four of them straightened. The Princess looked up at him, face unreadable. Despite her diminutive stature, when she spoke, her voice was loud and strong. "King Ethan. I have come to discuss the terms of your surrender."

"It might be easier!" Ethan yelled. "If we had this conversation face to face. Give me a moment and I'll be right there."

"You must take 3 people with you," Guinevere said and Nia nodded her head in agreement. "Otherwise, you will appear weak."

"Okay," Ethan said. "Guinevere, Nia and..."

"Me!" Michalus said. "She has a wizard, so you should have one too."

"Fine," he agreed. "Let's go."

Locking his eyes on the area right in front of the Princess's group, Ethan opened a portal. Nia, then Guinevere and finally Michalus went through. As soon as they appeared below, Ethan stepped through.

He was back in the Bifrost and once again, Merlin's face appeared. "Find me. Hurry."

Ethan blinked. It was different! For one, it was weaker. The image was almost completely translucent. The other thing that was different was, this time the message said to hurry. Ethan was trying to understand the ramifications of that message when he emerged in front of the Princess and her entourage.

42

"Tibold!" Michalus said enthusiastically. "It's good to see you again."

The man in robes frowned and furrowed his brow. "Do I... know you?"

Michalus looked hurt. "It's me... Michalus!"

Tibold tilted his head one way and then the other. "You can't be Michalus. He was... uh..."

"Old?!" Michalus shot back with a grin. "Not anymore. Thanks to... ah... some accidental magic, I'm young and fit as a fiddle!"

"Is that really you then?" the man said, squinting at Ethan's friend.

Princess Melody cleared her throat. "Gentlemen, while I can appreciate the reunion of two friends, we are here on another matter. One with a bit more gravity."

Tibold inclined his head towards the Princess. "My apologies, your highness."

Now that Ethan was close enough, he scanned all four of the people in his HUD.

Princess Melody Goldensun
    Elf
    Noble
    Level 8

Tibold Keldord
    Human
    Wizard
    Level 11

Zachus Ajosain
    Catling
    Warrior
    Level 10

Karlton Kross
    Human
    Warrior
    Level 7

Ethan felt *Mind* magic being used by Tibold and he slammed his mental firewall into place. Tibold didn't react, which meant he probably hadn't been trying to get into Ethan's mind. But he saw the Princess's eyes flick towards Tibold and his eyes to her. Were they communicating telepathically?

That was actually clever. A secret way to communicate

behind your enemies' backs, even though you were right in front of them. It would allow the Princess to get Tibold's advice without actually asking him. Why hadn't he thought of that?

Still, he would prefer everyone kept their cards on the table. Channeling his own *Mind* magic, he poked into Tibold's and the Princess's minds. There was no resistance from either.

Hey, he said. *Is this a private conversation or can anyone listen in?*

Both of their eyes went wide.

How dare you enter my mind without permission! the Princess snapped.

Funny, I thought it was rude to try a little under the table communication while under the flag of Parlay, Ethan shot back. *But I can pipe everyone in on the conversation, that way, we're all on even footing.*

Outwardly, the Princess's face was flushing with anger as she glared at Ethan. Tibold was also flushed but from embarrassment or anger, Ethan couldn't say. Ethan looked into the Princess' eyes. "What will it be, your highness?"

"Drop the spell, Tibold," she told her wizard. She narrowed her eyes at Ethan. "What are you? One of the channelers or warlocks we've heard about?"

"Nope." Ethan grinned. "I'm a wizard, just like Tibold and Michalus here."

"It's true," Michalus confirmed with a nod.

Tibold begrudgingly seemed to agree. "If he created a portal and did the magic of the mind, he cannot be a channeler or a warlock. They only have access to one school of magic."

"I see," Princess Melody said, looking Ethan up and down. "Before you so rudely interrupted our communication, Tibold was telling me that you must be extremely powerful to be able to create a portal large enough to fit a man. At least, I assume that was you."

"It was," Ethan confirmed. He really had no reason to lie to her. If she knew he was powerful, maybe that would help the negotiations. "But truth be told, I can create portals even larger."

"How is that possible?" Tibold blurted out.

Ethan just shrugged.

"And you have used your power to usurp the throne from Prince Marcus?" Zachus Ajosain, the lion man growled.

"Actually," Ethan retorted. "I used my magic to destroy the demon lord that idiot summoned."

"Demon lord?" Karlton, the other soldier with the Princess, said. "I thought they were summoning a goddess. Hel, if the reports were to be believed."

"I think they were duped into believing it was a goddess. But the entire time, they were actually summoning a demon lord," Ethan explained. He tried to recall the name of the demon lord, but failed.

"None of this matters," Princess Melody interrupted. "I do not recognize your claim to the throne! I have come to claim this city in the name of Moonpoint and put an end to the slavery and..."

"That's already done," Ethan interrupted. "The first thing I did when I became king. No more slaves. We're all equal again."

The Princess fumed at Ethan for a moment, anger

playing across her beautiful features for a moment before she mastered it. When she spoke, Princess Melody did in short, controlled words. "You will turn over the city to me, or you will all die."

"Why?" Ethan asked. "Why are you going to kill innocent people? For what?"

"You have oppressed..." she started but Ethan held up his hand and shook his head.

"I did nothing of the sort," he interrupted. "And neither did most of the people who are left - which aren't that many."

Ethan thought he could hear the Princess gritting her teeth. "The city of Castlehaven is responsible for the oppression of many people and the wholesale murder of hundreds - maybe even thousands!"

"That's over," Ethan told her. "We're under new management. My management. And that stuff isn't going to happen while I'm in charge."

"Do you think your little proclamation somehow makes up for all of the people who have died? Elves! Foxlings! Catlings! Halflings! So many others! Does it give compensation to their families? Their loved ones? Does it restore back the businesses that were stolen from those deemed as slaves?" Melody spat. "No! There will be justice!"

"Justice?!" Ethan chuckled. "What justice are you going to get from the few survivors in the city left? People who survived the same hardships you're describing. In the end, Marcus wasn't just sacrificing non-humans, he was sacrificing anyone he could get his hands on. Men, women...

even children. If the demon hadn't killed him, I would have done it myself."

"There must still be a reckoning!" the Princess growled.

"A reckoning against who?" Ethan asked, trying to make the woman see reason. "The crippled craftsman I pulled out of rubble? The orphan whose parents were sacrificed? The family whose home was destroyed by the demon? Huh? Which one of those are you going to force your reckoning on?!"

"Someone will pay for my sister's death!" the elven woman shouted. Almost immediately, she seemed to realize she'd said too much and snapped her mouth closed.

Ethan let out a breath. He now knew why the woman was so dead set on a reckoning. It wasn't justice she wanted. It was revenge. "I'm sorry about your sister. I really am. But the man who was ultimately responsible for it is dead. And if it's any consolation, he probably died in a really horrible way."

The elven princess set her jaw, eyes narrowed. "There will be a reckoning. There will be justice. You will relinquish the city to me, or I will take it by force."

"If I do surrender the city to you," Ethan said. "What happens to the people?"

"They will be tried for whatever crimes they are guilty of," she replied quickly. "If they are innocent, they will be set free."

"Wait," Ethan said, brow furrowing. "You're going to arrest everyone in the city and put them on trial?"

"Yes," the woman growled. "But they will be given a

trial and their accusers will be given a chance to bring accusations against them."

To Ethan, it sounded like the Spanish Inquisition or a Salem Witch trial. He shook his head. "That's insane."

"No!" she growled, her face twisting in anger. "You are insane. Proclaiming yourself king!"

"He drew Excalibur," Guinevere said. "He has the right."

"Children's stories do not grant the right to be called king," the woman spat. "And I, for one, do not recognize his claim! As part of your terms, you will surrender yourself to me to face justice for impersonating a king."

Ethan snorted. "I don't think so. I don't negotiate with idiots. The Parlay is over."

Before anyone could react, Ethan opened a portal directly beneath their feet. One minute they were there, the next minute they slipped through the portal and came falling out of the portal ten feet in the air, directly in front of their army. The lion-man soldier managed to land on his feet, but the others landed on their asses.

As childish as it might be, Ethan actually enjoyed watching the Princess falling on her holier than thou butt. But he knew he'd embarrassed her and insulted her in front of her army. She wouldn't forgive that. He cursed silently, knowing that he'd probably made an enemy for life.

Ethan opened a portal behind him. "Go! Quickly!"

The others dashed through the portal as the Princess got to her feet, screaming at the army. "Attack! Take the city!"

Stepping backwards through the portal, Ethan let it

snap closed behind him just as he saw the army starting to move towards them.

Appearing up on the parapet with the others, he saw Rollie look from the charging army to Ethan. "I take it the negotiations didn't go well."

43

A great shout arose from the enemy army as it charged forward. The frontline of the army was running towards the wall, followed by the lines of men and humanoids behind them. Ethan counted twelve of the tree trunks being carried towards them by the Moonpoint army.

Ethan knew the tree trunks would be used to scale the wall or to ram the doors. Those were the two things they needed to prevent. A breach in either the wall or the main gate meant fighting overwhelming numbers and that would spell their doom.

All they needed to do was keep the army outside the wall. From there, they couldn't do any harm. Well, not enough to bring down the walls. Unless they had brought siege engines. He frowned, searching the enemy army with his eyes. That would really change the game if they had.

The men carrying the tree trunks moved closer. He

saw them split into groups. Two trunks were headed to the doors, while the others were headed to either side.

"Bring out the big guns!" Ethan ordered. "Man your bows! Hold bow fire until they're scaling the wall or trying to ram it!"

All around the parapet, some men burst into action while others froze in fear, staring out at the charging army.

Rollie, slightly pale, ran over to the tarps and uncovered the two stone-covered crossbows. He passed one over to a soldier on his right and then ran back past Ethan to his left.

"I hope this works as well as it did when I saw you practice!" Rollie said, aiming the crossbow over the battlement at the approaching mass of people carrying the tree trunks towards doors.

Ethan saw the man touch the trigger of the crossbow, which had a Chymera crystal embedded in it. Blue light flared across the other crystals and a ball of flame the size of a softball sped from the weapon.

The flaming ball flew into the center of the men running at the door, exploding into a twenty-foot diameter fireball that tossed soldiers aside from the concussion. At the same time, another fireball exploded at the front of the two groups, doing the same.

Rocked from the two explosions, the tree trunks dropped to the ground as men were tossed aside by the blasts. Nearly at the same time, Ethan saw lines of men stop several dozen yards from the walls. He cursed as he saw the bows in their hands. "ARCHERS!"

Then enemy archers took aim and even from this

distance, Ethan heard the twang of bow strings as what had to be a hundred arrows suddenly took flight.

"Michalus! Air shield!" he called out.

One small advantage of having fewer men was that he didn't have as many to protect. He channeled *Air* into a protective barrier around his half of the wall, blocking the arrows and sending them scattering in all directions. Michalus did the same for his side.

His own soldiers and volunteers let loose a cheer as the missiles were deflected and Ethan immediately prepared to ward off another batch of arrows.

"Rollie! Pass the crossbow to the next person!" he yelled at the sergeant. "Now!"

The men at the gate were temporarily halted, but the other ten groups were not. They were already starting to raise the trunks towards the walls.

That's when Ethan saw branches hammered into the side of the trunks, like rungs of a ladder. He cursed. That was definitely going to make it easier on them.

"Aim at the men holding the trees! Aim at the base! Push the ladders away!" he yelled. A moment later, Guinevere echoed his cry to the men on the other side of the wall.

"Ethan!" Nia hissed, holding up her bow and pointing to the ground on their side of the wall. "I am out of arrows. I will run down and gather some of the ones deflected from the ground."

Ethan shook his head. His wife's aim and experience with a bow far surpassed any of their volunteers, and probably most of the soldiers as well. "Take over for one of the volunteers and have them do it!"

Nia nodded and hurried over to the closest volunteer and began shouting at him, pointing to the ground. The man nodded, seeming to be relieved to be asked to do something away from the battlements.

Two more explosions sounded just as the tree trunks began hitting the wall. Ethan cursed. Then he heard the twang of bows again and looked to see a swarm of arrows headed their way. "Air Shield!"

Once again, Ethan channeled *Air* to create a shield between the arrows and his men but this time he felt the *Mana* slipping away. Or perhaps, slipping away wasn't a good way to describe it. A better word would be: blocked.

"Duck!" he yelled, realizing he couldn't raise a shield in time and pressed himself against the parapet. As he went down, he saw the tell-tale blue glow of the Chymera crystal on a staff. Tibold! Tibold was blocking him!

The arrows whistled by and thudded around Ethan. He heard a strangled scream and turned his head to see one of the volunteers, who had been slow in reacting, struck in the throat with an arrow.

Ethan started to turn to yell for Par'karr. He'd given the kobold the portal pouch with the Grail, since he was small and maneuverable. Before he could call out to his friend, he saw the man stagger backwards and fall off the parapet, to the ground fifty feet below. Judging by the broken position of the body, there was no doubt the man was dead. Ethan cursed.

Growling, Ethan turned back to the bowman and picked out Tibold. The wizard was costing him lives. He had to be stopped.

"Nia!" he called out. "Target the enemy wizard, Tibold."

The foxgirl nodded, adjusting her aim and letting an arrow loose. The shaft flew towards the wizard but at the last minute, bounced against something solid. Ethan smirked. Tibold could use *Air* shields too. Fine. Two can play at that game.

"Again!" he told Nia. "But wait for my signal."

Two more explosions sounded from the base of the wall as his men continued to use the Fireball Crossbows to good effect. Several of his volunteers rushed a spot and shoved against a tree trunk, knocking it away from the wall. It swayed and then fell backwards, away from the wall. Good, one down... nine more to go.

Focusing back on the wizard, Ethan nodded to Nia. "Now!"

His wife aimed carefully and let her arrow fly. Ethan focused in on Tibold and as he felt the man conjuring *Air*, he shoved his own *Mana* into the spell, preventing it from forming. He felt the wizard trying again, this time more hastily but Ethan countered again.

Tibold's attempts stopped suddenly as Nia's arrow found its mark. The man's left arm went limp, his staff falling from his grasp. Ethan saw the enemy wizard drop to the ground, hiding behind the line of archers as he struggled to get to his staff with his right hand.

"That's not happening," Ethan growled. He winked at Nia. "Be right back!"

Before she could object, he activated his *Elemental Armor*, choosing Earth. As the protective coating of stone surrounded his skin, he conjured a portal and slipped through.

Ethan appeared exactly where he had intended, next

to Tibold. The wizard, on his hands and knees, looked up at him with wide eyes.

"I'd kill you right here," Ethan growled at the man. "But there are too few wizards left. But if you interfere again, I'll portal you out to the ocean."

Archers around him began to notice him and a cry went up. Ethan reached down, grabbed Tibold's staff and conjured a portal. He grimaced as he felt multiple impacts against his back, along with piercing pain.

```
Moonpoint archer pierces you for 2
damage.
   Royal armor absorbs 3 points of
piercing damage.
   Elemental armor (earth) absorbs 5
points of piercing damage.
   Moonpoint archer pierces you for 3
damage.
   Royal armor absorbs 3 points of
piercing damage.
   Elemental armor (earth) absorbs 5
points of piercing damage.
   Moonpoint archer pierces you for 2
damage.
   Royal armor absorbs 3 points of
piercing damage.
   Elemental armor (earth) absorbs 5
points of piercing damage.
   Moonpoint      archer      critically
pierces you for 7 damage.
```

>   **Royal armor absorbs 3 points of piercing damage.**
>
>   **Elemental armor (earth) absorbs 5 points of piercing damage.**
>
>   **Moonpoint archer pierces you for 3 damage.**
>
>   **Royal armor absorbs 3 points of piercing damage.**
>
>   **Elemental armor (earth) absorbs 5 points of piercing damage.**

Staggering, he slipped through the portal and back onto the parapet. Feeling his knees buckling, he grabbed onto the parapet for support. He looked around for the kobold. "Par'karr!"

Nia rushed over to him in a blur and tackled him to the ground just as another wave of arrows thudded into the battlements around him. He heard her yelp as one struck her leg.

Gritting his teeth, he called for Par'karr again only to have the kobold peek over Nia. His friend took one look at Ethan and scrambled for the pouch at his waist, pulling out the Grail. Par'karr grabbed a flask of water from his belt and poured a little into the chalice.

Ethan took the offered Grail but Nia shook her head. "Not yet! We must remove the arrows first!"

Ignoring her own wound, she crawled around to Ethan's back and hissed. "You are lucky! One of them just missed your spine! It looks like it might have nicked it."

Gritting his teeth against the pain, Ethan nodded.

"Yeah. That sounds about right. Just get the arrows out so I can use the Grail."

Nia looked at him grimly. "There will be pain."

"Just do it," he hissed through gritted teeth.

"Down!" Par'karr yelled, pushing himself against the wall as another wave of arrows landed all around them. Ethan heard a man cry out and twisted his head to see one of the soldiers with an arrow in his shoulder.

"Hurry so we can heal him too!" Ethan said and then screamed as Nia pulled one of the arrows free.

"Geez!" he said. "A little warning would be... Argh!"

She pulled another one out and he stopped talking and focused on not passing out. Instead, he listened to the men yelling around him and more explosions at the base of the wall.

After another minute and a lot more pain, the arrows were gone. Ethan gulped down the contents of the Grail. Instantly, he felt better. The pain in his back subsided and he felt his *Mana* and *Stamina* completely renewed. He sighed in relief and pushed the Grail towards Nia.

The twang of bowstrings drew his attention then and he looked over the battlement to see another swarm of arrows hearing their way. This time, Ethan was able to get an *Air* shield in place, sending the arrows skidding harmlessly around them.

A horn sounded in the distance and Ethan twisted his head around to see where it was coming from. A cheer went up from his men and he looked down to see the Moonpoint army was retreating.

"Hold your fire!" he yelled as some of his men shot arrows down at the retreating figures. He lowered his voice slightly. "Use the time to gather arrows. Collect any arrows that are good enough to be fired again. Do it now!"

Nia, having removed the arrow from her leg, drank from the Grail and handed the chalice back to Par'karr. "See to the injured man. Remember to have him remove the arrow first!"

The little kobold bobbed his head and then raced over to help the soldier with the arrow wound.

Ethan stood up, looking over the parapets at the retreating army. Guinevere and Michalus came to stand next to him and Nia.

"They're retreating!" Michalus said with a grin. "We've done it!"

"No," Guinevere said, pointing out at the large mass of soldiers. "They're sending them back into the trees to get more tree trunks."

Nia, whose eyes were darting back and forth, suddenly growled. "They are doing more than that!"

Ethan looked down at the foxgirl, her tail swishing angrily back and forth. "I can see men moving through the trees. Men without torches. They are circling the city!"

"Loki's Balls!" Guinevere cursed. "They must have figured out we only have a handful of men. They're going to attack one - perhaps both - of the other gates at the same time."

Ethan cursed. Things had just gone from bad to worse.

44

Ethan and his group had known this was always a possibility. They'd talked about it as they were preparing. After all, it was foolish to believe the enemy wouldn't eventually notice how few men they had. He'd hoped it would have taken longer but given their actions, they had figured it out sooner rather than later.

"Guinevere! Drorm! You take the men we designated to the south gate! You take the crossbows!" he yelled, pointing to the opposite side of the city. "Rollie! Take your team to the south eastern gate! Michalus, I need you to go with them and provide magic support!"

Ethan looked down at Par'karr and then back to the two teams. "If someone on your team is hurt or in need of healing, fire a fireball into the air and Par'karr will run to you as fast as possible."

Par'karr patted the portal pouch at his waist, looked around at the men staring back and bobbed his head. "Par'karr fast runner!"

"Go, people! Go!" he told them and the two groups split off from his own group.

As the men from the other groups climbed down from the parapets, Ethan looked at the sparsely manned wall. He barely had two soldiers and eleven volunteers now. Thirteen men, plus Nia and him. He also no longer had the Fireball Crossbows. That meant he would manually have to take care of any trees coming their way. He checked his HUD.

Mana: 118

The lull in action had given him enough time to regenerate most of his *Mana*. But once the fighting picked up again, he'd be limited to what he had. Since he'd already used the Grail today to heal his back, he no longer had the option of using it to restore his *Mana*.

Nia leaned in close to him. "If the enemy breaks through the gate, we do not have enough men to hold."

"I know," he replied quietly. Ethan looked out at the enemy army, visible only by their torches. They had killed some of the attackers and wounded many more. But even splitting up, the Moonpoint army still had hundreds of men.

Par'karr walked over to Ethan and handed him the magical shotgun and a pouch full of rounded stones. "Ethan use. If Par'karr run, Par'karr not able to use."

"Thanks, buddy," Ethan told his friend, taking the boomstick from the kobold. He looked out at the mass of torches. Compared to the sheer size of the army, he wasn't sure the shotgun would really make much of a difference.

They waited another half hour before men began to come out of the forest with fresh tree trunks. His men had used the time to gather any usable arrows. As it turned out, that was dozens of arrows. Unfortunately, they'd split the archers between the three gates.

"Par'karr!" he yelled, getting the kobold's attention. His friend looked up from gathering arrows. "Take the bundle of arrows you have now and three more and run them to the east gate. Drop off two bundles there and then drop off two bundles at the south gate."

Par'karr bobbed his head, gathered up the arrows and scurried down the ladder to the bottom of the parapets. Ethan watched his friend and his rabbits running down the road until they disappeared behind some buildings.

Turning, Ethan looked out at the men assembling in front of their gate. He did a quick count. Eight tree trunks. Less than before but still a lot. Someone was shouting and the men with the trees began to line up, just out of bow range.

Each tree trunk was being carried by a dozen men, six on each side. Behind the trees were groups of men Ethan recognized as archers. There weren't nearly as many archers as there had been before, but still four or so times their number. He would still have to expend a good amount of his *Mana* creating *Air* shields. Or would he?

Ethan looked around the parapets, cocking his head one way and then the other as an idea started forming.

"Are you well?" Nia asked, noticing his behavior.

"I have an idea," he said and then began channeling *Earth*. He reached out to the raised portions of the parapets and on every other parapet, he manipulated the stone and shaped it into a curved shield.

After he was finished shaping them, he looked at his handiwork. There were thirteen of the stone shields, enough for each man to hide under when the arrows came. He raised his voice so all of the men could hear him. "When they launch their arrows, duck under the shields. I'm going to conserve my *Mana* to take out the trees, so use them!"

There was a general muttering of agreement from the men, who all wore grim expressions.

"They are preparing to charge!" Nia growled, pointing out to the men. No sooner had she said it when a horn sounded behind the archers. Then another horn sounded to the east. After a moment, a faint horn sounded from the area of the east gate.

Setting his jaw, Ethan cursed. "Here we go again."

The men carrying the trees yelled and charged forward. Not for the first time that night, Ethan considered raising a wall of flame. He'd done a similar trick with the ogres to good effect. Unfortunately, a wall of flame that large would take nearly all of his *Mana*. He needed to conserve his magic. Unless he wanted to get down and dirty with Nia right here on the parapets, he had no way to replenish his *Mana* for the time being.

Ethan raised Excalibur and looked out at his men. Nia and the three bowmen drew back their arrows and waited for his command. "Fire at will!"

Bows twanged and arrows flew and one or two of the men carrying the trees fell. But the enemy archers moved up and released their own volley. Once more, arrows darkened the night sky, seeking out Ethan and his men.

"To the shields!" he cried and ducked under his own shield. A few moments later, arrows bounced off the shields and thudded around them. As soon as the arrow bombardment finished, Ethan looked out from the shield.

He cursed. The approaching men had covered half the distance. Two groups were running straight for the gate. They were the biggest threat. Without any sort of bracing, he had no idea how long the gates could hold out against their makeshift battering rams.

Ethan saw that he only had seconds before the archers released the next volley. Channeling *Fire*, he strained to reach the wood of the logs being carried. He furrowed his brow as he focused on heating up the wood. He kept channeling *Fire* until both logs burst into flames. The men carrying them immediately dropped the blazing tree trunks, stepping away to avoid the heat.

He started to grin and then Nia grabbed him and pulled him under the shield just in time to avoid being skewered by arrows. Around him, arrows thudded and bounced off the shield, some coming in at angles that threatened to get to them.

"You must pay attention!" she chastised him. "They are targeting you!"

He blinked. Ethan had been so intent on channeling the fire, he hadn't even heard the twang of the enemy bows or seen the arrows. He also hadn't noticed that they were targeting him. "What?"

"The enemy archers spread out," she said. She looked

down at the glowing blue gem in Excalibur. "They are targeting you from more angles now!"

Ethan cursed. The same thing that had given away Tibold was now giving him away and making him a target. He smiled at his wife. "Thanks."

"Just be careful!" she shot back and then ducked back around just as thuds sounded along the wall. At nearly the same time, a crashing of wood sounded at the gate.

Ethan stood up from behind the shield and looked over the wall. Two groups of men were backing away from the gate, preparing to ram it again. He cursed. They'd diverted two of the remaining tree trunks to the gate.

Once more, Ethan reached out and channeled *Fire* into the trees. This time it was easier and quicker since the logs were closer. After only a moment, the logs burst into flames.

He was turning to look at the logs up against the wall when he was tackled to the ground. He heard arrows whistling just above him as he hit the floor of the battlements with a thud.

Looking up, he saw Nia on top of him. She growled. "I told you, the archers have moved closer. They are targeting you directly now!"

"Great! Just..." Ethan stopped as he saw the pained expression on his wife's face.

Looking around her, he saw an arrow sticking out of her shoulder. "You're hit! I'll call back Par'karr!"

"No need," she said, gritting her teeth. "I already used it earlier."

Ethan cursed as he remembered. They'd both used the Grail. He cursed again. "Let me at least..."

She shook her head. "No! You must burn the other trees. I will be okay. It is not a deep wound."

He started to protest but she pushed herself off him. "I will live! You must stop the enemy from scaling the walls! Now!"

Growling, but knowing she was right, Ethan got to his feet but stayed crouched. He kept Excalibur and its gem below the parapet so he wouldn't be such an easy target. Fueled by anger at Nia's injury, he channeled *Fire* and his anger into the trees and set them ablaze, taking a perverse pleasure in hearing the screams of the men who had been trying to climb them. That would teach them to hurt his wife!

But it wasn't enough. He looked around and saw that Nia had been right. The archers had moved in closer, trying to get a better angle to target Ethan and the other defenders. They were close now. Their mistake.

He let a sadistic smile come over his face. They'd hurt his wife. *Mana* or no, it was payback time. Channeling all the *Mana* he could, he pushed it and his anger out onto the field causing a wall of flame to erupt under the line of archers.

The earth in front of the gate was suddenly bathed in orange and yellow flickering light as the fire engulfed the enemy archers. Screams echoed across the battlefield and Ethan saw the Moonpoint soldiers retreating back, beating out flames or writhing on the ground begging for someone to extinguish them.

Ethan might have watched the spectacle longer but his legs felt weak and he sank down behind the parapets next to Nia. She smiled at him. "They are retreating. You have done it."

Even as Nia was speaking, Ethan saw a large fireball launched into the sky from the east gate. At nearly the same time, he saw a smaller fireball above the south gate. He cursed. The other two gates were in trouble.

45

Ethan started to push himself to his feet, but Nia pulled him down. "Where are you going?!"

"I need to get to the other gates and see if I can help," he replied wearily. He brought up his HUD.

Mana: 3

He cursed as he saw how little *Mana* he had.

"What is wrong?" she asked.

"I'm basically completely out of mana," he revealed. "I have no magic."

Despite the pained expression and weariness in her face, she winked at him. "I know how to solve that problem."

Ethan chuckled despite the weight of the situation. Then he cocked his head as he saw her expression. "You're serious?"

"Yes," she said with a grim nod. "You need mana. I can help you get your mana back."

He shook his head. "We don't have that much time."

"We can be quick," she retorted, her expression showing that she was still serious.

Ethan opened his mouth to object but was interrupted by a man's shout. He perked up and tried to understand what the man was saying.

"Breach!" came the man's voice, about the same time Ethan heard the enemy horns from the eastern gate.

The man stopped a few dozen yards from them and looked up. It was one of the soldiers, but Ethan couldn't remember his name. He pointed east. "The east gate's been breached. We couldn't hold them!"

Cursing again, Ethan motioned to two men on the wall. "You, run to the east gate, tell them to fall back to the keep! You, do the same with the south gate!"

The men, neither of whom were soldiers, just stared at him wide-eyed. Ethan sighed. He pointed to the only two guards he had. "You two, go tell the gates to retreat. Now!"

Thankfully, the soldiers were more disciplined. The two nodded to him, keeping their heads low. "Yes, sire!"

"As you go, yell out that the enemy has breached the city!" he told them as they began to climb down the ladders. "Tell them if they want protection, they should come to the keep now!"

"Yes, sire!" the guards answered. They hit the ground, spun and ran off.

"We're retreating back to the keep too!" Ethan barked to the other men. "Grab your bows and all the arrows you can bring with you and head to the keep!" When the men didn't immediately move, Ethan yelled. "Now!"

Ethan turned back to his wife, who was twisting in place. She reached back and pointed to the arrow in her shoulder blade. "Pull the arrow free."

"But..." he started but she talked over him.

"I cannot use this arm very well until the arrow is removed," she explained. "I will not be able to climb down the ladder if you do not remove it."

Nodding, he grabbed onto the shaft of the arrow. She flinched as he did so but gave him a grim look. "Now, pull it out."

Clenching his teeth, Ethan pulled the arrow back as straight as he could. He felt his wife's body go tense as the shaft came free. She let out a low whimper but then rolled her shoulders.

The wound bled, but not as bad as he had thought. It should be okay until they got back to the keep and he could get a bandage on her.

"That is good," she said. "I will be able to climb down now. Come. We must go."

The two of them joined the men in climbing down. When they reached the ground, Ethan called out to the men with him. "If any of you have families, go to them now. Get them and bring them to the keep. Call out to anyone else to come to the keep or they'll have to take their chances with Moonpoint."

The men grunted and then most of them ran off. Ethan looked at the three men who remained. "You can go too!"

The men looked at each other and shrugged. "We ain't got no families to go get."

"Then each of you pick a direction and run that way. Shout for people to come to the keep. Tell them the walls are breached," he told them.

After giving him a nod or half-hearted salute, the three ran off in different directions, yelling at the top of their lungs. Ethan shook his head as he watched them go and then turned to Nia. "Come on, let's get back to the keep."

He and Nia walked quickly towards the keep, yelling as loudly as they could for people to come with them. A few people came out of their houses. Some just went back inside while others took a handful of belongings and ran towards the keep.

When they reached the keep, Ethan saw that the inside of the courtyard was already full of people. Several hundred people. He shook his head. For all he knew, this was all the people left in the city.

Pushing his way through, Ethan and Nia managed to make it to the door of the main hall. After pounding on the door for several minutes, combined with a bit of yelling, the door was finally opened. It was Lucius.

"Your majesty," he sighed. "Thank the gods it is you."

Ethan pushed his way into the hall, followed by Nia. Once they were in, Lucius slammed the door shut and barred it. He straightened himself and then turned to face them. "I take it things did not go as well as you had hoped."

"No," he replied. "They figured out we had no one

guarding the other gates and redeployed their troops. Separated, it appears we couldn't fight them off."

Nia was looking around the hall. "Have any of our other companions returned?"

"No, your majesty," the castellan replied to her. Ethan was happy to see that he also addressed her as "your majesty." She was queen, after all. At least, for the moment. Of course, a hostile army which vastly outnumbered them had just broken through the city gates. His days as king and her days of being queen might be coming to an abrupt end.

Even as the thought came to him, he wondered where Firestorm was. Ethan had wanted to reach out to the dragon to find out where he was. Unfortunately, the only way he could initiate contact with the dragon was to scry him first. Since the siege had started, he didn't have the *Mana* to spare to first scry the dragon and then start a telepathic link with him.

Either the dragon would show up in time or he wouldn't. For now, he had to act like the dragon wasn't going to show up. Ethan had to operate like everything depended on them.

Ethan turned to Lucius. "We're going to need to start letting people in here."

"Your majesty!" Lucius squeaked. "In here?! But... but..."

"Lucius," he shot back. "In a few hours, maybe a day... possibly two, this keep could fall. At that point, nothing in this place will matter. We need to get as many people into the keep as possible."

Lucius had turned pale. "But..."

"How about we stick with the elderly and the infirm,

plus any pregnant women," Ethan suggested. "Let's start with them and see how much room gets taken up."

Lucius closed his mouth and nodded. "As you wish, your majesty."

Ethan grabbed his wife's hand and started up the stairs. He looked back at Lucius. "I'm going to put a bandage on my wife's back and uh... work on recovering my mana... before the Moonpoint soldiers get here."

"As you say, your majesty," he replied stoically.

He led Nia upstairs to their bedroom and shut the door behind him. "Okay, take off your shirt."

She did as she was told and removed her armor and shirt. While she did that, Ethan found a silk shirt that belonged to the former prince. He ripped it into long bandages and then turned to face her.

Instead of just taking off her shirt, she had removed all of her clothing. He swallowed. "Uh... I was going to bandage your shoulder first."

His wife slid her hand across the wound and showed him her palm. "The bleeding has stopped. We must restore your mana while we have time. Come."

Knowing it was pointless to argue with her, and also knowing he desperately needed all of his *Mana* for the upcoming conflict, he joined her on the bed.

Quicker than he thought possible, they were done and he was dressing her shoulder injury. He was back to full *Mana* now and after washing out the wound with water from a basin, he wrapped it tightly with the silk bandages.

Once that was complete, they both got dressed again. They were heading towards the door when it burst open.

Drorm and Guinevere, both spattered with blood, entered the room.

"Recharging your mana?" Guinevere snickered. Ethan opened his mouth to answer but she held up a hand, her face becoming deathly serious. "That's good. You'll need it. Plus some."

"Are you two alright?" Ethan asked, waving at the blood that covered them.

"We're fine," Drorm snorted. "We ran into Par'karr on the way back here. Besides, most of the blood isn't ours."

"It looks like we lost the gates," Ethan said with a shake of his head.

"We never really thought we could hold them once they figured out we didn't have the manpower to defend them," Guinevere pointed out. "We knew that going in. It just happened sooner than we expected."

"How long before they're at the keep?" Ethan asked, grabbing Excalibur from the dresser and strapping the sword around his waist.

"It depends," Drorm said, scratching his head. "Whether they search the city first, or come right here."

Ethan remembered the pain, bordering on madness, he'd seen in the princess's eyes. "They'll come straight here."

"Then we don't have much time," Nia said, looking up at him. "We need to shore up our defenses."

"Nia's right," Ethan said. "Let's get the gate manned with as many archers as possible. I want to get up there too. Now that I have mana, I have a few ideas to make their lives miserable."

Drorm grinned. "I like the sound of that."

46

The keep was almost a tiny, walled city in itself. While it shared a wall with the city, the inner keep had two towers separating it from those walls. Combined with an indented gate, it gave the defenders a decided advantage against attackers trying to ram the doors. That was especially true if one, or more, of the defenders were mages.

Ethan met up with the rest of his friends outside the main hall, along with Mertin. The channeler saw him coming and immediately hurried over. "Ethan..."

"Your majesty," Nia corrected him. "He is king."

Mertin blinked at the foxgirl but then gave Ethan an apologetic expression. "Sorry, your majesty, I'm afraid I am a bit flustered by the recent events."

Waving the man's concerns away, he motioned him to continue. "It's been a trying night for everyone."

"Yes, yes," the channeler said, bobbing his head. "But... your majesty... the books in the library..."

"Are extremely valuable," Ethan finished grimly. "I know. I hope the people of Moonpoint have enough sense not to destroy knowledge like that."

"But..." Mertin started, clearly not satisfied with Ethan's answer.

"Mertin," Ethan stopped him, gesturing around. "The Moonpoint army is inside the city. We've gathered everyone who would come into the keep. There's nothing I can do about the library. I have no men and whatever magic I have, I need for the defense of the keep."

Mertin opened his mouth as if to say something but then glanced around at the men and women huddled together. Ethan didn't have Nia's sense of smell, but even he noticed the scent of fear in the air.

"I see your point," Mertin said flatly, his disappointment obvious. He belatedly added, "Your majesty."

"If we can hold out against them, we'll do what we can for the library," Ethan promised. "But I could use your help up on the gate."

"I... I... " the channeler stuttered before taking a deep breath and letting it out. "I guess nowhere is safe if they break in."

"No," Ethan agreed. "And your magic will be much more effective from up there than down here."

Mertin nodded slowly. "I will do what I can.... Your majesty."

"I appreciate that," he said. "I was heading up there now. You can come with me."

Catching sight of a weary-looking Michalus, Ethan turned to address the wizard. "You're looking a bit worse for wear."

"We had a lot of archers," Michalus replied. "I tried to keep up the air shield and fireball the attackers, but I'm afraid I don't have the stamina I once did."

Ethan noticed a bloody, ragged hole in the elf's robes, over his left pectoral. He saw more blood on his right shoulder. He gestured to the blood. "Are you okay?"

The wizard nodded. "I took a couple of arrows but I used the..."

"Potion," Ethan supplied, throwing a meaningful glance at Mertin. They hadn't told the channeler, or anyone outside their group, about the Grail. For now, he intended to keep it that way.

"Potion, yes, the potion cured my wounds," Michalus finished with a nod of understanding.

Looking around, Ethan checked out the rest of his friends. Nearly all of them had injuries of some type, most of which had been healed. That was good and bad. It was good because they had all survived and were healed. It was bad because none of them could use the Grail for another 24 hours.

"They're coming! To your posts!" came a cry from the gate. He thought it sounded like Rollie.

"Come on," he told the others. "Let's get up there."

Ethan and Nia headed to the ladders that led up onto the wall. Mertin and the others followed them. They climbed up and spotted a bloody Rollie. Walking over, he looked the man up and down.

"Yeah, I know," the sergeant said with a cocky grin. "My uniform's not up to muster."

"You okay?" Ethan asked, gesturing at the blood on his uniform.

Rollie's grin faded and he looked down. "I'm okay. Whatever potion you gave the kobold really does the trick." The sergeant bit his lip before continuing. "I lost a couple of my boys. They got hit in places that don't heal."

"I'm sorry, Rollie," Ethan said, putting a hand on the man's shoulder. "I'll do what I can for their families if we get through this."

The soldier shrugged. "Ain't got no families. That's why they joined the guard. But that's what happens in war. And this is war, right?"

"Yes, it is," Ethan agreed soberly. "A war your uncle started and we have to finish... one way or the other."

Rollie stood taller and nodded. "It's going to be tough for them to get in here. Place is, quite literally, a fortress."

"Where are the crossbows?" Ethan asked, looking around.

The sergeant grimaced. "We lost one when one of my men got hit. He fell backwards on the parapet and took it with him. It broke. The other one is in the guard house until we need it."

Ethan looked out into the city, at the sea of torches that were approaching them. "I think we need it."

Rollie left and his friends closed in around him.

"I take it you have a plan?" Guinevere asked, eyebrow raised.

He nodded, looking at the paved street in front of the keep. "I was thinking about completely covering the door in a couple of feet of stone."

Everyone turned and looked out at the approach to the keep. Guinevere tilted her head one way and then the other. "That might slow them down, but a good ram - even a shoddy ram, for that matter - is going to crack even a couple feet of stone eventually."

"But it might buy us some time," Ethan pointed out.

"We do not have much time," Drorm said grimly. He turned and pointed to the mass of people in the courtyard and surrounding buildings. "How much food stores do you have? How many days of food do you have for those people?"

Ethan frowned. He honestly didn't know. But he had a feeling it wasn't nearly enough. "We can portal out to get food."

Drorm chuckled and looked at Guinevere, who nodded. She smiled bitterly. "There's several hundred people down there. You'd need a dozen or more hunters hunting all day to feed them."

Looking down, he knew they were right. But what they didn't know was that they only needed to hold out for a day or so more - he hoped.

"There's also the fact that if you are using your magic for portals," Drorm explained, "you will not have magic for defending the gates. Our enemies will exploit that."

Ethan threw up his hands. "I'm open to suggestions."

"Send people away," Par'karr suggested.

Ethan blinked and looked down at the kobold with a frown. "What?!"

Par'karr shrank back, lowering his head. "Send people away."

"We can't just abandon these..." Ethan started but Michalus touched his arm.

"He has a point," the wizard said. "You could send

these people through a portal, somewhere safe, until the conflict is resolved - either way."

"Oh!" Ethan said, giving the kobold a sheepish look. "You mean send them through the portal."

Par'karr grinned and bobbed his scaly head up and down. "Send them to safe place. Not here."

Ethan looked back down on the hundreds of people. He frowned. "I can't send them all in one go. And I don't even know where I'd send them. I don't really have markers in any villages except Hawkshead."

Nia shrugged. "Any place might be better than here."

The approaching army caught his attention and he turned his head to see men carrying tree trunks as makeshift battering rams once again. He shook his head.

"I won't be able to send them away tonight." Ethan looked over to the horizon. There was a faint glow, indicating sunrise wasn't too far away. "Or should I say, this morning. Let me slow down the army first and then I'll.... Argh!"

Right in the middle of talking, pain suddenly exploded in Ethan's head. It hit him so suddenly, it took him a moment to erect a mental firewall. Even once he got his mental shield up, he could feel the attack on his mind hitting him over and over, making him feel like he had a nasty headache.

"Ethan!" Nia cried. "What is wrong?!"

He looked around and then looked at the approaching army. He grimaced. "Someone's attacking me with mental magic!"

"Are you sure..." Michalus started and then he went down to his knees, hands coming up to his head. "Ahhh!"

Remembering that the wizard didn't know mental magic, Ethan realized Michalus couldn't erect a defense. He cursed and hurriedly constructed a mental shield around him as well. But it cost him.

Mana: 91

Ethan cursed through the pain. "Someone's attacking us and they're powerful."

"Very," groaned Michalus, pushing himself back to his feet.

"Is it Tibold?" Ethan asked the wizard.

"I don't remember him having this sort of mastery over mind magic, but it has been a while," Michalus replied.

"You are well?" Nia asked.

"I'm okay," Ethan said with a frown. "But it's all I can do to keep the mental attacks away from Michalus and myself."

"That's probably the point," Guinevere growled.

"They must have a second wizard," Michalus said, rubbing the sides of his head. "Someone I don't know."

"Whoever they are, they're really strong with mind magic," Ethan acknowledged. He guessed whoever it was had specialized in Mind magic, like he had specialized in Aether magic.

Ethan scanned the incoming mass of people, trying to find the wizard attacking him but there was no tell-tale blue glow from a Chymera crystal. No sign of a wizard at all.

He growled, massaging his temples. "Well, this complicates things."

47

Ethan was still scanning the crowd, looking for the attacking wizard when he noticed something. He cursed.

"What is wrong?" Nia asked, her hands going to her weapons.

"Michalus," he snapped, getting the wizard's attention. "Did you sense any magic being cast?"

The elf cocked his head one way, then the other. "Now that you mention it, I don't. But I wouldn't necessarily sense it if it's a type of magic I'm not familiar with."

"Like mental magic," Ethan said.

"Right," the elf agreed. He gestured at Ethan. "But you can work mental magic. You should be able to sense a wizard casting it."

That's what he had suspected. But if that were the case, then why wasn't he sensing it? "What about channelers and warlocks? Can we sense them?"

"Channelers, certainly," the elf replied. Michalus

looked to Mertin for confirmation and the channeler nodded. "Now, warlocks. That's a different matter."

Ethan sighed. "Of course it is. Why can't we sense them?"

He took a moment to check his HUD.

Mana: 74

"It has to do with the way they actually get their powers," Michalus replied. "And to be perfectly honest, we're not sure exactly how that happens."

"Very true," Mertin agreed. "Channelers get their power through the transformation of their bodies. The more their body transforms, the more they are able to channel power inherently - just like the demon they make the pact with."

"And warlocks?" Ethan asked.

"Well," Michalus said, looking at the channeler. "No one's certain precisely how it happens. We suspect there is some sort of link between the two entities and the power is transferred through the link. That is why they... uh..."

"Go insane?" Ethan provided helpfully, remembering the warlock who had tried to kill him in Patheos.

"Not precisely technically correct," Mertin said.

"But close enough," the wizard said.

"They're about to start the bombardment!" Guinevere said, looking over the parapet and down at the men with the tree trunks. While they'd been talking, the Moonpoint soldiers had gotten into position.

Ethan tried to focus on *Earth* magic, to raise a carpet of spikes from the cobbled road. Unfortunately, he couldn't quite concentrate enough while maintaining the mental shield on both himself and Michalus.

The Moonpoint soldiers must have realized who he was and he heard the twang of bows as archers released a volley of arrows at them.

"Arrows!" he yelled and then threw himself atop Nia, low on the parapet. A moment later, he heard the whistle of arrows as they slashed through the air just above their heads.

Unfortunately, the arrows kept flying, gradually losing altitude until they dove into the mass of people in the courtyard. Ethan heard screams and cries of pain as the arrows fell upon hapless townsfolk. Then the first thunderous bang shook the air as the ram hit the thick, wooden gates.

"Return fire! Get that fireball crossbow out here!" Ethan cried out. He turned to Mertin. "Blast those men on the ram with all you got."

The channeler nodded, though Ethan could see the man was terrified. He was used to reading about wars in a book, not being right on the front lines of one.

"Michalus!" Ethan called, turning to the wizard. "Get into the main hall. Hopefully the wizard or warlock can't target you there and I won't have to keep the shield on you."

The wizard nodded and started for the ladder just as one of the soldiers yelled "Arrows!"

Everyone ducked behind the parapets as a fresh wave of arrows soared past them, only to descend into the crowd below. Ethan cursed.

"Return fire!" he shouted. He spun on Michalus. "Go! Now! I need to be able to counterattack!"

Nodding, Michalus hurried over to the ladder and hurriedly climbed down. Ethan tested the mental firewall but still felt attacks coming against both of them. He growled.

Looking around at his friends, he saw Par'karr reloading his shotgun. The kobold's rabbits were huddled around him, their eyes darting around the parapet. "Par'karr! Can you summon your rabbits below us and have them attack the men's legs?"

Par'karr looked down at the rabbits and then over the parapet. He gave Ethan a toothy grin and then nodded.

As Par'karr went about resummoning his rabbits at the bottom of the wall, Ethan realized he could still help out - even with his focus being on maintaining his mental defenses. Mustering his *Mana*, he used his *Summon Elemental* ability to summon a fire elemental at the bottom of the wall. He knew he could communicate mentally with it, but he shouted out anyhow. "Burn them all!"

Another loud crash echoed around the courtyard as the ram continued to thunder against the gates. Then screams began as demon rabbits and his fire elemental began attacking the men holding the tree trunk.

Another wave of arrows and they were all forced to duck back behind the parapets. He saw Michalus duck into the main hall, just before the arrows found marks in the people filling the courtyard.

He tested the firewall and, as he suspected, that must either be too far for the wizard or warlock - or it had

broken their line of sight. With a slight effort, he disman-
tled the defenses he'd put around Michalus's mind.

He checked his HUD again, looking at how much
Mana he had left.

Mana: 59

Ethan frowned then, brow furrowing - and not just
from the amount of *Mana* the mental defense had
cost him.

If the wizard was on the opposite side of the wall, why
had it taken so long for him to lose contact with Michalus.
Like portal magic, the wizard needed to either be able to
see the target, or they had to know the mind really well.
Which was it?

With some of his concentration now free, Ethan
popped up from behind the parapet and looked at the
scene below. The fire elemental, in the shape of a large
ferret or mongoose, was hopping around burning soldiers
holding the makeshift ram. At the same time, Par'karr's
demon rabbits were leaping in and out of their lines,
maiming men with their horns.

Both the rabbits and the fire elemental were still near
the front of the line. Ethan targeted the soldiers further in
line. With a burst of *Earth* magic, nine-inch stone spikes
erupted from the cobbled road.

Soldiers screamed as the spikes impaled their feet.
The entire back of the tree trunk collapsed as men fell to
the ground, writhing in pain. Unfortunately for them,
some of them fell onto even more spikes, causing grievous
wounds in their legs and torso.

But the victory was short lived as more men surged forward to take their place. They brought clubs and maces to smash down the spikes, beginning to clear the area for another attack.

He checked his *Mana* level after his little stunt and cursed.

Mana: 31

Ethan still had to keep his own mental defense up, so he couldn't risk any more magic. He chuckled mirthlessly. Whoever the wizard or warlock was mentally attacking him, they'd done their job well. He was now effectively useless.

Another wave of arrows hit and Ethan heard a strangled gurgle from one of the guards. He looked over just in time to see the man with the fireball crossbow go tumbling over the parapet to the cobblestone road below. The man had four arrows in his head, chest and throat.

"No!" he cried out, watching the crossbow shatter below. He cursed. It looked like more than just a random shot. They'd targeted the man specifically. Not good. "Par'karr! Mertin! Be careful! They're picking high-value targets!"

"High-value targets?" Par'karr repeated, cocking his head in confusion.

"It means," Ethan said, "if you or Mertin stick your head up, they're going to fill you full of arrows."

"Oh my," Mertin said.

"They have more archers," Nia said from behind him. "And better trained than these guards and volunteers."

Ethan nodded. The Moonpoint archers were actual archers. His people were just guards and volunteers that knew how to use a bow without hurting themselves. "We might be out of options."

"There are always options," Guinevere said from the other side. "They're just not always good ones."

He saw the wild look into the woman's eyes and frowned. "It looks like you're planning something crazy."

Guinevere shrugged. "I drop down there and cut a swath through those archers. My armor is impenetrable to anything but magical weapons. I could make quite a dent before they take me down."

"Your head and neck are still vulnerable!" Ethan protested. "They'd get you sooner than later."

"I'm a knight," Guinevere replied. "It was always sooner or later for me. At least I can buy you some..."

The light had begun to creep over the horizon, illuminating the area in a dim glow. But even that dim glow disappeared as a massive shadow fell across the keep. Around him, men and women from both sides screamed and pointed to the sky.

Ethan didn't even have to look up to know that Firestorm had arrived. Then the dragon roared. A loud, deep sound that rattled the glass windows in the main hall and something that Ethan could feel all the way to his bones.

As the dragon circled around the city, the mental attack that had been bombarding Ethan's mind stopped. Instead, he heard a familiar mental voice.

I am here, dragon-friend.

48

So relieved was Ethan to see the dragon, he let loose a chuckle that was on the verge of being a cackle. Nia looked at him and gave him a huge grin. Everyone else just continued to stare up at the mammoth form of the dragon as it circled the city.

Firestorm circled once, then twice, before coming down to land on the stone parapets of the gatehouse. His soldiers had scrambled away as the dragon flapped his wings above the parapet, so he did not squash anyone.

Ethan did notice that some of the stonework crumbled beneath the dragon's talons. He didn't care. The whole gatehouse could crumble for all he cared - preferably after he and the others got off it.

I am the one the orcs call Firestorm, the dragon's voice echoed in his head. By the looks of the shocked expressions in his own people and those in the enemy army, everyone was hearing the dragon's voice. *You attack one who has been named dragon-friend, the one called Ethan.*

Ethan saw with satisfaction that the Moonpoint army cowered. He might have been relieved if his own people had been cowering too. Then again, it was a freaking huge dragon. If he hadn't helped the dragon and spoken with it, he might be just as cowed.

Lay down your arms and surrender to the one you call Ethan or I will count you as my enemy, the dragon's voice said. *And destroy you utterly.*

The dragon glared down at the enemy army, extending his wings dramatically, making it look ever larger. *I am not without compassion. You may take a minute to decide.*

The dragon twisted his head around on his long serpentine neck and gave Ethan a wink with his right eye. *Humans are so easy to cow.*

Ethan smiled up at the dragon. He channeled some of his remaining *Mana* to open a mental connection. *Thank you so much for coming.*

I owe you a debt that can never be repaid. My mate is well again and we once again soar through the air together. The dragon inclined his head. *It is a glorious thing.*

I'm glad she is better, Ethan told the dragon, and he meant it.

The dragon turned his head back to the Moonpoint army, his smile replaced by a snarl. *What is your decision? Do you surrender to Ethan or do I dine well tonight?*

"We will not be intimidated!" came a female voice. Ethan thought he recognized it as belonging to the princess. "Moonpoint will avenge our fallen!"

The dragon didn't make a move but Ethan felt an incredible amount of *Fire* magic channeled. Much more than he could ever hope to use and certainly more than he could counter. All of the men near the ram and the archers were engulfed in pillars of fire.

So sudden was the magic and so hot was the fire that the men didn't even have time to cry out. They probably never even knew they had died. They were simply vaporized in an instant. The name Firestorm suddenly took on all-new meaning.

The dragon turned towards the place where Ethan had heard the princess. *If you have chosen death, then so be it.*

"We surrender!" a chorus of voices. It was the Moonpoint army. They threw down their weapons and raised their hands in the air. "We surrender! Do not kill us!"

"No you fool! It is only one dragon!" the princess's voice cried. "Fight it!"

You are the leader? Firestorm asked, head twisting towards the princess. Suddenly a woman's form hovered into the air and floated towards the dragon.

"I am Melody Goldensun! Princess and leader of Moonpoint! Release me this instant!" the princess screamed. Ethan shook his head. The woman had courage, he had to give her that. Not a single working brain cell in her head, but she did have courage.

The dragon left the princess suspended in the air and looked to Ethan. *Shall I end the foolish one?*

Ethan sighed and shook his head. "No, but perhaps she would be better in our custody for now."

As you wish, the dragon said and the princess floated to Ethan.

Nia rushed down the ladder to grab the woman as the dragon released her onto the ground. The foxgirl moved in, twisting the woman's arm behind her back painfully. "You wish me to lock her away?"

"You and Guinevere take her to the main hall, ask Lucius about the cells," Ethan told her. "He'll show you the prison area."

"You cannot do this!" the princess objected. "I am the leader of a free city!"

"If you wish to object to what we're doing," Ethan said. "I can give you back to the dragon. Your choice."

It was a long trip, I am hungry, the dragon said matter-of-factly.

The princess's mouth snapped shut, looking up at the snarling dragon. Firestorm stared back down at her and licked his lips.

Guinevere snorted and joined Nia. Together they escorted the princess to the main hall without another word.

Ethan let out a sigh of relief and looked back up to the dragon. *Thank you.*

The dragon made a motion that could have been a shrug. The dragon looked out at the Moonpoint army. *I go to hunt now. If anyone of Moonpoint is here when I return, I will feast twice today.*

A figure that Ethan recognized stepped into view. It was the catling, Zachus Ajosain, who had been with the princess when they'd met for Parlay.

"Dragon! I am captain of the Moonpoint guard and temporary general of the army," the lion-man said. "I wish to stay and speak with King Ethan about the terms of our surrender."

The dragon looked down at Ethan quizzically. *Do you wish this one to stay?*

"Sure," Ethan replied. He'd run out of *Mana*, so he was no longer able to communicate telepathically.

Very well, you may stay, the dragon replied. *But the rest of your army must leave the city. If they return, it will mean their lives.*

Zachus nodded and gave some hand-signs to his men. A moment later, the catling began walking up to the gate.

I go now, the dragon said, beginning to flap his massive wings. *But I will be close. I will return in one hour.*

The wind created by the dragon's beating wings forced Ethan, and everyone else in the courtyard, to look away. After a few moments, the dragon leaped off the battlements and slowly began to climb. After a minute, he circled the city once and then flew off towards the ocean.

Ethan smiled. If he was anything like his mate, Firestorm probably went to eat some of the pteranodons that frequented the water spouts.

"Open the gate!" Ethan called out. "Let the general in."

His remaining guards rushed to the gate to unbar it and open it just enough for the catling to enter. While they did that, Ethan climbed down himself, along with Drorm and Par'karr. The three of them walked over to the gate and waited.

Finally, the gate was opened and Zachus Ajosain stepped inside. He looked around at the huddled people and then his eyes found Ethan's. He inclined his head. "King Ethan."

"General Zachus," Ethan replied.

Zachus sighed. "I prefer Captain Zachus, or just Zachus. I was only made general for this... crusade."

"Very well, Zachus," Ethan replied. "Just call me Ethan. And this is Drorm and Par'karr."

"Hello!" Par'karr grinned. Drorm just grunted, keeping his eyes on the captain.

"Since the dragon asked that all of my people leave." The Moonpoint captain cleared his throat. "I wonder if I could ask you to allow the ones in here with you to leave as well."

Ethan tried not to look surprised. He had always known it was a possibility that some of the Moonpoint people might have infiltrated the townsfolk. He just hadn't had a way of figuring out who.

"Does that include the wizard?" Ethan asked. "You know, the one good with mind magic. Or is he a warlock?"

The captain's eyes widened only briefly but it was enough for Ethan to know he'd guessed right. He had thought as much when the line of sight hadn't been broken when Michalus climbed down from the parapet. He just hadn't had any way of figuring out who it was.

Zachus cleared his throat. "Soldiers of Moonpoint, we are abandoning this city. Leave now while King Ethan and the dragon allow it."

Ethan turned and watched as a half dozen figures rose to their feet and began walking to the door. They were dressed like normal townsfolk but their expressions were harder.

One of them wore a cloak with the hood pulled up and Ethan guessed it was the warlock. As the man walked by, Ethan reached and pulled back the hood, revealing a young-looking woman. But not a human woman, an elf. She stopped and glared up at him.

The elven woman was plain-looking, enough that she could go unnoticed in a crowd. In fact, her face and her clothes were so nondescript, no one would give her a second glance. He'd seen enough spy movies to know what a person like that was.

```
Meneka Syddi
    Elf
    Wizard
    Level 7
```

"Meneka Syddi," Ethan asked. "A wizard assassin?"

This time, Zachus couldn't hide his surprise. Neither could the woman.

"You know my name?!" she hissed. She glared daggers at the captain.

"I did not tell him!" the captain said, raising his palms. The captain licked his lips, looking from Ethan to the woman. "Meneka Syddi is a special agent for Moonpoint."

"With special skills," the elven woman shot back.

"Which did not seem to work," the captain growled.

Meneka looked at Ethan. He thought he saw respect in her gaze. Respect and curiosity. She shrugged. "His defense is stronger than anyone else I've met. Though I would have worn him down eventually."

Ethan scowled at the woman and then turned to Zachus. "They can all leave. Let's make sure none of them become a snack for Firestorm."

"See you around," the elf said as she left with the others.

Ethan frowned and made sure the elf went out the gate before turning to the captain. "Come, let's talk in the main hall."

Turning, Ethan strode to the main hall, not bothering to wait for the catling.

49

A half hour later, Ethan, Nia, Guinevere, Michalus, Zachus and Princess Melody sat around the dinner table in the main hall. After some convincing from the captain, Ethan had agreed to let the princess sit in on the negotiations.

"It's simple," Ethan had told her. "If you give me a hard time or go off on a tantrum, I will feed you to the dragon when he returns."

Skill increase: Bluff +1%.

The princess had reluctantly agreed at first but once they began talking, she went from an angry, reluctant watcher to a full-blown participant.

"You're willing to just... give the land to farmers who come to work it?" the princess asked for the second time, eyes narrowed.

"Not give," Guinevere corrected. She had been

correcting Ethan a lot during the negotiations. And that was a good thing. He was used to the way things worked on Earth, in a democratic society.

The strange feudal system this world used was wholly unfamiliar as well to Nia. Luckily, Guinevere, having been a queen, knew all about the politics and laws that governed the area - even if some of her experience came from the last millennium on this world.

"It would be a lifelong lease, with the understanding that they continue to work the land," Guinevere explained. "And pay taxes, of course. As is customary."

"Will you allow the farmers to pass it down to their children?" Zachus asked. "We do this in Moonpoint."

Ethan looked at Guinevere and the woman nodded. He smiled. "Yes, they can pass it down to the next generation, so long as they continue to pay taxes and work the land."

Guinevere gave him a small nod of approval and he actually felt like he was starting to catch on to some of this.

"And what about the shop owners you spoke of?" the princess asked.

"Provided no one comes forward within the next month to claim the workshops, and no families claim the tools or other assets," Ethan replied. "Any craftsman who comes to work will be given a year lease for free. After that, I will negotiate with them in good faith to continue the lease - should they wish to."

Once again, the princess' eyes narrowed. "But you will allow them to remain citizens of Moonpoint?"

"As long as they aren't spying, sure, why not," Ethan

said. "They'll still have to pay taxes here, and I assume probably taxes for Moonpoint, but if that's what they want to do, they're welcome to."

"And if they want to leave...?" the princess asked, leaving the question hanging in the air.

"If they've broken no laws here, are up to date on their taxes and aren't spies," Ethen retorted. "They can come and go as they please."

The princess looked pleased until Guinevere cleared her throat. "Provided they are gone for no longer than one month without notifying the crown. Any citizen craftsman who abandons their shop for more than a month without notifying us, will forfeit their rights to the shop and anything in it."

"That seems reasonable," Zachus said, earning a glare from the princess. He quickly shut his mouth. Ethan had a feeling that there would be some harsh words between the princess and the captain on their way home. He just wasn't sure who would come out on top.

"Yes, captain," the princess said, emphasizing his title of "captain." Ethan had noticed she hadn't referred to him as "general" since she'd entered the room. "It does sound... reasonable."

"We would also like to talk about trade," Ethan said. "As you can imagine, we will be in need of much in our efforts to rebuild."

The princess pursed her lips. "Yes, I imagine you do have need of a great many things. But the question is, what is it that you have to offer the people of Moonpoint?"

Ethan sighed inwardly. He had known this was coming. "Right now..."

"At the current time," Guinevere interrupted. "You can imagine that we are not in a position where we have much to trade but that will change soon."

The princess sat back in her chair. "Then what talk of trade can there be if you have nothing to offer."

"Ah," Michalus said, raising a finger up. "But we have something extremely valuable to offer at the moment. Something, I daresay, if impossible to find elsewhere."

Both the princess and Zachus perked up at the wizard's bold proclamation. The princess wrinkled her forehead. "And what is that?"

"The ability to move goods instantaneously," the wizard said triumphantly, giving Ethan a wink. "Imagine what the tradesmen would give to be able to move their goods from one city to another in the time it takes to walk across the room. Imagine the weeks or months that would save them."

The princess and the captain both snapped their heads around to look at Ethan. No doubt, they were remembering his appearance on the battlefield through a portal.

"There hasn't been a wizard who could open portals that large in..." the princess began.

"A hundred and thirty years," Michalus finished. "Gregarus. Nice chap. We never did find out where he disappeared to."

"Was probably assassinated," Guinevere said under her breath.

Zachus looked between Michalus and Ethan for a moment and raised an eyebrow. "Can both of you do it, or just the king?"

"Just me," Ethan said honestly.

"And you would be willing to provide that service yourself," the princess asked, forehead wrinkled even more. "Even though you are... king?"

Ethan shrugged. "If that's what it takes to get the city's economy back up and working, then yes. If I can find enough Chymera crystals, I might even be able to make permanent gateways between cities."

The princess chuckled and turned to Zachus. "I imagine the traders' guild will throw a fit when they hear about this."

Zachus nodded gravely and looked at the king. "You might find that offering magical transportation earns you no favor with certain groups who profited off the caravaning industry."

"Perhaps," Ethan said. "Or perhaps I will work with them. I'm sure I'll be faster and safer than sending a caravan overland, but there will still be a need for caravans."

"We will leave you to work out the logistics with the appropriate guilds," the princess said, a gleam in her eye. "But it appears you may have something of value after all. The question really becomes - how will you use this ability?"

"It does have the potential to disrupt the way things are being done," Guinevere agreed. "And people don't like change."

"Perhaps," Ethan said, thinking back to the advances in technology back on Earth and how each time there was something new, the people doing it the old way were oftentimes resistant to the change.

He thought of his own experience with customers who were still on old operating systems who got hacked or infected by a virus because they refused to upgrade to an OS that was being patched. In the end, they suffered for not keeping up with technology.

How would his ability to move people from place to place impact things? He didn't know. Ethan hoped it would make a positive contribution to the culture. If not, he could always stop it. Hopefully not before Castlehaven was on its feet again.

"Let's see how people receive the service I'm offering," Ethan said. "And we'll take it from there."

"You realize such ability would be of military concern as well?" Zachus said. "The ability to move troops in minutes instead of weeks would be concerning."

Ethan chuckled. "I would think the huge dragon who calls me friend might be more of a military concern."

Zachus cleared his throat. "There is that."

"Don't worry," Ethan said with an innocent smile. "He'll be heading home to his mate soon. They live down south...."

"There's two of those monsters?!" the princesses exclaimed.

"Well, yes," Ethan replied. "Firestorm's mate is the one I saved, so technically, I guess we're friends too."

"Odin's bloody eye," the princess hissed under her breath. "Two of them."

"Don't worry about them," Ethan said, making a dismissive gesture. "They won't bother the human or orc cities. In fact, as long as I answer when they send me a mental message, I doubt they'll come back at all. Of course... if I don't answer when they try to contact me..."

Skill increase: Bluff +1%.

"Is that some type of threat?" the princess asked warily.

He shook his head. "No, no threat. I have no idea what the dragons would do if they found out I was dead. I mean, sure, Moonpoint would probably be the prime suspect for them... but... I don't know what they'd actually do..."

Skill increase: Bluff +1%.

"I think we understand your meaning," Zachus said dryly. Ethan had noticed the catling sniffing during their conversation and wondered if, like Nia, he could smell a lie. Ethan had purposefully kept his talk of the dragon vague or speculative to avoid a direct lie. Hopefully it had worked.

Ethan let his smile slip and narrowed his eyes. "Good. Because if your little wizard assassin does manage to kill me, the dragons WILL know where to look."

Skill increase: Bluff +1%.

"What if it's not us?!" Princess Melody demanded. "Will Moonpoint suffer because some other prince or princess decides to take you out?"

"Pray that they don't," Ethan said. The princess and the

captain were quiet for a full minute before they resumed the negotiations.

The rest of the negotiations were fairly straightforward and Ethan let Guinevere take the lead. Despite insisting she was a knight, the woman had a head for politics and negotiation. He knew that he'd either need to keep her around or get a crash course from her.

Some time later, Ethan heard cries from outside and smiled. "It sounds like the dragon has returned. I'll be right back."

Ethan left the room, walked down the hallway and exited the main hall. Sure enough, Firestorm was back at the same perch he used the first time.

I am back, as I said I would be, the dragon said. *Do you require anything else from me?*

No, I think everything is good now. Thanks again for coming, Ethan replied to the dragon.

I am still in your debt, though I do not enjoy meddling in human politics, Firestorm told him. The dragon looked down at him, cocking his head. *You have not integrated the teachings I embedded.*

Ethan looked down at his chest, remembering the dragon-shaped tattoo on his chest. He frowned and wrinkled his forehead. *What do you mean? I learned Sigil magic when you gave it to me.*

Sigil magic? Interesting. You learned the type of magic that I used, but not the magic I passed on to you. The dragon replied. *The magic I shared is in the sigil. You will learn it when you are ready.*

What is it? More magic? Ethan was now curious since he had thought he'd already learned the magic the dragon had shared. He had just found out there was something else to learn. But what?

An ancient magic, the dragon replied. *One I have only shared once before, but one worthy of the service you performed for my mate.*

You're not going to tell me what it is? Ethan asked.

The dragon moved his massive head back and forth. *I think it is best that you discover it on your own. The magic integrates better that way. But now, it is best that I am getting back to my mate. I am weary of the stench of humans and the insanity of their politics.*

Ethan chuckled at the dragon's assessment of politics. That was one viewpoint they shared. *Don't worry, I won't make this a regular thing.*

If you do, the dragon chuckled as he began flapping his wings. *Make sure you have a herd of cows for me when I arrive. I do have a fondness for them.*

Ethan chuckled too. *Cows, huh? I'll remember that.*

Excellent, the dragon said, circling over the city. *Good bye, dragon-friend.*

Good bye, Firestorm, Ethan replied as the dragon soared to the south.

FROM HER HIDING spot in the trees to the south, the Queen watched silently as the dragon flew to the south. She had not moved for over an hour, keeping perfectly still - except for her multifaceted eyes. Her eyes tracked the dragon as it continued south and disappeared beyond the horizon.

She had seen the dragon leave before, only to return an

hour later. The first time, it had flown out into the ocean. Now, it went south. Would it come back again? The Queen clicked her mandibles together and then stretched out her limbs. Even as she moved, one of her eyes stayed focused in the direction the dragon had gone.

The Queen had many questions. Why had the dragon come to this human city? Why had it only stayed for a short while? What had it done while it was here? Of course, the most important question was: would it return?

The army that had assaulted the city was leaving now and she could easily sneak in, yet she dared not. Not if the dragon returned. She knew the dragons were hunting by smell and if she was in the city when it returned, the Queen knew it would smell her.

No. She would not go into the city after the human wizard. He would leave soon enough. If the past couple of weeks were any indication, he didn't seem to be able to stay in one place for very long.

She could wait.

50

A s the dragon was flying away, the Princess and captain came outside. Guinevere, Nia and the others walked with the two. Everyone looked south at the retreating form of the dragon.

"The dragon is gone?" Princess Melody asked.

Ethan turned to face her. He nodded. "For now. You never know when they'll be back though."

`Skill increase: Bluff +1%.`

Once again, he purposefully kept his comment vague. He thought it was interesting that vague comments sometimes earned him an increase in *Bluff*.

Without knowing for certain whether the captain could smell a lie, Ethan thought it was safer to keep his statements vague and let the Princess and captain read whatever they wanted into them. If that was *Bluffing*, then so be it.

"If everything you've told us is true," the Princess said. "Then you have nothing to fear from Moonpoint."

Ethan smiled. "Glad to hear it. Hopefully, this will be the beginning of a very beneficial friendship."

"We shall see," Melody replied guardedly. She looked him up and down. "Time will tell."

The Princess started to turn to leave but Ethan suddenly remembered something. "Princess. There was a group of refugees from the town of Silvershade that we rescued. We sent them north to Moonpoint..."

"That was you?" Princess Melody asked with curiosity, and perhaps a little more respect than just a second ago.

"Yes," Ethan said. "We rescued them from some slavers, then later found some children and Michalus was kind enough to take them up to Moonpoint as well."

"I do know of them," the Princess said. "It bodes well that you were the one that saved them."

"Be that as it may," Ethan said. "Please let them know that if they do wish to return and rebuild, they are welcome to. I can offer them some aid in the form of magic, but I'm afraid most of the resources will probably go to repairing the city."

Looking around at the smoke that still came from the temple district the demon had ravaged, the Princess nodded. "I will tell them."

"Thank you, princess. Have a safe journey back," Ethan said.

"Thank you," the Princess replied and with a nod to the captain, the two of them turned and walked towards the gate.

Michalus looked like he was about to say something

but Ethan held up a hand. He waited until the Moonpoint group had gone past the gate before turning to Michalus. "Sorry. I have no idea how good the captain's hearing is."

"Or his sense of smell," Nia agreed.

"Exactly," Ethan said.

"Oh, right," Michalus said. "The smelling truth thing. I didn't even think of that. That is why you spoke in generalities."

"Especially about the dragon," Guinevere added with a smirk. "I was wondering how much of what you implied about the dragon was actually true."

Ethan looked around, reaching out with his senses to see if there was even the slightest sense of being scryed.

"Is something wrong?" Nia asked, hands dropping to her weapons.

"Just trying to make sure we're not being scryed by the other wizards," Ethan said. "Because the truth is, I don't think the dragon has any intention of either checking up on me or coming around."

Everyone was quiet while they absorbed that news. Ethan continued. "I know the female dragon doesn't like humanoids at all, which is one of the reasons the orcs know next to nothing about her. But I don't think Firestorm is too keen on messing around with human politics either."

"Probably for good reason," Guinevere noted. "If he sides with any particular faction, it could make the dragons a target to the opposite factions."

"What can they do against a dragon?" Nia asked. "We are like fleas to it."

"True," Guinevere admitted. "But they might annoy it

with raids or a war. It seems like the dragons prefer to be left alone."

Ethan nodded. "I think Guinevere's right. The dragon told me as much. We're just fortunate that he felt indebted to me and chose to come this time. I don't think we can count on him coming again."

"That's too bad," a familiar voice said and Ethan turned to see Rollie. "A dragon would be quite a deterrent."

"Perhaps," Ethan said to the sergeant. "But we're going to need to stand on our own two feet."

"Easier said than done," Rollie said.

"That's why I'm making you captain of the guard," he told the former sergeant, watching with satisfaction at Rollie's stunned expression.

He'd been considering the idea since he'd assumed the role of king and the sergeant had thrown in his lot with him. Not to mention, Rollie was currently the highest-ranking guard he had. So it seemed like a logical fit.

"Your majesty," Rollie stammered. "I... ah... don't know what to say."

"Say thank you and say you'll take the job," Ethan replied with a smile. He held out his hand.

Rollie looked at Ethan's hand for a moment before grinning and taking it in a firm shake. "Thank you, your majesty. Yeah, I'll do the job."

"Good!" Ethan said. "Your first task will be to help the people of the city, and then to rebuild the guard."

"Yeah," Captain Rollie said. "I kind of figured you'd say that. I'll tell the boys to spread out and help where they can."

Ethan nodded. "Carry on then, captain."

"Yes, sire," Rollie said. He snapped to attention, saluted and then walked away. Ethan thought he saw a slight spring to the man's step.

Turning back to the others, Ethan received an approving nod from Guinevere. "Good choice."

"Well, I didn't think you would want the job." Ethan chuckled.

The former queen smirked. "Me, a captain of the guard? I don't think so. Now, maybe general, if we were at war."

Ethan raised an eyebrow. "General, huh? I'll remember that if we go to war."

Guinevere shrugged. "Let's see if we can get my father back first."

"Yes," Ethan retorted. "We will leave first thing tomorrow."

"I didn't mean that. I've been in that seat. Well, not king, but queen. You have a duty to your people first," she shot back.

He shook his head. "I think things will be fine for a day or two without me. I'm not sure exactly why, but I have a feeling your father is running out of time."

"Running out of time? What do you say that?" Guinevere asked in alarm.

Ethan bit his lip for a moment. "I'm not sure. Just a difference in the way he appears in the Bifrost."

The warrior woman frowned. "And you didn't say anything?"

"Sorry! I only really noticed it the last time I used the

portal," Ethan said defensively. "And we've been a bit busy since then."

Guinevere stared at him for a moment before nodding. "Perhaps we can go today then?"

Ethan looked around at the haggard expressions on everyone and shook his head. "None of us have slept. I don't know what we might run into when we try to pull him out of the Bifrost, but I want to be fresh."

"I agree with Ethan," Michalus said, covering his mouth to stifle a yawn. "Calibrating the portal detector will be tricky enough on a full night's sleep."

"Fine," the warrior woman said tersely. "But let's get going first thing tomorrow morning then."

"That's the plan," Ethan said.

"If we are going tomorrow, we will need food," Nia said. "I will find my bow and go hunt for something we can cook and take with us."

"Maybe we can get Lucius to have something made for us," Ethan suggested.

Nia looked disappointed and Ethan sighed. "But if you really just want to go and get out, go for it."

Brightening, his wife stood on her tiptoes, kissed him and then spun and strode away.

"I don't think she enjoys being in the city," Michalus observed.

"Probably not," Ethan said, remembering that her world had no big cities. He wondered how she'd handle being queen.

"Give her time," Guinevere said. "She'll adapt. Either that, or you'll need to give her responsibilities that take her out of the city often."

Ethan shrugged. "I guess we can figure that out once we rescue your father."

"Indeed," the warrior woman agreed. She looked towards the gate. "If we're not leaving until tomorrow, then I'll take a few hours to walk around the city and assess the damage."

"I think I will head to the library and see if any damage was done," Michalus said.

"Alright," Ethan said with a wave to both of them. "I'll see you later or I'll meet you here in the courtyard first thing tomorrow morning."

His two companions waved and then both walked off, heading to the gate. Looking around, Ethan realized he was alone. He yawned loudly. Maybe it was time for him to grab a quick nap and then go wander around the city and see where he could help out.

After all, tomorrow was going to be a big day.

51

The next morning, the group ate a breakfast of eggs and toasted bread. It wasn't much, but much of their stores had disappeared with the townspeople. Lucius apologized profusely but Ethan had waved his apology away.

"They probably need it more than we do," Ethan said with a shrug. He reached over and put his arm around his wife. "I can always ask my beautiful wife to go hunting when we get back."

Nia looked at him and sniffed, then smiled and nodded. She might be able to smell lies but the words hadn't been ideal flattery. He really did think she was beautiful, both inside and out. And he loved her.

He hadn't been sure for a long time. After all, he'd only had a half dozen serious relationships back on Earth. But her quiet strength and confidence had won him over. Well, that, plus her incredible body and insatiable appetite for, he smiled to himself, replenishing his *Mana*. That stuff never hurt.

After breakfast, the group gathered in the courtyard. Drorm, Guinevere, Nia, and Michalus all gathered around him, ready for him to open the portal. Ethan noticed that Drorm carried the pieces of the portal detector while Michalus had his arms filled with books.

"Are we ready to go?" Ethan asked, he raised an eyebrow at Michalus. "Do you need any more books?"

The wizard looked up at him hopefully. "I could use a few extra, but I would need someone to carry them for me."

Ethan sighed. "The extra books, they're for configuring the portal detector, right?"

Michalus shrugged. "Well, I have no idea how long we'll be there. I thought it might be a good time to read up on a few topics..."

"Hopefully, it won't take that long," Ethan retorted, noting that the wizard already carried over a half dozen tomes. He shook his head and lowered his voice. "We can hope."

Not wanting to give the wizard a chance to argue about how many books he really needed, Ethan focused on the runes he'd left in Patheos and opened a portal.

One by one, his companions entered the portal. Ethan looked back at Rollie and Lucius. He'd left them in charge while he was gone. Of everyone in the city, they were the two men he trusted the most at the moment.

"I'll try to return here at least once a day so you can give me updates," Ethan told the men.

"Don't rush back," Rollie snickered. "It ain't going to be nothing but cleanup for quite a while."

"Captain Rolland is correct," the castellan agreed.

"Rollie," Ethan said, giving the man a pointed look. "I wasn't kidding, make sure you send out..."

"Yeah, I know, your majesty," the man interrupted. "Send the guards who know how to actually hunt out to get food and then... just give it to the people... Are you sure we can't charge 'em?"

Ethan frowned at the captain.

"Okay, okay," Rollie said, putting his palms up. "Just give them the meat... after we take a bit for ourselves..."

"That's fine," Ethan told him. And it was. If anything, he needed the remaining guards well fed and ready to defend or work when the need arose. "And like I said, recruit more guards if you can. Perhaps having access to extra food will encourage some to join."

"Yeah." The captain rolled his eyes. "That's what we need, a bunch of hungry beggars on the Watch."

Ethan rolled his eyes. "I told you, we're only taking ones who know how to fight or who you think you can train. We're not taking just anyone."

"Yeah, I'll put them through their paces," Rollie assured him.

"Fine," Ethan said and turned to Lucius. "Keep an eye on things and make a list of the things that need to be addressed."

The castellan nodded. "Of course, your majesty. I'm already on my second piece of parchment."

"And on that cheery note, I'll see you tomorrow - hopefully." Ethan sighed and then stepped into the portal.

Ethan entered the Bifrost and the rainbow tunnel of light surrounded him as he moved without moving. As he expected, the ghostly head of Merlin appeared in front of him again. It was even more insubstantial than before. This time, when the mouth opened no words came out.

And then Ethan was stepping into the ruined city that had once been Patheos. He blinked. Merlin hadn't spoken at all this time. That wasn't a good sign. For whatever reason, Merlin was weakening. They needed to hurry.

Looking around, he saw that Drorm and Michalus were already reassembling the portal detector while Guinevere and Nia were scouting out their perimeter.

"You two need any help?" Ethan asked.

Drorm shrugged. "I have no idea."

Michalus bit his lip. "Not at the moment. I'm trying to put the pieces back together again. Once we do that, I'll need to re-enchant them one by one using the formulas in the book."

"And how long will that take?" Ethan asked.

"Most of the day, I'm afraid," the wizard replied.

It was Ethan's turn to bite his lip. He looked around to make sure Guinevere was out of hearing distance and then lowered his voice, just to make sure. "Do it as fast as you can, I don't think we have much time."

Michalus looked up, a startled expression on his face. "What do you mean?"

"In the Bifrost," Ethan explained. "I think... Merlin is getting weaker. This time, he didn't speak at all."

"What does that mean?" Drorm asked.

"I'm not sure," he replied. "But nothing good, I'm sure."

"It could be that his attempts to communicate with

you are draining his mana," Michalus theorized, scratching his chin. "He may not be able to regenerate his mana as quickly - or at all."

Ethan considered the wizard's words. Michalus had a point. Given the time distortion they experienced in the Bifrost, there could be some truth to the wizard's words. Something about what Michalus said jogged his memory.

He looked at the building that had once been the Library of Daemonium. Originally, there had been a portal that led to another planet. One with a very large red sun, not the twin suns of this solar system.

When he and Nia had gone to the other planet, Ethan hadn't been able to regenerate his *Mana*. They'd almost been stranded until he and Nia had discovered that sex also regenerated *Mana*. Had it not been for that, they might have died from dehydration or lack of food - or from the intense heat.

Perhaps Merlin was unable to regenerate *Mana* at all wherever he was. Perhaps he was in the same situation Ethan had found himself in, only without a woman like Nia to help him. What would happen when the legendary wizard was completely out of *Mana*?

Ethan saw Nia and Guinevere returning and he put his finger to his lips. "Don't tell Guinevere. She doesn't need to worry about something we can't change."

Drorm and Michalus exchanged glances but then they both nodded.

"There is no sign of any enemies," Nia said as they approached. "We are alone here, for now."

"Good," Ethan replied.

Guinevere was frowning. "Sure, it's good. But we have

no water and no food."

Ethan nodded. "I can portal Nia to Hawkshead and she can hunt there. We can also bring back some water."

"That might not be the only thing you need to bring back," Michalus said from behind him.

Turning, Ethan saw the portal detector was back together and Michalus had one of the large tomes open.

"What do you mean?" Ethan asked.

"I haven't started calibrating yet, but if I'm reading this correctly," Michalus retorted. "I need another measurement arm in order to find the spot in three dimensions."

"Three dimensions?" Guinevere asked, her brow wrinkling. "I thought you said this machine could detect portals."

"And it can!" the wizard replied. "But, I was only ever interested in the direction the portal was. Two dimensions are fine for that - like longitude and latitude on a map. I never designed it to find the exact origin point of a portal - or the exact point where someone might be trapped in the aether. For that, I will need one more dimension."

Nia frowned, also confused. "What is it you need?"

"Yes," Ethan asked. "What exactly do you need me to bring back that will help you?"

"I need to attach another arm to my detector, but one which will move vertically," Michalus replied, gesturing with his hands to show the motion.

Ethan wrinkled his forehead, trying to understand what the wizard was asking for. "So, you need some copper?"

"More than that I'm afraid," the wizard answered. "I will need someone with the ability to figure out the correct way to attach it and make it work. I'm afraid I have no aptitude for mechanical things. I need a craftsman... or should I say, a craftswoman..."

Rolling his eyes, Ethan finally understood what Michalus wanted. Or should he say, WHO the wizard wanted. "You want me to get Ainslee."

Michalus grinned and nodded. "Since the craftsman who helped me passed away a few years ago, and I don't know any others, Ainslee is precisely who I need."

THE QUEEN RAN through the forest, her large eyes and innate dexterity allowing her to move at blinding speed while avoiding trees and underbrush.

She had felt the human wizard use Aether magic again. She sensed him east and north. He had to be in Patheos again. She clicked her mandibles together in curiosity. Why did the wizard keep returning there? Was there something there? Something she had missed on her visit?

It didn't really matter to the Queen. Nothing mattered, except finding the human and drinking his brain. Then she would have his knowledge of portals and be able to open a portal to her own world.

Once there, she would kill the current Queen and then take control of the brood. After that, who knew. Perhaps she would be able to create portals to other worlds and take them over as well - expand her brood to other planets.

The Queen clicked happily. Yes. Soon, very soon, she would have all she desired. Picking up her pace, she adjusted her direction and headed directly towards the ruined human city.

52

"**I** told you! I ain't interested in no adventure!" Ainslee growled and then took another long draw of her ale. The dwarf finished it up and slammed the scratched pewter mug onto the table. She glanced over at Ethan expectantly. "Especially with a dry mouth."

Ethan sighed, and looked over at Fearghas. The innkeeper nodded and went to get a pitcher of ale.

Ainslee shook her head. "I think I'm far too parched for ale. Perhaps... spirits would quench my thirst."

Fearghas shook his head and chuckled. "Right for the good stuff, huh?"

"As long as I'm not paying," Ainslee replied with a grin and another glance at Ethan. She nodded her head towards the innkeeper.

"Go ahead and give her the good stuff," Ethan said with a roll of his eyes. "I'm good for it."

Fearghas looked from Ethan to Ainslee and then shook his head. He gestured to his wife, Elspeth, behind the counter. She'd been washing and putting away mugs but she stopped what she was doing and ducked behind the bar. A moment later, she stood with a hand keg.

"You better not drink it all tonight," the innkeeper's wife chided. "This is it, until the new batch is done."

Ainslee frowned and she slumped. "But why are the dwarven spirits gone?"

"Ha!" Fearghas barked a laugh. "Because you come in every night and have at least a glass! Most of the time two!"

"You need to make more!" Ainslee protested.

"You keep saying that!" Fearghas retorted. "But have you made me a new still yet?"

"I told you, I'm waiting for the copper from... Castlehaven," Ainslee trailed off, casting a sideways glance at Ethan. She shrugged. "Sorry. But trade from Castlehaven ain't exactly been reliable lately."

Ethan nodded. "And it probably won't be for a long time yet. We lost so many people - most to the sacrifices."

"And you're really the prince... I mean... king now?" Elspeth asked. "There hasn't been a king since..."

"Since King Arthur, I know," Ethan said with a resigned nod. Both Elspeth and Fearghas had both told him that twice now.

The innkeeper's wife smiled at him sheepishly. "The idea of a king takes a little getting used to."

"Especially you as king!" Ainslee said.

"Oh?" Ethan faced her, cocking an eyebrow.

His friend shrugged. "Let's face it, you aren't exactly the kingly type. Too practical."

Ethan nodded. On that much, at least, they agreed. He

certainly wasn't about to let being king go to his head. If anything, he knew it was a responsibility more than anything else. He'd gone from being responsible for only himself, to being responsible for his group, to being responsible for a village. And now, he was responsible for an entire city and the lands around it.

He sighed. This was too much like management. And he hated management and he hated managers. Well, most managers. Ethan had worked for a few good managers: people who had actually cared about their employees and treated them with respect.

It was that type of king he wanted to be. A king who treated everyone with respect. A king who didn't lord his power over the people but used his power to make things better for the people. Could he do that without the power going to his head?

Ethan thought he could. He was a wizard, and a thumping good one from everything he'd seen so far - especially when it came to portals. If he could create portals from Castlehaven to the other cities, he would be able to make it a trade hub.

If Castlehaven became a trade hub, then it would bring wealth and prosperity to the people living there, as well as their trade partners. That would hopefully give Ethan some sway over the other cities, even if only economically.

That was a start. Hopefully, he could reach some sort of pact of alliance with the other major cities and work on improving life for everyone. Hopefully.

"Uh... Ethan?" Ainslee asked, snapping him out of his thoughts.

Startled, Ethan looked around. "I'm sorry, what?"

"I said," Ainslee continued, rolling her eyes. "What exactly is this contraption that I'm supposed to do something with?"

"It's a portal detector..." Ethan started.

"Portals... those magical doory... things you make," Ainslee said, her face flushing as she took a very long sip of the dwarven spirits Elspeth had set in front of her. She finished up the alcohol in the cup and gestured to it.

Elspeth grabbed the small keg and poured another cup, then sat back down.

Ethan nodded. "Yes. Except we need to modify it so we can detect Merlin, who is trapped in the Bifrost."

Ainslee took a sip of the freshly poured cup. "Merlin? That's Guinevere's dad, right?"

"Yes," he replied. "And I think he's running out of time."

"What do you mean?" his friend asked.

"I think that whatever is keeping him alive in the Bifrost is starting to run out," he replied. Ethan wasn't completely sure, but he had come up with a theory.

If Merlin had been trapped in the Bifrost for over a hundred years, perhaps he was somehow sustaining himself with magic. If that were the case, he must have been slowly using up his magic with no way to really regenerate it.

When Ethan had appeared in the Bifrost with Excalibur, the wizard must have somehow sensed it and used some of his remaining *Mana* to contact him. If that were the case, then Merlin was slowly running out of *Mana*. If he used it all up, he'd die.

Either that, or the legendary wizard would be unable to contact him - or anyone else. That meant his chance of rescue would be reduced to almost no chance at all. A grim fate.

"This thingy," Ainslee asked, setting the empty cup down and gesturing to it.

Elspeth looked at Ethan and he nodded, holding up a single finger. "One more."

Turning to Ainslee he shook his head. "You'll have to come back with us."

"More adventuring," she whined.

Ethan blew out a breath. "It's not adventuring. It's going back to that dead city, taking a look at the machine, then I'll portal you back here so you can make the piece, and then come back to get you when it's done."

"So I don't have to stay there, right?" Ainslee asked. "You remember what happened last time we were there, right? I got captured, tied up like a pig, and almost killed! Killed!"

"No one's coming after us this time," Ethan told her. "We're just going there to get Merlin."

"Right!" she huffed. "Just like last time! There wasn't supposed to be some crazy warlock person or her little minions, either!"

"This time is different," Ethan promised. After all, there wasn't some crazy warlock person after them. No one was after them. At this point, he was fairly certain even Moonpoint wasn't after them.

All they really needed to do was to rescue Merlin, reunite him with his daughter and then go back to Castlehaven and start rebuilding. Simple, right?

"Sure, sure," Ainslee growled. "And why can't you bring the machine here?"

Ethan sighed. He'd explained this before to her but she'd either purposefully ignored him or she was getting too drunk to remember. "He's calibrating it right now, remember? We're running out of time. He needs to calibrate the sections he can and then once you bring your piece back there, he can calibrate it."

"And no fighting, right?!" the dwarf asked. This time, Ethan did actually notice a slight slurring to her words. He wondered how many ales she'd had before he and Nia had shown up.

"Definitely no fighting," he assured her. "There's no one in the city, except us."

Ainslee threw her hands up. "Fine! Fine! I'll do it!"

"Excellent!" Ethan said, standing up from his chair. "When can you leave?"

Turning over her cup to make sure it was empty, Ainslee let out a disappointed sigh. "I guess now is as good a time as any."

Ethan started for the door. "Great! Get your stuff and we'll meet you at the smithy as soon as Nia gets back from hunting."

Peeking inside the cup to make sure there were no dwarven spirits left, Ainslee muttered an acknowledgement.

"Thanks, you two," Ethan told Elspeth and Fearghas.

"Just bring our smith back in one piece," Elspeth said with a smile. "We've gotten used to her. The whole town has."

"No problem," he replied with a smile of his own. "Let me go grab the money from my place."

Fearghas waved him away. "It sounds like you're in a hurry, you can pay me later. After all, if a man can't trust his king, who can he trust."

Ethan wasn't sure if he heard sarcasm in the dwarf's words or whether the innkeeper was being serious. "Thank you, both of you."

With that, Ethan left the inn and went back to his place to wait for Nia. Soon, very soon, they'd have the portal detector ready and they could finally rescue Merlin. Unfortunately, when it came to the legendary wizard, time was their enemy. More than the others knew.

He hadn't told anyone, but on their journey to Hawk-shead, Merlin hadn't appeared at all. Ethan had no idea what that meant but he knew it wasn't a good thing. Time was running out.

An itching on his chest caused him to stop in mid stride. He looked down but nothing was on his tunic. Ethan frowned as the itching started again. It was a strange sensation but he wasn't quite sure what to make of it.

Just as he was about to start unbuttoning his tunic, the sensation stopped. Ethan waited for a moment and when the itching didn't reappear, he resumed his walk. He had more serious matters to worry about than a little itching.

THE QUEEN SWIVELED *her triangular head to the south and then back to the east. The wizard had transported south and*

she considered heading that direction. The wizard was no longer in the ruined city. He was now south.

As frustrating as it was to yet again have to run after her prey, she was happy he had left the city where the dragon had appeared. Of all the things on this world, the dragons were what she feared most.

They were unlike anything she had ever encountered. Physically, they were imposing. But even more than that, the dragons possessed magic. So much magic. More than any other beings on the planet.

And yet, she knew she had no chance against them. No. Their magic was too strong. She needed to avoid them at all costs.

The Queen swiveled her head back towards the east and then again to the south. For some reason, the wizard kept returning to Patheos. She didn't know why. Nor did she care. But if he did keep returning, did it make sense to adjust her course every time he created a portal?

If the wizard kept returning to the ruined city, she could go to Patheos and wait there for him to show up. She clicked happily. Yes. She could go there and wait for him. Wait until he was most vulnerable and then strike.

Soon, very soon, his brain would be hers. Clicking happily, she turned back towards Patheos and resumed her run. It would not be long.

53

An hour later, just before noon, Nia returned with a fresh kill. Ainslee was ready to go and the three of them portaled back to the ruins of Patheos. Once again, Merlin didn't show up in the Bifrost. It was the second time he hadn't seen the wizard as he portaled.

Ethan had hoped the first time was a fluke, but now he was worried. Were they too late? Or was Merlin just conserving power? Did the wizard know they were trying to rescue him? So many questions. So few answers.

After a brief reunion between Ainslee and the others, Michalus showed her his machine and explained what he needed. The dwarf listened intently, examining the portal detector and nodding as the wizard detailed his plans and even made some crude sketches in the ground.

Guinevere and Ethan listened to the exchange, each for their own reasons. Ethan was interested from a magical perspective. He suspected Guinevere just wanted them to get on with finding her father.

He had debated on telling Guinevere that he hadn't seen Merlin the last two times he'd used the Bifrost. There were positives and negatives to letting the warrior woman know but Ethan had eventually decided not to tell her.

Knowing her father hadn't appeared in the Bifrost wouldn't help Guinevere. In fact, it would most likely only cause her to worry. And in this case, worrying wouldn't serve any purpose.

Either Merlin was still alive, or he wasn't. If he wasn't, nothing they were doing would help or make a difference. If he was, they were already working as quickly as they could. Only time would tell which it was.

While Michalus and Ainslee reviewed the plans for the detector and the new arm that needed to be created, Nia and Drorm prepared dinner. His wife had bagged a small deer during her hunt outside of Hawkshead. They would eat what they could and then Ethan or Michalus would freeze the rest.

"Okay, wizard-boy," Ainslee's voice boomed from behind him. "Take me back!"

Turning, Ethan gave her a confused look. "Take you back?"

"I know what the old guy wants." The dwarf rolled her eyes at him and gestured around. "You expect me to make it here?"

Ethan glanced around and realized his mistake. "Oh, right. You'll need to smelt some copper."

"Yeah, about that," the dwarf replied, screwing up her face. "We ain't got no copper."

"Wait. What?" Ethan asked, shaking his head.

"We tried to get some copper, to make Fearghas a better still," she replied. "But with all the trouble in Castlehaven, it never came in."

Ethan sighed. He knew looking for copper in Hawkshead would be useless. Any copper they had would be used for necessities. That really only left one option. "We need to go to Castlehaven."

"You go to Castlehaven," Ainslee snorted. "Send me back to town so I can start stoking the forge - if it hasn't gone out completely."

Nodding, Ethan looked around at the others. They were watching the exchange between Ainslee and him. They were waiting for him to give them the next steps.

"Michalus," he announced. "You work on calibrating the machine. I'm going to send Ainslee back to Hawkshead to get the forge ready, while I go to Castlehaven to find some copper."

"I am coming with you," Nia announced and Ethan knew better than to try and argue with his wife.

He nodded. "Guinevere, you and Drorm work on getting the food prepared. Michalus will be tied up with calibrating the portal detector, so I will freeze any leftovers when I get back."

"Par'karr?" his kobold friend asked, looking at Ethan for his assignment.

There really wasn't anything for the kobold to do, but he knew Par'karr would feel left out if he didn't have something for him. He thought quickly. "Par'karr, I need you and the rabbits to make a loop around the ruins and scout them out. Make sure there are no surprises for us."

"Yeah! Like some crazy cultists!" Ainslee muttered, obviously referring to the followers of Hel they'd encountered the first time they were here.

"If you find something," he told the kobold, remembering how enthusiastic the little guy could be. "Don't engage it, just report back here to us."

"Par'karr scout!" The kobold bobbed his head up and down enthusiastically.

Once everyone muttered or nodded their approval, Ethan motioned to Ainslee and Nia. First, he opened a portal to Hawkshead and let the dwarf return. After she was gone, he opened a gateway to Castlehaven and he and Nia stepped through.

Their trip through the Bifrost was brief, with no appearance from Merlin. No one was in the courtyard to greet them as they walked through the portal. The emptiness reminded Ethan of how much work he needed to do to get things back to what passed for normal.

Normally, this courtyard would be bustling with activity for the keep. Not anymore. So many people had either fled or been sacrificed by the crazy ex-prince. The city was now a shadow of what it had been. He had his work cut out for him.

"Where do we get copper?" Nia asked, glancing around.

"Good question," Ethan responded. He racked his brain for things that were made out of copper - especially during medieval times. Pots and pans? He knew one person that would know.

Ethan led Nia to the door of the main hall and was about to open it when it opened itself.

A startled Lucius stood in the doorway, eyes wide. He recovered quickly, his features smoothing. "Your majesty."

"Sorry to scare you." Ethan chuckled.

"I was not expecting you back so quickly, your majesty," the castellan said, with an incline of his head. "I was about to go check with Rolland to see if some of his men had found any food for the larder."

"Before you go," Ethan interrupted. "Any idea where we could find some copper? I need some for... ah... a magical thing."

"How much copper?" Lucius asked. The man appeared completely unfazed by the question, as if someone asked him about copper every day.

Ethan frowned. He had no idea. Neither Michalus nor Ainslee had said anything about the amount.

Thinking back to the portal detector, Ethan remembered the other two arms, their approximate size and tried to guess at how much they might need for a third arm. He tried to think of it in terms he could relate to the castellan. "Maybe about the same amount you'd use in two or three frying pans."

"Frying pans," the castellan repeated, tapping his finger on the side of his head. "We certainly do have some copper pans."

"Excellent," Ethan said with a grin.

"However," Lucius said, holding the finger up in front of him. "If you're not sure of the exact amount, might I suggest one of the copper bathing tubs."

"We have copper bathing tubs?" Ethan asked. As he thought back to the first time he'd used a bathing tub in this world, he remembered back at the inn where he'd first discovered *Aether* magic. When he'd almost killed himself. That tub had been copper.

When he thought about it, it did make sense. Copper was a great conductor of temperature. It was what pipes had been made of for a long time, before everyone started using PVC.

"A copper tub sounds perfect," Ethan said. "Let's get one!"

Lucius nodded. "Follow me, your majesty."

Ethan and Nia followed the castellan upstairs, down a hallway and into a small room Ethan hadn't noticed before. Inside the room were supplies for the household, stacked on shelves. There were linens, towels, a solid metal iron, and two copper tubs.

The tubs were large, larger than the one he'd used in the inn. They had also been made with decorative patterns in the copper and trimmed in a gray metal he thought might be steel. They were, for all intents and purposes, works of art. He hated to just melt one down, but a man's life was at stake.

"That'll work," he told the castellan. "Thank you."

"My pleasure," Lucius replied. "Will you require assistance moving it, your majesty?"

Ethan shook his head. "No, I'll just portal us right from here."

"As you wish, your majesty," the man replied and stepped away from the door.

Checking his HUD, Ethan realized it might take a bit.

Mana: 47

From opening both portals, he was low on *Mana*. He shrugged. "We'll have to wait until my mana recharges."

"I see, your majesty," the castellan replied and gestured towards the hallway. "Do you require my assistance for anything else? If not, I will go check on the food for the larder."

"No, we'll wait until my magic is regenerated and then we'll head out," he responded.

Lucius inclined his head. "Then we look forward to your safe return, your majesty."

The castellan turned and strode back down the hall, disappearing around a corner. As Lucius's footsteps could be heard going down the steps, Ethan felt a tug on his arm.

Looking down, he saw Nia with a naughty grin on her face. She tugged him towards the hallway that led to their bedroom. Ethan grinned. He didn't have to ask her what she wanted. Apparently, they wouldn't be waiting long for his *Mana* to refresh.

∽

THE QUEEN WAS TORN and for one of the few times in her life, she was uncertain. She had felt the wizard portal from the ruined city back to the south. Yet, almost immediately afterwards, she'd felt him portal from the ruined city to the east. Most likely, he had returned to the city where she'd seen the dragon.

She hesitated, head and eyes swiveling between the west, the south and the east. Did she follow her original plan, go south or go back east.

Hesitation and uncertainty were not familiar feelings for the Queen. She had thousands of years of genetic memory to call upon to make her decisions. And yet, none of those memories had ever dealt with magic. Only her new memories - the memories she'd developed since coming to this world - knew anything of magic.

Mandibles clicking in uncertainty, she finally decided to stick to her original plan. Yes. She would go to Patheos and wait for him. And she could wait a very long time. She had patience.

54

———

Once Ethan's *Mana* was recharged, he opened a portal back to Hawkshead and delivered the copper tub to the dwarf at her forge. Ainslee eyed the tub and gave a nod of approval.

"Don't suppose there are any more of these lying around?" Ainslee asked with a cocked eyebrow. "One or two more and I'd have enough copper to make a new still for Fearghas."

"Once we rescue Merlin, I'll see what I can do," Ethan replied with a grin. His smile slipped as he thought about all of the abandoned buildings and belongings. Now that he thought of it, he would probably find some spare copper once they started going through things.

Ainslee rubbed her hands together. "That'd be nice. A new still means more dwarven spirits!"

Shaking his head, Ethan looked down at the dwarf. "Do you have everything you need to get started?"

The dwarf nodded. "This should be plenty."

"How long will it take?" he asked. He hated to rush the dwarf, but he knew how important the timing was.

"If I work through the night," Ainslee replied, scratching her head. "I can have it to you by tomorrow morning. Then an hour or two to modify the thingy and attach it. Then it's up to the elf."

"Are you going to be okay working through the night?" he asked. Ethan appreciated the dwarf's willingness, but at the same time, he didn't want to push her and have her make a mistake that cost them even more time.

Ainslee rolled her eyes. "I'm a dwarf. We can stay up for two or three days if we need to. We just don't like to, unless we have to."

"Alright," Ethan said with a nod. "Let me tell the others and see if Michalus needs any help."

The dwarf grunted, grabbed the copper tub and headed into her forge.

Ethan watched the dwarf disappear into the forge before turning to Nia. The foxgirl was frowning, which seemed uncharacteristic for her. "Something wrong?"

Nia blinked and looked up at him for a long moment. She looked down and bit her lip before answering. "I am Tal'Cha and I understand what is expected from Tal'Cha. You have told others that I am queen and I believe the queen is like Tal'Cha, but I do not fully understand it. I do not know what is expected of queen. I... do not know... if I will be a good... queen."

Ethan smiled down at the foxgirl. He also mentally berated himself for not having a conversation with her earlier. Then again, he felt like Guinevere had railroaded him into becoming king. He wasn't even sure it had fully sunk in yet.

While he wasn't completely comfortable with the idea of being king, he hadn't met anyone else who he would have trusted to do a good job. Anyone except Guinevere, that is. And she didn't want the job.

He had let himself be railroaded, not because he wanted the job, but because he knew it needed to be done. And because he hadn't found anyone else who was willing and able to do it. So for now, he would take on the role of king and would do his best at it.

But Nia had never asked to be queen and that was his fault. He hadn't once asked his wife what she thought of it. She'd always supported whatever decision he'd made and had rarely disagreed with him. Ethan had just taken for granted that she would fall into the role. He mentally kicked himself for not having the foresight to ask her ahead of time.

"I'm sorry," he told her. "I never even asked if you wanted to be queen."

Nia shrugged. "Tal'Cha supports her Alpha. This is the way of things. But I do not understand what is being asked of me."

"You mean, being queen?"

She nodded.

"As king, I will be in charge of the city... I will be its Alpha," he replied. "I will be in charge. I will make the laws and the people will obey them - hopefully. But it also means that I will do my best to make life as good as possible for them."

"That is like an Alpha on my world," Nia agreed.

"Right," Ethan continued. "And the queen is the second in charge. When I'm not around, you will be in charge."

"Of the entire city?" she asked.

"Yes, the entire city," he replied. "And possibly the surrounding area. Come to think of it, I really need to go over with Lucius what territory belongs to Castlehaven."

"What are the duties of a queen?" Nia pressed.

"Uh, duties?" he repeated. Ethan realized he barely had a grasp on the duties of a king, let alone the duties of the queen. And while that was true, he realized he had someone he could ask about them both. "To be honest, I'm not even completely sure of my duties yet. But I know someone who can hopefully tell us both what the expected duties are."

"Guinevere?" Nia asked, obviously thinking along the same lines.

"Yes," he replied with a nod. "She was a queen and her husband a king. If anyone could tell us, it would be her. We can also ask Lucius, though I suspect we'd get more answers on protocol and formal behavior than actual duties."

"She would make a good Sal'Cha'To," his wife said, suddenly looking thoughtful.

"A what?" Ethan asked, suddenly getting a bad feeling about what it might mean.

"Second wife," Nia clarified. "You are an Alpha and right now, you only have a single wife..."

Ethan held up his hands. "I know that's the way they do it on your world, Nia. But I don't think the people of this world would accept a king with two queens."

"Why not?" Nia frowned. "You are king. You are Alpha. Why would you not have more wives to show your dominance?"

He opened his mouth and tried to form a response but heard laughter from inside the forge. "Go on, wizard-boy, I'm dying to hear your answer."

Suddenly feeling embarrassed that the dwarf had been listening to their conversation, Ethan cleared his throat and tried to ignore the heat in his face. You'd think, after everything he'd been through on this world, he wouldn't be embarrassed as easily. Apparently, that wasn't the case.

"Perhaps we should talk about that part later," Ethan muttered, casting a glance into the forge. "We really should get back to the others."

Looking into the forge, he spotted Ainslee. "We'll be back tomorrow morning."

"Fine, fine, mister lover boy," the dwarf yelled back. He bellowed out a hearty laugh. "Go find yourself another wife."

Ethan worked his mouth soundlessly, unable to come up with a suitable reply. Instead, he turned. Dropping his hand onto Excalibur's hilt, he opened a portal to the ruined city with a thought and a pushing of *Mana*.

Taking Nia's hand, he stepped through the portal and into the Bifrost. One moment, they were in Hawkshead and the next moment, they were in the rainbow tunnel. Ethan and Nia speed through the multi-colored tunnel as usual. But like the last two times, there was no sign of Merlin.

The journey lasted for what seemed like minutes

before they were suddenly stepping out of the Bifrost and into the ruined city. While things looked no different than they had when he'd left, there was a strong aroma of cooking meat in the air that made Ethan's mouth water. He was suddenly aware of just how little he had eaten that day.

"You're back," came Guinevere's voice from over by the fire pit they had built. "Is the dwarf working on the piece we need?"

Ethan nodded, fighting the urge to lick his lips at the smell of cooking venison. "Yes, she's going to work through the night and have the piece ready to install tomorrow."

"Oh, excellent," Michalus said from the opposite side. Turning, Ethan saw the wizard sitting next to the portal detector with his book open. "I will have the crystals completely calibrated by then. Well, all except for the new arm..."

Ethan saw the wizard hesitate and guessed what the elf was going to say. He'd actually thought about it before but had forgotten to say something. To calibrate the new arm, Michalus was going to need a Chymera crystal.

Fishing into his pocket, Ethan pulled out the spare crystal he'd kept with him since the beginning. He walked over to the wizard and tossed it to him. "You need a crystal, right?"

Michalus broke out in a grin. "Just so! And you have a spare!"

Ethan chuckled. "Same one I've been keeping with me since I took it from the kobold shaman. Will it work?"

Michalus looked at it with a critical eye for long

moments before nodding. "It's large enough to hold the spell. It will work."

"Then we're all ready for tomorrow?" Ethan asked.

"We will be, my boy," the wizard said, looking from the crystal to the portal detector. "We will be."

55

Ethan retrieved Ainslee from Hawkshead early the next morning. The dwarf had dark circles under her eyes but otherwise, seemed her normal, grumpy self.

"About time!" she growled as he appeared. "I've been done for hours!"

"Well, you did say you'd be done in the morning," Ethan retorted in his defense.

"Morning started after midnight," she countered. "Anyway, it's done."

To emphasize her point, she pointed to a curved piece of copper that resembled the other two arms of the portal detector. Ethan cocked his head. "Wow, that looks just like the existing ones."

"Of course it does," Ainslee muttered, but Ethan saw the hints of a smile before she replaced it with a scowl.

The dwarf gave Ethan a hard look. "You gonna buy me

breakfast before we go? Elspeth makes a really good meat omelet!"

Ethan considered the request. He nodded. "Sure. Let's make it quick though. Michalus is waiting for the piece and then he still needs to do the calibration."

Ainslee looked back at the arm. "And you're sure this contraption is going to work?"

"No," Ethan admitted. He actually had no clue. He was trusting that Michalus knew what he was talking about.

For his part, Ethan was more powerful than anyone he'd met in creating portals. But he hadn't had time to really study the magical theory behind the portals. To him, it was still.... Magic. Sure, it was magic that obeyed him, but as to exactly how or why it worked, he didn't know.

The dwarf snorted. "I thought as much. I hope it does work. That Guinevere should be able to see her da again."

"Let's hope so," Ethan said and then the two of them walked over to the inn.

Ainslee was not wrong. Elspeth made a fantastic omelet. It had fresh vegetables and what appeared to be either rabbit or squirrel meat. It was quite tasty and he asked her to make a few to take with him for the others.

A half hour later, with a basket full of omelets, Ethan and Ainslee walked through the portal to Patheos. He handed out omelets to the others while the dwarf went to work attaching the new arm to the portal detector.

Michalus ate while he watched her work, occasionally saying something to the dwarf. This immediately prompted a retort from Ainslee, which then escalated in an exchange of words that always ended the same way.

The dwarf would put her hands on her hips, eye the wizard and ask him, "You want to do this?"

This went on for about an hour before she finally had the arm attached. Looking over her handiwork, Ethan couldn't help but notice that the thing really looked like a strange gyroscope now.

"And that will work?" Ethan asked, watching Michalus move the new arm one way and then another.

The wizard nodded. "I believe so."

"Of course it will work!" Ainslee growled. "He just needs to do his wizard stuff on it."

"Yes, indeed," Michalus said. "Let me get started on... my... wizard stuff."

The elf sat down next to the detector and opened up his book. "This should only take an hour and then we can give it a try."

"Excellent!" Ethan said and saw Guinevere smile. He flashed her a grin. "It won't be long now."

The warrior woman nodded. "It's hard to believe I'll see him soon."

Michalus looked up, his face shadowed. "My dear, I do want to point out - as I have before - that this is all theoretical. We have no way of knowing if this will allow us to portal to the same place your father is trapped."

"It will work," Guinevere said. Her voice dropped to a whisper and Ethan barely heard her next words. "It has to."

While the wizard went back to reading the calibration information for the final crystal, Ethan turned to Ainslee. "Come on, I'll take you back to Hawkshead."

The dwarf waved him away. "What?! And miss seeing this contraption work? Not a chance."

Ethan cocked an eyebrow.

"What?!" Ainslee shot back. "I ain't ever made nothing magical before. I want to see it work. Go get Merlin."

"Fair enough," he said.

"Par'karr want to see it work too!" his kobold friend said, feeding a bit of the omelet to his rabbits.

Looking around his circle of friends, he could see they were all anxious to see the portal detector work - and no doubt see him rescue Merlin. So was he.

Of course, seeing the machine work was only part of it. Ethan still had to figure out exactly what to do with the information it gave him. He could open a portal to some-place he knew or was looking at. But could he open up a portal to a place in the Bifrost? And if he opened a portal to a place where Merlin was trapped, could he get trapped too?

It was a question that he'd asked himself many times since first hearing the plan. The problem was, he didn't know the answer and the only person who might know, was Merlin himself.

Not that it mattered. Ethan knew he'd try. He had to. Not only had he promised Guinevere, but he couldn't just leave Merlin stranded in the Bifrost - not if he could do something about it.

THE QUEEN HAD REACHED the city and stealthily made her way to a point where she could observe the human wizard and

his companions. *There were several of them and she sensed magic from two of them.*

She watched the group intently, trying to figure out which one was her prey. She wanted both of their brains, but she needed to get the wizard who could portal first. If she didn't, he could use his portal magic to escape while she fed on the other one.

But which one was it? She was about to move closer when she heard one of them mention the Merlin. She froze. Both multifaceted eyes roamed over the party again, trying to be certain that one of them wasn't actually the Merlin.

The Queen had a memory of the Merlin. A memory from the drone who had seen the Arthur kill her. None of the humanoids appeared to be the Merlin.

She held back. The Queen needed to hear more about the Merlin.

THE NEXT HOUR went by painfully slowly as Michalus enchanted and calibrated the final arm of the portal detector. The entire time, the butterflies in Ethan's stomach continued to morph and grow until by the time the wizard finally told them it was finished, the butterflies had become a flock of pteranodons.

The machine was done and very shortly, it would be his turn to try and rescue Merlin. He was both excited and scared. But he had no choice. He had to at least make the attempt. Assuming the portal detector worked.

"How do we know if it works?" Ethan asked Michalus.

The wizard sighed and looked down at the machine.

"Once I activate it, it should detect any lingering portal residue in the Bifrost."

"Won't it detect my portal activity?" Ethan asked.

"No," the wizard replied, gesturing around the area. "The portals you've created should have had time to dissipate. If Merlin is trapped out there in the Bifrost, he should be generating some sort of anomaly. With the detector calibrated this way, it should give us an exact fix on where that is occurring."

"Then I just have to figure out how to portal to him," Ethan said under his breath.

"What was that?" Michalus asked.

"Nothing," Ethan said, putting a grin on his face. "How do we turn it on?"

"I just need to channel some mana into it to activate it and then it should begin doing its thing," he replied.

"Just do it already," Ainslee said, putting her hands on her hips. "Let's see this thing work!"

There was a mutter of approval from the others. Everyone was anxious to see it work.

Michalus cleared his throat. "Yes, well then..."

The wizard began channeling his *Mana* into the device. The three crystals in the arms all began to glow bright blue. Then, slowly at first but picking up speed, the arms began to move. The arms made a whirring sound as they rotated around the base of the machine.

With a snap, one of the arms stopped moving. The other two continued to whir around until there was another snap. A second arm stopped moving. Only one arm continued moving, the new arm. It moved around the base until finally, it snapped to a stop.

Ethan held his breath, looking at the machine. Waiting for something else to happen. It didn't. It seemed to be finished doing whatever it was supposed to do.

"Is that it?" Ainslee asked, giving voice to the question he had as well.

"Is that it?! What do you mean?!" Michalus asked, stunned. "It worked!"

"It worked?" Ethan repeated. He squinted at the machine. "What is it telling us?"

The wizard reached into his satchel and brought out a long, thin piece of charcoal. He also brought out a folded piece of parchment and smoothed it out on top of the book. He walked around the portal detector, taking note of the arms and their placement. As he did, he scribbled something down on the parchment.

Everyone was quiet while he did so, watching the wizard look at the arms. He examined it from one angle, then another. Ethan stared but wasn't quite sure what Michalus was looking at.

Finally, Michalus looked up with a big grin. "I have it!"

"Have what?" Ainslee blurted out before Ethan had a chance to ask.

"The relative coordinates of the anomaly!" the wizard said, holding up the parchment. "Follow me!"

Looking down at the paper and muttering to himself, Michalus began to take measured strides to the east. After two dozen steps, he stopped abruptly. He muttered something else to himself and then turned north.

The wizard took another dozen strides, taking him near the entrance of the library of Patheos, down into a crater that was on the side of it. Michalus walked down the slope of the crater and then stopped almost exactly in the middle.

Looking down at his parchment again, Michalus bent down and put one hand over top of the other about one foot apart until he was just about eye level. Ethan noted that the spot where he stopped with his hands was roughly even with the ground outside the crater.

"Right here!" Michalus said triumphantly. "Merlin should be trapped right here!"

56

Ethan looked at the spot the wizard indicated. He cocked his head. "Are you sure?"

Michalus glanced back down at his scribbled parchment. He looked back to where the machine was, then seemed to count to himself. Finally, he nodded. "According to the portal detector, yes, this is where the anomaly is."

"Uh... There's nothing there," muttered Ainslee.

"Well, of course we can't see anything, my dear," Michalus said. "Merlin should be trapped there, but inside the Bifrost. It's a place between worlds - possibly between universes. Theories conflict on..."

"And you're sure that's where my father is?" Guinevere interrupted, staring at the spot the wizard had indicated. Ethan couldn't help but notice the desperation that had seeped into her tone. Perhaps she somehow sensed they were running out of time. Or maybe, she just wanted to see her father again.

The wizard bit his lip, scratched his chin and then shrugged. "As sure as I can be. The theory behind the calibrations I made are sound. And I went over these latest calibrations several times. They're what I based the original design of the portal detector on. They take into account the..."

"He means, yes," Ainslee said, interrupting what Ethan guessed would have been a very long and boring explanation of portal theory.

"In other words." He took a deep breath and blew it out. "I'm up."

Michalus gave him a small shrug and a smile. "Yes, my boy. As you said, you are... up."

Guinevere's gaze pivoted to Ethan. "And you know how to get my father?"

"Not a clue." Ethan shook his head. He watched the woman's eyes go wide and her face starting to darken. He held up his palms. "No one does. It's never been done before."

"But..." Guinevere started.

Ethan held up his palms again. "But... I'm going to do my best. And I'll keep trying until I've exhausted all of my options. No matter how much time it takes."

He knew he would too. Even when he'd been a computer tech, he had never just given up on a job or a client until he'd exhausted all of his options. Most of the time, he'd brought back computers from the dead - but sometimes, there was just no coming back.

Something about the memory or his train of thought caused his chest to itch again. Ethan resisted the urge to peek under his tunic. He knew the dragon's sigil was still on his chest. He just had no idea why it itched or how he could "activate" the sigil to learn whatever the dragon used the sigil to teach him. He just didn't have time to think about it at the moment.

"Just give me some time to think about this," he told the warrior woman.

Ethan needed to focus on how to retrieve Merlin. He walked around the crater, staring at the space Michalus indicated. If the legendary wizard really was trapped in the Bifrost, how did he open a portal to him? Especially without knowing exactly where he was in the Bifrost.

At first glance, it didn't seem possible. Ethan had to know and focus on something unique about the place he was opening the portal to. That seemed to be some sort of "rule" when opening portals.

Without a clear idea of the destination, he could end up at anything that resembled the destination. And he had no clear idea of where the wizard was. And, if Ethan was honest with himself, he wasn't 100% certain he could even open a portal INTO the Bifrost. After all, how did you open a portal - which used the Bifrost - INTO the Bifrost. It would be like a door that opened into itself.

He paused. His door analogy made him think. If he took that analogy literally, then creating a portal between two places was like creating a door between two rooms. A temporary door, but still a door.

If he was right, Merlin was hit by the shockwave of his own explosion as he entered the doorway and was blasted - not into the other room, but into the wall. If someone were trapped in the wall and Ethan only had a door as a way to get to them, he wouldn't open a door into the wall.

He'd put the door THROUGH the spot in the wall where he knew the person was in the wall.

Admittedly, the analogy didn't work completely. But he did think he was onto something. If he created a portal between two points that intersected the spot where Merlin was, then he might be able to reach the wizard. Theoretically, of course. But it was the best plan he could come up with.

Ethan used his heel to put an "X" on the ground under the spot where Merlin was. Next, he climbed out of the crater. "Nia, go to the opposite side!"

The foxgirl looked at him curiously but scrambled out of the crater and then positioned herself directly across from him.

Ethan adjusted himself so that the invisible line between him and Nia passed directly over the "X" inside the crater. He smiled and put another "X" where he was standing. "Nia, make an X where you're standing right now!"

Everyone was watching them now as his wife made her own mark on the ground. She looked at him with a raised eyebrow. "Now what?"

"I'm going to open a portal from here to there," he answered, speaking loud enough that everyone could hear. "It should pass directly through the area where Merlin is. If I'm lucky, I can grab him as I go through the Bifrost."

Michalus scratched his chin and looked from one side of the crater to the other. "Seems plausible."

Drorm looked at the two points and shrugged. "That seems almost too simple to work."

Ethan sighed. He actually hoped it was that simple. If not, he wasn't sure how he was going to get to Merlin. "Let's hope it is that simple."

"Well, do it already, wizard-boy," Ainslee urged.

Nodding, Ethan focused on the opposite side of the crater. "Here goes nothing."

Bending the magic to his will, Ethan opened up a portal to the opposite side. Without hesitating, he stepped through and into the Bifrost.

As always, the journey into the Bifrost took longer to him than it appeared to the others. To them, he knew it would seem instantaneous. But for him, seconds passed as he sped through the rainbow tunnel.

He expected to see Merlin, floating or lying somewhere inside the tunnel but there was nothing. Merlin wasn't in the Bifrost where he thought he would... WAIT! He caught a shape just outside the tunnel but he had passed it too fast. But he was sure it had been the shape of a man. And then he was suddenly on the opposite side of the crater.

Ethan blinked.

"Uh... where is he?" Ainslee asked, face screwing up in confusion. "Weren't you supposed to bring her da back with you?"

He saw the disappointment on everyone's faces, but especially on Guinevere's face. He let the excitement he was feeling spread to his face. "I think I saw him!"

Guinevere brightened instantly, her eyes going wide. "You did? Can you get him?"

Ethan made a face. "I think so. He was just outside but

I caught a glimpse of him. If I adjust the path of the portal slightly, I should be able to intersect him!"

The warrior woman nodded enthusiastically and then gestured for him to get on with it.

Spinning to face his original point of origin, Ethan adjusted the angle of the portal slightly and then opened another one. Without a moment of hesitation, he stepped through.

Once again, Ethan sped through the Bifrost. The rainbow tunnel swirled around him but he kept his eyes darting around, desperately trying to see the man he'd come to rescue. He was hoping to see him in the middle of the tunnel so he could just grab him but that wasn't the case. Instead, he saw Merlin just outside the tunnel again, but this time to the opposite side.

Stepping out onto the ground, Ethan cursed. He was excited to have seen him, but for some reason, his calculations had been off.

"No luck?" Drorm asked and the question was echoed on Ethan's other companions' faces.

Ethan didn't understand it. He only adjusted it slightly and now Merlin was on the opposite side. He held up a finger. "Let me try that again."

Turning around, he adjusted his trajectory ever so slightly. Then, with a push of his will, he opened a portal and again stepped into the Bifrost. This time, Merlin was on the opposite side. The moment Ethan stepped out of the portal, he spun around. He tried twice more in rapid succession before finally letting out a loud curse.

"What is it now?" Guinevere demanded.

"Problems?" Drorm asked at the same time.

"Where Merlin?" Par'karr asked, looking Ethan up and down.

Growling, Ethan spun back around. "I don't understand. I keep missing him. I see him, just outside the tunnel, but I can't seem to get him in the tunnel. Sometimes he's on the right, other times he's on the left. But he's never in the tunnel."

Michalus scratched his chin, looking thoughtful but not offering any suggestions. Ethan looked around to the faces of his other companions but none of them offered a suggestion either.

"You can't just grab him as you pass by?" Ainslee asked, squinting at him. "I mean, you said you see him, right?"

"Yes," Ethan replied, trying not to let his frustration show in his voice. "But I can't grab him. I'm moving through the Bifrost, so I can't actually reach through it and grab him."

"Can you stop yourself?" she asked.

"No, I don't have any way of..." Ethan trailed off, cocking his head and looking at Michalus. The wizard looked back and pointed at himself.

"What?" Michalus muttered.

"You once told me that you could cast magic through a portal, as long as part of you was on that side, right?" Ethan asked, an idea forming in his head.

"Yes, I believe I remember saying that," the wizard replied, eyeing Ethan cautiously. "And it is possible to..."

"But part of you stays on this side," Ethan continued, cutting off the wizard.

"Well, naturally, the rest of you..." Michalus answered

but Ethan cut him off again as the idea matured in his mind. He checked his HUD.

Mana: 23

All of the portaling had really taken a toll on his *Mana*. He needed some time to regenerate. Either that, or a quick romp with his wife. Considering the lack of privacy, that was out of the question.

"I need your help," he told the mage, gesturing around at the ruins. "I'm low on mana but I need you to use air to move some stones to either side of my X down in the crater. Stack them high enough so that they are even with the top of the crater, which is where Merlin is."

Michalus looked confused but then understanding dawned in his eyes. "Yes, you know... that may work."

"Let's hope!" Ethan replied and gestured for the elf to begin.

"What are you planning to do?" Guinevere asked, though the others were looking at him with either confusion or curiosity.

"I'm not going to go all the way into the portal," Ethan told them. "I'm going to basically stick my upper torso in and try to get him without actually going all the way through."

"And that will work?" Drorm asked skeptically.

"It's the only other plan I have at the moment," he replied and then turned to watch Michalus moving the large pieces of stone and rubble with *Air*. The wizard quickly stacked them atop each other until, just as Ethan had asked, there were two piles to either side of the X in the crater.

Using a slight bit of *Air* to float himself to one of the piles, Ethan took a deep breath. Looking around, he could see everyone was watching him with anticipation. He sighed. No pressure.

With a push of his willpower, he opened up a portal in front of him, almost directly over the X down below in the crater. He took another deep breath and pushed his upper torso into the Bifrost.

Ethan was back in Bifrost, in the rainbow tunnel. He spotted Merlin to his left but before he could do anything, he was suddenly looking out the opposite side of the portal. But, the portal was still open since half of him was on the opposite side. He looked behind him to see his lower body halfway in the portal. It looked as if he had been sawed in half. Ethan shivered.

Taking another deep breath, Ethan pulled himself back through the portal. This time, he already knew where Merlin would be and he deliberately angled himself towards that side. Reaching out his arms, he brushed them against the side of the tunnel.

He felt a chilling electric sensation as his hands touched the side of the rainbow tunnel and it repelled him. Gritting his teeth against the sensation, Ethan pushed his hands through just as he passed Merlin.

His hands felt like they were being electrocuted but Ethan forced himself to grab onto the form of Merlin as he passed him. He felt his hands grab hold of something and he held on with all his might.

And then Ethan was back on the stack of stones but

now someone was with him, throwing off his balance. Releasing the man with him, Ethan windmilled his arms but it was no good. He lost his balance and fell off the stack of stones, into the crater below.

A moment after he impacted the ground, something - or should he say, someone - fell atop him.

Grunting, Ethan looked up into the face of a man who looked no older than he did. The man fluttered his eyes and forced a smile. "What took you so long?"

Then the man's eyes rolled back into his head and he slumped unconscious.

Ethan looked up at the faces of his companions, looking down on him from the top of the crater. He groaned. "A little help please!"

And that's when the Queen attacked.

*I*T HADN'T TAKEN *the Queen long to understand the talk of the bipeds. Nor had it taken her long to discover her prey. Listening to their conversation, she was able to determine which of the two wizards could do the portal magic. She could have struck then, but the conversation intrigued her.*

The humanoids believed that they could rescue the Merlin, bring him back to this world. The Queen didn't fully understand exactly where the Merlin was, but she did know they intended to bring him back here - to this world.

The Queen's mandibles clicked together hungrily. If she waited, she might be able to have her prey, the extra wizard AND the Merlin - all in one attack. With their combined knowledge, she would be powerful. Very powerful.

So she watched as her prey created one portal after another. All of the portals were within eyeshot of each other and then grew even closer. The Queen watched with fascination, having never seen portals actually created.

Finally, her prey went through the portal and this time he appeared with another humanoid. Both eyes fixed on the falling wizards as they disappeared into a crater. She only caught a glance but that was all it took. The prey had brought back the Merlin.

It was time to strike.

57

Everyone had been focused on Ethan's attempts to get Merlin from the Bifrost. They hadn't noticed the giant, but silent, praying mantis form of the Queen moving through the rubble. When she suddenly sprang from behind a mostly collapsed building, she took everyone by surprise.

Par'karr's rabbits were the closest and also the first to react. Unlike regular rabbits, which might have frozen at the sight of a twelve-foot-tall insect, the demon rabbits reacted like fighters. They sensed the threat and charged.

Ethan barely saw the rabbits move from his vantage point down in the crater, but he did see the head of the giant praying mantis and knew instinctively it was the Queen. It wasn't much of a glance, but it was enough for him to get an idea of her size.

The normal Doemenagg they'd encountered stood perhaps six feet tall, with their antennae and were equally as long from front to back. The Queen was easily twice that. She had to be twelve feet tall from the ground to the top of her antennae. Not only was she taller, she seemed larger, especially in the thorax.

She was a large and imposing figure that would normally scare him just in her sheer size and appearance. But Ethan also knew she had immense psychic powers. He'd felt them in his brief contact with her. And since the lesser Doemenagg had magical powers, he had to assume she did too.

A giant praying mantis - one with strong psychic powers and which wielded magic. Any of that by itself would be terrifying. Put together in one creature and it was something Ethan had hoped he would never have to face.

Scrambling up the side of the crater, he reached the top just in time to see the rabbits dodging under the Queen's thorax. They then launched themselves at one of her legs, only to have their horns rebound from the tough carapace. Stunned or surprised, they didn't see the Queen's scythe-like forearm coming down. The long arm skewered the rabbits, causing them to disappear in a puff of red-tinted smoke.

Par'karr, who had recovered enough to follow the movements of his rabbits, cried out when his pets were destroyed by the Queen. They weren't really dead. They'd only been banished back to wherever they came from. But it would take some time for Par'karr to re-summon them. For now, they were out of the fight.

But the rabbits had bought the others the time they needed to recognize the threat. Nia, Guinevere and Drorm were the first to react. They pulled their weapons free of sheaths and turned towards the incoming threat. All three of them had spun towards the Queen, ready to attack or defend.

The giant insect's large, triangular head swiveled back in Ethan's direction. The large bulbous eyes fixed on him, then the eyes rotated to look down into the crater, before fixing on him again.

Ethan swore. This enormous praying mantis creature was the Queen of the Doemenagg. It was the creature whose mind had touched him when he had invaded the mind of one of her drones. Somehow, she was in telepathic communication with her drones and had sensed him in the mind of her drone.

He hadn't given the Queen another thought since the dragons had made it their personal mission to destroy the Doemenagg. He'd assumed they had killed the Queen. It now seemed that, unfortunately, she had escaped the dragons' retribution.

"That's one of those Doemennie-thingys!" Ainslee yelled. She grabbed a small hammer from her leather belt. Unfortunately, it was more of a utility hammer than an actual weapon and Ethan doubted the hammer would be very effective against the Queen.

They'd fought the Doemenagg assassins the Queen had sent after them before. If the Queen's carapace was anything like theirs, it would be impervious to nearly any weapon. The only vulnerable parts were the joints, where the carapace didn't cover.

Other than those few vulnerable spots, the only other thing that had proven effective against the Doemenagg were the magical energy blades that Michalus had taught him. Ethan frowned and pulled up his HUD.

Mana: 18

He cursed again. Creating all the portals in rapid cessation had left him with nearly no *Mana*. The manablades were very *Mana* intensive. He didn't have nearly enough to create one.

The Queen's eyes moved one way and then another, each operating independently of each other. She seemed to be taking in Ethan's companions, possibly doing a threat assessment. Then again, Ethan really had no idea what an alien insect being like the Queen might be thinking. But her pause did give Ethan an opportunity.

He had almost no *Mana*. He didn't have time to let it regenerate naturally. And he doubted the Queen was going to let him "recharge" his *Mana* with Nia. That left only one other possibility. The Grail.

Not only could the Grail heal nearly any wound, it could also instantly restore all of his *Stamina* and *Mana* instantly. Unfortunately, the portal pouch he'd created to the Grail's resting place had been destroyed by the ogre channeler.

He checked his *Mana* again.

Mana: 18

Was it enough to open a small portal, just large enough for his hand to grab the Grail? He had no choice. He had to try. The Queen was still hesitating, her eyes looking from person to person. Ethan knew he had to do it now.

With a focus of his will, Ethan opened a small portal. It was just large enough to fit the Grail. But that was all he needed. He started to reach through. That's when he noticed that the Queen was staring at him. Her head had snapped in his direction and both eyes were fixed on him. He swore.

With speed that didn't seem possible for such a large creature, the Queen rushed forward. Had she been closer, she would have been upon them before they could react. As it was, the Queen had to cover about fifty feet. This allowed Nia, Guinevere, and Drorm to react.

Drorm stepped to the side, bringing his axe around at a slice aimed at the giant insect's leg. His intent had probably been to take out one of the legs and cripple her. Unfortunately, Drorm's axe was just steel. It bounced off the Queen's leg.

The reverberation caught the orc by surprise and he didn't react in time to avoid a swipe of the Doemenagg's forearm. The side of her arm hit Drorm across his torso, sending him flying away. He hit a pile of nearby rubble and rolled to a stop.

At the same, Guinevere stepped into the path of the creature, ducked between her legs and brought her sword up into the underbelly of the Queen's thorax. Or rather, that had been her intention. Like Drorm's axe, the warrior woman's sword couldn't quite penetrate the tough armored chitin of the Queen.

Guinevere's sword scraped against the creature's underbelly with a sound like fingernails on a chalkboard, but the Queen didn't even slow. She seemed to have a single-minded determination to get to Ethan but she did kick Guinevere with one of her hind legs as she went past her. The former queen was hit in the back and went sprawling across the ground.

As the Queen closed on him, Ethan's hand had closed on the Grail and pulled it through the portal. He conjured a bit of water into it as he brought it to his lips. Just as the Queen loomed over him, he took a sip. He felt the cool sensation of the healing magic and instantly saw his HUD flash with the update.

Mana: 128

Unfortunately, the Queen had reached him and it didn't appear it would make any difference. He watched as the scythe-like forearm came down at him. He started to conjure *Air* to deflect the arm but the Queen's antennae flicked together and he felt her countering his magic. His *Air* shield died before it even formed.

This was it. The razor-sharp forearm was going to skewer him and then it would be all over. He had failed. He started to utter what would probably be his last curse.

Then he felt something crash into him, knocking him to the side just as the forearm was about to make impact with him. He stumbled to the side, rolling out of the way and looking back just in time to see the Queen's forearm impaling Nia through the center of her chest. His wife looked down at her chest and then turned her head to Ethan. Then her eyes went dull and her lifeless body went limp.

Ethan screamed. The scream was something primal as he saw Nia's dead body and felt his heart breaking. But it wasn't just the pain in his heart. There was another pain from his chest. The pain burned into him and through him and he knew instinctively it was the dragon's sigil.

Knowledge flooded into his mind. It was knowledge from someone else's mind, but it was as if he had learned it himself. The information seemed to integrate with his consciousness even as a new message appeared in his HUD.

`You have gained: Time magic.`

Magic flared within him, activated at some unconscious level. Everything around him slowed and then stopped completely. The entire world suddenly frozen in the moment between a heartbeat.

And then, as if someone hit the rewind button, everything suddenly began running in reverse.

58

Ethan was suddenly thrust outside his body. Or rather, his awareness was thrust out of his body as he watched time rewinding in fast motion. The out of body experience was strange enough, but he was also trying to wrap his mind around the new knowledge he had. Knowledge that he somehow knew the dragon had accumulated over thousands of years. No, tens of thousands of years. And they had shared it with him.

He watched his body tumble out of the way of the Queen's forearm and saw it impale Nia. Instinctively, he reached out to her but he had no body. He was like an insubstantial ghost only able to witness what was happening, not actually act on it.

Frowning inwardly, he continued to watch things rewinding until he felt himself drawn back into his body just after he took a sip from the Grail.

He felt the cool sensation of the healing magic and

instantly saw his HUD flash with the update, just like the first time.

Mana: 128

Just as before, the Queen reached him. He watched as the scythe-like forearm came down at him. This time, he knew the *Air* wouldn't work and instead, he tried conjuring the manablade. Before it formed, he saw the Queen's antennae flick together. He sensed countering the mageblade was more difficult for her. It was as if she hadn't encountered it before and the complexity of the magic gave her problems. But she learned quickly. The Queen managed to counter it just before it formed in front of him.

Then he was knocked away from her incoming attack by Nia and he tumbled away, only to watch her die again.

Neither Nia nor the Queen had shown any recognition of the events that had transpired before. Only him. He knew this to be true somehow. Some memory that wasn't really his own knew this was the way it worked.

He knew it wasn't his memory. It was the memory of Firestorm. The dragon's memories about time had somehow been embedded in the sigil and had been transferred to him. He grimaced as the memories continued to integrate into his own mind.

And then things began running in reverse again, like some type of weird time loop. He watched himself, Nia, the Queen and everyone else move through their movements backwards until once more, he was back at the point where he'd just taken a sip of the Grail.

Mana: 128

Ethan tried another spell but the Queen countered it, Nia died and time reset. He cursed inwardly as time reset. Then he did the entire process over again. And failed again. And again. And again.

Mana: 128

He tried every trick he could think of. Once or twice, he even succeeded in hurting the Queen, only to get impaled himself. And time reset.

Mana: 128

Nia died. Time reset. He died. Time reset. And kept resetting each time he failed. It happened so many times, he began to despair that he was caught in some sort of endless loop that would never end.

Mana: 128

Yet, he knew from the dragon's experience that he could break it. But once he did, time would move on and whatever outcome happened would become permanent. And so far, he didn't like any of the outcomes since they all involved either Nia dying, him dying or the Queen plunging her brain-sucking appendage into his eye.

Ethan switched tactics, going from physical magic like *Air* and *Fire*, to *Portal* magic and *Mind* magic. Unfortunately, the Queen seemed to know *Aether* magic and countered his portals before they formed.

The *Mind* magic wasn't countered, but instead he ran into ironclad defenses and very powerful offensive capabilities as the Queen tried to take over his own mind. Luckily, some part of him reset time if she got close to breaking through into his mind.

Mana: 128

And thus, a game of cat and mouse began with him probing her defenses and her trying to infiltrate his mind. But now, he had a decided advantage. He knew how she would mentally attack him before she did it and could strengthen his mind or block off access before she got in.

Each time, he got closer to penetrating her defenses while lasting longer against her own attacks. And because they were attacks of the mind, they happened so quickly that every time loop, he made more and more progress against the Queen's fortress-like defense.

Finally, after so many tries and failures that he literally could no longer count them, Ethan found a weakness. A tiny crack in her mental defenses, but one which Ethan hammered into with experience of a hundred former attempts, possibly even a thousand. He'd lost count long ago.

Mana: 128

With the next time reset, Ethan slammed a focused beam of his will into the hole in the Queen's defense, pushing into her mind before she had a chance to stop him. He seized control of her body, freezing her arm on its way down. But even as he did so, he felt her mounting her mental defense, as well as an offense against his mind.

He considered killing her then and there, while she was frozen. He could have done it. With her antennae frozen, she couldn't counter his spells. He just needed to use some *Air* on Excalibur and he could slice her head off. Yet, he hesitated.

Ethan had questions. Why was she eating the brains of wizards? Why did she want his brain? Once she died, the answers would die with her. So instead of killing her, he delved into her memories. One memory at a time, one time loop at a time.

He couldn't sustain the connection for long at first, but time was on his side. She managed to break free and he reset time. He did the same thing again, but probed different memories. Once more she broke free and he reset time. This went on, over and over, time after time until Ethan had a clearer picture of the Doemenagg Queen and her motivations.

From what he could gather, the Doemenagg had some sort of genetic memory. The memories were somehow passed along to all versions of the insect creatures, but suppressed. Only a Queen could access all the memories. The others had the memories encoded, but lacked the ability to use the memories.

After dozens, or perhaps hundreds, of delves into the Queen's mind, he could see a long history of the creature's homeworld. How generation after generation of the creatures evolved, passing their memories to the Queen of the next generation. And when that Queen died, one of the drones was able to lay a new Queen egg, containing all of the genetic memories passed from the last Queen. It was a strange, but seemingly efficient, way of passing the memories from one generation to the next.

The creatures had also developed the ability to "eat" the memories of the other creatures of its world, making it the apex predator of its very large planet. A planet that had been completely subjugated by the Doemenagg.

Ethan shivered at the thought of living on such a world. Then he realized that this had nearly become that world, over a thousand years ago. The only thing that had stopped the Queen had been Arthur and his knights. But they'd paid the price.

He sifted through the memories, one by one, going back over a thousand years. He saw the drone abducted through a portal. He saw it lay an egg, a Queen egg. He saw the Queen hatch and begin the slow build-up of her nest and the creation of an army of Doemenagg.

The memories even included the fight with Arthur and the beheading of the first Queen born on this world. But there was no memory of the Queen actually killing Arthur. Ethan frowned as he searched for any memory of Arthur's demise. There was none. It must have been done by a drone or assassin after the Queen had died. A memory she hadn't inherited.

But there was something else. Something Ethan couldn't quite wrap his head around at first. The original drone who had come here had possessed a HUD. But when it laid the queen egg and the first Queen was born, she didn't possess one. He wasn't sure what that meant. He delved deeper, looking for answers.

Finally, after days or weeks of time loops, Ethan had the information he wanted about the Doemenagg. He had it, literally, from the Queen's own vantage point.

They were like locusts. Just highly evolved, brain-sucking, intelligent locusts. And they - or rather the Queen - seemed hardwired to want to dominate the planet. But yet, she wanted to return to her own world.

That was why she wanted Ethan's brain. She wanted his knowledge of portals. Little did she know it wasn't just his knowledge, but also his special abilities that he had through the character development that seemed mostly possible due to his own HUD. The specialization he'd taken in *Aether* magic.

Now that he had the information he needed, Ethan wondered what he should do with the Queen. He could kill her. It would be easy. He knew just how to break through her mental defenses and freeze her long enough to kill her a dozen different ways.

Ethan sighed. He'd seen and felt Nia's death so many times, not to mention his own, that he was sick of death. He really just wanted the Queen to go away and not bother them ever again. And he thought he knew how he could do that. He smiled and triggered another time loop.

Mana: 128

The Queen had reached him. He watched as the scythe-like forearm came down at him and he struck out with his *Mind* magic and froze her in place. Then he sent a mental message to the Queen.

Doemenagg, I've come to bargain.

THE QUEEN FROZE, *her body completely locked into place, unable to move. The human had cut through her carefully laid mental defenses as if they were not even there.*

She'd consumed dozens of wizards with the knowledge of mental magic. The Queen had integrated their knowledge of mental defense in creating her own mental defense. Her mind should have been impenetrable. It would take a master mental magician hours, perhaps days to unravel even the first layer of her defense.

Panicking, she tried lashing out mentally at the human wizard in front of her but he countered her every attack. His mind was incredibly quick. So fast, it almost seemed as if he knew what she was going to do before she did it.

Her panic grew. This human held her completely immobile. She was helpless. Out of the corner of her eye, she saw the sword. The sword that had killed her once before - wielded by the Arthur. Was that to be her fate this time, as well?

Then, the human spoke in her mind.

59

———

*D*oemenagg, *I've come to bargain,* he told the Queen.

I will crush you and devour your brain! Your knowledge will be mine, the Queen sent back. As she had done hundreds or thousands of times before, the Doemenagg Queen struck out again with her mental attacks.

Before, Ethan would have been hard pressed to resist her mental attack. That wasn't the case any longer. He'd been on the receiving end so many times, he knew exactly how to counter her predictable attacks.

The attacks came quickly, but like watching the reruns of a show on TV, he knew exactly what was going to happen. And he knew how to beat her. Within a few seconds, he had his own will wrapped around her inner core. He squeezed it, just to prove he could destroy her.

No! Wait! the Queen's mental voice rang out, tinged with panic and surprise. *Do not kill me!*

I will, if we can't come to an agreement. Ethan shot back. *Now stop struggling or I'll just crush you now!*

He sensed the Queen's reluctance. She was used to winning. Used to being the dominant one. Except with the dragons. He knew from examining her memories that the Queen had known she stood no chance against them. Ethan hadn't probed deeper, but somehow she'd sensed their power.

Finally, the Doemenagg Queen stopped her mental struggles. Ethan allowed her to lower her appendages.

"Stop fighting," Ethan told the others. "I'm talking with her."

Stopping just before she tackled him out of the way, Nia glanced at him and then the Queen. She watched the Queen through narrowed eyes as her forearm blades lowered. The foxgirl glanced back at Ethan. "Are you sure?"

"Yes," Ethan said.

Guinevere, who was scrambling back to her feet, looked at him like he was crazy. "What do you mean you're talking with her? Kill her! She killed Arthur!"

"No!" Ethan said, holding up a finger. "This isn't the same Queen. Arthur killed that one."

"Not that same Queen?" The warrior woman shot him an incredulous look. "Are you crazy?"

"I've seen into her mind. Into her memories," Ethan replied, still keeping the mental link with the Queen at the ready. The slightest thought from him and he would crush her instantly.

He did notice, in his HUD, that the use of the *Time* magic and then the *Mind* magic had dropped his *Mana* back down. It reset every time the time loop had reset, but now that he hadn't reset it, it appeared to have consumed quite a bit of his *Mana.*

Mana: 63

He couldn't sustain his hold on the Queen indefinitely. He needed to resolve it as quickly as possible.

"Just trust me on this," Ethan said. "All of you. Just stand down for a moment while I talk with her."

"Talk how?" Drorm asked. The big orc was up and bent his neck one direction and then another, obviously stiff from being tossed around.

"Mentally," Ethan replied. "Now, please, just give me a moment."

Your hive is eager to kill me, the Queen said.

Ethan frowned at the Queen. *Can you blame them after everything you have done?*

I have done what I have done for the betterment of my kind! the Queen replied, her mental tone full of righteous indignation.

Perhaps, Ethan said. He'd seen many of her memories. He knew she probably believed that. To her and her kind, they were little more than food - or vessels to lay eggs inside. But that wasn't the point right now. And he was running out of *Mana.*

I will send you back to your world, Ethan told her. And saw the two eyes, which had been looking around at the others, both snap towards him.

You will send me back to my planet? How? The Queen's

mandible snapped open and closed and the multifaceted eyes stared down at him.

How is not important. I can do it. I will send you back to your planet where you can rule the rest of your kind, he told her. *But. I want to know where all of your eggs are. I'm going to destroy them.*

He sensed anger briefly, but then it faded. The two eyes seemed to almost cross as the Queen stared down at him. *The dragons have already destroyed my hive. There are no eggs remaining.*

Ethan narrowed his eyes warily. *And you haven't laid any since?*

I have traveled here at haste to find you, I even consumed some of my brood when I was unable to hunt. All to reach you, she replied with a snap of her mandibles.

To suck out my brain. Ethan snorted.

Yes, the Queen replied simply. *I need your knowledge to return home. And then, to conquer other worlds.*

Ethan gave the Queen's mind a little squeeze. *That's not happening. I'll send you back to your own world. I know you possess some knowledge of portals, but if I find out you're invading other worlds, I will do something REALLY nasty.*

The Queen cocked her head in curiosity. It went all the way over at a 90-degree angle and looked very unnatural. *What will you do?*

Ethan grinned wickedly at her, not sure if she would understand the gesture. *I will tell the dragons where you went and open a portal to your world myself.*

The Queen's head snapped up, her eyes seeming to grow larger. *No, you must not.*

Firestorm's mate is still a bit upset at having gotten a whiff of your neurotoxin. Firestorm himself isn't too happy either. Imagine what they would do if I told them where your home-world was. Feeling panic through the mental link with the Queen, Ethan kept the smile in place. *They might just wipe out your entire race.*

He knew from the Queen's memories that more than anything else, she feared the dragons. He had been hoping the Queen would react as she had. First and foremost, the survival of her species seemed to be hard-wired into her. Ethan hoped he'd just used it against her.

From his time delving into the Queen's memories, Ethan knew she'd absorbed many brains - some of which might have been other aliens from other worlds. If she shared their memories and figured out how to open a portal, she could potentially invade all sorts of worlds. He wasn't going to let that happen. At least, he hoped the threat of the dragons would keep her from even attempting it.

In all honesty, he didn't even know if the dragons would care. Once the Queen was gone, they might care less what she did to other worlds. That was especially true of the female dragon. She'd barely said thank you for saving her.

From what Firestorm had said, his mate didn't really care for humans or any of the bipedal races. Ethan really had no guarantee that the dragons would really go after the Queen if she didn't keep her word. Luckily, she didn't know that.

There are no eggs left, the Queen repeated. *They have all been destroyed. If you send me back to my world, I will not leave it.*

Ethan didn't sense any falsehood, but he had no way of knowing for sure. Her emotions were alien so it was possible he wouldn't sense any lies. He nodded. Then he remembered something else.

You know you're not the original queen, Ethan told her. *You weren't even a queen when you were brought to this world. When you go back, there will be another queen in place. She isn't just going to abdicate the throne.*

There was a sense of annoyance at his words but then he felt a mental shrug. She fixed him with both her eyes again. *You are correct. But I am the stronger now.*

He started to ask why but he realized the answer. *Magic.*

Yes, the Queen said with a click of her mandibles. *With the magic I have learned from this world, I will dispatch the pretender and then I will be the one and only Queen.*

Ethan wondered if it would be the equivalent of killing her mother, a great grandmother, or perhaps even a sister. Then he realized something. He didn't care. He just wanted to get this creature off their planet. He looked her in the eyes. *So we have a deal?*

Yes, we have a deal. You will return me home and I will stay on my world and command my children, the Queen replied.

Then go, he said and pointed behind her.

Mentally, he opened a portal to the place he'd seen in her mind. He'd picked out a particular section of the planet that had been very unique because of the build-up of the hive. The portal formed and opened, showing him the image of her world with hundreds, perhaps even thousands of the Doemenagg drones coming in and out of the hive. Thankfully, the portal was invisible from the other side.

The Queen turned too, eyes widening as she looked into the portal. He sensed triumph in her mind for just a moment before she skittered through the portal without so much as a thank you.

The moment she crossed the portal, Ethan snapped it closed. He hoped that was the last he would ever see of the Queen or any other Doemenagg.

Michalus opened his mouth to ask a question but a voice from behind them startled them all.

"Anyone care to tell me what I missed," the voice said. Ethan spun to see Merlin. The man looked half dead and was holding onto the sides of the crater with both hands. Despite his haggard expression, he was smiling. "Oh, and if it's not too much trouble, would you mind if I had a sip from the cup you're holding."

60

Merlin recovered quickly after drinking from the Grail. The man, who appeared no older than his mid-twenties, looked like he could be Guinevere's brother. No doubt, his youthful appearance was the result of having drunk from the Fountain of Youth.

Ethan shook his head. He had carried this vision of Merlin as this bearded old man in robes, probably leaning on a staff. Instead, the legendary wizard was a young man, not so different from Ethan himself. He was medium height, skinnier even than Ethan, with a mop of unkempt brown hair and a thin beard.

"Father!" Guinevere cried, rushing into her father's arms. Merlin caught her and hugged her to him. "I thought you were dead."

Merlin just held his daughter for long moments without saying anything. Then he went into a coughing fit and pushed her away.

Concern creased Guinevere's features as she looked at her father. "Are you alright? Did the Grail not cure you?"

The brown-haired wizard coughed for a full minute before seeming to get it under control. He cleared his throat as he stood straight. "I'm afraid the Grail can't cure everything. I was burning my own body to keep my Mana up and stay alive in the Bifrost."

Ethan nodded. He knew from experience that the Grail didn't cure everything. He'd burned through one of his *Stamina* points when he'd saved Nia from a Cthulhu. Despite numerous uses of the Grail since then, the stat was gone permanently.

"How much did you lose?" Ethan asked him.

The legendary wizard turned towards him. "More than is good for me. Much more."

Merlin stopped and the man's eyes washed over him, taking in every detail. For a second, they seemed to go glassy. "Ethan, huh? Just Ethan? No surname?"

Cocking his head, he looked at Merlin. No one had said his name and he hadn't felt the wizard channel. He raised an eyebrow. "Did you just... use your HUD on me? Do you have a HUD?"

"The display? Of course I have one, all outlanders do," Merlin replied with a smile. He pointed into the sky. "The aliens that control the rifts..." Merlin snorted. "Or try to control the rifts - implant them into those that are sucked in through the rifts."

Ethan felt his eyes go wide. "So, wait! You were abducted too!"

"Indeed I was," Merlin replied. "Quite some time ago. Though, time moves differently here." The wizard pointed up to the two suns with the black hole between them. "Thanks to the vortex up there."

"The black hole?" Ethan asked, following the man's finger to the twin suns. He knew the basics of the theory of relativity, but no specifics. In fact, most of what he knew from black holes was from science fiction books. "It's warping time, isn't it?"

"Time." Merlin shrugged. "Or the perception of time. If the two things are indeed separate. But time isn't as relative to you any longer, is it?"

Ethan peaked an eyebrow again at the wizard.

"Oh, I might have been barely conscious," the wizard said. Merlin gave him an appraising look. "But I felt time magic being used. Quite powerfully, I might add."

"Time magic?" Michalus asked, walking over.

"Ah... uh... Michalus, right?" Merlin said with a smile and extended a hand to the elven wizard.

"Yes," Michalus replied. "You..."

"Helped you with the... uh... what did you call it again, oh yes, portal detector," Merlin replied with a nod. He broke into another coughing fit and held up a finger for them to wait.

"You should let my father rest," Guinevere said protectively.

Merlin stopped coughing and gave a kindly smile to his daughter. "Thank you, Gwenny, but it's been quite some time since I talked to anyone. The last thing I want right now is to be quiet or be alone."

Guinevere's face grew red and she gave her father an embarrassed look. "Father! I told you not to call me Gwenny in front of others!"

"Oh yes, sorry about that Gwenn... er... Guinevere," Merlin replied, though Ethan didn't hear any real remorse in the man's tone.

"What was that about time magic?" Michalus asked, resuming where he left off.

Merlin nodded. "Time magic. The branch of magic, or skill if you prefer, that deals with the manipulation of time itself."

Michalus blinked. "That's possible? I've never read... anything about that."

"I'm not surprised," the older wizard replied. "Until a few minutes ago, I believed the dragons and I were the only ones who knew it."

"The dragons know it?!" the elven wizard gasped. "You're sure?"

"Who do you think taught me?" Merlin asked and pulled down his tunic slightly to reveal the top of a curved tattoo on his chest. He nodded to Ethan. "Unless I miss my guess, you have one too."

Ethan nodded, pulling his own shirt down to reveal the top of his own tattoo sigil.

Merlin grinned. "You must have done something extraordinary to have earned that. I had to enchant an entire mountain to prevent portals!"

"I gave Firestorm's mate a sip from the Grail that cured her of the Doemenagg's neurotoxin," he replied.

The older wizard nodded gravely. "I'm sorry to hear that. The mind poison the Doemenagg produces has a profound effect on any living creature with a nervous system. Sometimes, the damage is so great that, even with the Grail, the person is never quite the same. It was the main reason I created the Grail - to help those in the Doemenagg War who had been affected."

"About that," Ethan said, pointing to the Grail that Merlin still held. "How did you..."

"How did I create an artifact of such power?" Merlin replied with a chuckle. "That's probably a topic for another time. I won't bore the others with all of the details."

The wizard looked around. "I assume we have some other place we can go? Someplace perhaps a bit more comfortable... with something to eat?"

"Ah, yes, father," Guinevere answered, gesturing to Ethan. "Ethan is now the king."

"The king? Is he really?" Merlin asked with a cocked eyebrow. Then he glanced between Guinevere and Ethan. "Gwenn... Guinevere, you didn't put him up to that did you?"

"What?" Guinevere shot back. "The place needed a new leader and this area needs a king. And he's the best man I've met since... since..."

"Arthur," Merlin finished, his tone gentle.

"Since Arthur," Guinevere said and then cleared her throat.

Merlin looked between Guinevere and Ethan, then his eyes settled on the sword at Ethan's hip. He nodded. "Well, you were able to retrieve Excalibur. And you know time magic. Probably a dragon-friend."

"You might make a decent king." The old wizard nodded. He cast his eyes from Ethan to Guinevere. "You know, if you need a queen..."

"Father!" Guinevere growled, face going red again. "You don't even know him and you're trying to set me up?!"

Merlin chuckled. "It's a father's prerogative to want to see his daughter happy..."

Ethan cleared his throat. "Uh... thank you, but I already have a queen."

He gestured to Nia who walked over to him. He put his arm around her waist. "This is my wife..."

"Nia," Merlin said after a moment of his eyes going glassy. "A pleasure to meet you. I hope you didn't take any offense to my suggestion."

Nia shook her head. "I am Tal'Cha, first wife. But she would make an acceptable second wife."

Merlin's eyebrows shot up. "Second wife, you say? And you would be fine with that?"

"Ethan is Alpha," she replied. "On my world, the Alpha has many wives."

"Fascinating," Merlin said with a smile. "I don't believe the foxlings on this world still observe that practice." He looked to his daughter and gave her a smile. "Second wife?"

"I will not be second to anyone!" Guinevere shot back. She seemed to catch herself and then gave Nia and Ethan an apologetic look. "No offense."

"Uh..." Ethan started and then shook his head. He needed to get off the polygamy topic as quickly as possible. "I think your dad was right. Why don't we go back to Castlehaven."

"Hopefully there is food in Castlehaven," Merlin said with a smile.

"If you want food," said Ainslee's gruff voice. "We

should go to Hawkshead! Elspeth can cook us up something real good! And you need to be returning me home before some dragon or ogre or something else shows up!"

Ethan looked around at his friends. "Hawkshead for dinner?"

"Par'karr like Hawkshead," the kobold squeaked.

Nodding, Ethan turned away from the group and opened a portal to the village of Hawkshead. One by one, his friends entered the portal until he was the last one. He gave one last glance at the desolation that had once been Patheos and then stepped through the portal to Hawkshead.

61

"Then you weren't really trapped for a couple of hundred years?" Michalus asked as he took another bite of the grilled venison Elspeth had made for the group.

Fearghas and Elspeth sat at the end of one of the tables they'd pushed together and listened as Merlin recounted his tale. Michalus seemed the most interested in it, though they all paid attention to the old wizard.

"Yes and no," Merlin replied, taking a sip of his mead. "Time moves differently in and out of the Bifrost."

"Which is why the journey seems longer when you're going through the Bifrost than when you're watching someone walk through a portal," Ethan added.

"Precisely," the old wizard agreed. He sighed. "When the explosion knocked me through the Bifrost tunnel and into the Bifrost itself, I found myself dying. Unable to move or open a portal from inside the Bifrost, I was effectively trapped there. I couldn't breathe and was quickly running out of oxygen. I used a bit of my own time magic to go into a sort of trance..."

"Like suspended animation?" Ethan asked, furrowing his brow. He hadn't even thought of using time magic for something like that. Now that Merlin mentioned it, his mind was already thinking about ways he could do it.

"Suspended animation?" Merlin repeated. "I'm not quite sure what that is, but it slowed my body down and allowed me to stay alive in there without being able to breathe."

Ethan nodded. "Suspended animation. Your body slows down so much, you're barely alive and can stay alive indefinitely."

"Oh, then yes, I put myself in... suspended animation," Merlin continued. "Until I sensed Excalibur in the Bifrost. Then I scryed it and sent a mental message." He looked at Ethan. "To you, apparently."

The old wizard smiled warmly at Ethan. "If it weren't for you, I'd still be trapped in there."

"I am still trying to wrap my head around how this time magic works," Michalus said.

"I stopped trying a long time ago," Ainslee muttered. The dwarf took a large swig of her dwarven spirits and wiped her mouth. "I don't really understand how you can manipulate time. I mean... time just... is."

"Well," Merlin said, holding up a finger. "It is... and it isn't..."

"Father," Guinevere interrupted, giving the man a pointed look. "Perhaps there's something other than magic you'd like to talk about?"

Merlin looked around the table and seemed to notice that Drorm, Ainslee, Elspeth, Fearghas, Par'karr and even Nia had glassy-eyed stares - and not from looking at HUDs. He gave an apologetic look. "Sorry, I'm afraid I could talk all day about magic."

"We know," Guinevere said in a monotone voice.

"Merlin." Ethan cleared his voice. "Now that you're back, what do you plan to do?"

Merlin glanced at his daughter and then back at Ethan. "I was thinking about going back to Earth."

Ethan blinked. "Earth?! Wait... What?! How?"

The old wizard cocked his head. "You haven't figured it out yet? I'm surprised. You visited the inside of the library, right?"

"Yes," Ethan replied. He'd mentioned their first visit to Patheos and his investigation of the library. Then it hit him. "Wait. So that portal went to a different planet. So... what? I can create a portal back to Earth?"

Merlin nodded. "Yes. And now that you possess time magic as well, you can return to whatever time you wish."

"Are you serious?" Ethan gasped. It hadn't occurred to him before, but it made sense. If he focused on a spot on Earth - one he knew really well - would he really be able to create a portal home? "Will magic still work on Earth?"

"It still works," Merlin said. "But, once you leave this planet, you won't regenerate your Mana naturally. But there... uh... are ways..."

Ethan looked at Nia beside him. He'd already discovered a way to regenerate magic off world.

Looking at Nia, he frowned. Ethan could return to Earth. If Merlin was right, he might even be able to return to the exact time he had left. But Nia wouldn't be able to come with him.

Technically she could come with him, but they would have to keep her hidden. He could just imagine the government swooping in, taking her away to Area 51 to run experiments on her. After all, she was an alien.

"What is wrong?" Nia asked, seeing his frown.

He didn't answer right away as he thought of various possibilities. Sadly, unless they moved out into the middle of nowhere, he knew Nia would never be truly accepted. Well, not outside comic conventions - possibly some renaissance faires.

No. If he went back to Earth, he'd have to leave Nia here. Ethan shook his head. That wasn't something he was willing to do. He smiled at her. "Nothing's wrong."

Ethan chuckled to himself, unconsciously looking down at his feet. Like Dorothy, he'd had the ruby slippers almost the entire time. He could have returned to Earth any time after he'd discovered *Aether* magic.

Yet, part of him never really wanted to go back. Here he was powerful. On this world, he was a wizard and now a king. What did he have back home? A dead-end job as a computer technician?

Of course, now that he had magic and magic would work back on Earth, he could probably make a killing in Vegas. He could become a millionaire overnight with a little well-applied magic at the craps table or roulette wheel.

He shook his head and glanced at Nia again. Ethan knew in his heart, he'd already decided he was staying.

This was his home now. But nothing kept Merlin from leaving.

"The Earth has changed a lot since you left," Ethan said. "It's like a different planet now. Things will be unrecognizable."

"I was thinking about returning back to the Earth at the same time I left," Merlin said. He looked at his daughter. "I was hoping you'd want to come with me."

Guinevere looked at her father without speaking for a long time. So long, the silence started to get awkward. Finally, she gave a small nod of her head. "I think I am ready for a change."

"Really?" Ethan asked, looking between the two of them. "You're both leaving?"

Guinevere gave him a kind, but sad smile. "Ethan, you're young yet. I have a lifetime - several lifetimes - of memories of this place, most of them unpleasant. I'm ready for a change."

He cocked his head. "Wait. Were you born on Earth?"

The warrior woman shook her head but it was Merlin who answered. "Her mother was pulled into the rift when pregnant. I jumped in after her and then Arthur's father, Uther, and an eight-year-old Arthur, not to mention a troop of knights, followed me thinking it was some sort of great evil to vanquish.

"Guinevere was born within the week and unfortunately, her mother did not survive," Merlin said sadly.

"So the founding of Camelot and all of the stories of knights, that all happened here?" Ethan asked. "Not back on Earth?"

Merlin shook his head. "No, Uther was just one of many warlords. He had never quite established himself before the rift. Once we appeared in this land, he and his men set about claiming a kingdom of their own but it was Arthur who finally realized that dream."

Ethan frowned. "So then, how are there stories about King Arthur back on Earth?"

"Are there now?" Merlin asked, his expression thoughtful.

"Uh, yeah," Ethan replied. "He's a legend. No one really knows whether he even existed but the legend of Arthur, Merlin and Excalibur is still popular today... well... in my time, back on Earth."

"Interesting," Merlin said, a slight gleam in his eye. "You know what that means?"

Ethan thought about it before chuckling and nodding to the wizard. "It means you do go back to Earth, back to your own time, and you must tell the story of Arthur and somehow it becomes a legend."

"Indeed, it does," Merlin smiled. "And Guinevere and I will have quite a long time to make sure our story becomes a legend."

Remembering that both Merlin and Guinevere were immortal, he nodded. "I guess you will... or already have. Maybe you could look me up... wait... no... don't do that."

"Don't?" Guinevere asked.

"No," he said. "In fact, best if you stay away from me back on Earth... you know... in the past."

"Why?" Merlin asked, forehead wrinkling.

"Time paradox," Ethan muttered, remembering all of the bad things that happened when you interfered with time in the science fiction books and movies. "If you meet me or change my life in any way, then I might not get abducted, which means I will never rescue you, which means you won't go back in time to change the timeline and... well... bad things can happen."

"Interesting," Merlin retorted.

"Sounds terrifying," Guinevere shot back.

"Well," Merlin said thoughtfully. "Whatever we do, or will do, must not affect your life, otherwise you wouldn't be here now, right?"

Ethan felt himself getting a headache as he tried to think of the possibilities with multiverses, timelines and interfering with things. He threw up his hands. "I have no idea."

"So you are really leaving?" Michalus asked.

"I'm afraid so," Merlin said. "I think I've had enough of this place. I'd like to settle down a bit, spend some time with my daughter and maybe explore Earth a bit more."

"It's a lot bigger than this world," Ethan chuckled.

Merlin raised an eyebrow. "How much of this world have you seen?"

Ethan quickly listed the places he'd been and both Merlin and Guinevere laughed. The warrior woman shook her head at him. "There's a whole world out there. We're on the west coast of Isolda. There are thousands of miles between here and the east coast."

"But I wouldn't go there if I were you," Merlin said. "The witch-kings, or should I say dukes, do not like other wizards. If they ever stopped warring with themselves, they might come this way and conquer these lands. Luckily, in the thousand years we've been here, they continue to fight amongst each other."

"Good to know. Don't go east," Ethan said. "I'll remember that."

Merlin's face grew serious. "And be careful. They haven't set their sights on the west yet, but the various Houses do have agents here. They'd been keeping this area destabilized since Arthur's time."

"How will I know their agents?" Ethan asked, suddenly getting a bad feeling.

"You won't," Merlin replied bitterly. "Not until it's too late."

Ainslee yawned and Ethan looked around. Everyone looked tired. "Why don't we turn in for the night and we can talk more tomorrow."

"Excellent idea," Merlin said, standing up. "Thank you for a wonderful meal, Mistress Elspeth."

With a flourish, he produced a dozen gold coins and Ethan only barely sensed the channeling of a small portal. He smiled. He had to admit, Merlin had style.

Merlin laid the pile of coins in front of the stunned innkeeper and his wife. He smiled down at them. "I hope that will be enough to cover the meal and perhaps a room for myself and one for my daughter."

"Uh, yes," Fearghas said with wide eyes. "That's plenty."

"Ah, good then," Merlin said and smiled at the others. "Until tomorrow then."

Realizing they'd been dismissed, Ethan and the others said good night to Guinevere and Merlin before Elspeth led the two of them upstairs.

"I guess we'll say goodnight too," Ethan said and

opened a portal back to Castlehaven. "Next stop, the castle."

His friends nodded and then stepped through the portal. Waving good night to Fearghas and Ainslee, Ethan stepped after them.

62

———

Since Ethan and his group had only been gone for two days, nothing in Castlehaven had changed. People were starting to clear out the rubble and rebuild. And, Rollie informed him, they were already asking for the king. Or rather, they were asking for his magic.

"Tell them I will begin helping this afternoon," he told Rollie. "Also, send a rider to catch up with the Moonpoint army and tell them that the creatures responsible for killing the wizards have been dealt with."

Rollie started. "Are you serious? What was it?"

"Big bugs!" Par'karr said from next to him. The kobold hopped onto his chair and held his hand up at about six feet. "Queen bigger!"

"Bugs?" Rollie frowned. "Big... bugs?"

"Large insectoid creatures that resembled a praying mantis. Do you have praying mantis on this..." Ethan was about to say world but he didn't think Rollie was ready to know he was an alien from another world. "In this area of the world. They're called the Doemenagg."

The captain of the guard scratched his head. "Can't say I've ever heard of any praying bugs. Or no Doemenagg."

"Suffice it to say, you're lucky you never met them," Ethan said. "But the dragon took care of most of them and I... uh... banished their queen."

"Huh," Rollie said, looking around at Ethan and his friends. He shook his head. "A really big bug, huh? Fine, I'll send Seejay. At least he knows how to ride."

"Thanks," Ethan said and gestured to the others. "We'll be back later to start helping out."

Rollie nodded. "I'll let them know... your majesty."

A thought popped into Ethan's head. "Also ask around, look around and search for any Chymera crystals."

"Chymera crystals?" Rollie frowned.

Withdrawing Excalibur, Ethan showed him the blue crystal embedded in the guard. "They're blue crystals that look like this."

"Like the crystals from the crossbows?" the captain of the guard asked.

Ethan nodded, impressed that Rollie remembered. "Exactly. In fact, if you can find any remnants of the crossbows, I might be able to salvage them. Also... go over to the library and ask Mertin if he has any."

"Sure," he replied. "Going to make more crossbows?"

"No." Ethan shook his head. "I'm thinking of portal pouches... uh... portal backpacks that will allow our hunters to place meat into them and it will appear here in the city."

Rollie looked impressed. "You can do that?"

"I can," Ethan said. "I had some already but they were destroyed."

"Huh," Rollie muttered, looking thoughtful. "Those could be used for other things too. Moving crops from farms quickly." He grinned. "Ale too."

Ethan frowned at the captain. "Let's stick with food first."

"You'd be surprised how ale brightens people's mood," Rollie said with a shrug. "People can go without the luxuries, sometimes even the necessities, as long as they have a good mug of ale."

"I'll think about it," Ethan told the man. "For now, let's see if we can find some crystals."

"You got it, your majesty," Rollie said with a little salute.

Rolling his eyes, Ethan motioned for the others to follow him outside. As soon as they were out, he opened a portal to Hawkshead. A few minutes later, they were all back inside in the inn with Ainslee, Guinevere and Merlin.

After they sat down, Merlin shot Guinevere a look. She nodded, and he cleared his throat. "My daughter and I will be returning to Earth. Today."

"Today?" Michalus exclaimed. "But... but..."

Merlin smiled kindly. "I'm sure you have a million questions, but both of us agreed, we are both ready for a change. And the sooner, the better."

"But there are so many things I wanted to ask you..." Michalus started but Merlin held up his hand.

"We've made our decision," he told the elven wizard.

He winked at Michalus. "But I did retrieve my diaries earlier this morning and I will leave them in your and Ethan's capable hands. I think you'll find that they contain quite a bit of my knowledge on magic. I hope they will help you both."

Ethan smiled and nodded. Like Michalus, he had a ton of questions for the legendary wizard. But he also understood the man's need to start over with his daughter.

When Ethan had been in the time loop, he'd seen all of his friends killed dozens - perhaps hundreds - of times, including Nia. He died too - many times. They'd all be dead if the dragon hadn't given him *Time* magic. It made him think about what was really important.

Like Merlin, Ethan didn't really feel like adventuring anymore. He thought he would be fine just spending time with his friends and trying to get Castlehaven back on its feet.

He nodded at Merlin. "I understand."

"I thought you might." Merlin gave him a wink. "What about the rest of you? What are your plans?"

"I'm going back to help out with Castlehaven," Ethan stated.

"I go with him," Nia added. "We will build the city of Castlehaven into a mighty empire!"

"Someone's got plans," Ainslee said under her breath.

Ethan turned to Drorm. "What about you? What will you do? Go back to your people?"

"I am not welcome there," Drorm said. "I will never be welcome there."

"What if you came back with an offer that would enrich your people?" Ethan asked with a smile.

The big orc narrowed his eyes. "What offer?"

"Castlehaven is going to need trading partners," Ethan told him. "And I really do intend to find enough crystals to create some portals to the various cities and make Castlehaven a hub."

"Crystals?" Merlin arched an eyebrow. "You need Chymera crystals?"

Ethan nodded, looking the wizard up and down. "I do. You don't happen to have some lying around, do you?"

"Better than that," Merlin said. "I can tell you where a mine is. There were still quite a haul of crystals left when... well... when things fell apart."

Ethan felt himself growing excited. An entire mine of Chymera crystals?! Imagine what he could do and build with a hundred crystals. Two hundred crystals! Maybe even three or four hundred! "Where?!"

Merlin chuckled and made a dismissive gesture. "It's actually in one of the volumes of my diary. I'll make sure I mark the page for you before we leave."

"Wow!" Ethan grinned. "That would be awesome!"

The old wizard's face became serious. "Just be careful what you build. Once an item is out of your control, it can be used against you."

Nodding, Ethan smiled. He already had some ideas on how to prevent the portals from being used against them. Some rather nasty ideas.

"It seems you will have something of value to offer my people," Drorm stated.

"Good, I will make you my ambassador to the orc nation," Ethan replied.

Drorm shrugged.

Ethan turned to Par'karr. "How about you?"

"Par'karr stay with Ethan," the little kobold said. "Par'karr ambassador too?"

"Actually," Ethan said. "It might be best if you stayed here in Hawkshead so you could start your rabbit farm. I don't think there will be enough room in Castlehaven for a rabbit farm."

Par'karr's eyes got huge. "Par'karr want to start rabbit farm!"

"I thought you might," Ethan said. "And you could sell some of the rabbits to Castlehaven, through a portal we can put here."

The kobold nodded. "Par'karr do that!"

Ethan looked at Michalus. "How about you?"

Michalus gave Ethan a serious look. "Oh, I plan to study Merlin's journals!"

"Is there... maybe something else you might want to do?" Ethan asked but saw that his friend wasn't getting the hint. "Maybe someone you might want to visit?"

"Ah, yes!" Michalus said, his face blushing. "Of course. I would enjoy seeing Yuliana again."

"I can arrange that," Ethan said. "We can even create a portal to the Camelot ruins from Castlehaven."

"From Castlehaven?" Michalus asked.

"Well," Ethan started, having already thought of his plans for the wizard. "Your home is destroyed and... well... I AM king. Kings have court wizards, right?"

"Court wizard?" Michalus said thoughtfully, rubbing his chin. "It does have a distinct ring to it."

"And I'm sure we can find an area for you to build a workshop in the city," Ethan said. That was actually the easy part considering the destruction. There were plenty of areas to build a new workshop or wizard tower. "What do you say?"

Michalus was already nodding. "If you are offering me the position of court wizard, I accept."

"Excellent!" Ethan grinned back at his friend. He turned his smile to the others. Making sure he hadn't forgotten anyone. He stopped on Ainslee.

"What about you, Ainslee?" he asked. "Are you happy here or do you want to come work in the big city?"

"I'm just fine, wizard-boy." Ainslee snorted. "At least for now. It's nice to be needed here and not just one of a hundred other smiths."

Ethan nodded. "Well, if you change your mind, you know where we'll be."

"Oh, I'll find you," the dwarf retorted, grinning back at him.

Smiling at his friend, Ethan turned back to Merlin and Guinevere. "Shall we have one more meal together before you leave?"

Merlin smiled. "Absolutely. I hate traveling on an empty stomach."

THE GROUP ATE a large brunch that Elspeth prepared. It was a full meal of sausages, eggs, beans, mushrooms, fried tomatoes and buttered, toasted bread. It was extremely filling and Ethan felt almost guilty for eating such a big meal when he knew the people in Castlehaven would be struggling to find food.

When they finished their meals, Merlin showed Ethan and Michalus a trove of familiar-looking journals in his room in the inn. "All of my journals. I retrieved them early this morning."

The old wizard walked over to one of them, fanned through the pages until he found what he was looking for and then turned down the corner of the page. He handed it to Ethan. "This is the page with the map to the mine. Some landmarks have changed a bit in the last 1,000 years, but you should have no problems finding it."

"Thank you," he told the wizard.

"No, thank you for saving me," Merlin replied.

Not sure what to say, Ethan just nodded and Merlin led them back downstairs.

The group left the inn and said their farewells. Then, Merlin opened up a portal to a lush green forest that Ethan didn't recognize.

"Thank you again," Merlin said.

Guinevere went around and gave everyone hugs. After she gave Ethan his hug, she stepped back and looked at him. "You'll make a good king. Just put your people first."

Ethan smiled. "Thanks! I'll do my best."

Guinevere rejoined her father and, hand in hand, the two stepped through the portal. Ethan saw them briefly on the other side before the portal collapsed and winked out of existence.

"Everyone ready to go back to Castlehaven? There's a lot of work to be done," he asked.

There was a general murmur of agreement and Ethan started to open a portal but Michalus made a strangled sound. "The books!"

"Oh, right!" Ethan said. The group quickly went up to Merlin's room and retrieved all of the journals. Each one had an armful of books as they gathered back in the courtyard, just outside the inn.

Ethan had magical knowledge to study, in the form of Merlin's journals. He had crystals to mine and gateways to create. And he had a city to rebuild.

More importantly, he had friends to spend time with and help him. He looked around at the group and smiled warmly. He opened up a portal back to Castlehaven.

Ethan took Nia's hand as the others entered the portal. He looked at her. "Let's go home."

She squeezed his hand and together they stepped into the portal.

EPILOGUE

he rubble shifted. The dragons had left the ruins of the Doemenagg nest days ago and hadn't been back. There was no need to come back. Everything had been destroyed. Or so it seemed. The rubble shifted again, this time exposing a small antenna that wiggled around. More and more rubble shifted, exposing more of a large, beetle-like creature.

It blinked its good eye. Its left eye had been destroyed by the falling debris but its right eye still worked. The drone looked around but saw no sign of any of its kind. It was not surprised.

The drone had been buried when the tunnel it had been crawling through had collapsed from a dragon attack. It had been completely buried under debris and had struggled for a short time before giving up and accepting that it would soon die.

Dying did not scare the drone. Its only function was to serve the Queen and the Queen had ordered it to distract the dragons while she had escaped. It had tried to do that. It had been on its way to the surface to act as a distraction when the tunnel collapsed.

It had struggled for some time before accepting that it could no longer fulfill its Queen's last command. That made it sad. Unable to follow out her order, the drone had simply stopped struggling and waited to die.

It had almost died. And then something had happened. It lost its link to the Queen. That could only mean one thing - the Queen was dead. That made it sad too. But more than sad, some deep instinct forced the drone to free itself.

After spending the last two days wiggling everything it could wiggle, the rubble had shifted and finally the drone had created a small opening. Meticulously, it worked on enlarging the opening until finally, it was free of the rubble.

The drone moved its head, looking for what it needed. It found it. A long tunnel that was still intact. A place where it could be alone. A place where it could do what was required of it. A place where it could lay its egg.

The egg had begun forming as soon as the link to its Queen had been severed. During the days it had taken for the drone to burrow out of the rubble, it had matured and was nearly ready to lay.

One leg broken, the drone hobbled down the tunnel until it reached a dead end. The tunnel beyond had collapsed but this would do. The drone could lay the egg here, away from the surface, where it would be safe.

The drone backed itself against the wall and its body, realizing it was time, excreted the egg. Unfortunately for the drone, the process killed caused a chain reaction that would kill it. It would die and become food for the new Queen once she hatched.

As darkness closed in on the drone, for the first time in its short life, it felt happy. The old Queen was dead. A new Queen would arise.

END

JOIN THE ADVENTURE

Thank you for reading this book! If you enjoyed it, please consider leaving a review on Amazon or tagging me on social media.
Tag me @authorjohncresı on Twitter and @authorjohncressman on Facebook and Instagram!
Reviews help readers like you find this book. More readers means more sales, and more sales help independent authors like me to be able to write more books!
To learn more about the author and his other books and projects, visit the author's website at:
https://www.johnecressman.com
Or visit him on Facebook
https://www.facebook.com/authorjohncressman/

LITRPG

To learn more about LitRPG, talk to authors including myself, and just have an awesome time, please join the <u>LitRPG Group</u>.

MORE LITRPG

For more information on this book and other exciting
LitRPG/GameLit books, please visit the following
Facebook groups:
LitRPG Books
https://www.facebook.com/groups/LitRPG.books/

and

GameLit Society
https://www.facebook.com/groups/LitRPGsociety/

ACKNOWLEDGMENTS

I'd like to acknowledge all the members of the LitRPG Authors' Guild who helped me in so many ways! Without your help, I could never have gotten this far!

I also want to acknowledge the 20Booksto50K Facebook group! I've received lots of help and inspiration from them and I recommend the group to new and experienced authors.

Also, a big thank you for everyone who had bought one of my books. Your support really means a lot to me.

ABOUT THE AUTHOR

John E. Cressman is an author, magician, mentalist, hypnotist, programmer, and longtime lover of roleplaying games and fantasy/sci-fi books.

As a teen, he wasted long hours creating D&D fantasy campaigns for his friends to play. He has tried several pen and paper roleplaying games from the original Dungeons and Dragons, Traveler and Star Frontiers to the new Pathfinder games.

He still enjoys computer RPGs and MMORPGs, with his current favorite being Elder Scrolls Online. He used to play Skyrim, but then he took an arrow to the knee.

www.ingramcontent.com/pod-product-compliance
Lightning Source LLC
Chambersburg PA
CBHW030656190726
48286CB00001B/56